"I've never thanked you for all this."

She paused before continuing, "For taking my case. For believing me when I came to you that day, when I wasn't even sure I believed myself. It's a lot, and I was up half the night thinking I'm kind of awful for not saying this sooner."

The idea they'd both been awake last night but not together made him sad.

"Are you usually this involved in your cases?"

Austin frowned. She couldn't mean what he thought she meant. Could she? "No. Not like this."

He'd never once been attracted to a client. Never wanted to get to know them personally or have them in his life. He'd always done his best to help, nothing more.

There had just been something about Scarlet from the start. And the more he'd gotten to know her, the more he wanted to know. The more he wanted her to stay when this was over. Which was what he should be saying to her right now.

But the risk could outweigh the potential gain.

ALWAYS WATCHING

—

JULIE ANNE LINDSEY

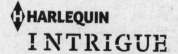

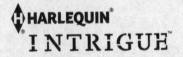

Recycling programs
for this product may
not exist in your area.

ISBN-13: 978-1-335-59058-9

Always Watching

Copyright © 2023 by Julie Anne Lindsey

For questions and comments about the quality of this book, please contact us at CustomerService@Harlequin.com.

Harlequin Enterprises ULC
22 Adelaide St. West, 41st Floor
Toronto, Ontario M5H 4E3, Canada
www.Harlequin.com

Printed in U.S.A.

Julie Anne Lindsey is an obsessive reader who was once torn between the love of her two favorite genres: toe-curling romance and chew-your-nails suspense. Now she gets to write both for Harlequin Intrigue. When she's not creating new worlds, Julie can be found carpooling her three kids around northeastern Ohio and plotting with her shamelessly enabling friends. Winner of the Daphne du Maurier Award for Excellence in Mystery/Suspense, Julie is a member of International Thriller Writers, Romance Writers of America and Sisters in Crime. Learn more about Julie and her books at julieannelindsey.com.

Books by Julie Anne Lindsey

Harlequin Intrigue

Beaumont Brothers Justice

Closing In On Clues
Always Watching

Heartland Heroes

SVU Surveillance
Protecting His Witness
Kentucky Crime Ring
Stay Hidden
Accidental Witness
To Catch a Killer

Visit the Author Profile page at Harlequin.com.

CAST OF CHARACTERS

Scarlet Wills—A real estate agent in Marshal's Bluff, North Carolina, being followed and tormented by an unknown individual.

Austin Beaumont—A private investigator who will stop at nothing to protect Scarlet from her stalker and help bring the criminal into custody.

Dean Beaumont—A private investigator and business partner with Austin, working hard to assist his brothers and local law enforcement in finding and stopping Scarlet's stalker.

Lydia Stevens—A friend of Scarlet and fellow real estate agent in the Coulter Realty office, Marshal's Bluff location.

Trina Wills—Scarlet's mother, a seasoned real estate agent in a neighboring county.

Mrs. Beaumont—The Beaumont family matriarch, who runs a restorative ranch with her husband and champions the interests of her five grown sons.

Detective Finn Beaumont—A Marshal's Bluff detective working with his brothers and local police to identify and capture Scarlet's stalker.

Officer Barrow—A police officer in Trina Wills's town, who responds to her disappearance and works with the Marshal's Bluff police to locate Trina and the stalker.

Cindy Reese—A real estate agent in Trina Wills's office.

Chapter One

Scarlet Wills paced the empty living room of the moderately priced two-story home on Wentworth Drive, hands clutched before her, heart rate on the rise. Thanks to a recent overhaul of the outdated Coulter Realty website, house hunters could now request a walk-through of any available property by completing an online request form. Scarlet had assumed this new feature would lead to an increase in appointments, showings, clients and sales. She hadn't, however, considered the lack of personal interaction meant never really knowing who was on the other side of the requests.

The contact form required only a name, phone number or email address, and the home a buyer wanted to see. Half the time, Scarlet didn't know who she was meeting until they'd arrived. Other times, like this one, no one arrived at all.

She rolled her tight shoulders and leaned her head side to side, hoping to alleviate the painful tension gathered there. This was beginning to look like Scarlet's third no-show in the five weeks since Coulter Realty's website changes went live.

And, like the other times, she felt distinctly as if she was being watched.

She'd breathed easier when she'd first arrived, glad to see another agent already at the home with a couple of potential buyers. Evan's familiar face and ready smile had been a welcome surprise. He'd even complimented her short-sleeved navy blouse and the way she'd worn her pale blond hair in a tight chignon. But now, he and his clients were leaving, and she would be alone.

According to her watch, it was nearing six o'clock. Hardly late, but the sky was already dark when she'd pulled her compact SUV into the long driveway. Autumn in her small coastal town of Marshal's Bluff, North Carolina, meant eating dinner after dark for more than a few months of the year. And Wentworth Drive was heavily lined with trees, the homes cloaked in shadows.

Ideally, Scarlet's potential client would've shown up before Evan left, but that, apparently, wasn't meant to be.

Now, she paced alone inside the eerily quiet structure, watching helplessly as gooseflesh climbed the exposed skin of her arms and Evan said goodbye to his clients on the lawn outside the dining room's bay window.

He waved a hand as his clients drove away, and Scarlet willed him to return inside. But he dropped into his car without another look in her, or the home's, direction.

A heavy, shuddered sigh escaped her as she checked her watch again. Pat Cranston, the contact who'd reached out to her, was officially more than fifteen minutes late, and her nerves were beginning to fray.

She refocused on the scene outside the window. October was once her favorite month of the year. The beauty that came with changing leaves and blooming mums was unparalleled. And her small coastal town thrived on harvest festivals, pumpkins patches and gratuitous, multicolored gourds on every doorstep.

Currently, however, it was hard to see past the early sunsets and shorter days. There was too much darkness and there were too many shadows.

Too much paranoia, she thought, chastising herself for the continued fixation on something unseen. Something that likely wasn't even real.

Moving to Marshal's Bluff four years ago had been an easy decision. She'd grown up in a neighboring county, where her mother, Trina, was a successful real estate agent. And in small-town North Carolina, one Wills woman selling homes was enough. In Marshal's Bluff, she didn't have to compete with her mother for home sales, and no one referred to her as Trina's daughter. Two big bonuses of setting up shop an hour away.

She stared at her SUV for long minutes, debating on when she could reasonably call it a night.

Soon the grandfather clock in the foyer gonged, and Scarlet's green eyes widened in the reflection of the glass. It was definitely time to give up and head home. Pat hadn't responded to any of Scarlet's texts attempting to confirm the appointment, and twenty minutes was more than enough grace time on Scarlet's part. Besides, she had a bottle of merlot, an excellent book and set of new satin pajamas just waiting for her at home.

She began the process of shutting off lights at the back of the home and moving forward, careful not to leave any unnecessarily on, extra grateful Evan had turned off the upstairs and basement lights before he'd left. Scarlet double-checked the locks on all exterior doors, then paused to collect her business cards and flyers she'd printed with details on the home and local market.

It really was a pretty home. Only three years old and full of modern charm. High ceilings. White woodwork and trim. Fancy, geometric-shaped light fixtures and marble everywhere marble was acceptable. Not her style, but lovely nonetheless.

The rooms, though flawlessly designed, were mostly empty now, thanks to a relocation that had taken the family to another state more than a week prior. Another similarity, she realized, in the homes where she'd been stood up. The appointments were always made online. Always for a home with limited neighbors and a family no longer in the area.

Her phone buzzed, and she flinched before rolling her eyes belatedly at the overreaction. The name of another client living out of state appeared on her caller ID.

"Good evening, Mr. Perez," she said sweetly, thankful for the bit of normal in her current situation. "How are you tonight?"

"Not good," he griped. "You assured me you could sell my house in a week, and it's been a month."

Scarlet headed into the foyer, tugging her purse onto one shoulder. "No, Mr. Perez," she corrected pleasantly. "I said I could sell your house in a week at the listing price I suggested. I told you I would do my best to sell your home at the price you insisted upon."

"I don't see the difference."

She highly doubted that. He was a businessman after all. And she'd explained the difference to him more than once. *Still*, she reasoned, *it would be nice to keep him on the phone a little longer.* "Your price is significantly higher than I recommended, which limits the number of prospective buyers. That's not to say the property won't sell at your price. I'm confident you can get the amount you're asking, but it won't happen as quickly. We're going to have to wait for the right buyer."

She stepped into the night and locked the door behind her. A cool breeze whipped the fabric of her blouse, sending a sharp chill down her spine. "If you can be patient a little longer, I'll brainstorm new ideas for spreading the word on a larger scale."

He grunted. Not happy, but not angry. With Mr. Perez, she'd call that a win.

Scarlet stilled as motion caught her eyes in the reaching shadows along the roadside. She stared and squinted into the darkness, begging the vague, sweeping movement to grow into something recognizable and harmless. A neighbor walking a dog, or a few wandering deer.

"I don't have forever on this," Mr. Perez complained. "My family's move was expensive, and we can't afford to pay two mortgages long term."

Scarlet made a break for her little SUV, racing down the steps and across the black asphalt driveway toward her vehicle. The lights flashed when she pressed the unlock button on her key fob. "Give me two more weeks to find a buyer at this price," she suggested. "Then we can revisit the subject of pricing."

"All right," he agreed reluctantly. "Two more weeks. But I want it sold. At my price."

"Understood."

She slid behind the wheel and dropped the phone into her cup holder, enjoying the satisfying snap of her power locks as the door closed. A few frantic heartbeats later, she reversed carefully away from the dark, empty home.

She queued up an audiobook at the nearest intersection, obeying a stop sign. A pair of headlights flashed on behind her, pulling her attention to the blinding reflection in her rearview mirror. Unfounded tension coiled through her limbs. "It's just a car," she whispered, pressing the gas pedal once more.

It didn't make any sense to assume the car was intentionally following her, so she motored on, shaking away the nonsensical thoughts. For good measure, she pressed the gas pedal with purpose, putting extra space between the vehicles.

Her company's online request form for house showings popped back into her mind. As did her three no-shows. Was it ridiculous to wonder if those requests had been made by the same person? Even if the names and contact numbers were different?

Above her an abundance of stars twinkled in an inky sky. Behind her, the glow of headlights grew until she had to look away. The other vehicle erased the distance she'd gained then crept uncomfortably closer before matching her speed.

Scarlet's grip on the wheel tightened, and she worked a little harder to convince herself the car wasn't following her and the driver wasn't trying to unsettle her. Whoever was back there probably always drove like a jerk, too close and too fast. It had nothing to do with her. She accelerated anyway, reaching nearly sixty miles per hour in the stretch of road marked forty-five. She'd cheerfully accept the speeding ticket if it meant seeing a cop anytime soon. At least then the car behind her would be gone, and if she played her cards right, the officer might willingly follow her home for good measure.

She decided to drive into town to be safe instead of heading straight home. As the downtown lights came into view on the horizon, she made a mental plan. She'd drive into the busiest parking lot and call a friend. If the car followed, she'd call the police. If the car went away, she'd wait five minutes, then take a roundabout and convoluted path home to be sure no one else was behind her when she arrived.

Paranoid? Maybe. But at least she had a plan.

She pulled her phone into her lap for good measure. If anything else happened, if the car hit her or the driver got out at the upcoming stoplight and moved in her direction, she would dial 911.

Her attention fixed on the rearview mirror as she slowed. The car picked up speed, and she braced for impact, until it suddenly peeled away, taking the exit ramp for the highway instead of stopping at the light.

Breath whooshed from her lungs, and a ragged laugh burst from her trembling lips. "Good grief," she whispered. "I'm losing it."

The other driver had simply been a jerk in a hurry to get somewhere, and she'd been prepared to call emergency services. For what? Tailgating? Clearly she needed a good night's sleep more than she'd thought.

When the light turned green, she drove straight home.

SCARLET SLID INTO bed that night with a glass of red wine and her favorite novel. A long, hot shower had washed the fear from her mind. "Just one chapter," she vowed. "Then it's bedtime."

She lifted the glass to her lips, and her cell phone vibrated, announcing an incoming message before she'd taken a single sip.

She didn't recognize the name, but that wasn't unusual. She'd printed her cell phone number on her business cards and shared it on the company website. Also, the new contact form pushed requests for home showings to their assigned agents via text.

She set her wine aside and raised the device reluctantly, hoping it was someone interested in the Perez property and willing to pay his asking price. She accessed the message with a swipe of her thumb.

Unknown: Nice seeing you again tonight

Not an offer on the Perez place, but at least it was a wrong number.

The phone buzzed a second time before she could return it to the nightstand.

Scarlet stilled, eyes fixed on the four little words.

Unknown: Thanks for the showing

Breath caught in her throat. Was it possible this too was a coincidence? A message meant for another agent? A confused buyer texting the wrong number from the website?

Or was this the point where she could no longer tell herself there wasn't anything to worry about?

A final text made her decision clear.

Unknown: CU soon

Chapter Two

Austin Beaumont leaned against the darkly tinted window at the front of his office, watching morning traffic creep along outside. His simple T-shirt and jeans reflected in the glass, as did the mug of coffee in his hands.

Every shop on the street had dragged out their autumn decor, complete with piles of pumpkins on hay bales and scarecrows with goofy grins. Even the private detective firm he owned with his older brother Dean had a bundle of cornstalks outside the door and a wreath of multicolored leaves with a Welcome sign. Not exactly the intimidating, highly serious, let us take your case vibe he imagined for his business, but there wasn't any use saying no to their mother. She insisted on making everyone comfortable.

She'd arrived with decor and a dinner invitation three weeks back. He'd declined the former and accepted the latter, but received both instead. The upside to his loss, he supposed, was the likelihood of making potential clients feel less on edge and more welcome. In his experience, when someone contacted a private investigator, they'd already made up their mind about getting help. He'd prefer his firm got the job.

A small SUV appeared in the curb lane, slowing by a fraction, then bouncing gently ahead. The warped brick streets of downtown Marshal's Bluff weren't built to handle the recent influx of vehicles. But a tax reduction for businesses had drawn the attention of several companies with ties to national corporations, which meant the town's population was experiencing a boom.

"What are you looking at?" Dean asked. The sounds of his brother's fingers on his keyboard underscored the words.

Austin peered over his shoulder at Dean's amused expression, and his partner stilled.

"What is it?"

"A dark SUV has passed here twice. It slows outside, then continues each time."

"What are you thinking?" Dean asked. "Lost commuter or possible trouble?"

Austin shrugged, maintaining the carefully disinterested facade he preferred to the tightly wound, barely suppressed, ball of tension he was. He'd perfected the act in the military and found it worked wonders in civilian life as well. People who looked cool and confident bred trust and put others at ease, exactly what a businessman wanted and what a calculating investigator needed. Being underestimated, or even overlooked, was often a golden ticket in his work.

He sipped his cooling coffee, which had become more of a prop than it had been when he'd poured it. Then flashed his brother a smug half smile. "Given the amount of criminals and cheating spouses we help bust every month, I'm hoping it's not the latter."

"That makes both of us," Dean said, doubling down on whatever he was up to on the computer.

The click-clacking of keys only lasted another minute before the office phone rang, and Dean's voice rose again. "Beaumont Investigations."

Austin returned the mug to his desk and grabbed a black ball cap from his bottom drawer.

The office was wide and rectangular, with two desks out front, bookshelves, chairs and other homey touches their mother had insisted upon. Two small conference rooms lined a corridor leading to the private employee section, where they kept a well-stocked kitchenette for long hours at the office and stakeouts.

Austin tugged the hat over his shaggy, sandy brown hair, reminding himself again to get a trim, and adjusted the bill low on his forehead. Then he strolled out the front door. He walked along the sidewalk to the end of the block and around the corner.

Brisk morning air swept along the streets between historic brick buildings, stirring up fallen leaves and setting a discarded plastic bag into flight.

He leaned casually against the wall at his back. The position of the building compared to the morning sun created a long shadow where he was likely to go unnoticed. He lowered his head, as if enraptured by his cell phone, just in case he caught a passerby's eye.

As predicted, the SUV reappeared, making its turn onto the street before him. And in a stroke of luck, the light at the corner turned red. Unfortunately, the same sun that had helped him blend into the shade, cast a bright glint off the vehicle's windshield, making it impossible to get a good look at the driver.

Austin murmured a curse and revised his plan. Better to know what he was dealing with than to be unprepared. He pushed away from the wall and strode into traffic, crossing the single narrow lane of moving cars with ease. He stopped on the yellow lines at the road's center and rapped his knuckles against the lightly tinted driver's-side window.

Clouds passed over the brilliant North Carolina sun, removing the glare from the glass and enabling him to get his first look at the driver, just as she screamed.

His hands flipped up in innocence, and he took in the shock and horror on the woman's beautiful face. Her pale green eyes flashed with fear, then red-hot anger.

"I'm calling the police!" she yelled, turning her phone to face him as if snapping a picture.

Austin reared back, stunned and a little amused, but earning a honk from an oncoming car. He raised a hand in apology to the vehicle, then returned to the double yellow lines.

When his eyes met hers again, the woman pointed pepper spray at her closed window, cell phone at her ear.

A hearty laugh rumbled unexpectedly from his chest, opening his lips into a wide smile. The light changed, and the SUV rolled away. He waited for a break in traffic then jogged back to the sidewalk at his first opportunity.

He took a minute to remove his hat and run a hand through his hair before securing the cap once more. And another minute to press back the smile still twisting the corners of his mouth.

"I am clearly Marshal Bluff's top investigator," he muttered, shaking his head as he made his way around the corner. Dean would never let him live this one down if he told him what had happened, and the story was too ridiculous not to share.

Instead of saving their office from an attack by a disgruntled criminal or cheater looking for retribution, he'd scared some poor, obviously rattled woman half to death, and nearly gotten a face full of pepper spray for his trouble.

With a little luck, she wouldn't panic and send that photo to the local police station. For starters, that would be terrible for business. And on a personal note, his younger brother, and Marshal's Bluff detective, Finn would surely print and hang the image on every telephone pole between Main Street and the coast.

He'd been certain the vehicle was paying special interest to the office as it passed. But maybe the driver really was lost, and he was losing his touch. He normally sensed trouble from a mile away, sometimes before the person who'd eventually cause the issue even knew that was the path they were on.

He shook out his hands, which had balled uncharacteristically into fists, curled by the tension and distaste of such a total error. He wouldn't blame her if she did call the police. A stranger had approached her in traffic. A guttural sound rumbled low in his chest as Beaumont Investigations came into view. Time to pull it together and focus on the full day he had ahead of him.

Vandalism investigations. A stolen stallion worth more than his truck. An allegation of hidden funds amidst a divorce dispute. And those were the tip of the iceberg.

Hopefully the call Dean had taken before Austin went outside to confront an unsuspecting woman was information on one of those cases. Anything to set his day back on course.

A gust of coffee-scented air rushed out to greet him as he pulled open the glass office door. His mother's festive leaf wreath swung wildly under the force.

The SUV driver's face flashed into his mind unbidden. She'd been angry and afraid, but beautiful, with the soft green eyes and plush pink lips of an angel. Maybe it was the morning he was having, or the way his instinctual sense of dread refused to let up, but he couldn't help wondering what had upset her. Why had she been circling the block?

Probably a marital squabble, he told himself. Women who looked like that didn't stay single. Even if she had the personality of a viper. Though he doubted that was true. She'd seemed vulnerable. And unnaturally quick to raise her pepper spray. Everyone else in town greeted neighbors, and strangers, with a smile and a nod.

He rubbed a hand against the back of his neck

and gave one last glance through the window before meeting Dean's curious stare.

"Everything okay?"

"Yep." Austin fell onto his desk chair as Dean rose from his.

"Good." He tugged on his brown leather coat and reached for his cell phone and keys. "Finn called. He's got some information on my missing person's case. I'm headed to the police station to check it out."

Austin nodded, attention fixed on his now tepid coffee. "That was Finn on the phone when I left?" He stretched upright again, in need of caffeine and something to busy his hands.

"No, that was a potential new client, which is why it's good there isn't a disgruntled nut casing this place. I have to take off, and you can handle the client. I've already opened a file and logged the basic information. It's in the shared drive. Give it a read before she gets here."

Austin shut his eyes for a long beat to stop them from rolling. This was hardly his first rodeo, yet something about the older brothers in his family made them think the younger brothers always needed help. Guidance. Or pointers. It wasn't personal, but it was habitual, and he made another mental note not to do the same to Finn and Lincoln. Besides, Dean's sage advice to be prepared was Scouts and cowboy 101. Austin had passed those life courses with gold stars years ago.

He forced himself to refocus on the more important information Big Brother failed to provide. "When's this woman getting here?" And did he have time to pour a fresh cup of coffee? "What's her name and problem?"

"Scarlet Wills, twenty-seven, unmarried, lives alone. Thinks she's being followed," Dean said, narrowing his eyes. "Read the file."

Austin frowned and headed for the coffee maker.

His brother moved toward the door.

The bell dinged, and Dean spoke again, but he didn't say goodbye.

"Ms. Wills?"

Great. She was already there. Austin's head fell forward on an exhale, and he straightened with resolve. No hot coffee for him then.

He forced a polite expression and turned back toward his desk as Dean shook the newcomer's hand.

"I'm Dean Beaumont. This is my brother and business partner, Austin Beaumont. He'll be meeting with you today and getting a feel for your situation. He's military trained, the middle-born of five rowdy brothers and an Eagle Scout. Not to mention he makes a mean cup of joe. You've never been in better hands, I assure you."

Dean's smile was warm and charming as he did his best to break the ice and put Ms. Wills at ease before walking out.

But her wide green eyes were already fixed on him in recognition, and Austin blew out a long, defeated breath. Hopefully the gorgeous blonde before him, the one he'd unintentionally startled in her SUV, would give him a chance to explain before making use of that pepper spray, wherever it was now.

He was definitely going to need that coffee.

Chapter Three

Scarlet froze as Dean Beaumont, the man she'd spoken to on the phone, walked away. Leaving her with his brooding brother. Dean had been kind and polite in person, and for a moment, the mounting tension inside her had faded. It probably helped that he was distractingly handsome. Unfortunately, she never went for the happy, congenial sort. One of her many flaws. Just ask her mother.

Not to ruin her perfect record of bad luck with men, she'd managed to threaten the private detective in front of her with pepper spray. The same man whose help she needed to figure out if there really was a stalker to worry about. Worse? Austin Beaumont looked exactly like the kind of guy she'd cheerfully hitch her wagon to, then get burned.

She scanned the room as he assessed her, taking the opportunity to gather her thoughts and resolve. The office was nicely decorated, with bookshelves and framed photos. Two mahogany desks faced the large front window and glass door, each with a leather executive chair behind it and two padded armchairs before it. The air was warm and smelled of delectable cologne and coffee.

"Ms. Wills," he said finally, tossing his black ball cap onto a shelf and running a hand through his shaggy brown hair. The soft locks fell over his forehead as he moved forward with an outstretched arm.

Manners lifted her hand to his before her brain had made the conscious decision to do so. "Please, call me Scarlet."

The air thickened and tingled between them as his calloused palm curled over hers. The heat from his touch sent sparks of attraction up her arms and into her chest.

He was unfairly handsome without his hat to shield his features, but not at all like his brother. Dean had been light and jovial. Austin had an air of danger around him. His dark, hooded gaze should've felt more like a warning than an invitation.

"I should apologize for frightening you earlier," he said.

Not actually apologizing, she noted and released his hand with some mental effort.

"And I should apologize for threatening you."

His lips quirked in amusement, without quite forming a smile. "Can I get you a cup of coffee?"

"Please."

"You can have a seat, if you'd like." He motioned to the desk on her left, then moved into a narrow hallway beyond the outer office where she stood. "I won't be a minute."

Unnerved by a torrent of emotions, from fear and hope to attraction and anxiety, she remained fixed in place. What did she hope would happen today? What would the PI say about her concerns? She certainly didn't want her fears confirmed, but hearing the danger was all in her imagination didn't seem ideal either. What would that mean about the state of her emotional health?

She bypassed the desk and chairs for a look at the bookshelves and photos. Images of the men she'd just met were accompanied by a collection of other friendly faces. A group shot included the PIs and three other men, roughly the same ages, each with a dauntingly attractive face. An older couple shared an embrace in the background. The Beaumont family?

Smaller frames featured individuals that looked nothing alike. All ages, with a variety of hair and eye colors and skin in every tone from ivory to ebony.

The top shelf held a shadow box with a Purple Heart medal and a dozen images of men in military uniforms or fatigues. A younger version of Austin leaned against a tank. Sweat had applied the cotton of his plain white T-shirt to every perfect muscle and plane of his chest like a sticker. Tan and brown camouflage-patterned pants and black boots completed the ensemble. A sheen of sweat was visible on his brow.

"Cream or sugar?" a low male voice asked, snapping Scarlet back to the moment.

She spun to find Austin barely three feet away, steam rising from the mug in each hand.

"No. Thank you."

He set the drinks on the desk and took a seat. "See anything interesting?"

"Just looking at all these faces," she said, demanding her traitorous gaze not return to the lucky white T-shirt. "You're from a military family?"

"I am."

"Is the Purple Heart yours?" Her voice cracked unexpectedly, and she cleared her throat. Something about the idea of Austin being wounded pressed the air from her lungs.

"No. That belongs to my youngest brother. He had it rough for a while and wasn't interested in keeping the medal around."

"But you were?"

Austin's brows lifted by a fraction, probably making a note of her nosiness. "I think that medal is a symbol of his survival. Not everyone who earns one lives to see it. I plan to honor and protect it until he's ready to take it back."

She wet her lips and swallowed. This man had heart. If the photos weren't enough to make things crystal clear, his speech had driven the message home. Austin Beaumont had served his country, and he clearly loved his family. Her crush on him was inevitable now. "And all these framed photos of children…" She looked at the images again. All so vastly different. Missing persons he and his brother helped locate? "Kids you helped bring home?"

"I'm afraid that credit goes to my folks," he said. "Those are my brothers and sisters."

Her smile sprouted. "Really? All of them?"

Austin rose and joined her at the bookshelves. "My parents run a ranch where they help troubled young people. They also foster and adopt. Most of these are grown now." He tipped his head toward the photos. "Some were adopted by other families, others aged out of the system, but for at least a little while they were raised by my folks. That makes them siblings for the long haul in my book."

A new warmth spread through her chest, and she turned to him. "Family dinners must be interesting."

"You have no idea."

She didn't, but she would love to. "There are five boys in your immediate family. How many were adopted?"

"Two," he said, stretching a hand in the direction of his desk. "We should get started."

"Oh." She'd nearly forgotten why she was there. "Right."

He hadn't clarified which of his brothers had been adopted, or if he was one of them, but it was clear that didn't matter.

Her heart gave another thud of appreciation.

She returned to the gray armchair in front of his desk. She'd always dreamed of having siblings, but it must've been hard to watch them come and go.

Austin sipped his coffee then moved the wireless mouse in a quick circle, waking up the computer. A moment later, he typed something with the keyboard. "Dean opened a file for you. I'm going to add additional information as we talk."

"Okay." Scarlet rested her hands in her lap, kneading her fingers to stall her nerves. "I'm hoping I'll laugh about this later," she said, planting both feet against the floor. She cursed the unforgiving pencil skirt she'd chosen for the day, unable to cross her legs and bounce her knee as she wanted. The material was too snug and short to make the move smoothly, and a second-rate flashing would be nearly as humiliating as having threatened the man with her pepper spray.

His trained gaze slid over her features and hair, along the length of her neck and torso to her hands. Probably sensing her thoughts and tension. "There's no need to be nervous. You're the one with the weapon."

A soft, unexpected snort of laughter broke on her lips, and her cheeks heated. "I guess you really can read my mind."

"Is that what you think?"

"Don't you know?"

The skin at the corners of his eyes crinkled with mischief, and his lips formed a lazy half smile.

She pushed the moment of lightness aside and hoped her imagined stalker wasn't any more real than mind reading. "I should probably start from the beginning."

She told the story as well as possible with the intensity of Austin's gaze on her, starting with an explanation of the company's website upgrade and her many calls to tech support, because attempting to navigate the system's changes was a low point in her recent career. She moved on to describe the three requests for home showings that had resulted in no-shows and carefully outlined the similarities. She included the homes' locations and absent owners. For her grand finale, she told him about the texts.

"May I see the messages?" he asked.

Scarlet unearthed the phone from her structured leather handbag and unlocked it with her fingerprint before accessing the texts. "The number doesn't match the one given on the contact form from last night. I checked as soon as the shock passed. It also doesn't match the number used for either of the other appointments when no one showed. Which is why I hope I'm overthinking all this."

"Burner phones are cheap and widely available." Austin took the device. His expression hardened as he read the messages but cleared before he raised his eyes to hers once more. "I'd like to take screenshots as evidence."

"Of course." Scarlet nodded woodenly and cringed inwardly at his word choice. Evidence made it sound as if he believed there was enough reason to open a case. As if she was already in the midst of a criminal investigation. "Do you really think someone would go to all that trouble to upset me? Using multiple numbers and sending me on three goose chases just to watch me roam around empty homes?"

Austin caught her in his dark gaze once more, jaw set and expression firm. "What do your instincts say?"

She blew out a slow sigh, deflating against the chair's backrest. She wouldn't be in his office if she could've found a way to let the suspicions go on her own.

"Instincts are rarely wrong," he said, apparently reading the answer in her body language. "People ignore their guts too often, especially women who tend to be more concerned about manners than men. Statistically you're more likely to be in danger of attack or abduction than I am and less likely to be able to fight off your attacker. That alone is reason not to take chances." He tapped the screen a few times then set her phone on his desk between them. "I would encourage you to walk away from anyone and any situation that makes you feel uncomfortable, even if you aren't sure why. Just turn around and leave. As far as these contact forms go, I'd tell your company it's an unsafe practice and you aren't showing homes to anyone else you don't meet in advance, at least by phone. Whatever you need to feel safe."

Scarlet considered his words and her situation for a moment, a new concern itching in her mind. "The contact form has only been in effect for five weeks. If someone is doing this, could they have been one of the first buyers I met through the site, then used the same method to make additional appointments?"

Austin leaned forward on his desk, appearing to weigh his response before giving it. "It's possible someone was watching you before the website changed, and once they realized the new contact form gave them direct access to you, they began to take advantage. He might even see these appointments as dates. Or think you're buying a house together."

Her stomach plummeted and the downy hairs on her arms and neck rose to attention. "You think someone could've been following me, watching me, for more than five weeks?"

"I think anything is possible," he said. "And if last night was the first time he's contacted you afterward, I think he's escalating."

Her mouth opened, and she snapped it shut. Escalating. There was another word she didn't like. A word that made her blood run cold.

"Is there anything else?" he asked. "Even if it's small, it could matter. Even things from before the website gained a request form? Things you dismissed at the time that might look more pointed now."

She shook her head, prepared to insist nothing else had happened, outside the texts and no-shows. Then something flashed back to mind. "Someone followed me last night when I left the home on Wentworth." She told the story slowly and in detail, watching Austin carefully for a reaction.

His jaw clenched and released several times before he spoke. "Can you describe the car?"

"Not really. It was dark, and I was shaken. I'm sure it was a car though, not a truck or SUV. Black or another dark color, I think. With those bluish headlights."

"That's good," he said, voice soothing and certain. "All those details will help if we come to need them."

Her tension eased by a fragment. She wasn't a confirmed victim yet, but if her fears did come true, she wanted to be useful.

"I'd like to look into this further," he said. "I have some things to tie up and off-load this morning, but I want to get started as soon as possible."

"Tomorrow?" she asked, both thankful and concerned by his decision to take her case.

"I was thinking I could meet you at your office after work today. Maybe interview your coworkers. Meanwhile, I'll check out the company website and do a little reconnaissance at the homes where you felt watched. Can you text me those addresses?" He pulled a sleek black business card from a holder on his desk and slid it in her direction.

She struggled to regain her breath as the reality of things attempted to flatten her to the chair. "You want to meet my coworkers?" She plucked the card from the desk and accepted her cell phone when he passed that to her as well.

"I do, but we can play that however works best for you. Tomorrow, I'd like to begin shadowing you for a day or two. I'll stay in the background. You won't even notice I'm there once we start."

Scarlet highly doubted that. In fact, now that they'd met, she was sure she'd notice him in a stadium full of people. And wasn't one person following her enough? "What do I tell people? My clients?"

He smiled warmly, the picture of calm.

She on the other hand was sure he could hear her erratic heartbeat across the space between them.

"You could tell clients I'm a trainee, if that helps. I'll even wear a suit."

Her mind went fuzzy at the thought of him in dress clothes, the crisp white sleeves of his shirt rolled up to his elbows. "And my coworkers?" she croaked, throat suddenly parched. "I don't want them to know what I'm worried about until I'm sure there's reason for concern."

"Long-lost cousin," he suggested. "New boyfriend? Just let me know what feels right to you."

She swallowed audibly and wished for a bottle

of iced water instead of cooling coffee. She took an eager sip anyway. "And your rate?"

"No charge until I know there's a case. We can talk more about it in a day or two."

Scarlet rose and slid her purse strap over one shoulder. "I guess I'll see you tonight. Six o'clock at the Coulter Realty office?"

"I'll be there." Austin walked her to the door and held it open as she passed.

When she buckled into her SUV across the street, he was still watching, and she tried not to stare. His tan, taut body leaned against the exterior wall. Autumn wind ruffled his hair.

Scarlet released a shaky breath and eased away from the curb, feeling the weight of his gaze on her as she passed.

If suspicions of a stalker weren't her complete undoing, the red-hot attraction she'd felt for Austin Beaumont would be.

Chapter Four

Scarlet drove to work feeling significantly lighter than she had when she'd left home, but also a little flushed. Austin Beaumont had put her mind at ease on the potential stalker situation and given her something altogether different to think about until she saw him again. He'd been a consummate professional in his speech and interactions, but something in his eyes had felt downright inviting. An unspoken dare or challenge.

Or maybe she was projecting.

Regardless, it'd been a long time since she'd experienced a physical reaction while speaking to a man. Yet, as she sat in that PI office, her heart had raced and her thighs had clenched. Her mind had even begun to wonder if he was as capable in private matters as he seemed to be in professional ones. More, what would his lips feel like on hers? What did he taste like? And was he open to entertaining her curiosity?

All thoughts she never had. Clearly the recent paranoia was affecting her mind.

She kept an eye on her rearview mirror as she made her way along familiar downtown streets toward the Coulter Realty offices. No one appeared to be following her, but she still breathed easier when she pulled into the lot behind a coworker. Now she wouldn't have to cross the lot alone.

Lydia Stevens, a newer and younger agent who'd grown up in Marshal's Bluff, climbed out with a grin. A collection of bags hung from her fingertips. Her brown hair was curled into thick beachy waves and hanging loose over her shoulders. The fitted red dress she wore emphasized her runner's figure, and an oversize cream-colored cardigan hung off her narrow frame. She hiked a black laptop bag and a designer purse onto one shoulder then slid a canvas tote and thermal lunch bag into her opposite hand.

Considering the tennis shoes on her feet, Scarlet guessed the canvas tote held Lydia's high heels for appointments. From experience she knew the lunch bag contained a reusable water bottle, a lidded bowl of sliced veggies and a ready-made smoothie or protein shake.

Scarlet admired the ambition, but she stuck with sensible two-inch pumps she could wear comfortably all day. And she ordered lunch on the go, when she had time to eat at all.

Lydia waved as she waited for Scarlet to park and join her. "Hey, you! How was the showing last night? Did you make another sale?"

"No. It was another no-show. My third in five weeks." She considered telling Lydia more about her suspicions and her visit with the local PI, but decided to wait until she knew more. Thinking she had a stalker if she didn't would just make her sound loopy. And telling someone else about her fears would make it all feel more real. Scarlet didn't want either of those things to happen, so she refreshed her smile and locked the car behind her.

Lydia pushed out her bottom lip. "Bummer. So you're still having trouble with the requests from the contact form?"

"Apparently. Have you had any issues?"

"No." Lydia followed her to the office door. "But I don't get a lot of requests that way yet. I'm still too new. I think the system checks senior agents' calendars first. So I only get the lead if everyone else is busy."

Scarlet paused to open and hold the door for her colleague to pass. "Do you ever get appointments through the website?"

"Only a few. Which is why I'm upping my social media game. I'm going to target potential clients by connecting with first-time home buyers, young couples and single career folk."

"Sounds like a plan," Scarlet said, making her way to her desk. She had to get something similar in motion to sell the Perez house before Mr. Perez pulled it from her listings.

A framed photo of Scarlet and her mother greeted her as usual, pulling a more authentic smile across her lips. In the image, the Wills women stood arm in arm beside a SOLD sign and in front of a big white farmhouse. Scarlet had just gotten her real estate license and, under her mom's guidance and tutelage, sold her first property at above the asking price. It was a moment worthy of its ornate silver frame.

She briefly considered calling her mom to tell her about the strange situation she might be in, but Scarlet also hated to upset her without reason. Having a mom for a best friend was wonderful but complicated. She wanted to share everything with her, but occasionally the stories needed editing. And others just weren't Mom appropriate. She couldn't even properly gush about the handsome man she'd met today because of his ties to the potential stalker.

Austin's lean, lithe body flashed back into mind, his dark eyes on her, a wicked half grin on his lips. It was enough to make her want to clutch her pearls, if only she'd been wearing them.

"I bet he has killer abs," she whispered to herself, setting up her laptop for the day.

"Who?" Lydia appeared with her breakfast protein shake, brows arched high.

Scarlet's face heated.

"Oh. You're turning red." Lydia pulled up a chair and sat, crossing her legs and leaning forward. "This is going to be good. Please dish. I love abs."

Scarlet laughed. "I didn't mean to say that out loud."

"But you did. So, let's discuss."

"I met a guy this morning," she admitted reluctantly. "He was…really nice."

Actually, she realized, *this is the perfect setup to our cover story.*

Lydia took a long swig from her shaker and waited for more.

"His name is Austin Beaumont, and he might stop by the office later. If you're here I'll introduce you."

Lydia's jaw nearly unhinged. "No. Way."

Scarlet wrinkled her nose at the strange look of shock on the other woman's face. "You don't want to meet him?"

"Scarlet," she said flatly. "You enormous out-of-towner." The younger agent spun in a dramatic circle on her chair.

"You know I've been here for four years—"

"He's a Beaumont. Of course I want to meet him. The Beaumont brothers are a main component in every Marshal's Bluff woman under fifty's secret fantasy life. And if they're being honest, probably plenty of the men too. The brothers are all older than me, but I've grown up hearing all about them. They're practically legendary. My grandmama says their dad and his brothers were the same way. The one called Dean got engaged last summer and broke a bunch of hearts."

Seeing one of the PIs taken off the market certainly would be heartbreaking, but not the brother Lydia had mentioned. "I met Dean today too."

Lydia threw up her hands. "Absolutely unfair. You know, that family did a calendar once to raise money for a local farmer who was losing his land. The photographer volunteered her services, and they sold enough calendars to save the farm and hire a crew for harvest."

Also not surprising. But a real missed opportunity. Scarlet would've cheerfully bought three copies of that calendar. One for her office, another for home and one for her mama, who was over fifty, but no one with any amount of good sense would ever mention it.

"How exactly did you meet them before work?" Lydia pressed.

A very good question. Scarlet considered her words. "Austin approached me on the street downtown."

Lydia's eyes bulged. "He just walked right up to you?"

"Yeah." She cringed, recalling him approaching her SUV in traffic. "He startled me, so I threatened to pepper spray him and call the police."

Lydia roared with laughter.

"After we got that misunderstanding sorted, he asked to see me again."

"Wow. Some people have all the luck," Lydia said.

True, though Scarlet had never thought of herself as that person.

Her laptop finished booting up, and she navigated to her email. The number of messages in her inbox knocked her back to reality. "I guess I'd better get busy."

Lydia rose and returned her chair to the empty desk beside her. "Fine, but I'm jealous. Of the guy and the inbox. One day my email will be full," she said, striding to her work space. "Until then, it's time for me to launch the social media campaign of my life."

Scarlet opened the newest email from Mr. Perez, following up on their chat by phone the previous night. He wanted a detailed plan for reaching more potential buyers with information on his property, and something in writing about selling the listing, at his price, in the next two weeks.

She chose to be thankful this was an email and not another phone call.

From there, the correspondences got easier. Past clients planning another move. Referral clients looking for advice. A few showing requests from families and couples she was already working with to find their new home. And three newly accepted offers, which meant a string of phone calls to banks and title agencies after lunch.

By three o'clock, her inbox was looking manageable, and her stomach was filling with butterflies. Just a few more hours before Austin showed up at her office.

An incoming message drew her thoughts back to work. Another showing request sent through the website's online contact form. She opened the email with trepidation and breathed easier to see a woman's name instead of a man's. Better still, the prospective client wanted to see the Perez home. The day just kept getting better.

"Lydia?" Scarlet said, checking the time and responding quickly to the request. "I've got a showing at the Perez home in forty-five minutes. I'm going to head out there now so I can set up before the potential buyer arrives. I want to grab some cookies from the bakery and fresh flowers from the florist. I should be back by six, but if Austin beats me here, will you let him know I won't be long?"

Her coworker smiled. "I will gladly regale him with my many wondrous stories of working with Scarlet Wills."

"I think offering him a bottle of water and a seat will be enough," she said, moving a little more quickly. "But since you said that, I'll definitely be back by six."

Lydia laughed as Scarlet made her exit.

The lines at the florist and bakery were short, and the drive to the Perez home was rural, so she easily avoided traffic.

The home was situated on multiple acres and set back from the road by about two hundred feet. A curving black ribbon of asphalt wound through a lush green lawn and past numerous mature oaks to a turnaround driveway outside the large two-story estate. The annual lawn and landscaping maintenance budget alone was more than Scarlet would make on the sale, and her cut of the asking price was more than some folks made in a year. Motivation to sell was high for more reasons than the owner's persistence.

She climbed out of the car, her purse on one shoulder, cell phone, car keys and a bag with cookies in one hand. A bouquet of fresh-cut flowers rested in the crook of the opposite arm. She closed the door with a flick of one hip and took a moment to admire the estate.

It was nearing five o'clock, making this the perfect time for a showing. There was still enough daylight for a potential buyer to appreciate the exterior beauty on their way inside, and by the time they headed home, an array of auto-timed landscaping lights would illuminate the home and driveway, showcasing the equally brilliant curb appeal by night.

She took two steps before something in the air seemed to change. The soft crack and grind of pebbles underfoot was her only indication she wasn't alone before an arm snaked around her middle and a gloved hand covered her mouth.

Scarlet's scream was squelched by the band of leather crushing her lips against her teeth. Air rushed from her lungs, pressed out by an unyielding grip across her center. The bag of cookies and fresh bouquet crashed to the ground at her feet. She jerked and kicked, fighting uselessly against an unseen attacker.

Hot, sticky breath blew across her temple and cheek. The scratch of his unshaven face scraped against her ear. "Stop fighting, Scarlet," he warned in a low, gravelly whisper. "I'm here to let you know I saw what you did this morning, and I won't tolerate you seeing him again." The rage behind the whisper stilled her limbs. "We can't be happy together if you won't be faithful. Understand?"

She nodded quickly, adapting as he changed the scenario. She'd expected to be dragged off somewhere and killed. Maybe there was hope after all. A warning meant a second chance. Didn't it?

That was all she needed.

"Good," he said, loosening his grip slightly. "Now, I'm sorry to do this, but you have to be punished. Otherwise you might forget we had this little talk or think you can try me again. You can't."

"No. No, no, no, no," she murmured against the glove. "I'm sorry. I'm sorry."

"Shh. This is going to hurt me more than it hurts you."

Scarlet's limbs tightened, and she braced for what would come next.

His hand left her mouth, and for one beat of her heart, she was free.

Then ten long angry fingers curved around her throat and squeezed.

Chapter Five

Austin wiped the back of one hand across his brow and adjusted the brim on his baseball cap to better block the sun. He'd scrambled to offload as much of his work as possible over the past few hours, clearing his schedule to better focus on Scarlet's case. He now owed multiple favors to Dean, and had a mere hour from meeting with his gorgeous new client again, he was baling hay at the family ranch and hoping his other brother Lincoln would agree to one little thing. "So, you'll handle it?"

Lincoln made a noncommittal sound.

Austin stifled the urge to toss the next bale at his brother.

There wouldn't be time to go home and shower thanks to this delay. He'd have to show up at the Coulter Realty office looking and smelling like someone who'd just filled the bed of a pickup truck with hay. Twice. He was on a real roll with bad impressions today.

"Lincoln," Austin pressed. "Just tell me you'll do it, so I can meet with the new client."

His brother sighed. "You're calling this a reconnaissance to make it sound more appealing, but I'll actually be sitting in my truck alone all night staring at a dark house and trying to stay awake. I can't even drink coffee to pass the time, because then I'd need a restroom, and I can't leave."

"But it's easy money," Austin said. "And it pays in cash."

"I don't need cash."

Austin tugged the work gloves from his hands and frowned. He always forgot that about his brother. Being an officer in the military for several years, most of which he'd spent deployed, had paid him well. And without actual expenses, the money had piled up. Then, he'd come home to reinvent himself as a hermit, working full-time for the ranch. Considering his earn-to-spend ratio and general lifestyle choices, Lincoln wasn't money motivated.

He eyeballed his brother—tan and fit, bearded face and overgrown hair. The picture of a guy with nowhere to be and zero cares to give. Very few things interested him. One was solitude and the other was a blonde. "No one said you had to go alone. Take a friend."

Lincoln's jaw set, and his gaze swept over the

stables, likely thinking of the young manager, Josie.

"And if you do this," Austin added, sweetening the pot before he said no. "I won't ask you for another favor for a month."

That raised one of Lincoln's eyebrows and snapped his attention back to Austin. "Six months."

"Two."

"Four."

Austin offered a bland expression. "I can say four, but we both know I'd be lying."

Lincoln rubbed a hand over the back of his neck. "Yeah, all right."

It wasn't abundantly clear if that was an acceptance of the offer or the fact that Austin would definitely need another favor in the next two months, not four, but he took it. "Thank you." Then he checked his watch again. "I might even have time to shower if I do it here instead of running home. And if I borrow some of your clothes."

Lincoln closed the tailgate and leaned against the old farm truck. "What's mine is yours, I guess." He scanned Austin, looking more interested than he had so far. "Do you think there's a real threat for this lady? Or do you just like her?"

"Both," he admitted. "She's beautiful. Successful. Smart. I looked her up online after she left the office. Based on her social media profiles, she doesn't seem to do a lot outside of work. Her personal posts are limited. The accounts for business are another story. I'm guessing that's how she attracted whoever's following her. I'd like to think she's being overly cautious, but if she's concerned enough to meet with a private investigator, there's almost always a problem."

"And you like her."

Austin looked over his shoulder toward their parents' home on instinct. "So far there's nothing not to like. Don't bring it up to Mama. I just met this woman. She's going to be a client. Not an addition to the family."

Lincoln grinned. "That's not what Mama would say."

The sound of tires on gravel pulled their attention to an approaching truck. Their youngest brother, Finn, waved an arm through the open window.

Austin moved in the truck's direction, a sensation of unease rolling down his spine. "Were you expecting him?"

"Yeah." Lincoln kept pace at his side. "One of the new boarders was involved in some petty crimes. The ranch took responsibility for her until the trial. Finn's been around every day or so to check in."

Finn parked beside Austin, then met his brothers halfway across the lawn. "Didn't expect to see you here." He adjusted the dark sunglasses over his eyes. The shiny detective badge on his belt announced his authority, even if he looked far too young for the role.

"I was just here asking for favors," Austin said.

Lincoln grunted. "He pawned his current work onto me so he can meet with some cute new client."

Finn turned widened eyes on Austin. "How'd you manage that?"

"I'm not allowed to ask him for anything else for a month."

"Two," Lincoln corrected.

Finn laughed. "Solitude beats cash, huh?"

"Solitude is priceless."

"Tell me about the cute new client," Finn said, still grinning.

Austin rolled his eyes and explained the situation with Scarlet Wills, then tipped his head toward the house. "I'm going to hit the shower here and try not to be too late reaching her office."

Finn looked up from his phone. He'd started scrolling the minute Austin had given Scarlet's name. "She's got a big web presence. Thousands of followers. If she's picked up a stalker, you're going to have your work cut out for you. She probably talks to a hundred people every week. Buyers, sellers, security companies, maintenance companies, landscapers, home stagers… Could be anyone."

"I'm aware." He'd already made lists to address categorically at their meeting tonight. "This is not my first rodeo," Austin reminded him.

Finn flipped up his palms in innocence. "You're right. You've got this. But let me know if you need an assist."

Austin took a few backward steps in the direction of the farmhouse. "Sounds good. I've got to get moving. I'm officially late."

"You're always late," his brothers called behind him.

They weren't wrong, but it was something he was working on.

Twenty minutes later, he'd showered and dressed in a new T-shirt and jeans from Lincoln's closet. Nice ones that Dean had purchased at Christmas, and Lincoln had promptly stashed in his closet without even removing the tags. Dean liked nice stuff. Lincoln found that entertaining.

Austin was glad for both truths, because now he didn't have to dress in Lincoln's worn-out and holey favorites. He ran a hand through wet hair as he made his way onto the porch.

Finn nearly knocked him down on the steps, more focused on his phone than where he was going.

"Whoa!" Austin sidestepped, barely avoiding the collision. "Where's the fire?"

His brother's brows were gathered low when he lifted his gaze. "The Realtor you're meeting with—Scarlet Wills—"

The chill he'd felt earlier returned to Austin's skin. "Yeah?"

"She's at the ER. Come on. I'll drive."

Tension coiled through Austin's limbs, and he shot a hand out to catch his brother's elbow. "What happened?"

"Someone attacked her this afternoon. Stole her phone, purse and car keys. She managed to get into her car and start it before the key fob was out of range. She locked the doors and used her onboard system to call for help. She was unconscious when they arrived. She had your card in her hand."

Austin was in motion, truck keys in hand. "I'll follow you. Use your lights."

Finn kept pace, making a run for his truck.

Scarlet had been hurt while Austin had bantered with his brothers. And her attacker had taken everything he needed to find or reach her anywhere she went. Which meant Austin had severely dropped the ball.

That wouldn't happen again.

Chapter Six

Scarlet woke with the sunrise the next morning. She'd been admitted at the hospital for observation after being rescued, treated for her injuries and given a battery of tests. Her head, neck and shoulders screamed with each small movement, but she was glad for the daylight creeping across her windowsill. It'd been a long night of interruptions and drug-hazed nightmares.

Thankfully, aside from being unprecedentedly sore and permanently traumatized, she was more or less fine.

She blinked against the reaching shafts of amber and apricot light and turned to stare into the even brighter hallway. A groan escaped her lips and the sound elicited fresh pain from her tender throat. Memories of the attacker's hands around her neck came rushing back, along with the pungent scent of leather. The once-pleasant smell would forever haunt her now. Just one more way the jerk would continue to ruin things for her, even after she'd physically healed.

Other details about the previous night were fuzzy. She'd spent the wee hours waffling between attempts to fill in the blank spots and not wanting to remember at all. She'd been strangled. That part was crystal clear, and the rest didn't matter.

She hadn't seen the person who did it. Couldn't identify him by face or voice. Hadn't even gotten a look at what he drove when he made his escape.

There had been pain and fear. Struggle. Then blackness.

She'd climbed into her car and locked the doors, then pushed the starter button, not realizing her keys were no longer in her hand or pocket. The next thing she knew, she'd been on a gurney headed into the hospital. A padded collar around her neck. Straps holding her torso to a backboard. Blinding light everywhere.

Kind of like now.

Except everything smelled of bleach and… flowers?

She squinted at a pair of bouquets beside a pitcher of water and small plastic cup on her nightstand.

"I'm headed that way now," a female voice said.

Scarlet spotted a redheaded nurse moving toward her open door with a wide smile.

Several other women in matching scrubs were gathered outside her room, clutching clipboards and smiling goofily at something unseen.

The redhead stepped inside. "Oh, and it looks like she's awake. Good morning, Scarlet. How are you feeling?"

Scarlet's throat was tight and raw, so she did her best to look pleasant instead of speaking.

"Pardon me, ladies," a familiar tenor declared, seconds before Austin Beaumont strode into the room behind the nurse.

Scarlet's heart rate rose, and her muscles tightened. A million insecurities raced through her addled head. This wasn't the way she wanted to look when he saw her again. Or when anyone who didn't work as medical staff saw her at all. She was hurting and battered, sleep deprived and wearing a hospital gown.

She wanted to order him out. Or at least brush her hair, but her eyes chose to fill with tears of defeat instead.

Austin's right hand curled around a disposable cup. His opposite hand plunged deep into his pocket. The congenial expression he'd worn a moment prior vanished.

"Good morning," the nurse said, turning on a light over the machines and checking the monitors before facing Scarlet. "Your pulse is elevated. How's your pain?"

Scarlet cleared her throat, wincing immediately at the dull throb in her temple.

"Take these," the nurse said, passing her a pair of white pills. "We'll send a prescription home with you." She poured water from the pitcher into the plastic cup and waited while Scarlet took the pills.

"All right. Everything else here looks good. I'll catch the doctor and find out where your discharge stands."

Scarlet watched the nurse leave then slowly turned her eyes to Austin, wishing she was at least wearing her own pajamas, and that she'd been wrong about someone following her.

"I'm sorry," he said, taking a cautious step in her direction. "Scarlet. I'm so very sorry."

Her bottom lip trembled as his compassion pushed her toward the edge. "I didn't want to be right," she croaked. "Celebrities and social media stars get stalkers. Not small-town real estate agents. I just can't—" Her throat ached and words failed her, so she pleaded with her eyes. "I shouldn't have gone to that appointment alone."

"This is not your fault." He set his coffee on the stand beside her bed and gripped the metal rail near her arm. "You did everything right. You sensed something was wrong, and you sought help. I started building your case file and off-loading my work as soon as you left my office so I could concentrate on this. You had no reason to anticipate an attack."

Scarlet bit her lip, knowing that was true. She'd never in her wildest dreams thought she'd be brutally attacked like this. Followed again, maybe, but she'd asked for help with that. "What are you doing here so early? The sun's still rising. How'd you even hear about what happened?"

"My brother Finn is the detective on the case. He filled me in on as much as he can."

She worked the words over in her mind. "I hope he didn't wake you. There isn't much you can do here."

He shrugged. "It seemed smart to come as soon as I could. I feel better knowing you have someone keeping watch."

Scarlet's mouth went dry, and she sipped from her cup again. Did he believe her attacker was still watching? That he'd come to the hospital for her? The thought coiled her gut. "I know it's important to make a statement as soon as possible, before I forget the details, but it's all just—" she moved her hands in circles around her head "—scrambled. Or missing."

"Don't worry about that right now. Finn will check in when he can. Rest. Heal."

A soft rap against the door frame made her jump. Apparently she was more on edge than she'd realized.

The doctor who'd cared for her upon arrival gave a slight nod. His white lab coat had a photo ID clipped to the pocket. The words *Dr. Lanke* were embroidered on the opposite side. "You're up early," he said, moseying forward with a warm, parental smile.

Austin offered the older man his hand. "Austin Beaumont."

"Dr. Lanke." He looked curiously at the PI then swung his attention to Scarlet. "Would you like your friend to step outside while we go over your details?"

Scarlet glanced at Austin. She wasn't sure which details the doctor planned to share, but she also wasn't in a hurry to be without him. "It's okay. He can stay."

Dr. Lanke explained the results of some tests they'd been waiting on and recapped things she already knew. "Nothing broken or fractured. No signs of a concussion. Bruising and swelling around the throat will reduce on their own. Rest and hydrate. Take the pills for pain as prescribed so your body can relax and heal steadily without becoming overwrought. Follow up with a counselor within a few weeks, even if you think you don't need further help. Sometimes these things sneak up on us when we're sure we've gotten past them, and something like this should be talked about."

She nodded. "And my missing memories? When will they return?"

He took a breath, releasing it slowly and donning the fatherly smile once more. "The memories will likely return in time. It's not uncommon for patients who've been through trauma like this to suppress the specifics. The mind is a complicated thing, and it will go to great lengths to protect itself."

She slouched, defeated and deflated. It was bad enough that this had happened, but she'd reasoned that everything had a silver lining, or at least a purpose. For example, if she could remember the attacker's face, his car or some other detail that would lead the police to his arrest, then maybe it was worth the trauma, because this would finally be over. But she couldn't remember.

"I'll get the discharge paperwork together, and one of the nurses will bring it around shortly. Alternate ice for swelling and heat for comfort on your sore muscles. Be kind and patient with yourself. Change the bandage on your shoulder daily. I'll send a tube of cream for the stitches."

"Stitches?" she asked, taking a mental inventory. Her shoulder was sore, but so was the rest of her.

"You fell," Austin said, before the doctor could clarify. "Police found blood on a landscaping stone near the driveway's edge. The impact was enough to split the skin."

Dr. Lanke frowned but nodded. "We cleaned the wound and secured it with a couple of stitches to reduce scarring. Nothing serious, but it will be tender as it heals."

"Thank you," she whispered. The words left her lips absently while her mind struggled to imagine the scenario Austin described.

"Pretty flowers," Dr. Lanke said, tucking his clipboard beneath one bent arm. "From you?" His eyes flickered to Austin.

"Yes, sir," Austin said. "My partner and I. The others are from her coworkers."

Scarlet's heart thudded, and her stomach dropped. Did everyone in her immediate world know what had happened? The possibility nauseated her. She wished no one knew, but keeping a secret like this for long in a town as small as Marshal's Bluff would be impossible. Her attack had probably made front-page news.

She rubbed her palms against her arms, trying to scrub away the sensation of her attacker's hands on her skin.

"You're lucky to have such a dedicated fan," the doctor said. "Most boyfriends don't stay all night like this. Not that any of the nurses minded having him around." He chuckled and winked then headed for her door. "I'll get that discharge paperwork moving. You'll be free to go later this morning."

Scarlet's attention snapped to Austin and her lips parted. "You've been here all night?"

Austin looked sheepish. "I couldn't leave you again. I stayed in the waiting room so you could rest. I can't stop thinking this wouldn't have happened if I'd started shadowing you sooner, instead of putting it off until the end of the day. It's possible this happened because you came to see me. If my presence in your life escalated your stalker, then I wasn't there to protect you—" He shook his head, expression darkening.

She let his words roll around in her head, unable to properly focus on or dissect them. Something else was already pressing to the front of her addled mind. "You told the staff you're my new boyfriend?"

"They assumed," he said. "I didn't correct them. I know we hadn't decided on our cover story yet, but I needed a good reason to hang around. Couldn't let them think I might be a stalker." He frowned. "That was very unfortunate and poorly timed wording. Sorry."

Scarlet's lips curled into a small, unexpected smile. She was certain the nurses she'd seen earlier would let Austin do just about anything he wanted without question, but she kept that to herself.

"If I've overstepped, I'm happy to set the record straight with the staff."

"No." She shook her head. "It's okay. I implied as much to my coworker, so—"

"So," he echoed, lips twisting. "I guess it's official."

Her toes curled beneath the scratchy bleach-white blankets. It was definitely official. She was into her new protector in ways that would surely get her hurt in the aftermath. "Yep."

SOMETHING IN SCARLET'S eyes told Austin she liked the sound of them as a couple as much as he did. The fact that she could manage a blush after all she'd been through gave him hope for her full recovery as well. Physical and emotional.

He'd met his share of people who'd experienced terrible things. They all healed at their own pace. Some never spoke of their trauma again. Others addressed their pasts only as necessary. He suspected Scarlet was the type to form an awareness group, hold rallies and raze offenders like hers to the ground. He liked that about her. More than he should.

"I had a second reason for letting the staff believe we're dating," he admitted in the interest of full disclosure. "I can't be sure if your attacker saw you at my office, if he saw us talking on the street or sidewalk, or none of the above. But

I don't want him to know you hired a PI. That knowledge could cause him to look more closely at the trail he's leaving while he follows you. We want to keep his focus on you, so Dean, Finn and the local police have the best chance of identifying and locating him quickly."

Scarlet swallowed audibly, and the pulse point in her neck beat faster. She sipped from her little cup again.

"I didn't say that to frighten you. I'm only being forthright." Austin leaned closer, expression firm. "I won't let him get near you again. You can believe that. He can't get past me, and he sure as hell can't go through me."

Her lips parted and her eyes widened as she watched and listened, hopefully realizing every word was true. Austin was more than capable of bringing down any enemy, and she could bank on that.

Satisfied, he nodded and straightened.

"But you can't stay with me forever," she said. "What happens when you're gone?"

It was a solid concern, but clearly she didn't know him. "I won't leave until this guy's caught or you order me away. Even then, I'll probably still be outside in my truck." He did his best to refresh his smile and lighten the mood. But he'd meant those words too. Whoever had hurt Scarlet was going to pay for it, preferably by way of extensive jail time.

She cringed.

Maybe telling a woman, who was being actively stalked, that he too planned to follow and watch her indefinitely wasn't the encouragement he'd intended. "That sounded less creepy in my head."

Scarlet gave a small laugh, and her eyes fell shut. She opened them a moment later. "Well, the pain pills are kicking in." She raised a hand to her temple, then frowned as her fingers traced the goose egg at the side of her head.

He'd seen worse lumps on himself and all his brothers at one time or another, but it was different seeing the knot on her. The pain of her wounds seemed to form an anvil in his chest.

She lowered her hand to her lap and looked through the open doorway. "What happens after I'm discharged?"

He considered his words before speaking this time, knowing whatever he said would be a shock on some level and wanting to ease that stress if he could. "I'll take you home, if you're comfortable with that. You shouldn't be driving or alone for a while. If you'd prefer someone else, I can call them for you. Or you can borrow my phone."

Her brows furrowed as she looked around the room. "I dropped my phone."

"We believe your attacker took it with him when he left."

She sank back against her pillows. "And my keys. I was in my car, but I remember being surprised when it started. I couldn't drive anyway. My vision was blurry. I was going to pass out."

He nodded, widening his stance for stability. The pain in her eyes might've knocked him back a step otherwise. "Paramedics broke your window when they arrived. You were unconscious. The police towed your vehicle, which is being treated as a crime scene now. Finn will have the window replaced when they finish. He'll let us know when it's ready, but that might be a few days."

"So I don't have a phone or car?"

"Not at the moment, but I can get you a phone," Austin said. He and Dean kept several at the office for situations like these. He might even have one in his go bag. "And I can be your chauffeur, assuming you don't mind riding in my truck. It's about ten years older than your SUV with none of the added comforts."

She wrapped her arms around her middle. "My purse had my driver's license in it. He's got my home address. And a key to my house."

Austin dipped his chin in acknowledgment. "You won't be alone there, and I'm going to change your locks as soon as we arrive."

"Delivery," a perky female voice called from the doorway.

He turned as a young woman stepped into the room carrying a tall glass vase and two dozen long-stemmed red roses. Austin frowned. "That's quite a bouquet."

"Isn't it?" the woman said, making room for the huge arrangement beside the other, more appropriate-sized ones. "Someone must really love you."

Scarlet's gaze jumped to Austin as the woman took her leave.

"May I?" he asked, already reaching for the card.

"Yes."

He plucked the small white rectangle from a thin plastic stake hidden among the baby's breath and greenery.

Two hastily scrawled words sent fire through his core.

I'm sorry.

Chapter Seven

Austin's focus jerked to Scarlet.

"They're from him, aren't they?" she asked, face pale and expression grim.

"I think so. I'm going to catch the woman who delivered these and find out. I won't be long."

She nodded, and he dove through the door.

"Excuse me," he called, too loud for hospital etiquette. A dozen nearby faces turned in his direction. "Wait," he instructed the woman who'd made the delivery.

Then he turned to the nearest nurse. "I need someone to guard Scarlet Wills's room until I get back. Don't let anyone in or out who isn't already assigned to her care."

The nurse nodded, eyes wide, then dashed toward Scarlet's room. Another nurse followed on her heels.

Austin jogged to the delivery woman's side, noticing the name Marie on her badge for the first time. He passed her the little card. "Did you take the order for these flowers?"

She stared in surprise and nodded. "Yes."

"Can you describe the man who wrote this?"

"I wrote that," she said. "I was in a hurry to complete the order and make my rounds." She motioned to a small rolling cart with an array of flowers, teddy bears and helium balloons. "I like to fill and deliver all the orders that came in after hours as soon as I get in each morning. He ordered the roses before I'd finished loading the cart."

Austin stilled. Marie had written the card. "Was the order placed online? Or did he come into the gift shop? Can you describe him?"

She shook her head. "He called."

"I need you to show me the receipt. Did he pay cash? Does the shop have caller ID?"

The woman looked skeptical, possibly border-line frightened.

"Please," he added, before she could make an excuse or do anything else that would cost him precious time. "I believe the person who sent those roses is the same person who attacked the woman in that room last night. I'm a private investigator, and I'm trying to find him." He pulled his credentials from his wallet as proof and waited while she looked at them. "Help me," he pleaded.

Marie grabbed her cart. "Okay. Let's go."

They hurried to the first-floor gift shop, where she passed her cart and delivery duties to a clerk behind the counter. She took the other woman's position and waved Austin to join her.

"Here." Marie pointed to the phone beside the register.

Blessedly, the device had caller ID.

Next she pulled the receipt tape from the register and matched the time of purchase to the time of the call. Another stroke of luck, likely thanks to the early hour. The phone only stored ten numbers, and his was still in the system.

Austin snapped a photo of the phone number before it was replaced by additional incoming calls. "I assume he paid by credit card. Do you remember the name on the card?"

She pressed her lips together. "It was a prepaid card."

Of course it was. Austin had to give the criminal credit. He was a planner and a thinker.

"May I have the number of the card?" he asked.

The woman frowned. "I think that's crossing some kind of line. I don't want to get fired."

"Can I ask your manager?"

"She comes in this afternoon."

Austin fought the urge to argue. Marie had her protocols too, and she'd already shown him more than she had to. "My brother is the detective on this case. I'll reach out to him. Maybe he can contact your manager."

She nodded. "Thank you. I'm sure that will work."

"Can you help me with one more thing?" he asked, pointing to the handset on the desk. "I'd like to call the suspect. He's more likely to answer if I use the gift shop's phone."

She glanced nervously around. "Okay."

Austin accessed the speaker function and dialed. He pressed one palm against the counter as he listened to the tinny rings.

"Hello?" a low and cautious male voice answered.

Marie's eyes bulged.

Austin motioned for her to talk then scratched a note on a flyer.

"Hi," she said, eyes scanning the paper. "This is Marie from the Marshal's Bluff Memorial Hospital Gift Shop. You placed an order for roses this morning, and I forgot to ask your name."

Austin nodded at her.

She'd done well.

The man's breathing became audible, and a rumbling laugh broke through the line. "Someone told you to call me. Didn't they?"

"No. I was just taking the flowers up and—"

"Don't lie!" he screamed.

Marie jumped back from the receiver, one hand pressed to her chest.

Austin set a palm on her shoulder. "Who is this?" he asked, raising the phone to his ear. "Tell me now, and I'll go easy on you. Make me work for it, and I'll be forced to remind you later that you blew this opportunity."

"Stay away from her," the voice warned. "Stay away. Or you'll regret it."

"I'm definitely not doing that," Austin answered, contrasting the other man's seething tone with a jovial one. "But I am coming for you." He smiled as he spoke, and Marie shot him a curious look.

Scarlet's stalker began to growl. The sound climbed into a wild scream. "She's mine! She's! Mine!"

A round of earsplitting cracks and booms made Austin cringe. It sounded as if the man was beating his phone against something hard, possibly until it burst into pieces, because the line went dead.

"Oh, dear," Marie whispered, moving her trembling hand from her chest to her lips.

Austin dragged a nearby stool from its position in front of the register to within Marie's reach, and she sat. "Do you need me to call someone so you can take a minute to gather yourself?"

She shook her head.

He wasn't sure she was all right, so he kept an eye on her while he dialed Finn and delivered the rundown, then sent the photo of the number on the memory display.

"You should've let me make that call," Finn said. "We could've traced it from the precinct."

"He wouldn't have answered a call from the police station," Austin said. "I called from the gift shop so he'd think there was a question about his order."

"This is the number?" he asked. "In the photo?"

"Yeah." Though Austin was certain that particular phone had been destroyed. "You'll have to come down here and talk with the shop's manager to get the credit card number, but they have it."

"I'm already on my way," Finn said. "If I'm lucky, he paid for the prepaid card with something linked to his name, but I'm rarely lucky. Still, I'll be able to track the card to the store where it was purchased. The store should have a time-stamped receipt. Then I can check the security camera feed from that time to see who bought it."

"He might've bought the card online."

"Don't say stuff like that," Finn said. "You're going to jinx me."

"Okay, Detective." Austin rolled his eyes and

waved goodbye to Marie, who was still shell-shocked behind the counter. "Thank you."

She nodded, eyes wide and skin pale.

He should probably send her flowers later for her help. Then again, the stalker might've ruined flowers for her. "I'm going back to Scarlet's room," he said, both to Marie and to Finn. "She's being released this morning, and I want to be there when she gets her instructions."

"Stay with her," Finn said. "I hate everything you've told me about this guy. I don't want you to leave her side again."

"Believe me," Austin said, breaking into a run for the nearest bank of elevators. "I'm not planning on it."

Chapter Eight

It was afternoon before Scarlet was finally discharged. She left in her dirty skirt, socks and underthings, plus a logoed T-shirt from the gift shop. Her top had bloodstains, and she couldn't bring herself to put it on.

The sun was high in the sky when a young man in scrubs wheeled her into the pickup area outside the hospital's sliding glass doors.

"Ready?" Austin asked, opening the passenger door of his truck and offering her his hand.

She didn't answer. She wasn't sure. Much as she wanted to leave the hospital, leaving made her feel vulnerable. She hadn't been hurt at the hospital. She'd been mended there. And going home with Austin meant a whole other set of problems. For starters, he was a perfect stranger, and while she didn't have any reasons not to trust him, she'd been through an ordeal. No one and nothing felt quite as safe as it had before.

In other, more mundane concerns, she didn't

have the capacity to be a hostess, and she wasn't in the habit of having company. Her home was her private domain. She met with friends at restaurants or visited their place. Now, she was on the spot to hold herself together and be congenial when all she wanted to do was cry or scream or pack up and move to Timbuktu.

And she still needed to call her mother. She quickly pushed that thought aside.

"Scarlet?"

Her name on his tongue pulled her back to the moment.

Austin stood before her, hand outstretched. The hospital staffer who'd been pushing her wheelchair waited for her to get up so he could move on with his day.

"Sorry." She gingerly set her hand in Austin's and ignored the instant buzz of chemistry as he pulled her onto her feet with ease.

He held the door while she climbed into the truck's cab, then shut it when she was inside.

The interior smelled of earth and hay, warmth and sunshine. The soothing scent of his cologne seemed to underscore everything else.

She winced as she fastened her safety belt; every muscle in her neck, shoulders, back and torso felt tender, overstretched and bruised.

Austin climbed behind the wheel, donned a pair of dark sunglasses and shifted into Drive.

She studied the space around her. He hadn't been kidding about the age of his truck. It was old, a model she remembered from high school, but well maintained. A pair of handcuffs hung from his rearview mirror, and she became suddenly thankful he couldn't read her mind.

"Do you prefer a certain radio station or type of music?" he asked, punching buttons as they turned away from the parking lot.

"I usually listen to audiobooks."

He pointed vents in her direction and turned on the cool air. "What kind of books?"

Heat rushed over her cheeks, and for the smallest moment, she considered dodging the question. Or lying. "Romance," she said finally, uninterested in bending truths. Even less interested in explaining her preferences. "I like books about families and happy endings." She turned her chin away and braced for the joke.

There was always a joke.

"Who are your favorite authors?"

She looked at him. "You know the names of romance authors?"

He shrugged. "A few. Mama is a huge fan. I try to keep up when she tells me about whatever she's reading. I know it's important to her, even if it's not my cup of tea."

"What's your cup of tea?" she asked, more curious about him than his mother's favorite authors.

He glanced at her, then away. "I read a little bit of everything."

"Such as?"

"Mostly nonfiction." He flexed his fingers on the steering wheel. Was he nervous to have the spotlight? "I like information. I don't even care what kind. Everything's fascinating if you give it a chance."

Scarlet waited, curiosity growing. "What have you read about most recently?"

"Cooking, gardening, fishing, aviation, unsolved crimes."

Scarlet smiled. The idea that Austin spent his free time reading was incredibly attractive. The fact that he read indiscriminately about everything from cooking to crime was even better. She wondered how many people knew that about him. And she liked the fact that she did.

"What?" he asked, noticing her stare.

"You're a nerd," she said. "You look like that, and you've still got a big inquisitive brain. I like it."

"You like how I look, or my big, beautiful brain?"

She laughed. Her throat ached in protest, but she couldn't squelch the smile. "I didn't call it beautiful."

"You called it big."

Another laugh broke free, and she grimaced at the pain.

She turned her eyes to the view outside her window, allowing herself a moment to recover while admiring the landscape. Slowly, the scenery morphed from busy downtown streets to quaint little neighborhoods, then to the sprawling countryside.

Within minutes, rolling hills of green grass stretched to the horizon, topped by a cloudless blue sky. Punctuated occasionally with a farmhouse, cattle or a big red barn. The sun was high and hot as it beat against the glass, combating the truck's comfortable AC.

It wasn't until Austin made the turn onto her road that she realized what was happening.

"How did you know where I live?" She hadn't thought to give him her address, and her driver's license was with the stalker.

"Dean put it in the new client file," he said. "But I could've found you without it."

She swung her gaze to him, befuddled and having completely forgotten about the details his brother had asked for when she'd made the appointment. Those moments and that phone call felt like memories from years ago instead of yesterday morning. Even more worrisome was what Austin had meant by the second statement. "How?"

"For starters, you bought your house." He raised his brows and his gaze flicked to hers. "Anyone can visit the county auditor's website and enter your last name in a property search. If they don't know how to do that, they can look at your social media."

"My accounts are all set to private."

"Not your business account." He looked her way once more. "You post daily about available homes, your life as a Realtor, and advice for buyers and sellers. You take pictures of your home and lawn, advising sellers to do this or that to spruce up their properties before listing them on the market."

That was true, but she was careful. "I never give my address or photograph the home directly."

"No, but you showcase landscaping features and additions recommended for curb appeal. Your house number is visible on the mailbox in more than one photo. It's small, but people can use their cell phones to enlarge the image. And anyone familiar with the area knows there are only so many sparsely populated streets with inlet views."

Scarlet rocked slightly as he turned onto her driveway. "You can see the inlet in photos of my patio?"

"Yes." Austin cut the engine and climbed down.

She flipped mentally through an array of her most recent posts, realizing how much she'd unintentionally given away. Sometimes she even took photos of a book on her legs while she sat in the sun. Did her stalker imagine those images were meant for him?

The passenger door opened, and she started.

Austin reached for her hand and helped her onto her feet at his side.

The air between them was charged, and if she hadn't looked like someone recently attacked, wearing yesterday's clothes, she might've thought the tightening of his jaw was a sign of attraction.

She turned to face the house. "Shall we?"

He pulled a large black bag from behind her seat then shut the door and followed her. "After you."

A warm heady breeze wafted through her freshly mulched flower beds, overflowing with native blooms. She inhaled and released several slow breaths, working her pulse back to a more normal range.

"You have a beautiful home," he said. His voice traveled to her ears from a few steps behind her. Appreciation colored the tone.

"Thank you. I got lucky on this one. I helped an older couple find a condo near their grown children, and they offered me first dibs. I bought it before it ever went on the market." And since they'd purchased the place for a tenth of its current value, they were happy with the fair market price she could afford. "I think they liked knowing I planned to preserve it." Anyone else would likely have demolished the little home and built something infinitely grander in its place.

Scarlet loved it just as it was.

She climbed the porch steps and leaned against the doorjamb. "I don't have any keys."

Austin set his bag down and removed a credit card from his wallet. He slid the card into the crack between the door and wall then gave it a shimmy. A moment later, the knob turned, and he opened her door. "Like I said, I'm changing the locks."

Scarlet blinked. Her stomach pitched. "The knobs are original," she said on autopilot. Nearly everything was original. She'd made sure of it, because that had been important until yesterday.

He squinted down at her, big hands on trim hips. "I can drill a hole in the door and add a dead bolt, so we can keep the knobs. Or I can replace the knobs with something more modern and secure. This," he said, tipping his head toward the open door, "doesn't cut it anymore."

"I can order new knobs online," she said. "They'll preserve the aesthetic while offering better security, but delivery will take a few days."

He seemed to consider her words. "Let's place that order tonight."

She nodded then led him inside, flipping on light switches as she moved, hoping her attacker wasn't hiding somewhere in the shadows. Austin closed and locked the door behind them as her limbs began to tremble.

Austin's hand brushed her back. "I'm right here," he said. "You're safe."

Her knees locked, and she looked at her home through new eyes. "What if he's here?"

Austin guided her to the sofa in her living space. "I'll be right back. If you see or hear anything that makes you uncomfortable, just holler, and I'll be back in seconds."

She kneaded her hands as he moved out of sight, listening as his footsteps softened in her adjoining kitchen then went silent in her dining room. She imagined him moving in and out of her two first-floor bedrooms and along the hallway in between. The bathroom and sunroom doors creaked open and closed on the far side of her home.

The steps groaned as he climbed to the second floor.

A few moments later, he reappeared and took the seat at her side. "It's just us. Can I get you anything? Tea? Water?"

She shook her head. "It's my house. I should—"

"You should rest," he said, interrupting. "That's the doctor's orders. Meanwhile, I need to secure your windows and find another way to reinforce your doors until the new knobs arrive."

"It's petty, I know."

"It's not," he said. "This is your home. You've worked hard to make it exactly the way you want it, and this guy doesn't get to change anything more about your life than absolutely necessary for your safety. I can stay here until the new knobs and locks are installed. Longer if he isn't arrested before then. As long as that's okay with you."

Scarlet wiped a renegade tear as it swiveled over her cheek. "Thank you. I'm grateful for your help. I just wish I could do something to contribute. He was close enough to me to do all this—" she motioned to her neck and torso "—and I can't even give the police a description. It's infuriating."

"You've been through a lot. Your memories will likely return. Give it time. I'm sure something will trigger them. Until then, focus on healing." He pushed onto his feet. "Are you hungry? I can make or order something."

"You're supposed to be my guest."

He wrinkled his nose. "I kind of invited myself, and you were just released from the hospital. I'm basically your caretaker," he said. "And if I don't feed you, someone is sure to revoke my privileges."

She kicked off her shoes and stood. "Well, we can't have that." She swallowed a wave of emotion, ready to escape to her room for a proper breakdown.

Of course Austin noticed. "Do you want to talk about it?"

"No. I'm going to take a shower and change into something comfortable and clean." She planned to burn the skirt, socks and underthings in the firepit out back or stuff them into the garbage can at her next opportunity. Anything and everything that could remind her of her attack needed to go. She might even trade in her SUV when it was finished being a crime scene.

"I can make some tea and sandwiches when you're ready," he said. "Or soup if that will be easier for your throat."

Scarlet shook her head. "I think I'll start with a large glass of red wine and go from there." She didn't wait for his response. She couldn't. Instead, she turned on her heels and marched into her bathroom, where the shower would cover the sounds of her cries.

Chapter Nine

Austin gave himself a second tour of Scarlet's home while she showered. On this round, he took his time to thoroughly inspect every nook and cranny. Not just the places an intruder could hide, but anywhere someone could gain access to the house or install an unnoticed camera.

It'd been too easy to break in, and that fact had stuck with Austin. No one was hiding inside, but that didn't mean someone hadn't let themselves in, done something nefarious then left without a trace. The possibility Scarlet's stalker could've established a way to watch her from inside her home made his skin crawl.

Thankfully, he found no signs of intrusion or surveillance.

He did, however, see an intense attention to detail on Scarlet's part. Visible in the design of each room and the maintenance of the original floors, baseboards and crown molding. It was as if someone had refinished every inch of wood, tile and marble in the place. No wonder she'd cared about the front doorknob. Her home was a personalized work of art.

The decor choices were more feminine than anyplace he'd ever lived, including the ranch, but he didn't object to any of it. It was like walking through a magazine spread. From the floral accents, to the soft color palette, the abundance of pillows, cozy throw blankets and art. It was a different side of Scarlet than he'd seen so far. The serious businesswoman he'd met at his office had shown no indication that she might also wallpaper a half bathroom in butterflies or sleep beneath a wildflower-print duvet. He added these things to the fact that she loved to read and preferred romance books, specifically ones with happy families.

Her small mudroom overlooked the rear patio and the inlet. A washer, dryer and shelf for folding stood before the window. A drying rack with a rainbow of lacy underthings hurried him along before his mind had time to formulate too many ideas.

He was there to protect her, not to want her. Not like that. Yet in two days' time, his ability to maintain professionalism was already being challenged, internally anyway. And that was before he'd essentially moved in with her.

He tried to imagine for the dozenth time how

she'd managed to drag herself into her SUV and lock the doors before passing out. Or how she'd had the presence of mind to use her onboard system to call for help. She'd just been attacked. Strangled. Most people panicked in situations far less dire, but she'd maintained a level head and her quick responses might've saved her life.

Satisfied the home's windows and doors were secure, he went to make coffee and pour her wine.

She'd been gone awhile, but he imagined she needed extra time to process what had happened, to appreciate being home and to get through her usual shower routine when she was still so bruised and sore. She likely also needed a minute to adjust to the fact that there was a practical stranger in her kitchen making coffee.

Her bedroom door opened, and she emerged a few short minutes later.

Austin carried a glass of merlot in her direction, meeting her in the small hallway.

Her blond hair was darker, still damp from the shower. She'd piled it on her head and pinned it there. She smelled of shampoo and lotion, a delectable blend of uniquely Scarlet scents. Her cream-colored top clung to her athletic form. A pair of loose pink pajama pants covered her legs. "You remembered," she said, accepting the glass and taking a sip. "Thank you."

He smiled, enjoying the blush that spread across her cheeks and hating the angry red welts, now fully exposed, on her neck. "How are you feeling?"

"Better. It's good to be home with my things, in my space."

"And an uninvited houseguest?" he asked.

She offered a small, sad smile. "As long as he brings me wine, I won't complain much." She glanced down the hall toward her mudroom. "I'm going to sit on the deck. Do you want to join me?"

"I'll meet you there." He turned back to the kitchen for a few things, including a fresh cup of coffee, then headed outside.

Scarlet's bras and panties were off the rack when he passed through the mudroom this time, tossed into a nearby basket instead.

He gave silent thanks for that mercy.

She looked up as he exited her home, wrapped in a soft-looking blanket. "I saved you a seat." She motioned to the white Adirondack chair beside hers; both faced the water.

"Thanks." He lowered onto the wooden seat and stretched his legs out before him. "I have something for you too."

"Oh?"

He lifted his cell phone into view. "I thought you might want to call someone. I still need to set up a phone for you, but you're welcome to use mine now. I'm sure there are plenty of people worried about you."

Scarlet stared at the device. "I think I'll wait. I'm not ready to talk about it."

"They're going to read about it in the paper."

She took another sip of wine. "I only care about my mother, and she doesn't live in Marshal's Bluff. I'll call her as soon as I can manage without crying."

Austin looked at her more carefully, noticing the puffiness around her eyes and slight redness of her nose. She'd been crying in the shower while he'd prowled her home. He should've—the thought stalled in his mind.

What could he have done? It was invasive enough that he'd come to her home and planned to stay. It wasn't as if he could've knocked on her door and offered her a hug.

"How's the wine?" he asked, pushing all thoughts of touching her from his mind.

"Exactly what I needed, though I probably shouldn't mix it with my pain pills."

He shrugged. The doctor had prescribed higher doses of the stuff readily available over the counter, nothing like a narcotic. "I'm sure a glass won't hurt."

"I doubt I'll even finish it," she said. "But a glass of wine on the deck has become symbolic to me. It's part of my routine, especially when I've had a hard day. It's peaceful out here. I swear some nights I can hear my tension rolling away in waves."

"The view is certainly beautiful." He looked away before she caught him watching her, fixing his eyes on the water instead.

"I don't always bring wine. Sometimes I have a cup of tea or a tall glass of ice water. It depends on the kind of day I've had. But the routine is tried and true."

Austin absorbed the autumn sun and salty breeze for several long moments, before moving on to his next gift. "I have something else for you."

She rolled her head against the backrest of her chair, an expression of relaxation on her features. "What?"

He shifted to pull the little weapon from his pocket and held it in the air between them.

She frowned. "What is it?"

"A compact stun gun. I thought you could practice using it a few times until you're comfortable, then keep it with you wherever you go. Especially until this is over."

"I have pepper spray and an air horn. And before you ask how well those worked for me yesterday, I want to point out that I wasn't able to get to them, and I wouldn't have been able to reach this thing either."

He bristled at her words, unhappy with whichever person in her life had made her think that would be anyone's response. "I wasn't going to say that."

She pursed her lips, eyes gliding cautiously over the device in his hand. "I'd probably just wind up shocking myself."

He also despised whoever had given her the idea there was anything she couldn't do right or well. "I'm sure that's not true."

She frowned, clearly unconvinced. "Can I think about it?"

"Absolutely. But just for fun, let me show you how simple it is." He hated pushing, especially now, when she'd finally found a moment of peace, but this seemed important enough to make an exception.

He held the small black cylindrical object on his palm.

"It looks like a flashlight."

"It does," he agreed. "And it even has a light, if you need it." He turned the device over until she could see one blunt end. "This little switch powers it on." He demonstrated. "This—" he pointed to a slider, flush with the side "—sets it to charge. And this—" he rested his thumb on a small red button "—stuns."

The device gave a menacing crackle, and Scarlet frowned.

"I have to be close enough to touch that little thing to the person's skin?" she asked.

He gave the device another look. He'd seen its small size as convenient. Looking through her eyes, it was easy to understand the problem. "I hope you'll never again be within arm's distance of someone who wants to cause you harm, but if that day comes, this will send them back a few steps and stop them long enough for you to get away."

He set the device on the small table at his side and turned his eyes to the inlet.

His peace was slowly slipping. He didn't like the thought she'd be alone if he wasn't there. She should be surrounded by friends and family while she pulled through this. If anyone in his family had been hospitalized, the waiting room would've been filled to capacity with folks hoping to wish them well. And a mile-long train of aunties bringing food would've wrapped the blocks outside their home. While her coworkers had sent flowers, the only person Scarlet had spoken of so far was her mama, and she hadn't even called her. "Are you and your mama close?"

She turned bright eyes to his. "Sure. She's my only real family and a great friend."

"And she doesn't live in town?"

Scarlet shook her head. "No. She lives in Holbrook. That's in the next county. Close enough to arrive quickly in an emergency, but far enough away to keep us from being competitors in the market."

He couldn't help wondering which part of the current situation she thought wasn't an emergency. "Have you considered visiting her for a few days while the police search for your stalker?"

"I have," she said. "I just haven't worked up the nerve to call and break her heart with this news."

Austin raised his coffee and returned his attention to the beautiful afternoon.

Wind rustled through her trees, jostling leaves in every shade from amber to crimson, and knocking a few handfuls loose. They fell like confetti against a backdrop of green grass and brilliant blue water. The view was enough to make him feel as if he was inside a painting. No wonder this was where she came to unwind.

"Do you think the police will find him?" she asked.

He didn't need to ask who she'd meant. And he was sure of his answer. "I do."

"And you'll stay with me until then?"

His heart softened with her wobbling words.

He couldn't explain it logically, but he knew he'd stay with her as long as she needed. "I will."

"What if it takes a year? Or ten? You can't just give up your life and all your other clients. What will I do then?"

"Let me worry about my life and my clients. You have enough to think about. Besides, it won't take a year to find him."

Scarlet turned, fixing him with the full intensity of her ethereal green eyes. "How can you be sure?"

Austin leaned in her direction, matching the weight of her stare. "Because whoever hurt you doesn't stand a chance against my family."

SCARLET WOKE THE next morning at nine. She hadn't slept past six in years, and it felt incredible, until she moved. Her aching body protested as she angled upward in bed.

A glass of water and a note sat on her nightstand, along with the painkillers the doctor had prescribed. The note had simple instructions a la *Through the Looking Glass*. "Eat me. Drink me," she read, smiling at the reminder that Austin Beaumont was running loose in her home.

She took the pills and headed to her bathroom to prepare for her day.

Memories of the previous night flashed in her mind as she combed her hair and brushed her teeth. Sitting with Austin on her deck until the sun had set. Watching movies with him in her living room while sharing snacks on the couch and talking about anything and everything to pass the time. She'd gotten to know him better in a few hours than she knew some of the folks who'd been in her life for years. And she hadn't learned anything she didn't approve of or admire.

He loved his family, all ten million of them. He was also smart, funny and kind. She'd felt safe in his care before, but now, she was looking forward to more nights like the last one.

She swiped her favorite tinted gloss across her lips and gave her lashes two coats of mascara before spending an extra few minutes on her hair. Soft jeans with frayed edges, fuzzy socks and a T-shirt from her office softball league completed the casual look. With any luck, he wouldn't realize how much she hoped he thought she was pretty.

Outside her bedroom, the house was quiet, save for movement in the kitchen.

"Good morning," she called, inching slowly in that direction. Hoping it was Austin and not her attacker shuffling around. "Hello?" she projected her voice as she drew nearer.

The scrape of a chair over tiles met her ears a moment before Austin said, "I have to call you back."

She exhaled in relief and pasted on a smile.

"Hey," Austin said, removing earbuds and rising from her table, where a laptop sat beside a pad of paper and a pen. The enticing scents of coffee and cologne filled the little room. "I hope you don't mind. I helped myself to the shower and your kitchen." He motioned to the pot of fresh brew on her counter. "Can I get you a cup?"

"Please."

"Cream or sugar?"

"Both."

He smiled. His outfit was similar to her own—faded jeans and a T-shirt with his PI company's name on the front. "This was all I had in my go bag," he said, following her gaze to his ensemble. "I borrowed something from my brother yesterday, which left this for today. We should probably visit my place soon for a few staples."

"Sounds good," she said, enthralled by the idea of seeing Austin's home. What did it look like? What secrets would it reveal? The thrill of curiosity thinned when she realized he might live like a frat kid, eating out of pizza boxes and sleeping on sheets he hadn't laundered since moving in.

He passed her a steaming mug.

"Thanks." She inhaled the delectable aroma and exhaled a pound of distress. "I can make breakfast since you made the coffee. As soon as

I get to the bottom of this cup and am officially awake."

Austin's gaze flickered to the clock on the wall then back to her. "I hoped to tell you sooner, but I've got breakfast covered."

"What do you mean?" She scanned the kitchen for an indication he'd prepared something already.

The doorbell rang.

"That's for me," he said, tipping his head to indicate she should follow. "Us, actually."

"You ordered breakfast?" She hurried along behind, shamelessly enjoying his use of the word *us*.

"Not exactly."

He opened the door and stepped back so she could move into the space at his side.

A middle-aged woman with a wide smile and milkmaid braids stood on the porch, a casserole in her hands and an insulated bag hooked over her wrist. "Good morning!" she said, big brown eyes swinging from Scarlet to Austin. "Hello, sweet baby boy."

Chapter Ten

"Morning, Mama." Austin stepped forward to kiss his mother's cheek before making room for her to come inside. "Scarlet just woke, and I haven't had time to warn her about your arrival."

She pinched his cheek. "Warn her? I'm here to help. Now, where's the kitchen?"

Scarlet blinked as the woman moved past, following her son to the stove.

"Scarlet," he said with an apologetic grin. "That's my mama. Mary Beaumont."

They followed on the older woman's heels. "Mama, this is Scarlet Wills."

"It's lovely to meet you," she said, setting the temperature on Scarlet's oven. "This just needs to be warmed a little. I hurried to get here so you wouldn't have to wait long."

"Thank you," Scarlet said, half amused, half in shock.

Austin's mom made casseroles and dropped what she was doing to race them to his clients?

Scarlet's mom never cooked, barely ate and only rushed to get to business appointments.

"I made your favorite," Mary said, speaking to her son. "Fajita breakfast casserole. I brought all the fixings and some things for lunch and dinner. Snacks too. But y'all can come to the ranch for dinner if you'd like. It must be dull staying here around the clock. It might be good to get out."

"Said the spider to the fly," Austin muttered, causing his mama's smile to widen.

Scarlet watched them, mesmerized at the ease of their interactions and the way they moved in practically choreographed steps around the room. Putting things into her refrigerator, sliding the dish into the oven, setting the table for three. Clearly Austin had familiarized himself with her small kitchen while she'd slept.

Mrs. Beaumont made small talk as they worked, complimenting Scarlet's home and asking how she felt. She asked about her mother too and if Austin was being a good houseguest.

The initial shock of her presence was gone in minutes, and Scarlet was unprecedentedly at ease with another stranger. Like with Austin, Scarlet suddenly felt as if she'd known the older woman forever. And she laughed when Mrs. Beaumont told stories about life on the ranch raising five boys.

"And that's how this one got a scar above his

eye," she said, poking Austin on the forehead. "He likes to say he fell from a bull, but that wasn't the story I heard."

Austin leaned away with a grin. "Dean said a blanket would work like a parachute if I jumped off the barn. He was fifteen, and I was ten. I thought he knew everything."

"Brothers," she said, pride evident in her eyes. "Do you have any siblings, Scarlet?"

"No, ma'am."

Mary reached across the small table and covered Scarlet's hand with hers. She searched her face a moment then said, "I know things probably seem pretty scary right now, but I promise you, my boys are working hard to change that, and they never fail."

She grinned, thinking of Austin's comment on her deck last night. "So I've heard."

"It's true," Mary said. "They're all very good at what they do, and they always get their man. Or woman." She winked.

"Mama," Austin warned. "Don't."

"What?" she asked, raising her shoulders to her ears. "I'm just offering her a little comfort. My boys never get involved unless they know it's worth the trouble, and they give 110 percent when it is."

Scarlet couldn't help wondering if Mary was

still talking about finding a stalker, or if she'd moved on to something else.

"Did Austin tell you Dean just got engaged?" she asked. "I can't wait for the wedding. And the grandbabies. Do you want children, Scarlet?"

Scarlet's gaze jumped to Austin, who dropped his forehead into one waiting palm. "Yes?"

"Excellent," Mary said. "I know it's every couple's choice, but I like to imagine the ranch filled with children one day when my husband and I are too old to keep all the teenagers. Then it will just be us, our children and our grandbabies."

Austin straightened with a laugh. "Mama would like to see my brothers and I populate a small town."

Mary beamed. "There's nothing wrong with wanting a big family."

"I always wanted five children," Scarlet said, unsure why the secret, silly fantasy slipped out.

"Really?" Austin and his mom asked in unison.

"Yeah." Scarlet laughed. "I don't know why five, exactly. Maybe it was a result of being a lonely only child, but I decided a long time ago five was the perfect number. Unfortunately, at twenty-seven and single, five is probably not in the cards these days."

"Well," Mary said. "You never know, do you?

Twins are a possibility. So is adoption and being pregnant a lot." She laughed.

Austin looked horrified. "Mama."

"We're just having a little girl talk," she said. "I suppose you'd prefer to talk shop."

He looked as if he'd prefer to talk about anything else, and Scarlet regretted her candor. It wasn't as if she'd included him in her fictional family of seven. Still, he looked paler than she'd ever seen him, and it felt like she was the cause.

"Have you given her a Taser?" Mary asked.

"I tried," he said. "I offered a stun gun, but she wouldn't take it."

Her thin brows furrowed. "How about a pistol?"

Scarlet laughed. "No, thank you. I think I'd sooner carry the Taser."

Mary smiled. "Then it's settled."

The apple really didn't fall far.

The oven dinged, and Mary popped to her feet. "Time to eat."

"She loves us with food," Austin said.

"I'd never say no to that." Scarlet smiled. She'd only known Mary Beaumont a few minutes, but it was evident she loved her family in every possible way.

Scents of roasted red peppers, eggs, onions and cheese floated through the room, and her stomach groaned in anticipation.

"Eat up," Mary said, setting the casserole on the table between them. "Because I think the next thing we should talk about is how soon you can relocate."

"We're going to my place later," Austin said. "I need to pick up some things if I'm going to stay here, but you can always see what you think while we're there." He looked to Scarlet, avoiding his mama's knowing eyes. "It might be the better choice."

AUSTIN KNEW THE moment he suggested his place as a possible location for Scarlet's respite, his mama would latch onto it. But the words had practically leaped from his mouth the moment she'd mentioned relocation, which was an idea he wouldn't argue with. And he couldn't back-pedal now.

His mama hitched a brow.

Everyone who knew the Beaumont family assumed it was their father, a former police chief, who inspired the boys to get involved in law enforcement or investigation. But anyone who'd spent any amount of time at the ranch knew Mama as the best detective among them. She saw, heard and sensed everything. The only time he or his brothers got away with something as kids and teens was when she'd decided to ignore it. Even then, she let them know she hadn't missed their transgression. Usually by doubling their chores for a week or two without comment.

Scarlet raised her mug, looking pleasantly calm on the outside, but her hand trembled as the drink reached her lips.

He didn't want to take her away from her home, and he'd been thinking of how to avoid it, but his mama was right. Scarlet's place wasn't the safest option. Changing the locks would help, but it would be days before the new ones arrived. Until then, the problem was sleep, or the lack of it. He couldn't remain perpetually awake and on the move for days, making his rounds from the front to back door all through the nights.

"Has Austin told you about our ranch?" Mama asked. "It's beautiful. Peaceful. There's always plenty of good food and even better people. There are animals too. A stable with horses if you like to ride. And you'd be safe. If you'd prefer someplace like that."

Scarlet returned her cup to the saucer with a soft clatter. "I'd like to stay here, if that's possible."

Mama tipped her head. "Anything's possible, but is it safe?" She looked to Austin. "How long before the door locks are changed?"

"By the end of the week," Scarlet answered. "I placed the order last night."

"And who will keep watch at your front and back doors until then?"

Austin fought a smile. He and his brothers had a running theory she was a mind reader. Times like these seemed to support that.

Scarlet's eyes darted to him. "How did you watch both doors?"

"I was on the move most of the night."

"You didn't sleep," she said flatly, and he could practically see the reality of the situation sinking in. The set of her mouth turned grim. "I slept better than I have in a long while."

Silence stretched around them.

Scarlet sat taller and turned to his mama. "I wouldn't want to risk bringing my danger to your ranch and the folks you're helping there. I hear you do wonderful things for young people with troubles of their own. I don't want to see this spread to anyone else."

His mama's gaze roamed Scarlet's features, and Austin wondered if she saw the things he did. Scarlet was brave and selfless. She'd been through hell, but still worried more about potentially exposing strangers to her attacker than about the added protection the ranch could offer her. "That's why you don't want to stay with your mama."

"Yes, ma'am."

"Hotels aren't ideal," Mama said, dusting her

lips with a napkin. "They can be hard to guard properly if they're breached. But if you can check in unnoticed, under a false name, you might not be found. If you decide not to stay with Austin. There will be an added expense of course. And he'd still need to be there. At least with adjoining rooms."

Scarlet nodded, accepting his mama's input, which had obviously been worded to sway her against the notion.

Austin rested his clasped hands on the table, drawing both sets of eyes. "I can talk to my brothers about setting up shifts to keep watch here for a few days. Staying won't be a problem if that's what you want to do."

Scarlet frowned. "I hate to put out anyone else. You're all doing so much already. And if they're here all night, they'll be exhausted all day. That will only diminish their ability to search for whoever did this to me." She sighed. "That's counterproductive."

He dipped his chin once in agreement. "My place is still an option. It's not listed on the auditor's website as owned by me. Very few people know where I live. Dean and I went to great lengths to hide our addresses when we opened the PI business. I keep a top-notch security system, and I'm an excellent shot."

He bit the insides of his cheeks, regretting the

comment about shooting trespassers, even if he had been joking. A little.

Scarlet snorted a small laugh, and his mother's smile widened at the poorly timed words.

"Well." Mama stood. "I should be getting back to help your father. Let me know what you decide and if there's anything you need. I've put a cowboy casserole in the freezer for dinner. Just take it out while the oven preheats, then pop it in for about half an hour, and it'll be ready to eat."

"Thank you," Scarlet said, rising to walk her to the door. "For everything. It was really nice to meet you, and your offer for me to stay at the ranch was very generous. I can see where Austin gets his kindness."

Mama's eyes flashed with pride, and she fixed him with a look over Scarlet's shoulder that could only be interpreted as immense approval.

He was sure to hear about it later.

Chapter Eleven

Austin and Scarlet waved from the porch as Mama drove away, and the moment felt so oddly natural, he wondered if his lack of sleep had pushed him toward delirium.

Scarlet turned on her toes, teeth pressed into her bottom lip and looking strangely excited. "I have an idea."

He frowned. "About?"

She shifted, averting her gaze before seeming to steel her resolve. "There's something I think we should do. You gave me the idea last night when you were encouraging me to relax and not worry."

His lips parted and all sensible thoughts left his brain. "What did I say?"

"That something would eventually trigger my memories, and they'd come back."

He fought a smile. He hadn't been sure what he'd unintentionally motivated her to do when this conversation started, but recovering her memories wasn't even on his radar. "What's your idea?"

"I want to go back to the place where I was attacked. Maybe being there will jar something loose." She pretended to knock on her forehead. "What do you think?"

Austin grimaced, uncomfortable for all new reasons. "Are you sure about that? It hasn't even been forty-eight hours. There's no need to rush. I think your memories will return on their own, if you're patient. Your doctor told you to rest."

"Maybe I don't want to rest." She crossed her arms and squared her shoulders. "It's not as if I'm asking to run a marathon." She winced. "That sounded angry, but it wasn't directed at you. I'm mad because I can't remember anything about this guy. Meanwhile, he's out there running free, doing whatever he wants, when he wants, and my life is a wreck. I'm hurt. I've got a live-in bodyguard. I might have to leave my home. I can't go to work. And I hate that I can't be more helpful to you and your brothers when everyone else is doing so much for me."

Austin stepped closer, leaving only a foot of space between them, unsure if she needed a hug, or if he did. He'd already assured her, multiple times, that she didn't owe anyone anything for their help. "Returning to the scene of your attack will likely be traumatic. Your mind hid what it did to protect you, and going back might feel a lot like unloading a dump truck of stress onto your brain."

"Or it might not."

Austin crossed his arms, matching her stance. He wouldn't willingly cause her distress. But he wasn't sure he could deny her either.

"You said you were here to help." Her expression softened and so did her voice. "I think this will help."

Austin sighed. She was right. Her happiness outweighed his concerns, and he was in way over his head.

An HOUR LATER, Scarlet was finally moving toward the front door.

She'd dragged her feet a bit while getting ready to leave. Mostly second-guessing herself, battling nerves and putting off the trip she'd suggested.

She stuffed her feet into brown suede booties and pulled her wool peacoat from the hook near her door. "Ready?"

"Yep."

She spun in the direction of his voice, hating the joy and comfort it brought when they'd only known one another a short time.

He stopped before her, having added a leather jacket and baseball cap to his ensemble. "I forgot to give this to you earlier," he said, reaching into his pocket. "You'd only been awake a short time before Mama arrived. By the time she left, you wanted to head out. Time got away from me." He passed her a cell phone.

She accepted the device, searching his eyes for more information.

"It's a new disposable," he said. "I had one in my bag like I thought. I opened it last night and set it up. I added myself, Dean, Finn and Mama to your contacts. Now you can call your mom when you're ready. Or a friend. Whoever you want."

A knot of unexpected emotion clogged her throat. It'd been her experience that most people said lots of things they didn't mean. But every time Austin made a promise, he followed through as if it was the most normal behavior in the world. He probably had no idea how much little things like reliability and truth meant to someone who'd been played, scammed and generally run around by men since the moment she'd started dating. "Thank you."

She gave herself an internal kick for her constantly increasing interest in him. He was here because she'd hired him. Not because he wanted to spend the rest of his life in her arms, watching sunsets from the deck, raising children who'd never doubt how much they were loved.

The sound of keys pulled her out of the fantasy, and she followed Austin across the porch toward the driveway.

They were on the road, closing the distance between her home and the scene of her attack, in minutes.

She stared at the phone in her hands, trying not to think too hard about their destination. It had been her idea after all, and it was far too late to chicken out now.

"Thinking of calling your mama?" Austin asked.

"Yes, but I might call the office first. Lydia sent flowers to the hospital, and I never thanked her." She dialed without letting herself overthink the decision. Whether she wanted to talk about what had happened or not, Lydia deserved to know she was safe and healing.

"Coulter Realty," Lydia answered on the first ring.

"Hey." Scarlet's throat tightened, and she had to clear it before going on. "It's me."

"Scarlet!" Lydia gasped. "Oh, thank goodness! I've been worried sick. I almost drove to your house this morning when I didn't hear from you. I stopped at the hospital after work, and they said you'd already been discharged."

"I'm home and doing well," she said. "The flowers were pretty and very appreciated. I'm sorry I didn't call you sooner."

"The morning paper said you were robbed. How are you doing? Do you need anything?"

Scarlet cringed, having forgotten to worry about what the paper said, and hating that Lydia's voice was laced with pity. "I'm fine. I didn't see the paper."

Austin glanced her way.

"The article was awful," Lydia said. "I cried reading it. I can't believe something like that could happen here, and to someone like you."

Scarlet wasn't sure what her friend had meant by the last part, but her eyes misted with unshed tears anyway. "I'm okay," she croaked. "Or I will be. I'm with Austin, and he's taking good care of me."

Lydia made a wild sound in the back of her throat then squealed. "Oh, now I am definitely coming to visit you."

Scarlet slid her eyes in Austin's direction. The slight upturn of his lips suggested he'd heard the squeal, if not Lydia's very loud words. "Don't do that just yet," she said. "We might stay at his place for a few days. The person who attacked me has my purse, so we know he has my address."

Lydia gasped again.

Had she always been so dramatic, or had Scarlet been emotionally numbed by recent events?

"Which reminds me," Scarlet added, pressing on. "I sent an email to the home office last night letting human resources know I wouldn't be in for the rest of the week. I can't exactly sell houses looking like I do." The knot at the side of her head seemed to throb on cue, and her fingers trailed up to touch the bruising around her neck. "I've reached out to all my appointments and asked if they'd like to reschedule. I've given your email to everyone who wasn't interested in waiting. I thought that was best. You can do the showings. Make the sales. Build your client list. And I won't look like a flake for canceling last minute. I hope that's okay."

"Are you sure?" Lydia asked.

"Absolutely. You're a fantastic agent, and I know they'll be in good hands. Call me back at this number if you need anything."

"Thank you."

Scarlet smiled. "Don't mention it."

She disconnected the call and refocused on the view outside. Her stomach tightened as Austin turned off the main road and onto Mr. Perez's driveway.

It was time to find her memories.

Chapter Twelve

Scarlet dropped the phone into the truck's cup holder, a rush of foreboding crashing over her as she stared through the windshield.

Austin cut the engine but didn't make a move to get out. Probably waiting for her to decide if she was sure she wanted to do this.

The Perez home was beautiful as always, a handsome estate on a gorgeous plot of land.

She was safe. She wasn't alone, and what had happened once at this location wouldn't happen again.

She repeated the ideas silently until they felt more like truth, then she reached for her door handle. "Okay. I'm ready."

"I brought the stun gun," Austin said. "In case you want to carry it for peace of mind or try powering it up while we're here."

She shook her head, releasing a slow breath. "One thing at a time."

Austin followed her lead when she opened her

door and climbed out. Then he hung back while she moved to the driver's side.

Sunlight glinted off pebbles of broken glass on the driveway.

"They had to break your window to get to you," Austin said.

She nodded, feeling his eyes on her as she walked along his truck, pretending it was her SUV. Her limbs began to tremble and her breaths quickened, but her mind went numb.

She scanned everything in sight, willing the blank spots in her memory to be revived.

"You doing okay?" Austin asked.

Scarlet clenched her teeth. "Everything looks different," she said, trying out reasons her stubborn brain refused to cooperate. "It's earlier in the day. My SUV isn't here. I know this is where it happened, but nothing feels the same."

"That's good," Austin said, stepping nearer and setting a gentle palm on her arm.

Scarlet turned to glare. "How can you say that? This place was supposed to give me answers."

"It's good because you're not losing your mind right now. Some people can't ever return to the places where things like this happened to them. Even seeing similar scenes in a movie can be enough to trigger their fear and panic. I'm saying I'm glad you're doing okay right now."

She considered his words, and the soft pressure of his palm against the fabric of her coat. "Yeah, well, I'm on a mission, and I'd hoped this would be easier."

He pulled his hand away and wiped it across his mouth, possibly fighting a grin. "All right. What's next?"

She wet her lips, making the procedure up as she went along. If being there wasn't enough, maybe the gruesome details would help. "Tell me what the police said," she suggested. "Maybe that will get the mental imagery going."

Austin looked skyward a moment, as if gathering his thoughts. "Finn said he spent about an hour out here walking the space, then circling the area in his car. There wasn't a lot to go on. He found some tire tracks in the grass along the road's edge, tucked behind that cluster of trees."

She followed his gaze and pointed finger to a dense cluster of pines. "I didn't come from that direction. I wouldn't have seen beyond the trees."

Austin nodded. "Your stalker probably knew that."

"He's smart," she said, wishing it wasn't true. "Like a conniving little fox."

"Pretty much. All the more reason to carry a stun gun."

She rolled her eyes. "You're persistent."

"I am," he said, releasing the mischievous grin

she loved. The one sure to do her in if the un-named stalker didn't.

Then another idea came to mind.

"I don't like that look," he said.

"What look?"

He stepped back. "The last time you made that face, you asked me to bring you here, and you wouldn't take no for an answer."

"Sometimes I can be persistent too," she said. "Especially when I'm right about something, which is most of the time. Like now." She twisted at her waist, scanning the area. "You won't like it, but I want you to humor me."

The apprehension on his face was nearly comical. As if she'd asked him to kindly remove his fingers. "Can you be more specific?"

"I want you to grab me from behind."

His eyes widened and his brows rose. "What?"

"Like an attacker," she clarified. "I think that could help."

"That is definitely not a good idea," he said. "For a whole host of reasons, I'm going to de-cline."

"You can't."

"I can." He took another step back. "I won't pretend to attack you. I don't want to upset you or put that terrible idea in your head, even if you think you want it. You don't."

"I decide what I want," she said. "Now, stop

backing up. That's where I was standing when it happened."

Austin's gaze fell to the broken glass at his feet.

"I'd just gotten out of my SUV. I'd barely taken two steps before his hands were on me. He dragged me back to where I'd started. I thought he was going to take me to a secondary location and murder me."

Austin paled as she marched forward then turned in front of him, putting her back to his chest.

"Scarlet," he warned.

She shivered at the sound of her name on his lips and the feel of his breath against her hair. "Hush, please." She reached back and caught his wrists then pulled them forward. "One arm came around me here." She curved his arm around her rib cage. "The other covered my mouth." She guided his fingers to her lips, but he tensed, refusing to actually touch her. "Put your face against mine. On the right."

Two long beats passed before he did as she'd asked. His skin was warm and smooth as it brushed against hers, and her heart rate quickened.

"I don't like this," he complained.

"Shh." She closed her eyes and imagined the scene, allowing the fear to build inside her. "I think he had a beard or hadn't shaved." Her breaths grew shallow as she chased the memories. "I felt stubble on my cheek."

"Good," he said, attempting to lower his arms. "That's something."

"Wait!" She caught his wrists and jerked them back into place, momentarily crashing one arm against her tender torso and the fingers of his other hand against her mouth.

Austin cussed and sprang back.

Scarlet's eyes flashed open, catching his reflection in the truck's side-view mirror. But it wasn't Austin she saw there.

He looked horrified when she spun to face him, hot tears on her wind-chilled cheeks.

"I saw him in the SUV's mirror. He was tall, but shorter than you, and he had a beard," she said, the words pouring out faster than she could sort them. "He wore a dark gray hoodie. The hood was up, pulled over his hair. I don't know what color it was, and his eyes were cut off in the image."

Joy and adrenaline flooded her system, and she bumped the toes of her boots against his. "His shoulders were narrower than yours. His arms were thinner. I didn't know him. Or he didn't seem familiar."

Austin's hands rose to grip her elbows as a tremor rocked through her. "Breathe, Scarlet.

This is all good, but you have to breathe. Do you want to sit?"

She shook her head, tears coming heavily as relief mixed with residual terror. "I did it."

"Yeah, you did." Austin pulled her against him, engulfing her in his embrace and resting his cheek against the top of her head. "You were fearless. And you're safe now. Okay?"

She nodded, tears soaking the thin cotton of his shirt. Her arms wrapped around him, beneath the unzipped bomber jacket. And another memory returned. "I think he wore leather gloves." A small, unexpected sob broke on her lips.

"It's okay," he whispered. "Just breathe."

AUSTIN CURVED HIS body around hers, holding her close and feeling his protective instincts surge. She'd been through so much, and she'd willfully returned to this place, hoping to make a difference, even knowing the experience could break her. That was a whole other level of bravery. And he admired her for it. He'd seen soldiers behave similarly during his time in the military, and the mental connection was jarring. Scarlet was a civilian, but she was fighting her own war, where the enemy was violent and invisible. And she was alone in her experience, but still, she persisted.

He stepped back, dropping his arms to his sides, stunned by the turn his thoughts continued to take. He was too taken by her, and he didn't like the way it left him unsettled.

"Sorry," she said, looking embarrassed. "I didn't mean to—" She motioned between them.

"No. You're fine. I just—"

They stared at one another, tension twisting in the air.

"What would you like to do now?" he asked, hoping to appear more calm and centered than he felt. "We can swing by my place to get some things, or your office if you have anything you need to do."

"Can we go to the police station?" she asked. "Maybe I can tell Detective Beaumont what I remembered."

"Finn," Austin said, raking a hand through his hair. "Yeah. That sounds good. I'll call and let him know we're on the way."

They climbed back into his truck, and the air seemed thicker as he reversed down the driveway. He hadn't intended to hold her. Hadn't expected her to hug him. But she had, and he did, and now he knew what her heart felt like beating against his.

And he had no idea what to do with that information, but it was all he could think about.

She looked at him as he pulled onto the road and pointed them toward town.

He dialed his brother.

"Detective Beaumont," Finn said, voice rising from the truck's speakers.

"It's me," Austin said. "You're on speaker, and I'm with Scarlet Wills. She's remembered a few details about her assailant and would like to meet with you if you've got some time."

"Nice," Finn said. "Did she remember what he looks like?"

"Kind of," Scarlet said, answering for herself. "I don't think it'd be worth meeting with a sketch artist, but I might be able to pick him out in a lineup."

"Can y'all meet me at the station in about twenty minutes?" Finn asked. "I'm headed that way now."

"Not a problem," Austin said.

"Good. Once we have some suspects, we'll call you in for that. How do you feel about taking a look in the mug shot database?"

A bright smile split her pretty face. "I can do that."

"Finn," Austin said. "Any news on the phone number used to order those flowers yesterday?"

"Unfortunately," he said, "it was a disposable unit like we suspected. Unregistered. I'm still working to track down the prepaid credit card's origin. So we could still get lucky on that."

Austin doubted it. This criminal was proving to be a real planner.

Chapter Thirteen

Scarlet trembled as she crossed the parking lot to the Marshal's Bluff police station. Her body couldn't seem to understand the reason for her recent jolt of adrenaline, and her fight-or-flight response was going haywire.

She took a calming breath with every step and hoped the rush would soon pass. She wanted to thank the detective on her case for all the effort he was making to protect her, and she hoped the news about her attacker's description would help speed up his capture.

She was also eager to talk to another member of Austin's family. Mostly because she was an only child, and siblings had always interested her. Nothing more.

Austin held the door to the lobby for her to pass, then greeted a uniformed officer behind a sliding glass window by name.

The men exchanged a few words while Scarlet

took in her surroundings. The space was pleasant, if she didn't get caught up in the fact that everything heavier than a magazine was bolted to the floor.

A nearby buzz set them in motion once more. Austin steered her through another door, one hand on her back.

They passed several offices in a narrow corridor before a ridiculously attractive man in a gray dress shirt, black slacks and a blue tie leaned into the hall ahead of them.

"Hey." His gaze moved from Austin to Scarlet, and recognition hit. This was Detective Beaumont.

Lydia was right. These men came from an unfair gene pool.

"Hey," Austin echoed. "Finn, you remember Scarlet Wills. Scarlet, you've met my little brother Finn."

Finn offered her his hand and she shook it. "I remember. You're looking well. It's nice to see you under better circumstances."

"Thanks," she said, following him into an office. He'd visited her on the night of her attack, but she'd been too out of sorts to hold much of a conversation.

Austin closed the door behind them then motioned for her to take a seat in one of the two chairs in front of his brother's desk.

Finn returned to the rolling chair on the other side.

She hadn't noticed before, but the resemblance between brothers was profound. Brown hair and eyes. Straight noses and teeth. Broad shoulders and square jaws.

Finn swiveled an open laptop to face her. "This is our mug shot database. It's fairly easy to navigate. You input the things you know here." He pointed to a set of drop-down lists on the left side bar. "Then click search."

Like online shopping, she thought. Except instead of sorting by price or pattern, she'd set the physical characteristics she wanted to see.

"It helps to sort by known offenses," he said. "Since we don't know if this guy has a criminal record, we'll have to work with what we've got. In the event he's never been arrested, this exercise will be futile, but at least it's somewhere to start."

Scarlet made a few selections and clicked search.

Finn slid a pad of paper and pen across the desk to her. "It might also be helpful to list all the men you see regularly or would recognize if you saw them on the street. Specifically those who live in town or nearby."

She straightened. "Like coworkers and clients? Or the barista at Java Jim's and the clerk at the grocery?"

"All of the above," Finn said. "Dry cleaner, mailman, guys from your gym. Anyone you've interacted with in the time since this began, or just before you started feeling watched. Even a simple exchange, a polite word or smile can be misconstrued as interest to these types of perpetrators."

She pursed her lips, hating that idea. She spoke to dozens of people every day. "Okay."

She switched gears, pulling the paper closer and starting a list while faces appeared in her mind like popcorn. She began with real estate agents and clients, then moved on to groundskeepers, bank representatives and title clerks, the man who cleaned the office, and a handful of workers at businesses she frequented. "You won't tell all these people I named them as potential criminals, will you?"

Finn chuckled. "No. And feel free to flag the ones you're sure don't fit the physical description. I'll still want to talk to them in case we're looking for someone peripherally connected."

She wrote until her hand cramped and she'd exhausted the list inside her brain. Then she returned the paper to Finn and her attention to the database search results.

"This is good," he said. "Thank you."

"Mom stopped by," Austin said.

Finn snorted a small laugh. "I had no doubt she would."

"She brought food."

"Uh-huh."

The brothers dove headlong into a discussion on their allegedly meddling mother, whom Scarlet thought was lovely. So she quickly tuned them out.

Her attacker's shadowed face, the hoodie and beard played on a loop in her mind. Little flashes. Tiny pieces of a larger picture. And something more. There was something about his mouth. She tried to hold on to the image for inspection. His lips hadn't been snarled or curled in anger as he'd choked her. The expression was flat, resigned. As if his strangling Scarlet was merely necessary. Something he simply had to do so he could go home and get on with his night.

She shivered, wondering what he was doing now. Was he afraid he'd soon be caught? Or did he like the chase? *Maybe*, she thought, *he's eating a hamburger with friends at the sports bar down the street*. Completely unaffected by what he'd done.

She forced her attention back to the screen where she'd been mindlessly scrolling. How many photos had she missed?

None of the faces before her now seemed right, and the more she scrolled, the more uncertain she became. Maybe she wouldn't recognize him after all.

A ringing phone broke her concentration once more.

The Beaumonts stilled as well, but no one made a move to answer the call.

A long moment seemed to pass before she realized the ringing phone belonged to her.

"Oh!" She pulled the device from her jacket pocket, having completely forgotten she'd tucked it in there when she left Austin's truck.

Her heart sank as she looked to the screen.

"Who is it?" Austin asked, swiveling on his seat with interest.

A reasonable question, considering she'd only had the phone for an hour or so, and she didn't even know its number. She did, however, recognize the digits onscreen.

"It's my mother."

Austin watched as Scarlet's expression moved from confusion to astonishment, then resignation as she answered the call. She scanned Finn's small office, likely seeking but not finding any place for privacy.

Finn raised his brows, noticing Austin's interest.

He shrugged.

"Hello, Mom," Scarlet said, turning slightly

away. "I'm fine. How did you get this number?" A soft groan left her lips. "Lydia."

Finn knocked gently on the desk, returning Austin's attention to him once more. "Is she close to her mama?"

He nodded. "I think it's the reason she's been putting this off. She called her office earlier. Lydia must've passed the number along."

Finn cringed. "Can you imagine if that was our mama?"

Austin matched his expression. "No."

"I'm serious," Scarlet said. "I'm barely injured. I was only kept for observations. A bump on the head and some bruising." She rubbed a hand over her eyes. "I asked them if they wanted to reschedule, and Lydia's handling the ones who don't."

Austin frowned. Had her mama moved on to shoptalk in the span of a couple sentences?

"Mom," Scarlet said, voice firming on the single syllable. "I'm at the police station right now, and I need to go so I can concentrate. We're trying to identify the man who did this." She glanced at the Beaumonts.

Austin and Finn looked at one another, both caught silent and staring.

"No, I don't need you to come to Marshal's Bluff. I'm staying with a friend for a few days… Because I didn't want to bother you."

Finn tented his brows. "Who's the friend?"

"Me." Austin slid his gaze away. "We might stay at my place until I can get her locks changed."

"We?"

"Yes," Austin said under his breath, returning his attention to his brother. "Obviously."

"When did y'all become a we?" Finn whispered back.

Austin scowled. "What?"

Finn raised his palms and leaned farther in his brother's direction. "You could've said you invited her to your place, or that she agreed to stay with you for now. You didn't have to use the word *we*. But you did."

"That's ridiculous." Austin mouthed the words.

"Sorry," Scarlet said, sliding the phone into her coat pocket. "That was my mom."

Finn dragged his gaze away from Austin and worked up a polite smile. "I hope she wasn't too worried."

"She took it better than expected," Scarlet said. "Of course, I didn't give her a lot of details, and apparently she hasn't looked online. Lydia said the morning paper covered things pretty well."

"It did indeed," Finn said. "Normally I would've played this close to the vest, but in your case I felt it was best to make an offensive move over a defensive one. By announcing this man's out there strangling women, folks will be cautious and vigilant. Hopefully people will be talking about him everywhere he goes and the spotlight will put a dent in his confidence."

She blinked. "You're trying to rattle him?"

"I want to make him think twice before acting out again. I need time to review all the materials related to this case, and considering how involved you are in the community, there are a lot of interviews to conduct." He lifted his notepad and turned it in her direction. "You have interactions with so many people on a regular basis that you broke them into categories. And each of these names is more than a potential suspect, it's a link." He looked at the paper then back to Scarlet. "You order coffee from Dustin a few days a week at Java Jim's, but when I talk to him, I might learn there's a cook in back on the days you normally visit, and a pastry delivery is also made around that time. Then I need to talk to the cook and pastry guy too."

She slumped in her chair. "So my list of fifty names could lead you to speak with a hundred people."

"Yep, and I can't have your attacker lashing out while I'm still doing the preliminary data collection."

"What if he gets a thrill from everyone talking about him?" she asked. "Like those bombers and pyromaniacs who stand around the crime scene, enjoying the trouble they caused."

"Right now, I'm willing to let his ego inflate a little, especially if that means he's not out there looking for you."

Austin rested a palm against the side of her chair, wishing he could squeeze her hand instead. "You okay? We can always come back later if you're getting tired or sore. Finn's got a nice long list of people to talk to now. He can use that to get started."

She looked to the screen then back. "Give me a few more minutes?"

"Sure."

He watched as she pushed herself to refocus. Then he dropped his hands into his lap and faced his brother. "Anything I can do to help you? I'll be at my place for a few days laying low, but I can research."

Finn worked his jaw, eyes seeking and hands clasped on the desk. "I'll let you know. Maybe I'll send you a copy of this list." He tapped the notepad. "Right now, you've got a witness to protect."

"Thank you," Scarlet said, still scrolling through mug shots. "For calling me a witness. Not a victim."

Finn opened his mouth then closed it and grunted.

Austin grinned. Scarlet Wills was a lot of things, but she wasn't a victim.

Eventually, her recent injuries got the best of her and she began to squirm, tipping her head side to side, stretching her neck and kneading her shoulders.

Austin nudged her with an elbow. "Let's go. You've done enough today, and we can always come back."

She sighed and slumped against the chair. "Yeah, okay."

Finn walked them down the hall and bid his farewell, leaving Austin to escort her back to his truck.

"You did a good job today," he said. "Did I tell you?"

She smiled. "I think I might've heard that."

"What do you think about getting that glass of wine and watching the sunset from my deck tonight?"

Her eyes lit. "You have a deck?"

"I do."

"And wine?" she asked.

He beeped his truck doors unlocked. "I've got hard cider. It's fruity, so that's a little like wine. Right?"

"Wine adjacent," she said. "I accept."

"Then let's call it a day. We can spend the

rest of the afternoon relaxing in a pair of rockers like retirees."

A sharp whistle turned Austin toward the police department before she could respond.

Finn jogged in their direction as Austin opened the passenger door for Scarlet. "Wait. I just got a call from Dispatch. A fire was reported at 1611 Inlet Way. The fire department is already en route."

Austin's eyes snapped to Scarlet.

She gasped. "That's my place!"

Chapter Fourteen

Scarlet sat numbly in the passenger side of Austin's truck as they raced through town, hot on Finn's tail. The detective's lights and sirens parted traffic for him, and Austin glided his truck through in the wake, like the second line to the world's worst parade.

Austin used voice commands to call Dean and a few others, attempting to get information about how bad the situation was, but everyone was still en route as they were.

Scarlet kneaded her hands, certain some part of her would die if her home was unsalvageable. She'd put her heart and soul into the restoration of the property, not to mention most of her money. Those walls were her safe haven. No amount of insurance money could rebuild it. The structure was historic. And some modern throwback or replica would never be the same.

Worrying about installing the wrong doorknobs seemed incredibly trivial when the place was on fire.

"We're arriving now," an unfamiliar male voice explained through the truck speakers. The sound of waning sirens faded in the background. "No visible flames," he said. "What's your ETA?"

"Three minutes," Austin reported. "See you soon."

The call disconnected, and Scarlet stared at his face. "Who was that?" she asked. "What did he mean? No visible flames. There's no fire?"

"Mark's a volunteer EMT. We'll know what he meant soon."

She swallowed a lump of fear rising in her throat and fixed her gaze outside the windshield.

The fire trucks were first to come into view. One had parked in her driveway. Another along the roadside. A police cruiser and an ambulance were angled into the space between the trucks.

"Someone called 911," Austin said. "I'm guessing it was the same person who set the fire, wanting to make sure you got the call while you were out and had to hurry back and find all this madness."

All Scarlet cared about in the moment was that Austin's friend had been right. There weren't any flames visible from the road. She placed a hand over her heart and sent up prayers of gratitude.

Austin parked behind the first responders. "Let's see what these guys know."

She hopped out and met him at the front bumper then hurried in the direction of her home.

Finn had jammed his vehicle into her driveway behind the first fire truck, two of his wheels on her lawn. He spoke to a passing fireman on his way to meet Austin and Scarlet. "We're going to get an update and report in a minute. Whatever happened in there, it looks like he's escalating again. I'm glad you made plans to stay elsewhere for a while."

Austin curved his fingers around hers, offering a small squeeze. "Do we have any idea how bad it looks inside?"

Scarlet's mind reeled. Fire could've ruined, charred or weakened the internal structure. There could be irrevocable smoke damage. Or chemical and water damage caused by whatever was done to stop the flames and smoke from spreading.

"Escalating," she said, repeating Finn's word. Her voice sounded foreign to her ears.

The word rolled in her mind, circling and itching.

"Yeah," Finn said. "And this is exactly the kind of lashing out I'd hoped to avoid."

Austin tugged her hand gently. "Are you okay? Scarlet?"

The Beaumonts' words sounded as if they were underwater. Flashes of her attacker holding her in place whipped in and out of her mind. *He is escalating.*

"I think he spoke to me," she said.

"Who?" Finn asked.

She shook her head, unwilling to be sidetracked as she clung to the sensation of her attacker's hands on her mouth and middle. "He whispered something into my ear when he pressed his cheek to mine." She closed her eyes, imagining the scratch of his whiskers, and her lids flew open. "He said he wanted us to be together." She looked from Finn to Austin, heart racing and stomach souring. "Something like that. There's more, but I can't—"

The brothers exchanged a look.

Scarlet's fuzzy thoughts suddenly cleared. Wasn't escalation supposed to move more slowly? "When I came to you, I thought I was being followed," she told Austin. "You said it was possible that had been going on for weeks. Then out of nowhere, he attacked me. Now two days later he lit my home on fire. It feels more like he's unraveling."

Austin rubbed his forehead then the back of his neck. "I think he saw you with me and became territorial. The attack might've been the warning you mentioned. Maybe that's why he let you live."

Her mouth twisted in disgust. "Then he tried to apologize by sending flowers."

"But I was there, and I called him."

Finn hooked his hands on his hips. "I'm guessing by all this." He motioned to the abundance of emergency vehicles surrounding her property. "He knows Austin spent the night here last night."

Nausea twisted in Scarlet's core. What if the person who'd set a fire in her home while she was away had acted last night instead? When she was sleeping and Austin was circling her home, trying to watch both doors by himself.

She stepped away from Austin and wrapped one arm around her middle, covering her mouth with the other hand.

A fireman strode in their direction, and Finn stepped forward with an outstretched hand. "How does it look in there?"

Their small circle turned expectantly.

The fireman made eye contact with her, then Austin, nodding to each, before returning his attention to the detective. "Small fire. No damage."

"I don't understand," she said. How could there be a fire without damage?

The fireman glanced over his shoulder at her house. "It appears as if a contained fire was intentionally started in the master bedroom. Nothing else seems amiss. It's safe to go inside and take a look when you're ready."

Finn tipped his head. "After you."

Austin turned to Scarlet, but her feet felt like lead.

He slid his hand in hers once more and gave that familiar, gentle squeeze. "Scarlet." He dipped his head closer. "I've got you."

Then they were in motion.

First responders milled around, chatting and watching as Scarlet and Austin passed. This small, contained fire was sure to be tomorrow's front-page news. It probably wouldn't take long for the dark cloud to settle over her name as a Realtor. The lady with a stalker. A bad luck human to be avoided. Then where would she be?

She'd have to start over. Again.

A million unkind words flooded into her mind. Nasty comments from her mother's many companions, snide words from Scarlet's former boyfriends. Unkind teachers who'd assumed she was the problem when her dyslexia made it harder for her to learn new material, before she'd gotten the help she'd needed. Anyone and everyone in her past who'd seemed to believe all their problems started and ended with her.

She'd overcome a lot of those burdens with regular trips to the therapist and remediation training for her dyslexia, but she was sixteen and miserable again as she marched into her home. Even with Austin at her side.

"No signs of forced entry," an officer stated to Finn as he reached the porch. The man in uniform nodded to her as she passed.

"He has my keys," Scarlet said, mostly to herself. There wasn't any reason to break in now. And if the criminal lost her keys, he could always use a credit card to gain access.

She followed the parade of men into her bedroom where another person in uniform took photos of the metal bucket, normally used to collect ashes from the living room fireplace. Now seated on her bed. Black soot marks marred the beautiful eyelet cover.

"Books were used to kindle the fire," the fireman said, pointing to the bucket. "A liquid accelerant enhanced the flames. Smoke detectors were going off when we arrived."

Finn made a path from one side of her bed to the other. "Who called this in?"

The fireman shrugged.

Scarlet supposed Finn already knew that answer, and the number was likely tied to another untraceable, disposable phone. "He wanted me to know he was angry," she said, feeling as if she was finally catching up, but very late to the game. "Another warning. Not a punishment."

The final word stuck in her head and itched in her throat. Another memory hovered just out of reach. Another awful thought pushed the curiosity aside.

The man who'd nearly killed her had been in her home while she was away. He'd been in her bedroom. Invaded her space, used her keys as if he belonged there. And for those reasons, this threat felt inexplicably more personal than the physical attack. If nothing more had gone wrong, she might've been able to convince herself she'd been in the wrong place at the wrong time when she was strangled. But there wasn't any way to deny this threat was intended for one person. This was absolutely about her.

Finn and the firemen left her room.

She turned to watch them go, having missed whatever they'd said.

Austin stepped closer. He released her hand in favor of sliding his palms along her forearms. "How are you doing?"

She exhaled a thin breath. "Not good."

He pulled her against him for a quick hug. "They have one more thing to show us, then you can gather your things and we'll get out of here."

Scarlet straightened and followed him through her open bedroom door.

Finn and the fireman stood before a small built-in desk in her parlor. Floor-to-ceiling bookshelves stood on either side. Several tomes were missing. Likely the ones used to start the fire.

A photo of Scarlet in a long white beaded gown centered her small desk. Her image beamed back at them. The gown had been spectacular, rented from one of those big LA shops and returned when the event had ended. The plunging neckline and slit up one side had made her feel confident and sexy.

The party had been amazing, attended by top real estate agents, bank execs and related industry stars. All to see her and a handful of others receive awards for excellence.

"When was this taken?" Finn asked.

"Last summer," she said, then thought better of it. "Not a few months ago," she clarified. "The year before. Maybe fifteen months back. It was a banquet thrown by Coulter Realty executives."

Finn stretched blue gloves over his hands and lifted the photo. "Fifteen months, huh?"

A slip of paper scooted across the desk in the picture's absence, revealed and set free by Finn's action.

The air thickened, and Scarlet's chest grew tight as she stared at the message and read the tidy script.

You betrayed me.

Chapter Fifteen

Austin spent the next half hour with his fists clenched and jaw set, taking in every comment and detail traded between Finn and the other officials. Hoping to hear some magic words that would give the stalker's identity away.

Scarlet had excused herself to collect her things and probably do some internal screaming.

The simmering rage was real and very thinly veiled, for him at least.

He'd promised to be her eyes and ears, so she wouldn't miss anything while she packed.

Eventually, the fire trucks and ambulance took their leave, carrying the first responders with them. Finn and his team stayed a bit longer, attempting to pull fingerprints from the doorjambs and knobs, as well as the desk, bookshelves and the fireplace bucket.

Austin hoped they'd find something but suspected they wouldn't. Whoever they were dealing with was meticulous. Worse, Scarlet said he'd worn leather gloves to attack her. He'd likely worn them for this as well.

Finn leaned against the archway between Scarlet's living room and kitchen. "I'm going back to the station," he said. "I need food and a little time to make sense of the information we have. Hopefully I can get it to lead somewhere."

"Good luck," Austin said, meaning it to his core.

"Thanks. I'm just glad he continues to leave clues." Finn sighed and tented his brows. "It's obvious I don't have to say this, but I will anyway."

Austin frowned.

"Keep her close." Finn flicked his gaze over Austin's shoulder, presumably toward the room where Scarlet was packing. "I know you like to get involved and take action. We all do, but this time your energies will be best used to entertain her. Distract her. Keep her away from town."

Finn was right. That didn't need saying.

Austin bit his tongue and nodded.

Finn released a small puff of air and rolled his shoulders. "I know you know what you're doing, but it's also my job to say the words. Speaking as your brother now," he said, voice lowering drastically. "She's hurting, scared and hunted. This situation could become an issue."

Austin crossed his arms and straightened. "You don't think I can protect her?" Was he kidding?

"That's not what I'm concerned about."

Austin narrowed his eyes, and the brothers exchanged a long silent look.

He imagined Finn was attempting to telepathically point out that Scarlet was vulnerable and Austin wasn't the sort to get serious about a woman, yet he'd been seen holding her hand by half the emergency responders in town. And that could be confusing for many people.

Knowing he'd probably think the same things in Finn's shoes, he settled for a curt dip of his chin.

Finn relaxed, glanced around the home then headed for the door. "Call if you need anything."

"Back at you," Austin said, following. "Keep us in the loop if something new comes up. Even a small thing. We want to know."

Finn stopped on the porch to puff out his cheeks. "We." He shook his head then jogged to his truck and climbed inside.

Austin stared after him. He had started thinking of himself and Scarlet as a we. He didn't want to think about why. It wouldn't end well. His relationships never did. Other than his mama, all the women he knew took issue with his job. It kept him out too late, gone too long and unable to discuss what he'd been up to most of the time. Since he couldn't imagine doing anything else for a living, he'd stopped trying to find a significant other.

A small crash in the next room set Austin in motion, heading toward the source of the sound.

Scarlet stood before her dresser, picking up a collection of books she'd apparently dropped while packing.

He crouched to help, but his heart stopped at the sight of her.

Tears tracked over her cheeks. Her eyes were glossy, her face pink.

They stood at the same time, and she wiped her face. "Sorry. I'm a little shaky, and I thought I had them stacked better."

He stepped forward without thinking and pulled her into his arms. A bad habit he couldn't seem to break. "You don't have to apologize. Let me help you."

"No. I've got it." She edged away, face cleared of emotion. "I'm ready." She tucked the books into a bag on her bed then lifted the handle of a large suitcase. "This looks like a lot, but it's not all clothing. I'm bringing some of the smaller things I wouldn't want destroyed in a fire if he comes back."

Austin pressed his lips together, feeling irrationally rejected by the way she'd pulled away. He'd crossed a line by hugging her, and he needed to be more professional. "It's no problem. Bring as much as you want."

He made a mental note to keep a more polite distance moving forward. He wouldn't allow her to be hurt again on his watch. Not by the criminal currently tormenting her. And certainly not by himself.

SCARLET BOUNCED ALONG in Austin's truck, moving away from town and the sea. It was strange to her, not to live near the water. But he'd grown up on a ranch, so maybe it wasn't as important to him as it was to her. Still, she'd be even more of a mess than she was if not for her deck and the inlet views to calm her.

The reaching limbs of ancient trees stretched over them, crowding the sky into little more than a pale blue ribbon above. The narrow gravel road ahead was spattered with autumn leaves in every color and utterly devoid of other vehicles.

He glanced at her as the truck waddled along, more and more slowly as the path they traveled grew infinitely less accommodating of their apparent trespass. "Are you worried yet?"

She dared a look in his direction, then returned her eyes to the road, if that's what she was supposed to call it. "Have I wondered if I accidentally let a serial killer drive me into the mountains to escape a stalker? Nope. That's never crossed my mind."

Austin chuckled, and the road began to smooth. Fresh chunks of gray gravel led to a short, covered bridge, then bent around another corner in the distance. Every board of the bridge appeared new.

"Wow." She leaned forward, admiring the structure. "There aren't many covered bridges left in North Carolina. What on earth is one doing here?"

"My brothers and I put it here," he said. "With a little help from our dad. It took us more than a decade."

She turned to gape at him.

He rolled onto the bridge's center and shifted into park. "Do you want to get out and look?"

"Absolutely." She climbed down and ran her hands over the treated wood, taking in the obvious craftsmanship. "You really built this?"

His smile was proud as he approached. "We started when I was a kid. My grandma owned the land, and she liked covered bridges. She had a lot of memories of the one in the town where she grew up. Grandpa proposed there. So, when she was getting older, Dad made her foreman on this project, and he enlisted my brothers and I for free labor. We took turns leaving for the military and college, but eventually we got the job done."

"And your grandma?"

He shook his head. "She was around for most of it, but she was too ill to see it finished. We promised to bring her here on the next nice day, but she passed during the winter. I guess it wasn't meant to be."

Scarlet moved to his side and folded her hands in front of her, determined not to touch him like she wanted. All the touching only made things more confusing. "I'm sorry you lost your grandma. She must've felt so loved, seeing you do this for her." Scarlet couldn't imagine. The possibility love like that existed, even between a grandparent and their grandchildren, tightened her lungs and filled her heart with hope.

"I like to think so," he said. "She was very special to us all."

Scarlet moved to the bridge's edge, drawn by the sounds of running water. "I can't believe your dad knew how to do this. And that he was able to teach children."

"Grandpa was a carpenter. Dad learned a lot growing up with him, and we learned a lot working with Dad. Our family didn't always have tangibles to pass down, like family jewels or antique whatnots. But our parents and grandparents did what they could to give us their morals, values and skills."

She rested her hands on the wide railing and

peered through a cutout in the bridge's side. Initials had been carved into the wood. D.B., F.B., A.B., L.B., J.B. She traced the set in the center. "Is J.B. your dad?"

"My oldest brother, Jake."

She wondered which face was Jake's in the family photo at Austin's office, but the image had already faded in her mind.

Below them, water burbled over rocks and around fallen trees, cutting an arched path through the hillsides. A hundred yards ahead, on the freshly graveled road, stood an old mill, its waterwheel motionless in the creek.

Austin leaned a hip against the railing. "These aren't quite inlet views, but they make me happy when I've had a tough day."

She turned to squint at him. "You live nearby?"

He hitched his chin toward the mill. "Grandma left the property to me. My brothers got other things. They wouldn't have wanted this, and I wouldn't have wanted anything else."

"And you live here now?" she asked, attempting to make sense of it.

He nodded. "I'm restoring the place a little at a time. I'll have the rest of the road repaired and covered with gravel in the spring. Living back here is the main reason I keep my old truck. I've never gone anywhere it couldn't take me."

Scarlet smiled, fitting another piece of the

Austin Beaumont puzzle into place. She already knew he loved his family, history and the outdoors. Now she knew he was good with his hands.

He smiled, and her face heated. "Are you cold?" he asked, likely mistaking the color in her cheeks.

She shrugged, unwilling to lie and not trusting her mouth while her brain felt a little on the fritz.

"Let's go inside." He opened her door and waited while she climbed in. Then he drove the rest of the way to his home.

The former mill was a two-story rectangle with a triangular roof, like the ones children draw on paper. Weathered old boards ran lengthwise like a log cabin, making up the body of the structure. Red metal panels replaced the original roof. Thick beds of black mulch and a row of brightly colored mums lined the brick walkway. A grapevine wreath with a burlap bow hung on the painted black door.

"Pretty," she said, climbing steps cut from stone as old as time.

"Mama decorates everything," he said, unlocking and opening the door. "She says pretty things put folks at ease."

"She's not wrong," Scarlet said, following him inside.

Battered hardwood floors spread out before

them to an exposed brick wall. A small table sat against the stone with a framed sketch of the mill hanging above and an empty vase. A set of steps anchored the wall to her left. A pass-through arch in the bricks drew her forward.

The space beyond was wholly unfinished, covered in dust and fallen plaster from a crumbling ceiling. A row of tall, skinny windows lined the far wall and overlooked the waterwheel.

"This will eventually be my office," Austin said, motioning to a set of sawhorses topped with a sheet of wood and a stack of files. A ladder-back chair stood behind it. "Come on. Let's get you settled upstairs."

He led her up the sturdy, visibly reinforced staircase, past strips of insulation rolled between two-by-fours. Clearly a work in progress with much more to be done.

She began to worry about what she'd find on the second floor.

Those fears subsided as she rounded the bend in the stairs.

A spacious, open floor plan rolled out before her. On this level, the exposed bricks from below became a fireplace dividing the studio. A small island stood before multiple sets of French doors overlooking a rear deck. Stainless steel appliances and painted cabinets hugged the corner, careful not to interrupt the view. Living room furniture had been arranged on an earthen-colored rug before the fireplace, and a large bed with scrolled iron head and footboards anchored the wall opposite the creek views.

"There's only one bedroom and bathroom," he said. "I can set up a cot in my office or sleep on the couch if you're okay with me being up here. You're welcome to the bed, and the bath is around the corner there." He pointed.

She stared, trying to reconcile what lay before her with the exterior views and the barely passable road.

He frowned. "You don't like it."

"No. I love it. It's like living in a tree house." A really modern, very cool tree house. She moved to the bank of glass doors, mouth hanging unashamedly agape. "How do you ever make yourself leave?"

"I'm money motivated. I like to eat and keep the lights on. Plus, there's a lot still to be done here, and that all takes cash."

"Have you applied for historical property grants?"

He smiled. "I have. I might be able to get some help with restoration of the wheel and road, but not the mill. I've altered too many things, and the updates have negated eligibility."

She gazed at the granite countertop and Edison lights over the island. She supposed he had changed a lot, but the structure was still original. Wasn't it? Not the roof. Her mind whirled with new purpose. Maybe when her stalker was jailed, she could help Austin look for available funds.

Assuming he wanted to remain friends.

Austin's stomach growled, and she grinned.

"I don't suppose you get pizza delivery here?"

"No." He moved toward the fridge and opened the doors. "But I've got a grill and some free time. How do you feel about burgers?"

"I feel very good about burgers," she assured him.

And Austin went to work.

Chapter Sixteen

They sat on Austin's deck long after the meal was finished and the sun dipped low in the sky. Scarlet actively reminded herself that the last few days, and the current moment, were real. She wasn't dreaming and wouldn't wake up to her formerly predictable and satisfying life. That era was over. It wasn't safe to go home.

Austin excused himself and returned with two brown bottles. "As promised, my special wine."

She smiled as he approached with the hard cider. "Those look perfect for fall."

He twisted the cap from one bottle and passed it her way. "What?"

"What?" she repeated, accepting the offer.

"You made a face when I took off the cap. I'm sure you could've done it yourself. I was just being—"

"Kind," she said. "I know. I'm starting to pick up on the pattern."

He returned to the rocking chair at her side. "I've noticed some of your routines too."

"Like?"

"You frown a lot when anyone does anything for you. The simplest things. Like when Finn held the door. Or Mama brought breakfast. When I breathe."

She smiled and took a sip of her cider. "Habit. I'm not used to the help, I guess. I've been on my own a long time, and I don't have siblings or close friends. So I just do everything myself."

He looked offended.

She bristled. "There's nothing wrong with being self-sufficient. Don't look like I just told you I hate your truck."

He kicked back in the chair, swigging from his bottle before speaking. "What about your mama? You must've been her top priority, since it was just the two of you."

Scarlet debated her response. She hated talking about herself, and especially about her life before moving to Marshal's Bluff. But she also longed for someone in her life she could be real with. *And if Austin has a problem with my truth, he doesn't have to stick around when this is over*, she reasoned.

She watched the water flowing through the creek below, letting it soothe her nerves and urge her on. Maybe it was time to be transparent for a change. Time to stop putting on a show. Everything else was changing. Why not this too? Besides, she was almost certain Austin wouldn't hold her past or secrets against her. If not because he was genuinely honorable, then because she'd soon be out of his life if that was what he wanted.

He waited patiently while she chose her words.

"My mom started selling homes when I was in elementary school. I don't remember much about my dad, but after he moved out, she told me he only came back to ask her for money, and we didn't have any. He'd threaten to take me with him sometimes, and Mom would empty her tiny bank account for him. She said whatever amount she had was always enough to make him go away, but never enough for a lawyer."

Austin's jaw flexed. Unhappy or uncomfortable. She couldn't be sure which, but he'd asked, so she was answering.

"When Mom heard how much money she could earn selling houses, she made it her mission to be the very best agent she could. We drove all day once, visiting every thrift store in three counties looking for suits and costume jewelry on the cheap. Then she studied every night after her shifts at the diner and got her real estate license. She was my age then, beautiful, witty, motivated. She did well and made a shrewd businesswoman. I never doubted I'd follow in her footsteps."

"Why do I sense a but?" he asked. "I know you sell real estate."

Scarlet inhaled deeply and released it slowly. "She was busy making a living and thriving on the attention that comes with mastering something, and I was home alone more often than not. I was rarely her priority, but I couldn't complain without feeling guilty because I knew I was the reason she worked so much. She was making ends meet for me. But she was never very...maternal. She did the best she could, and I doubt she has any idea she could've done better."

"You raised yourself and ended up caring for her too," he guessed.

"I did what I could, which wasn't much while I was small, but I got older and I learned. She hired a lawyer to protect me from my dad in the times he was out of jail and on the take." Scarlet forced herself to meet Austin's eyes, waiting for the judgment that came when anyone found out one of her parents had been in jail.

He nodded in understanding, processing without judgment. So, she carried on.

"I was in high school when I discovered I had dyslexia. Until a kind and attentive young teacher caught it, everyone else just thought I wasn't very smart, or that the girl with the uninvolved mom didn't try. By that time, I'd already decided who I was, and I wasn't proud of her. And Mom's continued absence seemed to say I wasn't worth the time. Having dyslexia made it all worse, because once I'd been diagnosed, I couldn't just pretend my grades were low because I was too cool to care. Everyone knew my grades were low because something was wrong with me. I didn't want a label, and I hated being pulled out of class for extra help. I tried to quit school my junior year. Mom wasn't having that, so I rebelled however I could and our relationship suffered for a while."

"Rebelled?" he asked.

"Endlessly." She smiled a little at the lengths she'd gone to push back at a life she thought had pushed her too far. "I got a fake ID, then a tattoo and piercings. I dyed my hair jet-black then cut it off. I skipped classes, and some nights I didn't come home. And I always dated the wrong kinds of men."

Austin rocked in his chair, head turned to face her, the picture of ease. "I'm not going to pretend to know what it's like to be you, then or now. But I will say I grew up on a ranch for troubled youths, and what you've described is practically troubled teen 101. Kids try to regain control however they can. My brothers and I all did similar things too."

She frowned. "Sure."

"We did," he assured her. "We didn't even have it rough in life. We just hated rules and authority. And living on a ranch for struggling kids put a spotlight on us. There was pressure to be some kind of models for appropriate teen behavior. None of us were good with spotlights."

She tried to imagine the pressure he described and wondered if it wasn't easier for her in the house alone. No one caring if she slipped up. She probably would've failed her teen years either way. "I think I dated bad boys to goad my mom. It never worked, and I wound up wanting them to care about me, but they didn't."

"You were young, angry and trusted the wrong people," he said. "Then those people perpetuated your low self-image."

She looked away, hating the truth. "I created my own misery."

"You were a kid, and you were hurting," he corrected. "You turned out pretty great, so it might be worth forgiving yourself."

She opened her mouth to say she already had. Of course she had. She was twenty-seven years old. But she couldn't say the words. Because maybe they weren't true.

"Is it why you listen to so many audiobooks?" he asked. "Because of the dyslexia?"

"I can read as well as anyone now," she said.

"I like audiobooks because I spend a lot of time in my car, driving from showing to showing. The books help pass my time. And I listen at an advanced speed, which means I read more books a year than I could otherwise."

Austin took a deep pull from his cider, tipping his head back as he drank.

Her eyes dropped to the long, tan column of his throat. Then, a little lower, to the bit of exposed collarbone, where his shirt was tugged down at the side. "I started over when I moved here," she said. "I put the past behind me, and I began a new story."

"I get that," he said, setting the bottle aside. "You faced some demons in your teen years and you conquered them in your twenties. Sounds like victory to me."

"I have a tattoo of a broken heart on my hip." She bit her lip hard, unsure why she'd told him, but needing him to understand her past wasn't behind her—it was etched into her heart and inked on her skin.

"As far as any men who broke your heart," he said, shifting forward on his seat and glaring at her. "They didn't deserve you and probably didn't deserve the company or attention of anyone, especially a woman. They probably also had their own emotional issues and mistreating you made them feel a little bigger. Either way, you weren't the cause of their behavior. That was all on them."

Her eyes stung, and she blinked back the tears. "It's very nice of you to say." No one else ever had.

"It's very true of me to say."

"Why aren't you dating anyone?" she asked, unable to quench her curiosity, and hoping he'd be as candid with her as she had been with him.

Maybe he'd say he hated marriage, believed in open relationships or didn't want kids. Maybe then she could get her head on straight where he was concerned.

He rolled his eyes, looking unprecedentedly self-deprecating. "I live in a small town with three eligible brothers relatively my age. The dating pool got incredibly small, really fast. Aside from that, women don't seem interested in a partner who works long hours, stays out late, often overnight, and can't talk about who he's with or what he's doing."

"So you aren't opposed to dating?"

"No." A small smile played on his lips. "Why? Are you asking?"

She laughed. "It's just good to know there's at least one nice guy out there, willing to treat a partner right."

Austin made a disgruntled sound. "There are lots and lots of men like that. You found the bad ones because you were in a bad place. Those guys were the exceptions, not the rule. I promise you. Now you've got me rethinking my life's mission."

She gave a startled laugh. "You have a life's mission?"

"Don't you?"

She rocked and smiled. "I guess I try to do the best job I can every day at whatever comes my way."

"See?" he said. "And I help and protect anyone I can, however I can. I'm adding you to this list. I will convince you good men exist and there's one out there for you, if you want him."

She wet her lips, hoping that man was him, and not caring that it was silly to want him. Even if they were from two very different upbringings. "You've got lofty goals, Beaumont."

His lips twitched. "More than you know."

Chapter Seventeen

Austin woke groggy and restless the next morning. He hadn't slept well following a long night of research on the potential stalkers in Scarlet's life. And countless replays of his conversation with her before she'd gone to bed.

They'd talked about deep and real things on his deck, things he didn't generally discuss. Not with his friends. Not with his brothers. Absolutely not with someone he'd only known for a few days. Yet, there he was. Scarlet made it so easy to open up, and he could see some of her shared stories had cost her as well. The worst things she'd confided were about her father and the boyfriends of her youth. Too many men had treated her poorly, and those experiences had evidently chipped away at her self-worth. Though no one would know it by talking to her more casually. She hid the dark and bruised parts well. And he wanted more than anything to spend as long as it took to help her heal every past scratch and scrape, because those injuries had nothing to do with her and everything to do with unworthy men.

She'd been especially understanding when he'd shared his reluctance to settle down over the years. He'd been in love once, but she'd had no patience for his work and no trust when he was away. The relationship had gone from the best days of his life to the worst in less than a year. And evoking the fool-me-once motto, he hadn't planned to waste his time, or offer his heart for another punching, ever again.

Scarlet had just nodded and said the whole experience must've been hard.

He'd spent a long while wondering if he was an unintentional hypocrite. He'd insisted Scarlet be open to the possibilities that her bad experiences were exceptions to the rule. Yet he hadn't been willing to take the same chance himself. At least, not before meeting her.

Worse, what if she held him to his challenge? Was he actually supposed to introduce her to someone else so they could fall in love?

His fingers flexed and curled, tempted to knock the hypothetical other guy's lights out.

Living with Scarlet Wills was going to be the death of him.

He sighed in relief when the shower in the next room finally silenced. Knowing she'd been naked and wet on the other side of the wall had conjured a thousand unbidden ideas. The concentration it'd taken to push the thoughts from his mind was exhausting, and he blamed his lack of sleep.

He poured a glass of iced water from his pitcher in the refrigerator and started a fresh pot of coffee. Finn and Dean were on their way over, and they'd likely be exhausted. They too had been working on Scarlet's case long into the night. In fact, everyone he knew with the ability to look for this criminal was on the job and taking it seriously. Austin had never been so thankful for his network of lawmen and related professionals.

The coffee finished brewing several minutes later, and Scarlet still hadn't made an appearance. Something about her prolonged absence struck him as odd.

Maybe he was just looking for a reason to see her sooner, but he went to check on her anyway.

He crossed the floor to his bedroom then rounded the corner to a closed bathroom door.

A low curse and sharp yip sounded inside.

Austin's heart thundered, but he knocked casually. "Everything okay?"

"No!" Scarlet snapped. "It's this ridiculous cut on my shoulder. Of all my injuries, this is the one I hate most."

His muscles tensed. He hated every bump and

bruise on her body, but he'd admittedly forgotten about that one. "Are you in pain?" he asked. "Is it bleeding? Should I call your doctor?"

The lock clicked, and the bathroom door crept open. "No. It's healing fine, I think. I just can't reach it to use the cream," she said, shame thick in her voice. "I've only been replacing the bandage for the last couple of days, but it's itchy now, and I have to deal with it. Except I can't."

He looked at the door, now cracked open by an inch, and he imagined her bare shoulder. The long line of her neck, the gentle sway of her hips. The supple fullness of her breasts. He swallowed a groan. The universe was testing him. "Can I help?"

"I feel like a completely helpless human, which I hate," she said. "But yes. Will you please?"

His hand was already on the knob. "Of course."

Scarlet stood inside, looking sheepish and frustrated in a pair of navy blue leggings and a plaid flannel shirt. The buttons at the top were unfastened. She gripped the material at her breastbone, allowing the shirt to drape loosely over her shoulder and down her back. "I can get the bandage on if I prepare it first, then kind of slap it in the right direction, but I can't see what I'm doing to get the cream on. I don't think I could reach it properly, even if I could see."

He stepped inside and closed the door, hoping that would make her feel less exposed. "Just tell me what to do."

She turned her back to him, loosening her grip on the shirt. Their gazes met in the reflection of his bathroom mirror.

An inch or two of slightly puckered skin was visible on one shoulder blade, striped with three small stitches. "It's healing," he said. "That's why it's beginning to itch."

"That's good news, I guess." She sighed, apparently still coming down from her frustration. "I'm supposed to put this cream on the stitches then replace the bandage." She slid a tube of prescription medicine around her middle to him. "The new bandage is set up on the counter, but I can't get this part accomplished."

Austin checked the cluster of materials near his sink. As promised, one square gauze pad was outlined with medical tape and waiting, sticky side up, on the counter. Her shoulder was smeared with the cream nowhere near the wound. "I've got this," he said, smiling at her reflection. "Someone's always injured on the ranch. I've had my fair share of first-aid experience."

"I haven't," she said. "I've never broken a bone, needed my tonsils out or been admitted to a hospital before the other night. I never even needed braces."

He guffawed at her reflection. "Brag a little, why don't you?"

She laughed.

"Hold still." He lifted the tube and squeezed a dollop of cream onto her little wound, thankful the injury wasn't any worse and that the doctor had chosen stitches. Austin had suffered much worse without stitches, but those wounds had left scars. He hated the thought of her being scarred for life by this creep. The emotional and mental aftermath alone would be bad enough. Scarlet didn't need physical reminders too.

Her body swayed closer, leaning back as he gently dabbed at her shoulder, then smoothed the bandage on. He took his time wiping the extra, accidental spots of cream she'd applied before he came to help, and shamelessly savored the feel of her soft, supple skin.

"I'm happy to make this my daily job, if it reduces your stress," he suggested, lingering where he shouldn't.

"I accept," she whispered, relaxing fully against his chest, eviscerating the space between them from hips to shoulders. Her head lolled to one side, and their gazes met in his mirror once more.

Tension ratcheted in him as he watched for signs of uncertainty in her eyes. When he found only curiosity and interest, he stroked his fingers over the curve of her shoulder, tracing her honey-scented skin to the crook of her neck. "Is this okay?"

"Yes." She sighed softly, and his body stiffened.

Austin's heart rate doubled as he thought of a dozen other ways he wanted to touch her and elicit those little sounds. But he was supposed to be her protector. She was hurt, scared and vulnerable. The things he wanted weren't right. At least not right now.

She turned to face him, and his hands fell to his sides. Her chin lifted, and she fixed him with those beautiful moss green eyes. The longing and trust he saw there twisted and tightened his core.

His hands rose again, cupping her hips. He warned himself not to cross a line.

Not to take her mouth with his. Not to toss her unbuttoned shirt and everything else she wore onto the floor so he could worship her. He definitely shouldn't lift her onto the countertop and lose himself inside her.

Scarlet's hands glided over his chest and shoulders, fingertips tangling in his unshorn hair. Her pink lips parted and she rose onto her toes. The slide of her body and warm press of her breasts against him tightened his grip on her hips.

The heat in her gaze set a fire in him, and he felt a fissure form in his already too thin resolve.

"Austin," she whispered, her breath dancing on his lips, inviting them closer.

The sound of his doorbell pushed a curse through his gritted teeth. He forced his hands away from her with the final frayed tether of his self-control. "My brothers are here," he said, voice too deep and gravelly. "Excuse me."

He turned on his toes and headed for the door, forcing his mind and body back into submission with each measured step. And knowing his brothers would still see right through him.

SCARLET STUMBLED BACK, gripping the countertop and wondering what had happened. She'd imagined Austin's mouth on her a thousand times, and she'd practically thrown herself at him in the hopes of experiencing the real thing. But he'd walked away.

Hot, delicious tension seemed to coil around them anytime they were near, and she'd been sure he'd felt it too. She'd spent a long, restless night wondering if the mutual attraction had been only in her mind, but his assistance this morning had been electrified. He'd touched and held her as if he wanted her too.

Hadn't he?

He'd practically run away when the doorbell rang. Actually, he'd cussed first, then run. Had he been upset about the interruption or about what they'd almost done?

The latter seemed silly since he'd offered to find a good man for her, so she'd see they still existed. When he'd said it, she'd hoped he meant himself. Maybe she'd misread everything. Maybe her confused, overwrought emotions had made her brain unreliable.

She shook the circling thought away and buttoned her shirt. She left the bathroom with her shoulders square and expression flat.

Male voices rose up the staircase as she moved through the bedroom. "What do you look so guilty about?" someone asked.

She thought the voice might belong to Dean, but she hadn't spoken to him since their initial meeting and phone call.

"I don't know what you're talking about," Austin said.

Was Dean right? Did Austin feeling guilty? Why?

Maybe she'd completely misread it all.

"I've been waiting for you guys," Austin said. "I'm just impatient."

"That doesn't explain the look on your face," Dean pressed. "What happened?"

"What happened to you?" Austin asked. "I don't live that far out of town."

"No, but it's not as if it's easy to get here,"

Finn answered as a herd of footfalls arrived on the second floor. "Where's Scarlet?"

She waved. "Here."

The brothers stopped in a cluster at the top of the stairs. And they all looked a little guilty in her opinion.

Chapter Eighteen

Dean was first to speak, seeming to break the spell around them. "Hello." He stepped toward her, hand outstretched. "We met at the office. Dean Beaumont."

"I remember," she said, accepting the shake and fighting the urge to more fully cover herself despite the yoga pants and long-sleeved top. She felt exposed, as if all three brothers could see far more than she wanted them to see.

Finn simply raised a hand then slid his eyes at Austin before heading into the kitchen and helping himself to a mug of coffee. Dean followed.

Austin seemed frozen for a long beat.

Scarlet's heart squeezed when their eyes met. Humiliation and confusion heated her cheeks. She'd come on to Austin, and he'd made a polite, but speedy, escape.

Would he ask her to leave now? Maybe send her to his family's farm?

Did his brothers know?

"Looks like you're healing up nicely," Dean said, kindly breaking the silence once more. "How do you feel?"

Scarlet jerked her attention away from Austin and forced a polite smile for the slightly taller, older Beaumont brother. "Thank you." She hadn't noticed how bright his blue eyes were before. After looking into Austin's deep brown gaze for so long, the contrast was slightly jarring. "I'm feeling better. It's been good to get out of town, I think."

Finn unpacked a bag she hadn't noticed him carrying and set up a laptop on the table. "I thought you might want to give the mug shot database another try while I'm here."

She moved in his direction, eager to be useful and glad to have a purpose. The strange energy moving between brothers put her a little on edge. "Sure," she said. "I'd love to."

Finn ran his fingers over the keyboard briefly, then looked at her once more. "All set." He pulled out a chair at the table and motioned for her to sit. "Can I get you some coffee?"

"That sounds nice. Thank you."

The oven dinged, and Dean grabbed potholders from a drawer. "Tell me this is Mama's ham and cheese quiche."

"It is," Austin said, striding stoically into the kitchen to help.

A few minutes later, the four-seat table was covered in plates, mugs and food. And three-quarters of it was surrounded by Beaumonts.

The conversation flowed between small talk and shoptalk seamlessly, each brother easily keeping up as the direction ebbed and flowed, moving in a half dozen directions.

She tried to concentrate on the mug shot database and her coffee. She'd made short work of her breakfast, including two servings of chopped fruit from a bowl.

"I'm hung up on the photo of you in white," Dean said, catching her eye over the laptop's screen. "You looked like a bride."

"Afraid not," she said, glancing up at him. "It was a company event."

Finn shifted. "I've contacted Coulter Realty's home office and asked for a guest list from that night. Can you identify everyone visible in the photo with you? Including folks in the background? It might help us focus our search."

Her knee began to bob beneath the table, unsettled by the implication. "You think it could be someone from my company?"

"Or someone peripherally related, yes."

She wasn't sure why that information made her situation feel worse, but it did.

"Do you commonly use the same service people when you're preparing homes for sale?" Finn asked.

"Frequently." Scarlet took a big drink from her coffee. "We have preferred companies for lawn maintenance, home inspections, stagers, bankers and title companies to name a few. Representatives from all of those companies were at the party, plus Realtors and their guests, event staff and valets."

Dean wiped his mouth with a napkin. "Sounds like a lot of interviews to arrange."

"Will you discount the people from my daily life now?" she asked. "From the list I gave you before the fire?"

"Not completely," Finn said. "I'm just shifting my focus a bit. That photo is significant to your attacker. I want to know why and how he came to have a copy."

"Have you checked online?" she asked. "The company website sometimes uses shots from special events to build the Coulter Realty brand."

"I have, and I didn't see it. I'd like to start contacting the people you remember seeing at the party."

Scarlet nodded, hating that everyone she knew professionally would receive a call from a detective regarding her attack. She returned her focus to the database and soon refilled her coffee.

Dean was the first to leave after breakfast. He

offered fist bumps and warm smiles when he headed out. The love and respect between brothers were something she admired. If she'd had siblings, she would've wanted to be their friend too.

Even if her interest in Austin was one-sided, she'd always remember that he showed her what a family could be. And that families like those she read about in books really existed. Because if this existed for the Beaumonts, it could exist for her too one day. That kind of hope was priceless.

Scarlet rubbed her eyes a long while later, tired and stinging from screen fatigue. The mug shots were endless, but she'd begun to wonder if her attacker had ever been arrested. Maybe he was too young. Or too careful. Maybe his stalking tendencies were new, or maybe he'd been content to just watch until now. There were too many unknowns. Too little she could control and too few assurances.

Austin's phone buzzed on the table and Finn's phone rang.

Austin frowned. "Well, that's not good."

"Dean?" Finn asked, phone already at his ear.

Scarlet tensed, hoping nothing bad had happened to their kind, congenial, blue-eyed brother.

Austin stared at his phone then at Finn.

Finn tapped the phone's screen and lowered the device onto the table, speaker function engaged. "Say that again."

"Y'all better come down to our office," Dean said. "I just got here, and there's been trouble."

AUSTIN WAS GETTING tired of following Finn through town from crime scene to crime scene. He hated that all these awful events led back to Scarlet's attacker, and that his office was now involved in something sure to make the paper. Whatever they were driving into this time was a double whammy. Scarlet would be unfairly rattled. And his business would receive bad press.

No one wanted to hire a private investigator everyone was talking about. The most important thing a PI could do was be discreet. But that was out the window now.

He parked his truck along the curb near his office, behind a police cruiser and Dean's truck. A small crowd lined the sidewalk. Several onlookers snapped pictures.

"Take a look at the people," he told Scarlet. She'd barely said ten words to him since asking for help with her bandage this morning, and he needed to apologize, but now wasn't the time. "Let me know if you recognize anyone in the crowd."

"Okay."

"We might want to adjust our plan moving forward," he said, drawing her eyes to his.

"What do you mean?"

"We think this guy was following you for weeks, but he attacked after you met with me. I think he saw us together, either at my office or outside it. Then, he apologized by sending flowers to the hospital, but I called him back and he lost it. I stayed at your house overnight and he lashed out again the next day when we left. He said you betrayed him. There's a pattern forming, and it's not a good one. I think he imagines himself in love with you and doesn't like you spending so much time with me."

"Are you sending me to the farm?" she asked. The words came quick and flat, as if she'd been expecting the possibility to arise.

"No." He frowned. "I won't suggest that again. You want to stay with me, and I want you with me. Now we're making the detail decisions together."

She unbuckled her seat belt and turned on the seat to face him. "Okay. So, what are you suggesting?"

"Maybe we should go out in public as a united front. It might be a good idea to make it clear that I'm not going away soon."

Scarlet chewed her bottom lip. "How?"

"I'd like to stay a little closer to you, if you'd be comfortable with that. Hold your hand, keep you near. Disrupt the misconstrued fantasy that you're his somehow. Make it clear he cannot lay claim to you."

She blinked and scowled. "Like when I tell a guy I'm not interested, but they won't leave me alone until I lie and say I have a boyfriend? Because they have more respect for a fictional boyfriend they've never met than me, the woman they're trying to hit on?"

Austin rubbed a hand against his cheek. "Seriously. We've got to introduce you to nicer people."

The anger bled from her face, replaced by something that looked a lot like hope. "Like you and your brothers?"

"Not my brothers."

Her lips quirked, and the teasing little motion was nearly enough to make him lean in and kiss her.

"About earlier," he said instead. "I'm sorry. I shouldn't have run away."

"I wish you wouldn't have," she whispered.

The urge to kiss her hit again.

Someone rapped on his window, and he turned slowly to see who'd ruined his very pleasant moment.

Dean grinned and waved through the glass. "Are y'all getting out, or did you just come to be near the action?"

Beside him, Scarlet's door opened. She cast

a knowing look in his direction as she rounded the hood toward him and his brother.

Austin climbed out as well.

"Ready," she said upon arrival. Then she offered Austin her hand.

He folded his fingers with hers and drew her closer.

"Mama's going to hear about that," Dean muttered, leading the way through the crowd. "Half the people out here know her in one way or another. And everyone knows how she is."

Scarlet stopped short a few paces later, and he did as well.

Big red letters had been spray-painted across the office windows, spelling three familiar words.

SHE IS MINE

Dean stuffed his hands into his pockets. "Our security camera was down, so we don't have any footage of who did this."

Austin struggled to maintain his calm. "What do you mean our cameras were down? That's a top-notch system." He'd made sure of it, chosen every component with exacting care.

"I don't know." Dean frowned, eyes trailing over the red-lettered threat. "It doesn't make any sense. Everything was working fine, then it just...wasn't. At least the glass wasn't broken. The office wasn't breached."

He didn't care about the windows. Those could be replaced. But he loathed the fact that some unhinged, dangerous individual was out there, watching and believing that Scarlet was his. That he had some twisted claim to her. As if she was property instead of a person. And that she was his.

Finn cut through the crowd in their direction, scratching his head. "One of the officers on my team found a few neighbors near Scarlet's place and the Perez home who are willing to share video footage from their doorbell cameras around the times of those crimes. We'll talk to business owners on this block too. If we're lucky, we might catch the same vehicle near more than one crime scene at the times of the crimes."

Scarlet stared at the big red letters. "This feels less significant than his earlier attacks. Doesn't it? Spray paint instead of fire or destruction."

"Only at first glance," Finn said. "Yes, the person who vandalized the windows could've easily chosen to destroy the office or smash the windows instead, but that destruction would've been open to interpretation. He wanted to leave an exacting message. And it's for Austin this time, not you."

Austin clenched and flexed his jaw. "This is what he said when I called him from the hospital gift shop."

Scarlet squeezed his hand, a small, silent, secret gesture.

And he felt a bit of the tension ease.

"If he's moved on from heartbreak over his imagined loss to rage at Austin for his interference, this could get much worse before it gets any better," Finn said.

Dean snorted a small laugh as his keen gaze drifted over the onlookers. "Keep coming at us, guy. You're only creating more chances to be found."

Austin nodded. He didn't like the idea of a criminal's rage pointed anywhere near Scarlet, but it would certainly help Finn and his team if the stalker continued to lash out. Everything this guy did provided another clue. Another sliver of his identity. And soon the pieces would come together enough to see the big picture.

"Finn?" Scarlet asked.

All eyes in their little circle turned to her. "I thought I was followed away from a home showing the night before I decided to meet with a private investigator. I don't know if it was or wasn't the stalker, but it was a car, not a truck or SUV. I don't know if that will help your team as you review the video footage, but I wanted to say it."

Finn's gaze slid from Scarlet's face to their joined hands. "I'll let the team know." He raised his eyes to Austin and shook his head. "And I can almost guarantee you about five people on this sidewalk have already let Mama know about that."

Dean covered his mouth, failing to hide a wide, toothy smile.

"I've been warned," Austin said.

Scarlet wiggled her fingers, but Austin cupped his free hand over their joined ones and leveled her with a no-nonsense grin. "I'm not worried about Mama, and you don't need to be either."

His brothers broke into laughter and walked away.

Chapter Nineteen

Scarlet rolled her tender shoulders and rubbed the bunching muscles along the back of her neck. Sitting inside the Beaumonts' PI office had red flags of panic flying high in her head, and tension building steadily in her muscles. The last time she'd been here, sitting at this desk, a brutal attack followed, and the trauma from that night sizzled inside her. She might've been followed long before meeting Austin, but it felt as if this was where her nightmare had begun.

Austin placed a bottle of water on the desk before her. "Did you bring your pain pills?"

"Yes." She dug into the small purse she'd brought from home, large enough to carry everything she needed, which was only a phone and pills these days. "Thanks. I almost forgot they existed."

He took a seat on the edge of his desk and watched as she took the medication. "Are you hurting? We can take off anytime if you want to get out of here and lay down. You're supposed to be resting, but I feel as if we're constantly on the move. That must be taking a toll."

"No. I'm okay," she said. "I'd rather be here than somewhere else waiting to know what happened. I can work with facts. The waiting and wondering are worse."

Dean clicked the mouse at his desk, reviewing the feed from their security camera before it went offline. Finn hovered at his side.

Scarlet's phone rang as she tucked the pill bottle back into her purse, and she glanced at the screen. "It's my mom."

Austin nodded and moved to join his brother, giving her space to talk.

"Hey," she answered, forcing enthusiasm she didn't feel into her voice. "How's it going?"

"That's what I called to ask you," her mom said. "I've been thinking of you, and I wondered if you want to come and visit. I can't get out of town because I have a showing first thing tomorrow, but I'm home for the rest of the day, and you said you were taking a little time off, so why don't we meet somewhere for dinner?"

"I'm not sure that's a great idea," she said, gaze flickering to the window washers attempting to scrub the most recent threat off the glass. "The police haven't been able to identify the man who attacked me, and he's making it clear he'll try again."

Her mom was silent.

Finn looked her way, an expression of apology on his handsome face.

She made a mental note to remember she had an audience.

Austin returned to her and waited for acknowledgment.

"Hold on a second," she told her mom, lowering the phone from her ear.

"It might be a good idea to get out of town for the evening," he said. "If your mom wouldn't mind an extra guest, we can head that way now. Spend a few hours. If you want."

She squinted, unsure if seeing her mom was what she needed right now.

Austin bent forward at the waist. "I would love to meet your mama," he said, voice low. "Besides, I already showed you mine. You've got to show me yours."

One of his brothers snorted, and she smiled.

"I suppose fair's fair." She delivered the news to her mom, with one caveat. "Mom? Sounds like I can come, but I'm bringing a friend, and I'd be more comfortable if we had dinner at home, considering the circumstance."

"That's fine," her mom answered. "I'll get my carryout menus together and see what's for dinner."

Scarlet said her goodbyes and disconnected, then she stood.

"Looks like we're taking off," Austin announced.

"Yeah, yeah," Dean said, motioning him away with a teasing smile. "You take the pretty woman to dinner, and we'll stay here working."

Finn shook his head in feigned remorse.

Austin held her hand as they walked to his truck and opened her door. "Don't be afraid to let me know when you're ready to leave your mom's place. Even if we've barely arrived. Or if you need to lay down while we're there. I can entertain myself and your mother if necessary."

"You will definitely entertain my mother," she said dryly. She only hoped her mother wouldn't make an obvious show of her delight when she saw him. Handsome men were on the top of Trina's favorite things list. Having their undivided attention was another.

He smiled. "I'm just saying that I'm here to help, and you're not a bother. Sometimes I get the feeling you could use the reminder."

Scarlet nodded as she climbed inside and buckled up, deeply grateful fate had brought her to this man, and equally sad for the day they'd say goodbye.

AUSTIN PARKED OUTSIDE a grand two-story estate in the historic district of Trina Wills's town. He whistled appreciatively.

"Yeah," Scarlet agreed, looking up at the large Tudor-style home through the windshield. "I spent my teen years here. Mom got a good deal and worked hard to restore it."

"Just like you," he said.

"I picked up a thing or two from the project that made the work at my house a lot easier." She reached for the door handle and paused, as if steadying herself. "I've learned everything I know from her. The good and the bad."

Austin wanted to respond but didn't know how, so he climbed out and walked with her to the door. Scarlet rang the bell.

It only took a few moments for the large wooden barrier to swing open. An older version of Scarlet appeared before them with a smile. She wore dress pants and heels with a crimson blouse. Her fair hair was blown out and teased like a pageant woman, and her makeup was fully done.

"Baby," the older woman said, pulling her daughter into a hug. "I'm so glad you came. It's been too long. Come in. Come in." She motioned them into the two-story foyer. "Let me take your coats."

They removed their coats, and Mrs. Wills examined Scarlet. "Are you wearing pajamas?"

"No, Mom," she said. "This is Austin Beaumont, my—"

He stepped forward, offering his most respectable smile. "Nice to meet you, Mrs. Wills. I've heard so many nice things."

"Me too," she said. Her gaze traveled the length of him, appraising. She placed a stiff hand beside her mouth, as if to hide her next words. "You're right. He is handsome."

Scarlet's lids drifted momentarily shut. She reopened them with a resigned expression. "Dinner smells delicious."

Her mom cast another look in Austin's direction. "Call me Trina." Then she turned to lead them to a dining room table large enough for twelve. "I ordered Italian. Hope you like it."

Trina sat at the head of the long table, pushing salad around a plate while Austin and Scarlet each took a chair on either side of her and enjoyed two helpings of stuffed shells.

"How's Lydia doing with your clients while you're out?" Trina asked.

Scarlet paused, a forkful of pasta halfway to her mouth, and tension zinged in the air. "I haven't heard from her today."

Trina blinked. "You didn't call her? Have you at least checked in with the clients to see if they're happy with her level of service?"

"No." She returned her fork to the plate. "It's been a busy day."

"Every day is a busy one," her mom said. "Either that, or you aren't making the most of it. Am I right, Austin?"

He narrowed his eyes, certain he'd been snared in some sort of trap. "I'm not sure that's always the case," he said, unwilling to support her, but trying hard not to flat-out disagree. "Scarlet's right about our day. We've been on the move since breakfast. The only call she made time for was yours."

Trina stopped pretending to eat her salad and rested her hands on her middle. "My. I'd better stop before I need stretchy pants too."

Scarlet rolled her eyes, and Austin stifled a laugh. She changed the subject to her mom's workday, and things got lighter.

Trina obviously loved talking about herself, her sales and the new clients she'd be working with soon. She also mentioned a new boyfriend who thought she could stand to lose a couple of pounds and who was currently between jobs.

Scarlet's expression implied this was all par for the course with Trina.

Austin made a mental note to hug his mama a little tighter the next time he saw her. And to thank her for all the fussing she did to make his life nicer just because she could.

Despite the strange dynamic between mother and daughter, they seemed to enjoy their time together, more or less. And Trina boxed up the leftover food for them to take home.

She asked very little about what Scarlet was going through, and while he didn't understand that either, he was glad not to rehash it all. Scarlet seemed like she needed the break.

He drove home in the dark, Scarlet dozing beside him, and he couldn't help wondering what it would be like to have meals with Trina more often. And to see his family include Scarlet as well.

He was thankful for the peek inside her life, and he felt as if he understood her a little better now. Scarlet was the focused and giving one in their mother-daughter relationship, while Trina was the workaholic, driven by attention and supported at home by her child.

Regardless of their differences, it was clear they loved one another.

In hindsight, it made sense Trina hadn't asked more about the hell Scarlet was going through. The conversation would've steered too far away from her as the topic. And Scarlet had a lifetime of doing what she could to keep the spotlight on her mother.

A long practiced dance.

All the more reason Austin would work to make Scarlet the center of her world and his.

And he planned to tell her as much in the morning.

Chapter Twenty

Austin finished his third cup of coffee on the deck after breakfast. Scarlet sat beside him, still in her pajamas and bundled in the woven throw from the back of his couch. It was an image he wanted to see for years to come. And he'd promised himself he'd say so today. Which was the reason he planned to pour a fourth cup of coffee. He'd been up all night trying to decide how to broach the subject.

I know your life is in constant danger right now, emotions are high, you probably feel overwhelmed and confused about many things and my timing is terrible, but I'm falling in love with you. Let's discuss.

"You okay?" she asked, peering over her steamy mug. "You look stressed. Not that we don't have enough reasons for that. I've just never seen you actually look rattled until now. And we're here. Doing this." She extended an arm toward the mountains around them, the rocking chairs, the blue sky and the picturesque view of the creek rushing beneath. "So, what's up?"

He thought of a few reasonable ways to say he'd developed an attachment to her and didn't want to see it end, but none of them seemed right or worthy.

He'd become far more than attached.

"Lost in thought, I guess," he said, forcing a smile. "You?"

"A little," she said. "I've never thanked you for all this. For taking my case. For believing me when I came to you that day, when I wasn't even sure I believed myself. Then showing up and staying the course when everything went promptly to hell. You've catered and comforted. Now you're hosting me. It's a lot, and I was up half the night thinking I'm kind of awful for not saying this sooner."

The idea they'd both been awake last night but not together made him sad. He liked being with her and talking to her. They could've been happy instead of restless.

"Are you usually this involved in your cases?"

He frowned. She couldn't mean what he thought she meant. Could she? "No. Not like this."

He'd never once been attracted to a client. Never wanted to get to know them personally or have them in his life. He'd always done his best to help, nothing more.

There had just been something about Scarlet from the start. And the more he'd gotten to know her, the more he wanted to know. The more he wanted her to stay when this was over. Which was what he should be saying to her right now.

But the risk could outweigh the potential gain.

If Scarlet didn't feel the same way, there was a chance she wouldn't be comfortable staying with him. He'd regret her absence in his home, but more importantly, he'd worry about her safety anywhere else. After what had happened at his office yesterday, he wasn't convinced the culprit wouldn't go to his family's farm for her. And the farm was the only other place he'd consider safe enough for anyone under constant threat of attack.

All reasons to wait until the criminal was captured and the danger gone before making an already complicated situation worse.

"So, your past girlfriends didn't get upset about your job because you'd started living with other women?"

He barked an unexpected laugh. "No. It's the time involved. Unless I'm on a stakeout, I always come home. Alone. But it's still a lot of long hours. Even after I get here, I work online, create files, paperwork, process contracts. I don't have a lot of time to go places. To date. I work, make time for my family and this place, then scrape together a little sliver of downtime when I can."

She set her coffee on the table at her side and turned to him, expression caught somewhere between contemplative and resolved. "I need to ask you something important, and I need you to answer me directly. Will you do that?"

He shifted, matching her position in the chair beside his. "If that's what you want." He swallowed and braced himself for what came next.

Her green eyes flickered away then back. "Yesterday, in the bathroom," she began. A blush spread across her face, pinking her cheeks, and her gaze dropped to his lips for one quick beat. "I thought you might've wanted to kiss me. I've spent the time since then wondering if I read everything wrong, or if something changed your mind. I stepped up and put my arms around your neck because I wanted you to kiss me, but if I misread you, I think I should apologize and let you know it won't happen again." She wrinkled her nose. "You've been so kind, and if I crossed a line or made you uncomfortable, I'm sorry."

His mouth opened to speak and his mind raced. He hadn't been able to make himself broach the subject, and she'd simply put it out there. No wonder he was falling for her. Scarlet was fearless. Unlike him, apparently. "I definitely wanted to kiss you in the bathroom yesterday."

Her eyes widened and her lips twitched. "Well, then I'm not sorry."

He smiled. "If I'm being fully honest, I've been thinking of kissing you a lot more often than I should."

She blushed, and his gaze dropped to her full pink lips.

He could practically taste them, almost feel them pressed to his. When his gaze returned to hers, she was watching him.

And like magnets, they both began to lean closer.

She laughed and pulled away when the distance between rocking chairs proved too much.

He stretched to his feet as Scarlet fell back into her chair, shaking her head at the temporary defeat. He offered his hand and pulled her up beside him, then wound an arm around her back. "We can't give up that easily."

"Agreed," she said. "We should try that again." The delight in her eyes thrilled him, and her contagious smile parted his lips as well.

Austin cradled her jaw in his palm, memorizing the lines of her face and absorbing this moment.

She closed her eyes and tipped her chin, then rose onto her toes.

The simple, openhearted gesture cracked something loose inside him, and he knew there wasn't any going back from there. He could only hope she'd feel the same when all was said and done.

And his phone rang.

Scarlet stepped away, brows raised. "Whoever's calling you right now is the absolute worst."

He laughed, dipping forward quickly and pressing a kiss against her temple before pulling the phone off the table at his side. "It's Finn."

She sighed, sobering a bit. "It's back to reality then."

He puzzled briefly at her meaning as he answered. "Hey, what's up?" Did she know being with her was the only reality he wanted?

Probably not because he'd yet to say so.

"I'm at the Coulter Realty office in town," Finn said. "Is Scarlet right there, or do you need to get her?"

"She's here."

Scarlet's brow furrowed.

"Hold on." Austin tapped his screen and lowered the phone between them. "All right. You're on speaker," he told his brother.

"Morning, Scarlet," Finn said, his voice oddly flat. "I'm at your office."

"More window paint?" she asked.

"No," Finn said. "A woman was attacked here

this morning, and there's a threat at your desk. You two should probably get down here."

Fear flashed in Scarlet's eyes, and Austin's heart ached for her.

The stalker had crossed another line, bypassing destruction of property and trespassing. He'd attacked again, and this time it was someone Scarlet knew and likely cared for.

"What woman?" she asked, voice quaking.

"Lydia Stevens."

SCARLET BOUNCED DOWN the gravel lane on the seat in Austin's old truck then flew with him over paved country roads into town. Her heart raced and stomach lurched with flashbacks of her attack and fear for Lydia. Would she be hospitalized too? Would she be okay?

Did Lydia know Scarlet was the reason for her attack?

She was sure Austin would tell her this wasn't her fault, but he couldn't deny the truth. Scarlet's stalker wouldn't have been at the Coulter Realty office if not for Scarlet. He wouldn't have been so upset if she wasn't hiding out with Austin. And even if Scarlet wasn't sure what she could've done differently, Lydia's suffering was still directly linked to her. Scarlet should've predicted this somehow and protected her.

Austin covered her hand with his on the seat

between them, gently stroking his thumb over her clenched fist.

"Did he say how badly she's hurt?" Scarlet asked. She'd barely heard anything Finn had said after Lydia's name.

"No. The paramedics were still working on her when he called."

Scarlet closed her eyes and sent up endless prayers for Lydia's well-being. For her stalker's capture and for no one else to be hurt this way.

The crowd outside her office was thick and deep, significantly larger than the group that had gathered outside the PI office the day before. The full gamut of emergency responders were there as well. An ambulance, a fire truck and three police cruisers crowded into the employee parking lot. Red and white lights flashed against the surrounding buildings on repeat, reflecting off the glass of nearby windows.

She and Austin jumped down from the truck and met at the hood, catching one another's hand then jogging the rest of the way to the building.

Uniformed officers had formed a barricade on the sidewalk. Thankfully, they recognized Austin and let them pass without question.

A moment later, he held the door so she could enter the office.

The space was full of people in uniforms. Cameras flashed and low voices murmured.

Time slipped beneath her, and the world seemed to tilt.

Lydia was laid out on a stretcher, eyes closed and a padded collar around her neck. Dark bruises and fresh cuts peppered her jaw, forehead, eyes and nose.

Scarlet pressed her lips together, willing herself not to be sick on the office floor. And she hurried to the gurney's side. "Is she going to be okay?" she asked, clutching Lydia's hand.

Her friend's fingers didn't curl or grip back in response.

And Scarlet's tears began to fall.

The gurney inched forward as an EMT dislodged its brake. "I'm sorry," the man said, looking as if he meant it. "We'll do everything we can, but we have to go."

Scarlet pulled her hand away, and the paramedics guided an unconscious Lydia through the door.

Austin's arms curled around her, and she turned to bury her face against his chest. "We'll go to the hospital when we finish here, and I'll see if I can learn more."

"Thank you."

He stroked her hair, and she fought the urge to break down.

A sharp whistle cut through the air, and Scarlet forced herself upright, shoulders square and chin high.

Finn waved a hand overhead.

Austin pulled her against his side. "Time to see what he found."

The sea of uniformed personnel parted as they made their way down the aisle toward Scarlet's desk.

Finn stepped back, making room for her and Austin to take a look.

Her chair had been overturned and everything had been scribbled on. Her files, papers, the monitor. Even the fabric of her rolling chair and the desk itself. Two haunting words repeated again and again.

She's mine. She's mine. She's mine.

Chapter Twenty-One

Austin swore under his breath as Scarlet fell against his chest, breath rushing from her body. Even while doing all he could to protect her physically, the stalker was still getting in his jabs. Taking mental and emotional hits wherever he could.

"I can't believe this is happening," she whispered.

Austin wound his arms around her, gritting his teeth and pulling her in tight.

A storm of fury and heartbreak thundered inside him. Whoever was responsible for these attacks had clearly snapped. And wherever he was, he was a danger. The expressions on the medics' faces had made it clear that Lydia wasn't as lucky as Scarlet had been. Her injuries were more severe and would take far longer to heal. Though, she too would carry a lifetime of trauma from this man's hands.

The mere idea that Scarlet, who'd been strangled and left unconscious, was lucky compared to anyone was another sign of just how bad things had gotten.

Her fingers curled against his back as she clung to him. Her ragged breaths vibrated his chest and pierced his heart. Whatever thread of connection he'd imagined between them before had fast become a heavy rope. One he was sure could tow freight trains without a single tear.

"I've got you," he whispered, lowering his mouth to her ear. "Finn and the others are going to find the man who did this."

A camera flash straightened his spine. Behind her, a member of the crime scene unit documented evidence of the struggle.

Finn's and Dean's eyes were on Austin. They gave nods of understanding and acceptance before turning away. They saw what he'd yet to verbalize.

He was in love with Scarlet Wills.

"Come on," Austin said, sliding his hands onto her biceps. "Let's go to the hospital and see what we can find out."

Finn took a step in their direction as they broke their embrace. "I'll be there as soon as I can. We'll touch base then if you're still around."

Scarlet curled her arms around her middle, eyes haunted. "I want to stay at the hospital until I can see her," she said. "Her siblings are out of state now. I think I should wait with her mom until the rest of the family arrives. She shouldn't be alone."

Austin checked his watch. If they hurried, they'd arrive before his favorite volunteer headed home. "We'd better get moving." He guided Scarlet back to his truck and helped her inside. "You're very kind to think of Lydia's mother," he said. "She and Lydia will appreciate that."

"It seems like the least I can do." Scarlet's eyes were woeful as he closed the door.

He rounded the cab to the driver's side and climbed behind the wheel. "There's only one person to blame for any of this," he said softly. "And that person isn't you."

The drive to the hospital was silent, save for the sounds of Scarlet's unsteady breaths and tires on warped brick roads. He parked beneath the nearest streetlight just outside the visitors' lot and held her hand as they hurried inside.

Curious eyes turned briefly in their direction then away, not finding whoever or whatever they'd been seeking.

"What now?" Scarlet asked. "We're not family, so the staff won't talk to us. Do we wait for Finn to arrive?"

"We can, but it's a small town," he said, steering her toward a pair of chairs near the interior doors. "We won't have to wait long for information."

She offered a quizzical look, but sat.

"Do you know Mrs. Thatcher?" he asked.

"No. Does she work here?"

"She's a volunteer who makes those little knitted hats for newborns and fills in just about anywhere she can."

One of the paramedics from the real estate office moved into view before Scarlet could ask more questions.

Austin stood and offered his hand. "Were you able to get her stabilized?"

The other man nodded, expression grim. "She's undergoing tests, then they'll admit her for monitoring. She's stable, and that's something."

Scarlet rose. "Is she awake?"

"No, ma'am. Not yet." He opened his mouth to say something more, but his partner appeared behind him moving double time.

"We've got another call," she said. "One of the Briar kids fell from his horse."

The man gave a quick goodbye nod and hustled away.

Scarlet sighed. "Maybe I can steal a lab coat from the back of a chair and sneak around until I find her. It always works in sitcoms."

Austin fought a smile. "No need," he said, gaze locking on the woman he'd hoped to catch. "Here comes Mrs. Thatcher."

The older woman carried a large, quilted bag in one hand with an array of yarn strands hanging over the edge. Her white hair formed a crown on her head, and her milky blue eyes twinkled at the sight of him.

"Mrs. Thatcher," he said, lifting a wide smile. "How are you?"

She kissed his cheek and beamed. "Very well. Thank you. How's your mother?"

"Missing you," he said. "When will you get out to the ranch for lunch again?"

"Oh." She shrugged. "It's hard to say. I spend all my time knitting lately. This town has become a baby factory. There were four new little ones born since I arrived this morning." Her gaze slid to Scarlet. "All girls."

Scarlet offered a small smile.

"You remember Scarlet Wills," Austin prompted. "You were here when I got here on the evening she was attacked. You knew where I could find her."

The woman's eyes widened, and her gaze moved to Scarlet's throat. "I remember. Why are you back? Are you unwell?"

"I'm worried about my friend," Scarlet said. "The man who did this to me attacked another woman today. She was brought here a few minutes ago, and we're waiting to see her, if someone will allow it."

Mrs. Thatcher released a puff of air. "Oh, dear. You should sit."

Scarlet and Austin returned to their seats, and Mrs. Thatcher sat beside Scarlet. She took her hand and offered a cautious look in Austin's direction.

"Did you see her come through?" he asked.

"I might've," she said. "Would she have arrived in the last fifteen minutes?"

Austin nodded. "She was with the paramedics who left as you arrived just now."

Mrs. Thatcher's expression fell. "Then I know the one you mean. I thought she'd been in a car accident."

Austin shook his head.

The older woman turned her eyes to Scarlet, who was listening silently. "I'm so sorry."

"Mrs. Thatcher is the eyes and ears of this hospital," he said. Even better, she was a shameless gossip, and a little flattery usually loosened her lips.

"My husband was the chief of surgery," she said proudly. "Rest his soul. He practically lived here, and so did I until our children were born, then again after they'd grown. I know everything about this old girl." She glanced around the room. "Always changing. Full of life and tragedy."

"And the woman?" Austin asked. "Any chance you know where we can find her?"

"I don't want her to be alone," Scarlet interjected. "And I'd like to be with her mom when she arrives."

"They took her straight to the CT room for a scan," Mrs. Thatcher said. "The paramedics told the doctors she'd had severe head trauma, was unconscious, and they were concerned."

"How'd the scan look?" Scarlet asked.

"I don't know about that, but she's in the ICU now for observation. You should go up to the third floor waiting room. They keep fresh coffee and hot water for tea. I'll bring something sweet when I come around tomorrow."

"Thank you, Mrs. Thatcher," Austin said.

"Anytime, dear." She rose, and Austin did as well. "Now, I'd better go see how the ladies at intake are doing. Tell your mother I'll call soon."

"I will." He reached for Scarlet and pulled her up with him. "This way."

HOURS SLOGGED BY in the little waiting room outside the ICU. There wasn't anything to do and no real reason to stay, but Scarlet insisted, so Austin did his best to accommodate.

He requested a pillow and blanket from a volunteer to help Scarlet sleep more comfortably, and he'd even begun to refill the waiting room coffee when it ran low or got cold.

Finn had come and gone with minimal news to share. Lydia's head scans had been clear, but she'd had significant neck trauma and was sedated to help with the pain. Her mother, who was local, had been visiting Lydia's brother in Texas. The family was flying in as soon as they could.

Yet another reason Scarlet wouldn't leave. She couldn't bear the thought of Lydia not having anyone waiting for her when she woke.

A guard had been positioned outside Lydia's room for due diligence. Just in case the attacker returned to silence her, if she'd seen his face.

The whole set of events had pushed Austin to his limits, and he'd spent a long while reviewing the evidence available while Scarlet slept. He'd seen his share of awful things, but he'd never seen them keep coming like this, and not at someone he loved.

He pulled the compact stun gun from his pocket and slid it into her jacket. She didn't want it, and he hoped she'd never have reason to use it, but knowing it was within her reach, even while she was safe beside him, offered a world of comfort. Only then, as the sunlight of a new day began to climb the windowsills, did Austin finally fall asleep.

SCARLET WOKE WITH a stiff back and aching neck. Her head pounded and her throat was dry. Austin was asleep in the chair beside her, long legs stretched out before him, while she and her pillow had leaned against his side.

A travel pack of pain pills sat on the table before them with a bottle of water.

She rubbed her eyes and rolled her shoulders, working out the kinks in her tender muscles, then opened the pain pills and water to take the medication.

The hospital bustled around her, and she was thankful for every hushed voice and hurried footfall. The halls had become eerie in the night, too quiet and still. Occasionally punctuated by a tragedy, racing crash team or other emergencies that left Scarlet on edge. Fearing Lydia had taken a turn for the worse and knowing no one would tell her if she had.

A trio of swiftly moving men appeared in the hallway, visible through the wall of waiting room windows. Her heart raced at the sight of a familiar face.

"Finn!" She clutched Austin's hand to wake him then creaked to her feet, wincing at the discomfort.

Austin stood instantly. "What happened? Are you okay?"

"Finn's here," she said, tracking the detective with her gaze. "And he's not alone. That means something, right?"

She moved into the hall as Finn and the officers approached.

"You're still here?" Finn asked, brows furrowed. He motioned the officers to continue on.

"I couldn't leave," Scarlet said. "Lydia's family isn't here yet." She glanced at the empty waiting room to be sure that was still true, and they hadn't arrived during the night.

His gaze shifted to his brother. "I'm on my way to see her now. Why don't y'all come back with me? It might soothe her to have a friend present when we talk. Officer Pratt is here to relieve Officer Grant of his shift, and Officer Meade will speak with the nurses."

Scarlet's heart swelled with hope. "Speak with her?"

"Yes. Lydia's awake."

Scarlet stifled the urge to hug him. She settled for following him into Lydia's room with Austin at her side.

Her friend's eyes opened and shut several times before opening to stay. "Scarlet?"

"Yes." Tears burst into existence as Scarlet hurried to Lydia's side. She clutched her right hand, avoiding the one with an IV, and did her best to remain calm and composed. "I'm here."

Lydia made a weak attempt to hold on to Scarlet's hand. "He came for me," she whispered, voice rough and raw.

"I know. I'm so sorry."

"Lydia?" Finn said. "I'm Detective Beaumont.

I was assigned to Scarlet's case and I'll be working on yours as well. I promise I'm going to do everything in my power to apprehend the man who did this as soon as possible."

Lydia turned to watch and listen as he spoke. The wide red marks on her face from the day before were now swollen and black. A deep cut on her lip had been patched with a stitch, and there was blood on the white of one eye. A thick padded collar still circled her neck.

She released Scarlet's hand, brows furrowed and gaze distant, as if the reality of things was just filtering in. She lifted her fingers to the injuries on her face, and her expression crumbled.

"It's going to be okay," Scarlet said, voice quaking. "I'm here now and you're safe. No one will hurt you again. I promise. And I won't leave unless someone makes me. Even then I won't be far." She glanced to Austin, who'd made a similar promise to her once.

Finn pulled a little notepad from his pocket. "Were you able to get a look at the man who did this?"

She nodded then searched the ceiling with her eyes. "I think he was—" Her gaze snapped back to Scarlet. "He was looking for you. I said you weren't at work, and he said he knew that. He wanted to know where you were, but I didn't know. I said maybe at home."

"Can you describe him?" Finn asked again, rewording the question and working to regain her attention. "I know this is hard."

A sob broke on Lydia's lips and tears began to roll.

Her monitors beeped and a nurse came to check the situation. "Lydia? Morning, hon. Can you breathe for me? Nice and slow?" She frowned at Finn, then Austin, and slid her eyes over Scarlet. "This is an ICU. She's permitted to have one guest at a time, and all guests should be family. You know that, Detective."

"Her family is en route," he said. "Scarlet went through something similar this week, and we hoped her presence would put Lydia at ease."

"How's that working?" she asked, gaze hard. "Wrap it up."

Austin raised his palms in innocence. "I'll step outside." He moved into the hall just beyond the door, outside Lydia's sight, but within Scarlet's view.

Lydia's lips quivered and her face contorted, fighting the tears. "He was tall with a beard. Not old. Not a kid either. I don't know. He wanted Scarlet. It was all he would say. Over and over. Where was she? Who was she with? Why was I lying?"

She sobbed.

Scarlet passed her a tissue. "I'm so sorry." The words were small and pathetic, but they were all she had to offer. The horror of the moment was too heavy to bear.

Lydia wiped her eyes, sucking in shallow, shuddered breaths.

Finn cast a cautious look at the nurse before trying again. He worked his jaw. "Was he familiar to you?"

"No." She shook her head and cringed, presumably at the pain. Her gaze flipped back to Scarlet. "But he knew me. He said my name."

"That's good information," Scarlet said, hoping to look calm and reassuring, while inside she cracked apart. "Detective Beaumont can use all of this to build a profile. To try to find him."

"Can you think of anything else?" Finn asked. "Even something small. A limp or lisp. A logo on his hoodie? A scar or tattoo?"

Lydia's eyes shifted, possibly sorting her thoughts or searching her memories. Her monitors beeped more frequently.

The nurse's expression tightened. "Remember to breathe, sweetie. Last warning, Detective."

"He went to your desk," Lydia said. Her hand latched onto Scarlet's with unexpected fervor. "He left me on the floor and I watched—I watched him—"

"I saw," Scarlet said, covering her squeezing hand. "It's okay. We were at the office yesterday. Everything's been photographed."

"Photograph," Lydia repeated, gaze distant, as if recalling the moment.

"That's right. It's all being processed."

"No." A tear slid over her cheek. "He took your photograph."

"When?" Finn asked, voice harder than it had been since entering the room. "At the office party? Could he have been the photographer?"

Lydia shook her head again, skin paling and a sheen of sweat breaking across her brow.

"All right. That's enough." The nurse stretched her arms wide, as if to herd and push them from Lydia's room.

"No!" Lydia shoved onto her elbows. "He took the photograph from your desk."

The words hit Scarlet like an anvil as images from the day before returned. Everything had been covered in ink. Scribbled with that horrid message. *She's mine. She's mine.* Her desk had been overturned. Her papers scattered.

Austin stepped back inside, eyes darting from Scarlet to his brother. "Did you find a framed picture with her things?"

"No," Finn said, turning to Scarlet. "Why? What was in the photo?"

Her world came crashing down with the answer. "Me and my mother."

Chapter Twenty-Two

Scarlet dialed her mother for the thirtieth time as she and Austin raced along the highway between Marshal's Bluff and Holbrook. "Voice mail," she reported. "She's not answering her landline or cell phone. And no one at her office has seen her yet today."

"Hang in there," he said. "Finn's been in touch with her local police department, and they're looking for her too. All we can do is get there and help. Meanwhile, we have to keep trying."

"What if we don't find her?"

"We will," he said, reaching across the seat to grip her clasped hands, which were kneaded into a ball on her lap. "Can you think of anyone else she might've spoken with recently?"

Scarlet shook her head. Her mother didn't have friends. She had coworkers and clients, plus the occasional boyfriend. "I knew some of her co-workers before I moved, but there's a lot of turnover in this business. I don't know how many still work with her."

"If you know how to reach them, give it a try. Meanwhile, we'll stop at her home, then move to her office," he said. "We'll talk to neighbors and anyone else who might've seen her coming or going at either location. And we'll visit the local police department to introduce ourselves. Whoever is on this case will want to talk to you too."

Scarlet closed her eyes, combatting a swell of nausea and fatigue. Each time she was sure things couldn't get worse, they did. And this was far more horrible than anything she'd imagined.

This guy had her mother.

"He attacked Lydia yesterday," she said. "He's had enough time to drag my mom into another state and do anything he wants to her."

Austin gave her fingers a squeeze, and she braced for more words of false comfort that didn't come. "I know."

And those words were even worse.

Her mom's historic Tudor home appeared a while later, tucked neatly behind its brick fence. The limbs of mature trees swayed on the lawn, losing hordes of multicolored leaves with each bluster of the late fall wind.

Scarlet made a run for the front door. She rang the bell and knocked then peered through the windows, praying for signs of life inside. Hoping her mom would trundle into the foyer with a new man on her arm and a mimosa in one hand, having turned off her phone's ringer to embrace irresponsibility and new love.

"Car's gone," Austin said, hands cupped near his eyes as he peeked through the narrow garage windows.

"That's good," she said. "Right? I don't see any signs of a struggle inside the home, so maybe she's just…out."

She wrapped icy arms around her middle, recognizing her words as a lie. The unseasonably cold day burrowed ice into her veins. Her mother wasn't out shopping or meeting someone for an early dinner. She wasn't with a new boyfriend. She was gone. Taken against her will.

"Do you have a key?" Austin asked. "We should check inside if we can."

Scarlet shook her head and glanced toward the home. "No." She hadn't had a key to her mom's place since the day she'd moved out and Trina had asked for it back. Scarlet tried the doorknob just in case. "Locked."

"All right." Austin moved toward the waiting truck. "We'll check her office next."

The drive into town was short. A cruiser sat in the parking lot when they arrived.

"Why do you think the cops are here?" Scarlet asked, climbing down from the truck and hoping she didn't already know. Her teeth began to chatter as her exhausted body flooded with adrenaline she had no way to process.

The last time they'd arrived at an office like this with a police presence, they'd found Lydia beaten and unconscious.

"This is routine," Austin said, matching his stride to hers across the parking lot. "No flashers. No other first responders. My best guess is that these officers are just following up like Finn requested."

She exhaled, shaking her hands out hard at the wrists. "Okay. That makes sense."

"I always make sense," Austin said, drawing her eyes to his.

A small smile tugged her lips.

"I've got you," he told her, swinging open the glass office door and waiting for her to pass. "Whatever comes, we'll face it together."

Her heart swelled, and her lips quivered. "Thank you."

Unlike the more modern satellite location in Marshal's Bluff, her mom's office was set in a historic brick building with a row of curtained windows and tidy flower beds along a stone walkway.

The homey theme carried through to the interior. Each agent had a large wooden desk on a colorful rug with two armchairs positioned before it and a matching chair on wheels behind it. A refreshments area with coffee, tea and a mini-fridge for bottled water and juices anchored a wall near the restrooms. Vases with fall-colored blooms sat on side tables with framed photos of top-selling agents and printed lists of company attributes.

"This is cozy," Austin said, pausing in the entryway to look around.

"Each office is designed to be most attractive to the clientele in that area," Scarlet said. "It's all about the outdoor views in our town. People move there to enjoy the seaside."

The Marshal's Bluff office was utilitarian, mostly glass and metal, meant for brief visits on a client's way back outside. The interior was pale blue and the art featured boats, gulls and images of the sea. No one wanted to be indoors in Marshal's Bluff. Whereas Holbrook was all about history and hospitality.

A uniformed officer spoke to a woman at a desk near the back. "And this is her calendar?" he asked.

"Yes. We keep our own schedules. Trina's is always full. We don't see a lot of her, unless it's a paperwork day and she's here playing catch-up." The woman's gaze jumped to Scarlet and Austin as they stepped forward. She gasped. "Oh, my stars, I thought you were her."

The stern-faced officer looked their way. His pale blue eyes were creased at the corners and tight with concern. He was older than Scarlet, probably older than her mother, but fit with an air of authority that gave Scarlet hope. "I'm afraid this isn't a good time," he said. "Can Ms. Reese take your name and number and give you a call in a bit?"

"No." Scarlet moved in their direction. "I'm Scarlet Wills. This is Austin Beaumont. My mother's Trina Wills."

The man's expression morphed from politely patient to apologetic. "I'm sorry. Come on in. I'm Officer Barrow and this is Cindy Reese, a coworker of your mother's."

"Please sit," Cindy said, pointing to a seat at the desk beside hers. Her white sweater set and long, shapeless blue skirt reminded Scarlet of her elementary school librarian. Her gray bun and pencil tucked through the knot finished the look perfectly. "That's your mama's desk," Cindy said. "You look just like her. Anyone ever told you?"

Scarlet tried to smile. "It's been a while, but I used to hear it all the time." She lowered herself into the seat and covered her mouth at the sight of her mother's things. All neat as a pin. All untouched, waiting for her return. And the same framed photo that Scarlet kept on her desk stood beside her mother's monitor as well. "Austin," she whispered. "Look."

He placed his hands on her shoulders, and she did her best to soak up his strength.

Scarlet ran a fingertip over the glass, tracing her mother's cheek.

The large paper calendar beneath her opposite hand was lined in client names, addresses and times. The color-coded system had been in use for her mother long before the realty company they worked for had a website and apps to organize an agent's schedule.

"It looks as if your mother had an appointment on the books for first thing this morning," the officer said, drawing Scarlet's eyes to the paper calendar. "I'm guessing she went straight to the home on Elm after leaving her place. We've tried the number for the client, but no one answered." He pointed to the digits written with the name and address where her mother planned to meet a client at 9:00 a.m.

Austin set his hands on his hips. "He's been using disposable phones for related crimes in Marshal's Bluff."

Officer Barrow grunted, clearly unimpressed but unsurprised. "Detective Beaumont gave me a pretty solid rundown," he told Austin before returning his gaze to Scarlet. "I'm very sorry for what you're going through. My team and I are working in tandem with the Marshal's Bluff police force, and we'll do everything we can to locate your mother and make sure she's safe."

"Thank you," Austin said.

Scarlet nodded, throat tight.

The desk phone rang, and the room stilled. Air thickened around her shoulders as she stared at the screen.

"That's the number I called earlier," Officer Barrow said. "From the morning appointment. Let's see if your mother arrived as planned." He leaned forward, arm outstretched, as if intending to answer the call.

Scarlet lifted a hand to block him. Her gaze swept the caller ID screen then the paper calendar under her hand. And a sense of foreboding curled around her spine. She pressed the speaker button on the phone. "Coulter Realty," she said warily. "Scarlet speaking."

"Hello, darling," a low voice seethed. "I knew you'd answer my call."

Austin was at her side in the next moment, his cell phone poised before the speaker, a recording app already in use.

Scarlet gripped his arm then pushed on. "You did?"

"I know everything about you. And I see you right now," he said. "Still with that man. Still unwilling to listen."

"Is my mom with you?" Scarlet asked, ignoring his menace. "Can I talk to her?"

"Not while you're keeping him around."

"What if I ask him to go outside?" she asked, cringing slightly at the thought.

"Tell him you're mine!" he roared, voice vibrating the little speaker and sending Scarlet's hammering heart into her throat.

She reeled back, feeling as if she'd been slapped and remembering women got hurt when he got angry. "I'm sorry," she said, rising to lean over the phone and beg. "I'm so sorry. Please don't be mad at my mom. I didn't mean to upset you. It's not her fault. I'll do better."

"You will," he said, voice lower and assured. "Because infidelity has a price."

The line went silent, and Scarlet's world collapsed around her.

Chapter Twenty-Three

Austin sent the audio recording to Finn, then he turned his focus to Scarlet, who looked as if she was in shock.

Officer Barrow had cracked immediately into action, voice rumbling through the quiet office as he recounted the details to Finn and his team. The front door quickly opened and closed as he moved outside.

Cindy Reese stared after him. "Where's he going?"

"Looking for the caller, I imagine," Austin said. "Are you okay?"

She nodded woodenly then cast her attention to Scarlet, staring and motionless, before heading to the refreshments table. "I'll find something for her to drink. I think she's in shock. Heaven knows I can't blame her."

"Thank you."

"I'm not in shock," Scarlet whispered, still staring blankly ahead.

Austin crouched at her side. "Are you sure?"

Her chest rose and fell in steady breaths. The hairs on her arms stood at attention, bolstered by a cascade of goose bumps.

"Scarlet?"

Cindy returned with a steaming mug and a half-sized bottle of water. "I wasn't sure you liked tea, so I brought water too," she said, setting both on the desk.

Scarlet didn't move or respond.

"Is she okay?" Cindy whispered. "Should she see a doctor?"

"I'm thinking," Scarlet said.

"Oh." Cindy set a packet of crackers beside the water and backed up. "That's good. I'll leave you to it."

Austin raised his palm in thanks as the older woman turned away.

"Do you think he's still out there?" Scarlet asked. "Parked across the street or lurking on the corner?"

"I'm sure he's already moved on," Austin said. Leaving them to chase their tails as usual.

"He knew I was here. Sitting at her desk. Knew I'd answer the phone. How?"

Austin looked at the windows, each with a slatted wooden miniblind and sheer curtains parted at the center. "I don't know. He likely guessed."

"After following us here," she said. "Knowing I'd look for my mother."

"That, or he saw my truck in the lot. From there he could've assumed you were at her desk. Just because he said he saw you, doesn't mean he did. And there's a chance he was speaking figuratively when he said he saw you. As if he knows you, not that you were literally in view." Though even Austin had trouble believing that theory. Whoever this guy was, he'd been clinging to Scarlet like a second skin from day one. And he'd yet to figure out how he was doing it.

And now he had her mother.

The door opened again, and Officer Barrow strode back inside, cell phone no longer at his ear. "There weren't any signs of the caller on the street, but he could've easily walked or driven away. A team's been dispatched to review local security footage in search of a car matching the description provided by Detective Beaumont. For now, it's probably best that Ms. Wills find someplace safe to stay out of sight."

Austin nodded, his mind already working through their prospects. His place was the safest, but it was back in Marshal's Bluff, and he knew better than to ask Scarlet to leave this town, where her mother had gone missing. She'd want to stay close to the places and things in her mother's world. There were a handful of inns on the way into town, but those wouldn't be any easier to guard than any other house, which only left hotels. Something outside Holbrook, but not as far as home, would be best. Some place within a ten-to fifteen-minute drive, in case they were needed in a hurry.

Scarlet tugged on his coat sleeve, gaze still fixed on the paper calendar under hand. "Look."

Officer Barrow moved to his side. "What is it?"

One slender finger touched a set of initials at the top of Trina Wills's schedule for the prior day. TS.

Austin examined the script, then looked to her for explanation. The letters were written near the date without indication of time or purpose. "What does it mean?"

Scarlet turned bewildered green eyes to him. "Tech Services."

His mental wheels spun as the pieces of the puzzle began to fall into place.

Cindy returned, an expectant look on her brow. "Trina has been having issues with her company laptop and accounts. Maybe she scheduled a meeting to sort it out."

Scarlet paled. She'd had her share of similar problems not long ago. "What if the person who left the image of me from the party didn't actually attend the party or take the picture?" she asked. "What if he had access to the photos from that night because he was the one selecting which ones to use?"

Austin recalled the Coulter Realty website, where images from events like the one in question were featured on the About page.

"Tech Services would've been given all the images, so they could upload a few to the site."

Austin's fingers curled. The culprit had been in Scarlet's life all along. Tucked neatly into the background.

"I'll call Detective Beaumont," Officer Barrow announced.

Scarlet moved her cell phone onto the desk and navigated to Coulter Realty's corporate page, then to the staff directory.

"Smart," Austin said, crouching for a clearer view over her shoulder.

"Tech Services," she said, zooming in on a candid shot of the men and women who made up the department. "I talked to someone from TS almost every day during the transition to the new website. Something was always going wrong or haywire with my new email or the password. I must've had it reset a half dozen times. Then I needed help with the contact form when I began to receive showing requests. They were assigned to me, but I didn't always get a notification in time to make the appointments. It was a long process filled with hiccups. But what if they weren't all hiccups?"

"Who did you talk to?" he asked. "You said you spoke to someone every day. Was it always the same person?"

"Yes," she said, the word barely a whisper. "Him."

Her hand trembled violently as she passed the phone to Austin, nearly dropping it in the process. She'd zoomed in on one man in a group of smiling, carefree faces around a table. Sandy hair. Dark eyes. A narrow face and build. "Greg. I've never met him in person or seen him before now." An ugly sound ripped from her core. "That's the man who attacked me."

Austin returned the image to normal size, temper raging silently beneath his surface. The man who'd attacked two women, threatened, stalked and now abducted someone looked just like everyone else in the photo. A perfect wolf in sheep's clothing.

He wrapped Scarlet in a hug.

"Tech Services," Officer Barrow said, back on his cell phone nearby. "I need the contact information on a man called Greg."

A tremor spread through Scarlet as they listened to the seasoned officer command someone at Coulter's corporate location.

"That's the one." His gaze flickered to Scarlet then Austin. "Greg Marten."

Austin held his eye contact, jaw locked, and a silent understanding passed between them. Greg Marten's reign of terror was ending now.

"I need Marten's contact information and everything you know about him. I'd also like to speak with the other members of his department... He's a person of interest in several ongoing investigations with both the Holbrook and Marshal's Bluff police..." Barrow rubbed his forehead, apparently unhappy with the response he received. "Then I'll be there with a warrant inside the hour." He disconnected the call and made another while heading for the door. "Get her somewhere safe while I run this guy down," he told Austin, before pulling his attention back to the phone. "This is Barrow. I need to speak to someone in Judge Touran's office." He raised a hand in goodbye and strode back into the day.

Scarlet stood, gripping Austin's elbow for balance. "Greg tampered with my account and had access to my schedule. That's why he always knew where I would be. He could've even watched me through my laptop camera. It was company-issued after all. So was my phone. And I'll bet he's the reason your security cameras weren't working when your office windows were vandalized."

"We've got his name now. Finn will know everything else about him soon. Let's go somewhere and lay low."

"I don't want to leave town until my mom is found."

"I know," he said. "I have an idea."

SCARLET FOLLOWED AUSTIN into the lobby of an upscale boutique hotel on the edge of town. The building was grand, with a crimson awning, doorman and the year 1912 carved into a stone beside double-glass doors.

The parking lot had been relatively full considering it wasn't tourist season, and they didn't seem to be near anything of significant importance. But she supposed staying here was a treat any time of year.

The arching foyer was inlaid with golden accents and a mural of the sky. Crimson carpet ran underfoot, outlined in large marble squares. An ornate round table centered the space, topped with a massive floral arrangement that had probably required two people to carry it.

A man in a suit stood ready at the desk beyond. "Welcome to The Carolina Grand. How can I help you?"

"Hello," Austin said. "We'd like a room."

"You're in luck," he said, without referencing the computer screen at his side. "We have one left."

Men and women crisscrossed the space around them in bunches, all clearly delighted. Their voices and laughter echoed off the high ceiling, walls and floor.

Austin frowned at the busyness. "Is there something going on?" he asked. "A convention?"

"A weekend wedding," the man said. "If you're looking for peace and quiet, it might not be the right place for you. But, if you're fans of music, there'll be a live quartet at meal times in the house restaurant and a local band in the bar, which could make for fun evenings."

Austin grinded his teeth in consideration, keen eyes scanning the exits and doorways. "Where is the available room located? Which floor?"

"First."

His frown deepened, and he glanced at Scarlet.

The man behind the counter furrowed his brow. "Is that all right?"

"Maybe," Austin said. "Does your restaurant have a private entrance?"

"No. All guests use the main doors. Why?"

"What about the bar and kitchen?" Austin asked. "How many entrances are on this floor?"

The other man reared back his head and looked to Scarlet. This time, a bit concerned.

"I'm okay," she said, offering a small smile. "He's just incredibly diligent."

The man's attempt to match her smile failed.

"How many entrances in total?" Austin repeated.

"Four. One on each face of the building. North. South. East. West." He moved his hand from wall to wall, as if the exits were visible from where they stood.

"And on which side is the room located?"

He pointed again. "The Thurston Suite is east facing and well equipped. Anything you don't find there can be delivered to you from our pantry or closet, and our concierge is full-service. Anything you need, he can acquire."

"I doubt that," Austin muttered.

The man leaned forward, looking pointedly near their feet. "Do you have any luggage?"

"No."

Scarlet sighed at the ridiculousness of the conversation, and how utterly bizarre they must look and sound to this man. Eager to take the last available room, but worried about the building's entry points, and all the while without a single duffel bag or suitcase between them.

"We didn't expect to stay in town when we arrived," she said. "But circumstances have changed."

"And you want the room?"

"Yes," Austin answered. "And I'll need to speak to your manager."

The desk clerk took his time checking them in, probably wishing he'd told them the hotel was full. Then, Austin spoke briefly with the shift manager, delivering the details of their situation. He promised to pass the information on to the hotel manager when her shift began.

The walk to their room was long and slightly convoluted in the historic building. They turned left twice before finding the hallway with the last available suite. They were each given a key card to access the door, though she had no intention of going anywhere without Austin. And he let them inside with a swipe.

The space was small, as promised—a large four-post bed at the center took the lion's share of space. An armchair in the corner shared a stand with the bed. A table with two chairs stood before a window at the far wall, and a restroom was just inside the door from the hallway. Plush blue carpet covered the floor, and large oil portraits in gilded frames adorned the walls. A minifridge and small television were the only signs of the millennium.

In another life, in a room like this with a man like Austin Beaumont, she'd never have time to turn the television on. But in that life, her mother wouldn't be in the violent hands of a deluded, dangerous man.

Chapter Twenty-Four

Scarlet showered and slipped into a T-shirt and underthings they'd ordered after settling in.

Austin had arranged for anything not provided in the room, like clothing, to be picked up from a local store by the hotel concierge, who really did handle everything. He'd also ordered a tray of soups and breads from the restaurant for their dinner, and he hadn't forgotten her glass of red wine.

He'd met her every need without being asked, and though Scarlet's world was crumbling, she felt utterly cared for. A new sensation she never wanted to let go of. In fact, she hoped to do the same for him someday.

Austin rose from his chair at the table when she stepped away from the steamy bathroom in her big T-shirt and fuzzy socks. Damp hair hung loose over her shoulders, and she shivered, suddenly regretting not wrapping herself in the cushy terry cloth robe.

"It's all yours," she said, hoping to look less self-conscious than she felt and moving to one side of the bed to peel back the covers.

A new show had started on the television, which had been playing softly for hours since their arrival. They'd watched a marathon of sit-coms from her childhood while intermittently eating and touching base with Finn for new information. He never had much to offer, but he and Officer Barrow were exhausting even the tiniest leads, which made a terrible situation slightly better.

The last update had come more than two hours before, and all that was left for her to do now was wait. She wasn't sure she'd be able to rest well, but it was late and sleeping was the fastest way to pass the time until he called again.

"Thanks." He gathered his things and headed for the bathroom, which was still seeping steam.

The closet door was ajar in the corner, and a stack of folded blankets sat on the armchair, topped with a pillow. Somehow, the time they'd spent collecting updates on the search for her mother and watching television had distracted her from the implications of sharing a room with one bed. She'd felt comfortable and safe, despite the overarching circumstances, just as she had in the days shared at her home and his.

Now thoughts of their sleeping arrangements

were front and center in jarring and slightly thrilling ways. She couldn't ask him to sleep in a chair while she had a queen-size bed to herself. That was just bad manners. And impractical.

She dragged her attention to the bathroom, where a shower had started running, then made up her mind. She put the pillow and blankets away, closed the closet door and slid into bed as planned.

Every splash of water in the next room brought an image with it that she couldn't ignore. Memories of his arms curved gently, protectively around her. His hands on her skin offering comfort. His breath on her lips when they'd nearly kissed.

She squirmed beneath the cool cotton sheets, restless for something she didn't want to name.

When the bathroom door opened again, Austin appeared in pajama pants and bare feet. His hair was wet and a T-shirt clung to the damp planes of his chest.

Scarlet felt a rush of heat from the crown of her head to her toes.

He stared at the empty chair then turned his eyes to her. "You put the blankets away?"

She nodded and pulled the comforter back. "I think we should share the bed. It doesn't make any sense for you to sit in a chair all night. Given the days we've had lately, we both need some rest, and you won't get it there." She nodded to the place where his blanket stack had been. "We need to be ready for whatever the morning brings."

Austin released a breath. "You're not wrong there." He dropped the pile of clothes he'd worn all day onto the table then climbed into bed beside Scarlet and turned out the light. A moment later, he rolled over and leveled his face with hers.

The soft glow from the television flickered in the darkness.

"On or off?" he asked, raising the remote he'd grabbed from his nightstand.

"Off."

Her eyes adjusted quickly to the darkness, and she smiled at him lying so close to her. "Do you think we'll hear any more from Finn tonight?"

"It's possible," he said.

Finn and his team were working every angle. Interviewing Greg's friends, family and coworkers. Looking for properties he or his family might own that went unused this time of year, like a cabin or lake house. Checking the vehicle databases for anything he could be driving, including boats he could use to hole up on the water. On top of that, Tech Services had spent the day digging into his work computer, and Marshal's Bluff officers had combed his home.

"It's just a matter of time now," Austin said.

She nodded, liking the way that sounded. "It seems impossible for him to hide."

"I think it is," Austin said confidently. "It would be hard enough for someone in their right mind to stay out of Finn's grasp for long. Add in the fact that Greg's juggling some kind of mental break, and he's got your mom in tow, and I don't think he'll last another twenty-four hours. I suspect they'll close in soon. He'll know he's caught and be forced to leave Trina behind to make a break for it."

Scarlet raised a hand to wipe a renegade tear. "I hope you're right. I hope he won't hurt her before he leaves her." At least no more than he'd likely hurt her already, forcing her into his control.

"Hey." Austin brushed hair away from her face with the backs of his fingers. "You okay?"

"My emotions are everywhere, but I'm fine. It's a lot to think about, and it's been a long week."

"All the more reason to rest." He tucked the lock of hair behind her ear then stroked his palm over her shoulder and down her arm.

Heat from his touch sizzled a path across her skin, and she shivered.

Austin pulled back, but she caught his fingers

and rested their joined hands on the blankets between them.

Their eyes locked and breaths mingled in the darkness. Electricity charged the air.

"Are you still thinking about kissing me?" Scarlet asked, releasing his hand. "Because I'm thinking of kissing you." She slid her fingers along the curve of his neck then stroked his jaw with her thumb.

He stilled beneath her touch, and his Adam's apple bobbed. "I am."

"And?" she asked, somehow closer to him than she'd been a moment before.

He crooked one arm beneath the pillow supporting his head and let his free hand trail the curve of her hip. Then he pressed against the small of her back, eviscerating the little space left between them. Austin's lips curved into a small, mischievous grin as he pressed his mouth gently to hers.

Scarlet's body melted against him. She'd never wanted to be kissed by any man so much in her life. And unlike so many people liked to say, the anticipation was not better than the reality. It was as if his mouth was made for hers, and every fiber of her ignited at his touch. The soft moan that escaped her drew a full smile across his lips.

He pulled back and stared, heat and longing in his eyes. His heart hammered beneath her palm on his muscled chest. "I won't ever let anyone hurt you again," he vowed, voice low and thick with truth. "And I don't want to leave you when this man is caught. I'm hoping you'll ask me to stay."

Emotions rose and bloomed in her as she kissed him in response. His perfect words filled her, because she didn't want him to go. She found the hem of his shirt and tugged until he pulled it over his head and tossed it onto the floor. She removed her shirt as well.

Austin cussed at the sight of her bare breasts. He cupped them reverently in his hands as he kissed her once more.

When her head was light and her body boneless, he moved his skilled tongue along the plane between her breasts. She gasped as he stroked and suckled one taut nipple, angling his body more firmly against hers.

Her hands fisted in his outgrown hair and his mouth drifted lower. "Austin."

"Still okay?" he asked, as he continued to explore.

She arched in answer and invitation.

"Yes?" he asked between kisses, working a magic rhythm with his touch.

"Yes."

He dragged his lips up the column of her throat.

The gentle slide of his tongue on her skin sent shock waves of pleasure through her limbs. She rocked her hips with every pulse of his hand. Austin's kisses were devouring and he swallowed her needy moans. She wanted nothing more than to be consumed by every inch of him.

She gripped the waistband of his pajama pants, desperate to feel more of his bare skin on hers.

"Scarlet?" he whispered, as her body tipped toward the brink of unraveling. "Are you sure this is what you want?"

"You are the only thing I want," she said, and his eyes flashed hot with pleasure.

Then he brought her swiftly over the edge.

AUSTIN WOKE THE next morning with Scarlet's hand in his. Her lithe body curled against his side. He stroked the hair from her cheek, pressed a gentle kiss to her forehead and hoped like hell she'd want him today the way she had last night. Because there wasn't anything he wanted more than her, and he didn't see a future where that would change.

He longed to kiss her awake and love her once more, before the busyness of their day began. More than that, he needed to reiterate his feelings and intentions so there'd be no questions or misunderstandings by the light of day. His heart was hers for the taking.

A shrill ring interrupted his thoughts, turning his eyes to the phone on his nightstand.

He grabbed the receiver quickly, silencing the sound, but his shifting body roused Scarlet anyway.

"Who is it?" she asked.

"I don't know." He pulled the phone to his ear. "Hello?"

"Mr. Beaumont?" a strained male voice asked.

"Yes." He slid upright against the headboard, senses on sudden alert. "Who's this?"

"This is the hotel manager," the voice continued. "There's a man in the lobby looking for the woman you arrived with yesterday. He has her photo and is claiming that she's his wife and she's been abducted. He's making quite a scene."

"What does he look like?"

"Sandy hair, brown eyes. He's wearing jeans and a hooded sweatshirt."

Adrenaline surged in Austin's body as he swung out of bed and began to dress on autopilot. "Where is he now?"

"In the lobby. He's arguing with the desk clerk who's refusing to give any information. I sneaked into my office to call you."

"Good work. I'm on my way. Call the local authorities and tell them what you've just told me." Austin returned the receiver to its cradle and swiped his cell phone off the nightstand.

Scarlet sat, clutching blankets to her chest. "What's going on?"

"Greg's in the lobby trying to find out which room we're in. The hotel manager is calling local authorities, and I'm going out there to see if I can get my hands on him before he gets away." Austin tucked a pair of handcuffs into his pocket and grabbed his wallet and key card. "Get dressed and be ready when I come back. Don't answer the door for anyone."

She nodded, already scrambling for the bathroom. "Be careful."

SCARLET WAS IN turbo mode. She dressed in seconds and headed back into the main room, preparing to stuff their things into bags in case they needed to leave in a rush.

The door clicked again, stilling her in her tracks. Austin had barely been gone a minute. What had he forgotten? Or had something big already gone wrong?

She pulled on her coat as she hurried to meet him. "Everything okay?"

A familiar figure moved into view as she rounded the corner.

Greg Marten glared, wild eyed, and raised the gun in his hand.

Chapter Twenty-Five

"This way," Greg said with a flick of his wrist, pointing to the door with his gun.

Scarlet held her ground, mind racing. If he shot her, everyone would hear and she might live. If she went with him, her odds of survival would be infinitely thinner. What she needed to do was stall. Austin would be back soon. "How did you get in here?"

"Key card." He grinned. "They're not hard to copy if you know what you're doing and can get close enough to the one you want. I know what I'm doing, and it's surprising how careless the housekeeping staff is these days."

She struggled to swallow. The harmless guy from Tech Services had somehow become the ultimate modern-day villain. "The manager is on to you," she said. "He called the police. You'd be smarter to run now than to add another crime to your spree." If he valued being clever, maybe he'd take her advice and go.

Greg grimaced and marched forward, extending his gun in her direction until her eyes closed. "I am very smart." A hand clamped over her wrist, and he jerked her hard, nearly knocking her off her feet. "Don't give me any trouble, or I will leave without you, and I'll kill your mother as punishment."

Scarlet's ears rang, and her thoughts clouded. Everything dissipated from her mind except her mother. And she let Greg tow her into the hall.

"No one's coming to save you this time," he said, guiding her along with a stern hand. "A bunch of hotel guests are in the restaurant making a ton of noise, and your PI is chasing his tail in the lobby. I've got you all to myself. Now, out you go." He shoved her through an exit door, into a small lot where a large truck was making a delivery.

She scanned the traffic-packed streets nearby and winced at the sight of the old navy sedan local police had been searching for.

Greg opened the passenger door. "Get in and climb over. You're driving."

"What?"

He pushed her across the armrests and into the driver's seat then planted the keys on her lap. His hand lingered unnecessarily. "Drive. Make a left onto Main Street and hurry, or we'll be too late to save your mother."

Terror seized her lungs as she dug the key from

beneath his palm and started the car. She glanced through the window as she shifted into gear, wishing for Austin to burst from the hotel and save her.

"Do you hear any sirens?" Greg asked, turning her attention to his smug face.

She blinked away the tears forming in her eyes. "No."

"That's because I'm the one who called your room, not a manager. I'm the one who drew your PI away. No one called the cops. There's no help on the way. Right now, your friend is standing around wondering what happened. He'll probably demand to speak to the manager who will have no idea what he's talking about. I've outmaneuvered all of them. Now you and I can start the life we're meant to have."

AUSTIN RACED DOWN the hallway, past a housekeeping cart. The staffer's lanyard hung from one side. He considered stopping for a fleeting moment, to tell her not to disturb his room, not to frighten Scarlet who was already terrified and alone, but he couldn't spare the time. Not if Greg Marten was in the lobby and local police were on their way. This was Austin's time to take down their enemy and see that he was cuffed and charged.

The hotel restaurant was packed as he jogged over the crimson carpet to the desk. Guests spilled from the open French doors, bringing a cacophony of voices, laughter and music along with them. Greg could blend easily into the rambunctious morning crowd and vanish through a side door if Austin didn't hurry.

"Where did he go?" Austin called, erasing the final few yards to the welcome desk.

The young man behind the counter blinked. "Who?"

"The man who was here looking for his wife. Your manager called me. I'm Austin Beaumont." He dug his wallet and PI license from one pocket and flashed it across the counter.

The man frowned. "I don't know anything about that, sir."

"Who was working here a minute ago? I need to talk to them. No." He waved a panicked hand, feeling the world tilt beneath him. "I need to speak to your manager."

"Can I help you?" A regal-looking blonde woman in a black pantsuit and heels strode confidently from a nearby doorway. "I'm the hotel manager, Eva Branson."

Austin stilled then stumbled back, realization gripping his heart and chest like a vise. The hotel manager he'd spoken to only minutes before had been a man. "Call the police," he demanded. "Tell them Austin Beaumont said to get here. Now!"

He tore back through the cavernous lobby, down the hallway and past the housekeeping cart to his room. He pressed the key card to the door and swung it open, his heart and final thread of hope in the balance.

But as expected, the room was empty.

"WHERE IS MY MOTHER?" Scarlet asked, fingers aching from her grip on the wheel, fear stiffening her posture.

The old sedan smelled of motor oil and cigarette smoke. Both scents likely permeated the fabric seats long before Greg made the purchase. A pair of orange tree-shaped air fresheners dangled from the rearview mirror on white springy cords. The back seat was empty, the car otherwise immaculate.

"Turn right," he said, ignoring her question and pointing to the upcoming highway entrance. "Get on the interstate, then stay in the left lane and keep up with traffic until I say otherwise."

She looked at the car beside her, wishing the other driver would make eye contact and see her distress. The young man behind the wheel of the SUV sang along to the radio, oblivious to her terror. She changed lanes, losing hope, and something thumped softly in the trunk.

"Good," Greg said, satisfied she was cooperating.

Her heart sank. Getting on the highway would mean disappearing, maybe permanently. Somewhere Austin and local law enforcement would never find her.

A flash of red and white in her side-view mirror caught her eyes. Austin's old truck appeared, cutting in and out of traffic with ease.

"Use your signal," Greg said. "Make the turn."

She shot him a venomous look and eased her foot off the gas pedal. Surely he wouldn't kill her while she was driving. "First tell me where my mother is!"

The muted thumping she'd heard earlier grew louder and more fervent. Scarlet jerked her head around to face the back seat, earning her a honk as she swerved.

"Is someone in the trunk?" Scarlet gasped. "Is that my mom?"

Greg pressed the gun's barrel to her ribs. "She's fine. Now pay attention and drive. Getting into a car accident won't be good for her."

Scarlet bit her lip, eyes darting to Austin's truck in her rearview mirror. He was a block away but gaining on them. She slowed, poking along, allowing cars to pass her.

"What are you doing?" Greg demanded. "Drive faster!"

"I'm nervous," she snapped. "I don't like traffic or having guns pointed at me. I think you locked my mom in the trunk. How am I supposed to handle this? Why did you even take her? Do you want me to hate you?"

"I want you to do what I say. She's your motivation," he said. "Mommy stays safe as long as you obey and stop seeing that man. She's in the trunk so you stay calm and don't try anything ridiculous while you're behind the wheel."

Scarlet's mouth opened then shut. She could be angry, and she could be mean. But her mom would be the one he punished, and she couldn't allow that.

"Get on the highway."

She checked the rearview again. Austin had moved ahead by another car length, but the traffic light was yellow. He wouldn't make it through the intersection with her.

Greg pointed the gun into the back seat then cocked it. "Run the light or a bullet goes into the trunk."

Scarlet released a defeated sob as she jammed the gas, launching them onto the highway.

Austin pounded his hand against the horn as the sedan carrying Scarlet and her abductor made the turn onto the highway.

The phone rang as he angled out of line and onto the berm, tossing dirt and gravel into the air behind him.

"Beaumont," he answered, skirting around waiting traffic.

"This is Officer Barrow," a familiar voice announced. "What's going on? One minute Dispatch has me en route to The Carolina Grand, and the next minute, I'm told you're in vehicular pursuit of Greg Marten."

"I made both calls to Dispatch," Austin said. "He tricked me, came right into the hotel and took her. They're headed southwest on Highway 17." His truck hit the on-ramp with a growl and shot him up to speed. "They're in his Toyota with a two-or three-minute head start I plan to eliminate."

"We've got his vehicle registration. I'll put a notice out on the car and access cameras along 17 to scan for his license plate."

Austin pushed his truck's engine to its limits, determined not to let Scarlet and her abductor get away.

Soon, a car resembling Greg's appeared.

"I think I see it," he said, nudging the gas pedal lower. "They're passing the Camden exit, heading toward Elizabeth City."

"Copy that."

A caravan of semitrucks appeared on the horizon, stretching down the center lane. He'd barely considered the possibility of the trucks becoming a barrier and obstacle when the sedan began to change lanes, cutting in front of the convoy as Austin drew alongside the second truck from the rear.

When he reached the front of the line, the sedan was gone.

A FORK APPEARED on the highway, dividing one interstate into two. "Where are we going?" Scarlet asked. "What do I do at the fork?"

She needed information, and she needed a plan.

"Stay right. We'll get off at the next opportunity."

Scarlet used her signal and began sliding across four lanes in a mess of traffic, barely avoiding a caravan of 18-wheelers. "But where are we going?"

"I don't know."

"What do you mean you don't know?" She pursed her lips, reeling in her temper. "You said we're going to start a life together. Where are we doing that? You have to talk to me."

"How can I trust you?" he snapped. His formerly placid expression suddenly filled with rage. "After you spent the night with that man? How can I ever trust you?"

She winced, hoping he hadn't somehow seen what they'd done. Like he seemed to see everything else she did.

"I warned you and warned you," he said. "I told you to knock it off or you'd be punished.

And it's as if you don't even care!" he screamed. "What is wrong with you?"

Scarlet focused on the road, muscles tight.

Spittle flew from his mouth with each lament, and he pounded his fists against the dashboard.

"I'm sorry," she said, voice wobbling and tears threatening. "Please don't be angry."

"I thought we had a connection," Greg complained. "You called me for help with the system, with your email, with passwords, and I helped you. I thought we bonded. We got to know one another. You even helped me pick out our house."

"You bought a house?"

His glare burned the skin of her cheek. "I bought the one you told me was perfect for a new family. One that could grow with me."

Her stomach dropped, and the severity of her situation grew infinitely clearer. She remembered the conversation about the house. She'd encouraged him to buy the bigger home, because he had his eye on someone special and hoped to settle down. Maybe start a family.

Greg's expression became affronted, and his mouth set into a grimace. "I can't believe you don't remember."

"I do," she croaked. Suddenly, she saw all those innocent chats with a stranger at the corporate help desk in a drastically different light. And she couldn't help wondering if all her computer issues had really been a result of the new system, or if they'd happened at his hand and by his design, so she'd have to keep calling.

"You said I was your hero," he whispered. "And I believed you."

Heat climbed Scarlet's neck, and nausea rolled in the pit of her stomach. She struggled to breathe, certain she'd be sick or black out and kill them all in traffic. She'd been so thankful for Greg's help every time. She might've even been flirty. And he was right, after a particularly frustrating issue with her email password, she'd called him her hero.

Had that been his tipping point?

"I saved you before, and I'm saving you now," he said, voice lighter. "You see the kinds of choices you make on your own. How easily someone can get to you. Harm you." He lifted the gun from his lap, as if she could've forgotten it was there. "I'm going to keep you safe. You just have to stop fighting me. I can make you happy."

She made eye contact with another driver as she reached the far right lane. The other driver pulled swiftly ahead. A hundred witnesses and no one saw anything, when it felt as if the entire car should be flashing with her distress. Why couldn't others see the dark cloud preparing to consume her?

Greg's hand landed on her thigh again, and her stomach pitched. "Take this exit."

Rolling fields of grass spread into the distance. A forest rose on the right.

Her foot eased off the pedal a bit, not ready to leave the safety of a hundred moving cars.

He pointed his gun into the back seat again, and she took the exit to nowhere.

They rolled along the curving county route with no homes or businesses in sight, and infinite reasons not to go any farther.

Left without options, she burst into a dramatic round of tears. She was out of time for making a good plan, so she'd have to improvise and settle for making any plan and hoping it worked.

Since he seemed hung up on being her hero, tears felt like a good start.

She breathed harder and faster, making each puff audible, and shuddered. Then she pulled onto the side of the road with a series of desperate sobs.

There weren't any cameras to find them here. No passing vehicles to notice they'd stopped. Just them and a whole lot of nature. So she'd focus on getting him out of the car. Then she could drive away with her mom in the trunk and not stop until she found a police station.

"What are you doing?" he demanded. "Drive!"

"I can't," she cried. "I can't. I can't." The tears ran freely now, her true emotions mixing with the show. "Help me. Please!"

Greg swiveled on his seat, looking through the

rear window then back to her. "What's wrong? What do you want me to do?"

"You have to drive. I'm shaking. I'll crash if I keep going. I'm—" she considered her believable options "—I think I'm having a panic attack." She shifted into Park and pressed her palms against her face, hoping to make her skin redder, eyes puffier and her overall look more unwell.

"What do you need?" he asked. "A paper bag? Water?"

"Just drive," she said. "I can't do it."

A long beat of silence passed before he spoke again, distrust evident in his voice. "I know what you're doing."

Scarlet steeled her resolve, unfastened her safety belt and reached for him across the armrest.

It was possible he'd take a shot at the car after he climbed out and she drove away. Possible a bullet would hit the trunk. But at least if that happened, she'd already be in motion, able to find a hospital for her mother. She had to take the risk, because staying with him was a death sentence.

"You're still my hero," she whispered, swallowing bile that rose with the words. "Help me. Please."

Slowly, his tense muscles relaxed beneath her hands, and he pressed his gun-free palm against her back. "Shh," he cooed. "Breathe."

The shudders of repulsion that followed

seemed to convince him she truly wasn't in any shape to drive.

"Okay," he said. "But no one's getting out of the car to make this switch. We'll have to slide across the seat to trade places." He pushed the armrests up, creating a flat bench between them, and patted the space.

Scarlet released him, heart thundering, mind racing. She couldn't actually let him drive. He'd have all the control.

Greg scooted into the center of the seat and swung one foot into the well beside hers. "Come on."

She turned and rose, attempting to awkwardly climb over him, but he caught her hips and drew her onto his lap in a straddle. Gooseflesh crawled over her arms like a thousand baby spiders and another hard round of shivers racked her form. She dropped her hands to her sides.

"Hey," he said softly, peering into her eyes. "I've got you." The handle of his gun pressed against her left thigh.

Something heavy registered inside her jacket pocket on the right. An impossible thought rose in her mind, a tiny sliver of hope.

She maintained eye contact with Greg as she felt the cylindrical shape with her fingertips, then slid her hand into the pocket.

Austin had given her the Taser.

Chapter Twenty-Six

Scarlet wet her lips in concentration as she located the narrow switch at the bottom of the stun gun and slid it into the on position as Austin had shown her. Then she pushed the slider along the device's side to arm it. Now she'd have to choose her moment and be quick.

Greg's gaze moved to her mouth, and his hand skimmed her ribs, apparently misinterpreting her still exterior as submission. He leaned in for a kiss, and she let her head fall to the side, allowing him to access her neck instead.

Ignoring the nauseating feel of his lips on her skin, she gripped the compact stun gun and rested her thumb on the button. When Greg finally sought her mouth, eyelids at half-mast and an eager expression on his face, she thrust forward, connecting her forehead with his. The teeth-rattling collision drew a shout from her captor. His hands flew to his forehead.

The gun's barrel angled toward the roof.

Scarlet squinted against the pain and grabbed his raised wrist, holding the handgun in place while she pressed the stun gun to his neck.

A sickening crackle carved the air, and Greg's gun went off in a burst. The bullet ripped a hole through the roof before his hand opened and the weapon toppled into the back seat.

Scarlet grabbed the keys and threw herself toward the passenger door.

He sputtered and roared, fingers clutching at her shirt as she scrambled away.

She pressed the trunk release button on the key fob, and the lid swung open.

The car rocked as Greg raged, pounding a hand against something inside.

Her mother's curled form came into view as Scarlet reached the trunk.

Trina blinked against the sun. Her usually perfect hair and makeup were in unprecedented ruin. Her skin was pale, and a large bruise marred her cheek. "Scarlet!"

"We've got to go," she said, reaching for her mom.

The driver's door opened, and Greg bumbled into the grass, still spewing horrific strings of swears and clutching a palm to his neck.

"Stay back," Scarlet warned, releasing her mother in favor of resetting her stun gun. "Stay away from us."

Trina wobbled at her side, shaken but alive, then clutched her daughter's arm for balance.

Their assailant glared as he yanked open the door to the back seat. "Oh, I'm going to stay far away from you now. I'm done trying to set you straight. So it's time to end this instead." He stretched inside, and Scarlet spun away, pulling her mother with her.

"Run!" she cried, and the women headed for the trees.

Trina struggled to keep up with Scarlet, despite the fact that she was in far better shape.

Scarlet added that to her ever-growing list of concerns.

"Come on, Mom," she panted. "Just a little farther." They had to make it into the trees before Greg. "We need to find somewhere to hide."

Soon, shade poured over them, and a small measure of relief set in. The forest stretched in three directions, providing plenty of options for cover.

"Here," Trina rasped, pulling her daughter sideways. She ducked behind the broad trunk of a moss-drenched oak then doubled over to vomit on the forest floor.

"Oh, my goodness." Scarlet crouched at her side. "Are you okay?"

"I think I have a concussion," she said, sliding down to sit in the leaves and dirt. "I can't keep running. My head is pounding and spinning. It might explode, if I don't straight-up collapse."

Scarlet pressed a gentle palm to her mother's sweaty face. They couldn't stay there long. They'd be sitting ducks if they didn't keep moving. "How long were you in the trunk?"

"I don't know. Hours maybe," she said. "I was attacked outside my morning showing. I don't even know if that was today. I woke up in a trunk."

Scarlet smoothed her mom's hair away from her eyes. "That was yesterday."

"Scar-let!" Greg's voice echoed through the trees. He broke her name into syllables and sang them like a nursery rhyme. "You can't hide from me, Scarlet," he taunted. "Don't you know that by now?"

She pressed a finger to her lips, and the women became still as statues.

Leaves crunched and twigs snapped in the distance.

Scarlet held her breath as she peeked around the ancient tree.

Greg was visible through a dense thicket of brush and patch of evergreens. He scanned the forest in the opposite direction.

Her mother tugged her arm then pointed away. A massive boulder stood near the tree line. "Do you still have the car keys?"

She nodded. If they could get to the boulder, they could take another break for Trina's sake then make a run for the car.

She locked eyes with her mother, and Trina stood on trembling legs. Scarlet used her fingers to count to three.

They burst into crouched runs, darting toward the massive stone.

Maniacal laughter erupted behind them. "There you are!" Greg jeered. "No need to bother running now. I've found you, and it's time for your punishment."

The earsplitting crack of a gunshot sent birds into flight from the treetops.

And her mother fell to the ground.

AUSTIN EXITED THE HIGHWAY, certain the sedan must've done the same. He'd only lost sight of it for a few seconds, and it had to have gone somewhere. He slowed to consider his options, which were few. He could return to the highway, but if they were there, his detour would've afforded them a more than generous lead, one he'd likely never make up. Or he could continue on the winding country road, hoping to catch them, assuming they had gotten off the interstate.

Another set of questions crowded into mind before he could sort the last. If Scarlet and Greg had taken the rural exit as suspected, where were they now? And where were they going? According to the big green signs at the bottom of the ramp, the nearest town was twelve miles away. The nearest town with a population over a thousand was nearly fifty miles farther.

A gunshot broke the silence, and Austin went on alert. His truck rocketed forward as he listened carefully for another round of gunfire to break the silence. And he prayed he wouldn't discover a fatality along the roadside. He redialed Officer Barrow.

"What do you know, Beaumont?" the cop asked, answering on the first ring.

"I'm heading east on a county route off exit 113. There's been a shot fired."

"Any sign of the cause?" Barrow asked.

"Not yet," Austin said, floating around the next curve.

Greg's sedan appeared as the road straightened. Trunk lid up. Three doors open.

"I've got eyes on the sedan. Two miles east of the exit. I'm approaching now."

Austin skidded to a stop behind the sedan, and he leaped from the truck's cab, cell phone in one hand, sidearm in the other. "No signs of the passengers."

He turned in a small circle, scanning the scene in all directions. Wondering what to make of the abandoned car. Hoping things weren't as bad as they appeared. "I think she got away somehow and made a run for the trees." That was where he'd go if he needed cover and time to make a plan.

"Copy that," Barrow said. "Help's on the way."

Austin pocketed the cell phone and jogged across the field toward the tree line, phone tucked into his back pocket, sidearm in hand.

Scarlet's ears rang, and the breath left her body. She fell to the earth beside her mother, scooping her into shaky arms. "Mom!"

Trina's eyes opened, then shut.

Scarlet scanned her body for a bullet wound, then frantically searched the forest for signs of her shooter. Trina wasn't bleeding, but she also wasn't responding.

Scarlet's world tilted, and tears fell from her eyes as she imagined all the scenarios where they didn't make it out alive. And all the things she wished she'd told her mother long ago. "I'm so sorry," she whispered.

A gut-wrenching wail rose through the forest.

Scarlet froze, unsure what to make of the sound.

Then someone called her name.

She lifted her head, straining to see without being seen. A familiar silhouette came into view. "Austin?"

"Scarlet!"

She stretched onto her feet and ran to meet him, careful to watch for signs of the shooter.

Austin caught her in his embrace and cupped her face in his hands. "You're okay," he said, stroking her head and holding her tight. "I thought I'd lost you. I don't ever want to lose you."

Emotion clogged her throat and fresh tears stung her eyes. "Mom's hurt, and Greg's got a gun. We have to get her out of here."

Austin shook his head. "I shot Greg and took his weapon. He'll live, but he won't go far. I aimed for his knee."

Scarlet fell against him in relief as sirens wound to life in the distance.

"Let's get your mama," Austin said, and he followed her back to Trina's side.

Chapter Twenty-Seven

Three months later

Scarlet jammed the sale sign into her front yard with equal feelings of relief and remorse. Greg Marten had been charged with multiple counts of assault, attempted murder, abduction, stalking and a bevy of lesser crimes. He'd been convicted of them all. And though she knew, logically, that he'd be behind bars for many years to come, she still felt his eyes on her some days. Especially in places she knew he'd been. Like her beloved waterfront home.

"You okay?" Austin asked, rubbing her shoulders and gazing at the historic cottage he'd tried to help her redeem.

Weekly counseling sessions for her trauma and a thorough cleansing of every room on the property had made a dent in her unease. But she knew now that nothing would fully erase the unsettling sensations she felt there. Not even the brand-new locks and dead bolts had brought her peace.

She raised one gloved hand to cover his. "It's bittersweet," she said, her breath rising on the frigid air in little white clouds. "I love this place, but I can't stay."

"Well," Austin said, moving to stand before her. "How about we go home and get warm? I have a surprise there for you."

"I love everything about those suggestions," she said, curling into his embrace.

He pressed cool lips to her forehead. "Let's go."

The sun was setting as they climbed back into his truck and cranked the heat and defroster. She'd moved the bulk of her regular-use items to Austin's house weeks before, and the Beaumonts had helped her transport the last of her other things into storage last weekend. Now all that was left to do was sell her home.

She peeled off her gloves and held her icy hands in front of the hot air vent. "I hope your surprise involves a fire, a glass of wine and lots of naked cuddling with my favorite human."

"Please let that be me," he said breathlessly.

Scarlet laughed and leaned closer, planting a kiss on his handsome face. "Take me home, Mr. Beaumont."

The drive to Austin's place was borderline perilous in the winter. An exceptionally cold snap had created ice in the ruts and grooves before the covered bridge. Driveway repair would be top priority come spring, or she'd be stuck there permanently.

"What on earth?" she asked, tipping forward as an abundance of twinkle lights became visible on the bridge and in a number of surrounding trees.

Someone had also lined the road with candles burning inside canning jars.

"Do you like it?" he asked.

"I love it! Can we get out? Is this the surprise?"

Austin chuckled and rolled on.

Scarlet twisted on her seat, seeking the beautiful lights and making plans to take photographs from his deck when they got home.

A collection of 4x4s had gathered in the parking space outside the mill.

"Is this a party?" she asked, recognizing a few of the vehicles as belonging to his family. "Or just dinner?" She could never be sure with his family. There were just so many of them, and they gathered for any reason.

Austin parked then turned to grin at her in the darkness. "I'm hoping it's a celebration."

She narrowed suspicious eyes on him. "What are we celebrating?"

"Us." Austin leaned in her direction and kissed her absolutely senseless.

The porch lights flashed on, and Scarlet took a moment to regain her composure.

Hopefully partygoers weren't planning to stay long. She had plans for snuggling that couldn't be ignored.

Mrs. Beaumont waved one arm overhead on Austin's front step. A wool cape clasped around her shoulders. "Come in!" she called, her words muffled through the glass. "It's cold! What are you doing?"

Austin ran the pad of one thumb across his bottom lip, returning her gaze to what she was missing. "Ready?"

Oh, she was ready. Not necessarily for a party, but she would like to see the Beaumonts. Austin's family had embraced her as one of their own, and she loved every encounter. She especially looked forward to his mother's hugs and his brothers' banter. And she deeply appreciated her new sort-of sister too, Dean's fiancée, Nicole.

Scarlet opened her truck door and slid into the cold. Austin met her with a kiss on her nose.

"Finally," his mama said, greeting them with hugs before ushering them inside.

The air smelled of cinnamon and vanilla. Merry chatter rattled down from the second floor.

"Hurry up," Mrs. Beaumont pushed, nudging them toward the stairs. "Everyone's waiting."

Austin took Scarlet's hand and escorted her to the party.

A round of cheers erupted as they reached the little crowd. At least two dozen people raised their glasses. Dean and Nicole, Mr. Beaumont and Finn. Lincoln and Josie, the stable manager at the family ranch. Plus a fully recovered Lydia and Scarlet's mother, to name a few.

"Mom?" She moved in Trina's direction and pulled her into an embrace. The time they'd spent in the forest together had sparked a sort of healing between them that had been long overdue. "What are you doing here?" she asked, grateful and downright shocked to see her outside Holbrook on a work night. Then she remembered the treacherous road. "How did you manage it?"

"Wisely," Trina said, answering the latter question first. "I left my car at the Coulter office in town, and I rode here with Lydia and Finn."

Lydia beamed at Trina's side. The pair had formed a bond in the days since their ugly run-ins with Greg Marten. "Hi, Scarlet. Austin."

Austin shook the ladies' hands.

"Thank you for being here," Scarlet said. "I had no idea we were having a party, or I would've invited you myself." She turned to pin Austin with a playful look of reproach and found him pulling a small velvet box from his pocket.

"It's happening!" Mrs. Beaumont yelled.

Austin laughed, and a hush rolled over their guests. "Scarlet," he said, voice warm and thick with his sexy southern drawl.

"What are you doing?" she whispered, staring at the box and certain she must be wrong.

"I love you," he said. "I was lost for you the moment you walked into my office, and I just keep falling a little further every day you're around. You are strong and smart. Steadfast and sexy."

The crowd chuckled, and Mrs. Beaumont covered her mouth with obvious delight.

"I can't imagine my life without you in it," he said. "And I don't want to. I hope you feel the same way."

"I do." She nodded, head and heart so light she could blow away.

His eyes misted with emotion as he opened the little box and lowered to one knee. "Marry me," he pleaded.

Hot tears swiveled over Scarlet's cheeks as she pulled him up to kiss her.

Then she said yes.

* * * * *

If you missed the first title in Julie Anne Lindsey's Beaumont Brothers Justice miniseries, look for Closing In On Clues, *available now wherever Harlequin Intrigue books are sold!*

"Twenty seconds!"

Livingston looked at the men. "I'll go first, then Weyers, Lambert, Ogan, and Colon."

"Ten!"

Weyers yelled through the cloth covering, "Don't hesitate! Go out, turn facedown, count to ten, then pull the cord."

"Go!"

When he hit the ground, reality returned with a jolt. Livingston didn't see the parachute, but he heard and felt it. It drew him to his feet, and he limped forward as he struggled to pinch the quick-release hook. When the chute finally came off, he scooped up the lines and hauled in the deflated canopy.

Lambert was chattering from the cold. Livingston handed him his own gloves, then bundled up the parachute and stuffed it behind a skimpy bale of hay. They started toward the field; as they passed the house, a shotgun blast was heard.

"Ahdyeen meenootah pahzhahloostah!"

Livingston looked toward the house, at the silhouette of a man standing in the doorway. He had no idea what the Russian had said; all he knew was that before he could reach his Luger, either Lambert or he would be dead. . . .

FORCE FIVE
Destination: Stalingrad

Jeff Rovin

LYNX BOOKS
New York

DESTINATION: STALINGRAD

ISBN: 1-55802-165-5

First Printing/April 1989

This book is published by Lynx Books, a division of Lynx Communications, Inc., 41 Madison Avenue, New York, New York, 10010. The name "Lynx" and the logo consisting of a stylized head of a lynx are trademarks of Lynx Communications, Inc.

Printed in the United States of America

0 9 8 7 6 5 4 3 2 1

FORCE FIVE
Destination: Stalingrad

Prologue

Lieutenant Clayton Livingston sat at the desk in his London hotel suite, completing his report as he waited for the government liaison officials to arrive.

He shook his head. Just back from Algiers, from their first mission, everyone newly released from the hospital, and they were being sent away again.

That's the price you pay for being good. Getting another chance to be shot at.

Not that he was complaining. Compared to the desk job he'd left behind in the States, even KP would be an improvement.

Livingston finished writing about the destruction of the German airfield that had made an Allied landing in Algiers possible. Then he read what he had written: about having to fight the Germans after landing on the beach, sniffing out a traitor in the Algerian resistance, and working with erroneous intelligence, stolen explosives, and an airfield far more heavily fortified than reconnaissance had suggested.

He doubted that the new mission, whatever it was, would be better planned. Force Five had been put together *because* of problems in the system. There had been cracks in security, and men had had to be brought in from outside the intelligence service. Independent men who could think on the run. Two Americans—himself and the scrappy marksman Colon. Ogan, the by-the-book Englishman. Lambert, the conniving Frenchman. Weyers, the crackerjack South African pilot with fists the size of anvils.

An international team, to satisfy all the Allies. Expendable men, to satisfy the units that had given them up. Angry men, who didn't like the Axis or any of the crap they stood for.

Better planned? Who needed a better plan than a burning need to right the wrongs over here.

Livingston signed the report, then sat back. The satisfaction of having pulled off the Algerian mission was profound, and he savored it—though his gratification was tempered by the knowledge that as sharp as they'd been, they'd barely escaped with their lives, and would be damned lucky to do so again.

But he told himself that very few soldiers got to affect the outcome of the war single-handedly, and as different as each member of Force Five was from the other, that challenge had bound and inspired them like no other Allied fighting unit. It would do so again.

All things considered, he was looking forward to the return of his men from their one night's leave, and the arrival of liaison officers Sweet and Escott with information on the new mission.

Chapter One

"What do you think, Rotter? Has the blighter got the guts to show up?"

The speaker, a burly, young baldheaded man, ground a fist into his palm. Though Corporal Arthur "Wings" Weyers of the South African Long Range Desert Group was dressed in nothing but loose-fitting khakis, he didn't appear to feel the stiff, late fall wind that knifed across the wharf. He seemed aware of nothing but The Admiral's Pub on the other side of the dock.

Beside him stood a short, slender Frenchman with lively eyes. Corporal Jean-Pierre Lambert—known to his intimates as Le Rodeur, the Prowler—was dressed more sensibly than his companion, wearing a sweater and corduroy pants. He ground a cigarette under his boot.

"It isn't a matter of guts, *mon ami*. It's a question of brains. If he's smart, he'll stay in the bar. If he's brave, he'll come out and take his lumps. Either way, we win."

Weyers continued to punch his open hand. "I hope he comes out. I'd rather win by beating his brains out."

Several paces away, the third member of the party, Private Ernesto Colon, squatted on the icy wooden planks facing the Thames. Like Lambert, the American was dressed warmly, in a brown leather jacket and jeans. Un-

like the wiry Lambert, however, his posture, even in
repose, was taut, dangerous. He wore a brooding expression and said nothing, only stared out across the water.

After several minutes, the door of the pub opened and
three men walked out. Lambert recognized just one of
them, the red-bearded man on the left. He was Geoffrey
Thorpe, captain of the submarine *Saphir*. Just over a
week before, Thorpe had carried the five members of the
Force Five espionage team to Algiers, where they had
destroyed a German aerodrome. There had been no love
lost between the passengers and the captain, and tonight,
when Thorpe had happened to walk into the pub where
three Force Five men were celebrating their safe return,
Lambert had wasted no time inviting him and any two
of his crew members to come outside and air their grievances. Thorpe had agreed, and while the Force Five men
went outside, the captain had gone searching the smoke-
filled room for men.

Lambert whistled when he looked from Thorpe to the
captain's two companions. They were even brawnier than
the huge-shouldered officer.

Weyers muttered, "I didn't know they let bulls on sub-
marines."

"They don't," Lambert sneered. "Neither of those
men was on the minelayer. Looks like the bastard went
and got himself dockhands."

Colon came over, his concentration intense. "Does
that bother you?"

"No . . . it makes me *mad*. You can't even trust your
Allies to fight square."

Weyers drilled his palm one last time. "Doesn't matter. Let's go and knock out some—"

"Don't." Colon grabbed his arm. "I want you to stay
here."

"What?"

"When they get closer, grab the guy on the right, toss him to me, then hit the lug in the middle."

"Where will you be?"

"Behind you. We'll make it three-on-one before they know what hit 'em."

"*Et moi?*" Lambert said. "I get to handle Captain Le Porc?"

Colon nodded, then ambled behind Weyers.

As the sailors neared, their eyes reflected the searchlights that scanned the skies on the other side of the river. The men looked unearthly, like machines, and reminded Lambert of a robot he'd once seen in a German sciencefiction movie.

"I found some mates," Thorpe said, grinning when they were just a few meters away. "Moby and Punch. They load mines for me—"

"—an' chew up airy-fairies like you in our free time," chortled the man who Weyers was supposed to grab. Lambert noticed an M tattooed on his forearm. This one must be Moby.

"I'll warn any fairies I run into." The Frenchman smiled. "Now then, monsieur, do you happen to know what we do in *our* spare time?"

"Sell yer mothers to sailors?"

"*Mais non*, monsieur. You mistake us for Englishmen. No. We go searching for blubber-gut mariners like you, and then we *harpoon* them."

The huge man glowered at Lambert, his heavy brow shrinking his eyes to small, black spots. "Why, you snivelin', goddamn frog—"

Before the man could finish, Weyers bolted forward and locked iron-strong fingers around his wrist, then tugged him ahead. Caught off balance, the man stumbled forward, where Colon was waiting. Sliding one hand in the man's belt and grabbing his shirt with the other, the American used the big man's momentum to pull him across the slick wooden dock. Moby hit the river with a

heavy splash before his companions even realized what
had happened.

The instant Weyers lunged, Lambert drove the toe of
his boot into Thorpe's groin. The captain doubled over,
and an uppercut to the jaw put him on his back. Meanwhile, rolling to the left, Weyers plowed his shoulder
into Punch, sending the seaman to the ground. A knee
drop to the stomach made sure he stayed there.

It was over in less than ten seconds, after which the
three Force Five men gathered around Thorpe. The big
captain was curled, fetuslike, and was clutching his
crotch.

"Y' cheatin' bastards!" he moaned.

Colon's expression grew dark and he straddled the
captain. "You're wrong, sir." He flipped out a switch-
blade and put it to the man's chin. He had Thorpe's complete attention. "A cheating bastard woulda *stuck* you.
All *we* did was teach you peaheads some manners."

Folding the knife away, Colon walked to the edge of
the dock, where Moby was grasping at the pilings. Colon
helped him from the icy waters, while Lambert went
over to Punch. The man was winded but didn't seem
badly hurt.

The captain climbed painfully to his feet. He smacked
aside the helping hand offered by Weyers. "Tomorrow
night, y' rat-bastards. I want ta see ya here same time—
fair fight."

Weyers shook his head. "Sorry, but tomorrow night
we head for parts unknown."

"Then when you get *back*," Thorpe growled. "We're
in for a week o' repairs, an' we'll be waitin'."

The South African shrugged. "Fine with me. But I
suggest you wait until the sub is fully operational." His
wide mouth twisted into a vast, ungainly grin. "The only
way you're going to knock down a Force Five man is
with a torpedo. And you'd be smart to make it a direct
hit, at that."

When Moby had been dragged onto the pier, and Punch roused with a flurry of slaps, the victors headed for the side street where they'd parked their black sedan.

"I liked that," Weyers said, pausing at the car and looking back. "Damn, Rotter, but you know how to show a body a good time."

They were unaware of a man who was standing in the shadow of an old shuttered burlesque house, watching their every move.

Wearing a tweed jacket and puffing hard on his pipe, Inspector Bertram Escott of Scotland Yard marched stiffly before his associates. His hands were locked behind his back, and thick folds of flesh wagged to and fro beneath his outstretched chin. Puffs of smoke rolled past his thinning white hair and collected in a tester near the low roof of the hotel suite.

"It's incredible!" he blustered. "Unconscionable, really!" He stole a look at Lambert and Weyers, who were sitting backward on bridge chairs. "Bad enough my own men attacked fellow soldiers, but now we're spying on each other!" His eyes shifted to a memorandum that lay on a plain end table. "There's sabotage in our factories, leaks in spy networks on the Continent, fifth columnists everywhere—and the Secret Intelligence Service wastes manpower watching *us*! It's obscene!"

Weyers and Lambert nodded in agreement. Sunk in a plush wing chair, Colon sat still, staring at his knees. Behind him, the team's English member, Sergeant Major Kenneth Ogan, stood beside drawn drapes. His arms were tightly folded, his lantern jaw rigid. Livingston stood beside him. A shade over six feet, he wore a sharply pressed captain's uniform and a rugged, commanding look.

Escott stopped his pacing and glowered at the seated men.

"Needless to say, I'm most disappointed in you. Inspector Sweet and I give you a night's leave, to relax, and what do you do?''

"Just what we were supposed to do," Weyers rejoined. "We relaxed!"

"That'll be enough of that," Livingston cautioned.

Escott flushed. "What you *did*, Corporal, was start an altercation which resulted in one man nearly drowning, and another suffering a pair of broken ribs!''

"Don't forget Captain Thorpe's *goullions*," Lambert said under his breath.

"What was that?''

"Nothing, sir. I was thinking aloud.''

"Thinking? That's a matter of opinion, Corporal. Your problem is that you think too little! At the Yard, if any of my men had acted so recklessly, I would have suspended him without . . .''

Before he could continue, the door opened and a man walked in. He was tall and lean with horn-rimmed eyeglasses and a bowler. "They're not going to reprimand us," he said. "Or watch us anymore.''

The portly inspector pressed his palms to his eyes and sighed. "Thank the Good Lord.''

Sweet shut the door and pulled off his hat. "Actually, that's exactly who you should thank. Lord Oliver Caldwell came over from Whitehall and sat down with us, with the Secret Intelligence Service, and with Military Intelligence. The long and the short of it is that SIS has agreed to stop spying on Force Five and trying to give us a black eye. In exchange, our superiors at MI have agreed not to put together any more special units.''

"What! After what we accomplished in Algiers—''

The lanky William Sweet slipped off his trench coat. "No, Bertie, *because* of it. SIS understands that our unit is unique, created because a leak in their ranks compromised all of their operatives. But they're very protective of their territory, and now that the leak's been plugged, they don't want our success to spur the creation of similar teams.''

Escott threw up his hands. "Madness. All the enemy has to do to win this war is to sit back and let us destroy ourselves!''

Livingston pulled over an armchair. "From what Inspector Sweet tells me, there's just as much infighting at Scotland Yard.''

"Why do you think we were glad to be seconded to MI? With so much at stake, it seemed reasonable, dare I say *imperative*, that there would be nothing but cooperation between the branches. God, we are the most *idiotic* creatures on this planet. Even my *dogs* have the good sense to chase the fox and not each other.'' He looked at Lambert, Weyers, and Colon. "But if my Jack Russells can learn discipline, then by God so can you. And if balmy Algiers didn't do it, then maybe a few days somewhere less inviting *shall*!''

Weyers and Lambert exchanged uncomfortable glances as, trailing clouds of pipe smoke, Escott strode to an easel beside the console radio. He drew back a sheet of paper and picked up a pointer, tapping it several times on the map of western Russia. He took some delight in the fact that Lambert buried his face in a hand.

"For three months now, a massive German army has laid siege to Stalingrad—which is here, some nine hundred kilometers southeast of Moscow. The Germans went in with the notion of taking the Lower Volga to control both the oil traffic and access to Russia's industrial centers. But Hitler saw Stalingrad as a splendid prize, a city of a half million souls to be taken and enslaved, and diverted the Sixth Army under General Paulus and the Fourth Panzer Army for this purpose.

"Despite heavy losses, the Russian defenders have held. Unfortunately, now that winter has come, Hitler is impatient and Paulus is desperate. As a result, they are prepared to add a new leaf to an already thick book of wartime atrocities.'' Escott stepped from the map, his eyes on the floor. "According to radio transmissions intercepted by an operative in Turkey, Berlin has already shipped massive amounts of dichlorodiethyl sulfide to the city.''

Sweet said, "Mustard gas.''

"Quite—but it's worse than the stuff with which you men may be familiar. We believe this is an experimental batch, one which we know they've been working on at Farben. It's far more concentrated and lethal. It literally hangs in the air wherever it's released, possibly for days. It'll burn the skin off anyone who comes in contact with it, destroy the lungs of anyone who breathes it. It's damnable, barbaric stuff.

"The point is," he continued, "if we can prevent the shipment, the Russians have a good chance of breaking the siege and driving the Nazis from Russia.''

After the men took a moment to digest what they'd been told, Livingston said, "I assume there's a reason the Russians can't handle this mission by themselves.''

"It's a question of manpower, really. Everyone who is able—man, woman, and child—is busy trying to get supplies and ammunition to the defenders. These people aren't trained saboteurs, and to divert the numbers that would be necessary to attack the convoy would be catastrophic for Stalingrad.'' Escott paused. "And there's another reason. When this business with Hitler is eventually finished, Stalin and the Bolsheviks will still be the same treacherous bunch they've always been. Whitehall and Washington both agree that it would be *unwise* to allow the gas to fall into their hands.''

"In short," Sweet said, "Force Five is going to Stalingrad to save the city . . . and to make absolutely certain that the shipment from Berlin ends up on the bottom of the Volga.''

"Any questions?" Escott asked.

Lambert raised a hand. "Just how cold *is* it in Stalingrad during the winter?"

"Well below zero," Escott said. "Or to put it another way, does the word *tundra* mean anything to you, Corporal?"

It was well below freezing as Sweet, Escott, and the five Force Five team members stepped from a pair of sedans onto the small military airfield outside London. Strong winds tore across the tarmac, and Lambert pulled the collar of his parka tightly around his neck. He and Weyers went to the back of the car. With one hand, the big South African pulled his duffel bag and parachute from the trunk, while with the other he handed Lambert his gear.

"There's no doubt about it," Lambert said as they headed toward the waiting B-17. "When we get back, I'm going to insist that I be transferred to warm, sunny North Africa."

"Under Patton?" He swore in Afrikaans.

"Why not? He treated us very well—"

"We'd just blown up a German airfield. When that wore off, he would have treated us just like everyone else."

"Meaning?"

The two men stepped aside as Livingston, Colon, and Ogan collected their gear.

"While we were recuperating in Casablanca, I heard that the bugger raided a food locker and gave the steaks to his dogs, the beets to his men. I'd rather be on my own *anywhere* than serve under that kind of bastard."

Lambert squinted into the harsh wind. "Not me. I believe it's better to serve in heaven than to freeze *mon derriere*!"

Escott smiled as he stood to one side and eavesdropped. Despite the Frenchman's grievances, he, like the others, was not a man to shy from the rigors of war.

Each man had been selected for Force Five due to his survival skills, abilities that had been expanded by Sweet and Escott to include training in espionage and self-defense.

The inspectors had had a week to work with the men before shipping them to Algiers; ideally, they would have liked some time to prepare them for Stalingrad. The men spoke German, but no Russian; they had limited experience with naval vessels; and only Weyers had ever used a parachute. But the orders had come from Military Intelligence just the day before, and as it was, there had been barely enough time for Sweet, Escott, Livingston, and Ogan to work out the logistics of the mission—and get the SIS off their back.

Lambert and Weyers followed Colon, Ogan, and Livingston through the forward entry hatch under the plane. As Weyers, Sweet, and Escott climbed up, the pilot came from behind the cockpit armor plate.

"Captain Kane?" Escott asked.

The tall newcomer nodded once. He wore a faded flight jacket capped by an equally leathery face; a mop of gray hair atop his head underscored the weatherbeaten look. But he was smiling, and Escott seemed encouraged.

"Are you Inspector Escott?"

"I am."

They shook hands. "It's rather cramped up here, Inspector. Let's go to the back, shall we?"

Heading from the nose section, he led the men through the bomb bay into the fuselage. There, Escott introduced the others. The pilot shook their hands in turn.

"It's going to be quite a run," he said with enthusiasm, "a spot of excitement after all those boring flights over Germany, dodging antiaircraft fire, enemy fighters, and the like."

Escott grinned. "Vice-Marshal Park tells me you have a strange notion of what constitutes excitement."

Kane shrugged. "I enjoy flying and I enjoy hurting the Hun. And this mission—frankly, sir, it's going to be a challenge. I don't think the Almighty's winged angels *themselves* could get into and out of Latvia. The Germans *own* that region. And we have to do it twice!"

Escott forced a smile. The B-17G bomber had a range of 3,200 kilometers, which was barely enough for a one-way trip. The plan called for them to fly to Latvia, on the Baltic Sea, where Kane would refuel on a barren stretch of field nearly fifty kilometers east of the seaport capital of Riga. On the return trip, he would have to stop and refuel a second time. If the mission in Stalingrad wasn't dangerous enough, getting there promised to be even riskier.

Kane turned his wrinkled face to Livingston. "Make yourself at home, Lieutenant—as much as you're able." He pointed to the plain, gunmetal benches bolted to either side of the fuselage. "They shake like the blazes, and your bum'll go numb from the cold. The loo's in the back—the big iron drum with the lid but no seat—and if anyone needs a rest, the auxiliary crew member's seat'll be empty. It's forward, right next to the radio operator."

Livingston thanked him, after which they began stowing their gear beneath the benches.

"See you in a few days," Escott said as he shook Livingston's hand.

"Peut-etre," Lambert said. "If I find someplace warm over there, I won't be leaving it."

"The cold will be good for you," Sweet said. "It'll toughen you up."

"For what, my next trip to the Arctic? I'm not going to like this, messieurs. Not at all."

Escott said gravely, "The cold should be your worst problem, Corporal."

Wishing the men well, the two inspectors departed. A crew member shut the door, and the four 9-cylinder, turbo-supercharged engines were started up; the plane rattled as promised, and Lambert pulled his collar over his ears to muffle the drone.

"At least there's one thing to be thankful for, *mes amis*."

"What's that?" Weyers asked.

"At least the pilot's enthusiastic. We won't have to teach him *manners* when we get back."

Chapter Two

His eyes shut, Sergeant Major Ogan was nestled between a portable oxygen bottle, which was lashed to the wall, and a 12.7mm Browning M2 machine gun, which sat on a pole to his left and faced a shuttered, rectangular slot.

Though it was early, just six in the evening, he was exhausted; the combination of the droning and the vibration of the fuselage relaxed him. As soon as they were airborne, he drifted asleep. The only time he woke was when the bomber hit turbulence. His chest was still bandaged from the wounds he'd received in North Africa, and though they'd been less severe than bloody, they stung whenever he made any jerks or sudden, twisting motions.

During those periods when he was awake, Ogan knew that what he was feeling was partly mental and physical exhaustion from the long hours of planning the mission to Stalingrad: working on a flight plan that would bring them into Riga under cover of midnight, and helping to arrange, with Sweet, for Russian partisans to meet them at the field, and for two more to meet them in Stalingrad.

But part of it too was emotional exhaustion. Ogan still

had difficulty accepting the fact that he'd been relieved of the command of Force Five. He didn't resent Livingston for having been promoted to second lieutenant. If anything, he respected Livingston more for having saved both the team and the mission in Algiers; his own decisions in North Africa had been too cautious, too inexperienced. But it had been a humiliating setback for the handpicked British member of the team, the inspectors' fair-haired boy. He was glad that, upon his return to England, his wife had been able to make a quick trip from Coventry. Without her support, picking himself up and dusting himself off would have been more than emotionally draining. It would have been impossible.

Across from Ogan, Livingston opened his duffel bag and retrieved the thin dossier Military Intelligence had put together on the situation in Stalingrad, and on the operatives they would be meeting there; there was also a psychological profile of General Paulus. Beside him, Colon was reading a Human Torch comic book.

"You played football at Benning, didn't you?" Livingston asked.

"Yes, sir. And for four years at Duquesne."

"Tell me—what went through your mind when you had to face a goal-line stand."

"A thinkin' question, huh?" The private bent down the corner of the page, shut the magazine. "What happens, sir, is you stand there sayin' to yourself, 'The crowd's expectin' us to be able to move the ball a couple of yards.' So you start thinkin' about *their* expectations, and that's usually enough to distract you and *stop* you from doin' it."

"And when you're a defender?"

"Just the opposite. You take each down as it comes, focus on every second, every inch. I always found it easier to score from *our own* two- or three- or four-yard line than to punch in from theirs."

Livingston nodded. "That's something Hitler doesn't understand."

"Football?"

"The psychology of winning."

Colon gave him a puzzled look. "The bucket-heads have done well enough, considerin' how Hitler's pushed 'em—"

"No argument. But what you just said makes sense. They're less concerned with winning than with living up to Hitler's expectations. That's a helluva distraction."

Colon nodded inconclusively, then returned to his comic book.

Livingston riffled through the papers, looking for the history of the conflict in Russia. He'd learned many things during six years of fighting—first with the Abraham Lincoln Brigade, against Franco in Spain, and then with the French resistance before Pearl Harbor. However, the most valuable lesson he'd learned was that ambition and ability alone are never enough to win a war. As even Colon understood, it takes a will that comes from somewhere inside.

He found the two-page summary of the invasion of Russia and began reading.

When the U.S. finally agreed to join the war, Hitler was already waging war on two very difficult fronts: against the British and against the Russians. Of the two, the Russian front was far more draining on men and matériel. The defenders had their entire eastern section to draw upon, and they simply replaced the hundreds of thousands of soldiers as they fell. When Germans died, their comrades were expected to fight that much harder.

Hoping to effect a swift victory against the Russians, Hitler regrouped. He sent the massive Army Group A and the Fourth Panzer Army into the Caucasus, to capture the oilfields, while ordering the powerful Army Group B to take and hold the River Don. Taking it, Army Group B was ordered to cross the river and head south-

east, to Stalingrad—which produced nearly one-third of
the tanks, guns, tractors, and other vehicles used by the
Russians.

It was at this point, Livingston noted, that Hitler made
a catastrophic error. Encouraged by the progress of Army
Group A, he ordered the Fourth Panzer Army to leave
the Caucasus Front and help the struggling Army Group
B. Just shy of their goal, Army Group A found itself
stretched too thin, and was stopped dead by the Russians.

Meanwhile, the Germans at Stalingrad underestimated
the determination of the defenders not to lose the city
that bore their leader's name. After months of bitter
fighting, without a victory, Hitler ordered the city razed
with artillery fire and Luftwaffe bombing raids. When
the smoke cleared, General Paulus's Sixth Army encir-
cled Stalingrad, expecting an easy victory. Instead, the
fighting became even more vicious. It was hand-to-hand,
measured in meters, as the Russians fought from
bombed-out buildings, from hastily dug tunnels, and
from behind heaps of rubble.

Finally, November came, and desperate to give Hitler
Stalingrad as a Christmas present, Paulus took the unprecedented step of requesting the poison gas. In defi-
ance of the rules of warfare set down in Geneva, Hitler
agreed.

Livingston flipped past the statistics and maps, reread-
ing the scant material about their two contacts. After
parachuting in, they would link up with Masha Vlasov
and her younger brothers Andrei and Leonid. The Russians were lifelong residents of Stalingrad, and were
couriers in the underground lines that brought food and
ammunition into the besieged city. MI knew little else
about them, save that only Masha spoke English. Their
father had been a theatrical impresario, and she had traveled widely with him throughout Europe. Resourceful

and daring, she was one of the partisans most sought after by the Germans.

For the Germans to acknowledge that a woman was hurting them, Masha *had* to be exceptional. Livingston was looking forward to meeting her.

After going forward and reviewing the flight plan with Captain Kane and his navigator, Livingston, Lambert, Weyers, and radio operator Forbes Rathbone crowded into the transmitter room to play poker. Copilot Derek Abel joined them for several hands, winning them all, after which Lambert joined him in the cockpit for a smoke. Two hours later, at a few minutes past 11 P.M., Abel and Lambert came back to the small but warm transmitter room. The copilot informed them that they were flying over the Baltic Sea on their approach toward Riga.

"You might want to go back and buckle in," he said. "We'll be dropping fast from thirty-two thousand feet, and will soon be within range of enemy guns. If we're spotted, things could get bumpy."

Livingston thanked him, and as soon as they entered the fuselage, their breath froze.

"Definitely the Pacific Theater next time," Lambert said. He dropped onto the bench and pulled the belt across his chest. "I was talking to the copilot, and did you know, the Romans used to fete their soldiers before sending them into battle? What did we get? A night at a dockside tavern. Where were the women, the confetti?"

Weyers said, "Better you should ask where the Romans are."

Without looking up from his magazine, Colon answered, "I agree with Rotter. Gimme a few hours of sun and a dame instead of a bulkhead and a *cavallo* like you."

Weyers's wide mouth turned down. "Those things'll

make a man soft." The frown deepened. "And what the hell did you just call me, ya runt? A cava*what*?"

Colon bristled, but before he could answer Livingston ordered the men to be quiet. Though they'd gone through the plan for Riga in London, Livingston asked Ogan—who had made the arrangements—to review the procedure again.

"Two small bonfires will be lit on the field by partisans," he said, "and the plane will come down between them. An oil truck will be waiting, part of the stores the Russians hid in June of last year, when the Nazis came from East Prussia into Lithuania and Latvia. Lambert and Weyers, you'll man the Browning machine guns here"—he pointed to the weapons on either side of the fuselage—"while the rest of us take up positions outside, to watch the perimeter while the Russians pump the fuel."

No one had any questions and, as the plane rocked and lurched, radio operator Rathbone poked his head from the transmitter room.

"Captain Kane says we're just about one hundred kilometers out of Riga, and about to go down through the clouds. Keep a sharp lookout."

Livingston glanced at his watch. "Eleven thirty-five. Right on time."

There was a great deal of turbulence as he and Lambert slid back the metal doors and peered through the machine-gun ports on their respective sides. As soon as they penetrated the thick cloud cover, the searchlights of the port city were visible some thirty kilometers to the south. Their own lights doused, inside and out, Kane held to a course well north of Riga. Before descending farther, he waited until they were twenty kilometers east of the city, then doubled back.

The men looked out carefully. After they circled the area twice, the fires flared on Lambert's side of the plane.

"We've got them below," he said.

A moment later, the stocky Abel came back. "Lieutenant, the captain says there may be a problem."

"What kind of problem?"

"Well, we've circled the field once, and make it out to be roughly a thousand meters long. That's over a hundred meters more than we need to land—but some fifty less than we need to take off again."

"Shit."

"Precisely. Now just to play it safe, he suggests you lighten the aircraft while we refuel; about a thousand pounds should do it."

Livingston nodded, and as the big main wheels and tail wheel were lowered, the team scanned the fuselage for anything that could be taken out quickly. As soon as the huge aircraft thumped down, Weyers and Lambert swung the machine guns toward the ports while Livingston, Ogan, and Colon unfastened everything from the oxygen bottles to the fire extinguishers to the toilet lid.

After less than a minute, Rathbone looked in on them. "Excuse me, Lieutenant, but Captain Kane would like to see you."

Livingston looked up from the cover of the auxiliary direct current generator, which he was in the process of detaching. "What is it?"

"Well, sir, it would seem that there are no Russians and no gasoline truck."

Livingston hurried through the transmitter room and empty bomb bay. Rounding the navigator's bench, he dropped through the open hatchway. His feet smarted when they hit the hard ground. Ignoring the eye-tearing cold and propeller-driven winds, he went over to Kane. The captain stood with his hands on his hips, staring into the adjacent woods.

"Nothing?" Livingston asked.

"Not a peep, not even a bloody squirrel. And if they aren't out there, I'd say we're in a bit of a jam—and not just because of the petrol."

Livingston understood. "Someone lit those fires."

"Exactly."

Livingston went back and pulled himself halfway into the plane. "Lambert! Weyers! Keep a sharp lookout! This may be a setup!" He dropped back down.

Kane asked, "Was there supposed to be a signal of some sort?"

"Nothing. The whole idea was to get in and out as quickly as—"

Sharp reports and white streaks burst from the dark woods, and Lambert's Browning cracked to life. Kane and Livingston jumped behind the main wheel as enemy fire dug up chunks of earth less than a meter from their feet. The guns fell silent, and they peered into the woods on the starboard side. Above, Weyers sent a warning burst into the woods on the port side.

"They must want us alive," Livingston said, "or they'd have picked us off when we first stepped out."

Ogan and the navigator appeared in the open hatch. Ogan lowered his hands.

"Come on!"

"You first," Livingston said, giving Kane a push. The pilot ran for the hatch, bullets tearing up clods of earth as Ogan grabbed his arms. Looping his legs inside, Kane pulled himself up.

Ogan bent out again for the lieutenant. "Let's go, sir!"

When Lambert and Weyers set up covering fire, Livingston jumped around the landing gear and literally dove up into the hatch. Ogan caught his arms and pulled him up as bullets tore the cuffs of his pants and raked the outside of his left leg.

"Get us the hell out of here!" Livingston hollered as he and Ogan shut the hatch.

Bullets chewed at the sides of the aircraft as Kane

throttled up. Ogan helped Livingston back, the aircraft turning before they even reached their seats. Livingston fell onto the bench, and Ogan, kneeling beside him, examined his leg.

"Doesn't look serious—"

"Forget it," Livingston barked. "Is anyone on the tail gun?"

"Colon."

"Then you get to the chin turret, Ken—just in case they try to roll something in front of us."

Ogan saluted and hurried forward. Livingston hobbled behind him and stood behind the copilot, leaning on the cylindrical hydraulic accumulator for support.

As they taxied, Livingston saw flashes of white close in from both sides of the field. Bullets scraped cometlike smudges on the bulletproof windshield; behind him, the sharp clanging was constant as gunfire riddled the fuselage.

Suddenly, a Waffenwagen bolted from the woods, its 20mm cannon blazing. The small armored vehicle raced toward the aircraft, Ogan's return fire bouncing from its iron shell; as the B-17 rushed by, there was a pop and the plane listed to one side.

"They got the bloody landing gear," Kane said through his teeth.

The copilot quickly adjusted the flaps to try to give them additional lift as they raced ahead. The aircraft leveled, and with the trees at the far end of the field less than one hundred meters away, Kane pulled back on the controls.

"Get Ogan up here!" he yelled.

"Why?"

"The damn chin turret may not clear!"

Swearing, Livingston limped around the armor plate and shouted down as the huge bomber nosed up. Kane immediately put the plane into a steep climb, listening as the tops of the trees slapped against the plane's underbelly. He heard the grinding of metal, first below and then behind him as they cleared the woods.

He exhaled loudly, and moments later, Livingston and Ogan staggered into the cockpit. They were followed by the navigator. Several charts were gathered in his arms. The wind tore in from the ruptured nose section.

"How much did we lose?" Kane asked.

"The chin turret and cheek guns both," the navigator answered, "along with the floor under my table. I saved what I could."

"Good show." He patted him on the arm, then said to Livingston, "You know, Lieutenant, we really do owe the Jerries our thanks."

"For what?"

"For not letting us refuel. Even after ditching a half ton, there isn't a way in hell we'd have done it with a full tank of petrol."

Despite the cold, Livingston wiped sweat from his brow. As in Algiers, it seemed as if Force Five was cursed. Once again, from the very start, nothing was going as planned.

Slumping against the hydraulic panel, the American noticed a red light burning beside the pilot's left foot. "What's that?"

Kane looked down. "Landing gear warning light. It means the struts are stuck halfway between extended and retracted."

"Can we fix it?"

"Not if the trees tore either of them out of alignment. In any case, why bother? I'll be very much surprised if there's anything left below the shock absorber. Whether they're up or down makes very little difference."

Livingston had to admit that that made sense.

"And now, sir," Kane went on, "it's up to you. We've got enough fuel to turn round, or else go most of the way to Stalingrad. If we go home, the plane can be saved."

"And if we don't, Stalingrad can be saved. From my point of view, there isn't much choice."

Kane looked from his copilot to the navigator. "Yes, well—the crew and I are up for a little adventure. Southeast, then?"

"Southeast," Livingston said, smiling and then heading back to take care of his leg.

Chapter Three

"How do you think they found out about us?"

Livingston's question, though expected, caused Lambert to shift uncomfortably, and Weyers to look away. The landing had been Ogan's responsibility. As with those parts of the Algerian mission that had gone wrong, he was the one who had to answer for it.

"Ken? Was there any possible way the Germans could have intercepted your communiqués?"

"Possible, but unlikely. We broadcast on a frequency that no one uses or monitors any longer."

"Then what happened?"

"If I had to guess, I'd say the Germans had no idea we were coming. The remnants of the Russian Eighth Army have been in the hills since Hitler invaded. Rather than send troops after them, the enemy probably waited for them to show themselves, to attempt something bolder than cutting telephone lines and sabotaging tanks and planes."

Livingston stretched his bandaged leg along the bench. "And this was it."

"That's my feeling," Ogan said.

"Then chances are good they don't know about Sta-

26

lingrad. They must've captured those poor bastards right after they lit the fires.''

"Most likely.''

Lambert said, "If I may, Lieutenant—what are our plans now for Stalingrad? Do we jump, or are we really going to try to land in this wreck?''

"Weyers, you've done both. What do you say?''

The big man leaned on the machine gun. "Me? Call me practical, but I'd put my faith in a working parachute before I'd trust a plane without landing gear.''

Livingston nodded. "That's how I feel. We can arrange to meet Kane and the others after they set down. What's important is that *we* get as close to the target area as possible, and in one piece.'' He looked at his watch. "We've got six hours. I suggest everyone try to get some shut-eye, since I doubt we'll be getting much rest once we land.''

Colon, Weyers, and Lambert curled up beside their machine guns, and Ogan pulled a small book from his jacket pocket. Pouring them both some coffee the radio operator made, Livingston sat beside him.

"What're you reading?''

Ogan turned the cover around. "A Russian-English dictionary. Just in case.''

Livingston smiled. "Glad someone around here's thinking ahead.''

"For all the good it does. I want you to know, Lieutenant, I'm sorry about what happened back there.''

"No reason to—''

"But there *is*. The *entire* mission was placed in jeopardy because we failed to ask ourselves, 'What if?' ''

"And if you had? What could we possibly have done any differently?''

"We might have planned a straight-through flight to Stalingrad and tried to refuel there, or we could have had a fighter go into Riga first. A mustang could have made the trip—''

"And been snookered, just like we were. Ken, we only had thirty-six hours to pull this together. Besides, you heard what Kane said. What happened was a blessing in disguise."

"Not for the Russians."

Livingston's voice was somber. "No, not for them. But like it or not, that's the price of doing business. We're risking our necks to save Russians; I can't hurt for the couple of Russians who let down their guard and got their necks wrung."

Ogan returned to his book.

"You're not convinced."

"No, sir. I hate to sound like a tyro, but I don't think I'll ever be able to just shrug it off when someone dies because of something I did or didn't do."

Livingston stretched out his bandaged leg, pulled his cap over his eyes. "Well, maybe a little compassion is good for the team, just as long as it doesn't interfere with one thing."

"What's that?"

He lifted the edge of his cap. "Killing Nazis. As long as you don't hurt for *them*, I can live with the rest of it."

The lieutenant could feel Ogan's eyes on him as he settled back into the seat. But that didn't bother him. He himself had felt righteous, once; it had died the first time he'd had to execute a saboteur in Spain, a young woman. And it had been buried for good when he saw an enemy chaplain pick up a bayonet and drive it into a man's back for raping a nun. Sometimes it took a few battles, but in the end, war turned everyone into a survivor.

"Lieutenant. *Lieutenant!*"

Livingston's nose was numb. That was the first thing of which he was aware. The second was that perspiration had literally frozen his fatigues around his body. He barely felt Lambert's prodding.

"What time is it?"

"Just after four, sir—but we've got a problem. Captain Kane asked to see you, *tout de suite*."

Livingston was instantly alert. He jumped up, his leg smarting, his clothing cracking loudly as he hurried to the cockpit. He stood in silence as Kane and the navigator shouted numbers to each other over the drone of the engines.

"The situation is this," Kane said when they were finished. "We're nearly three hundred kilometers northwest of Stalingrad, and I don't think I can stay aloft for more than another hundred kilometers. How long will your people in Stalingrad wait for you?"

Livingston turned around. "Ogan! Up front on the double!"

The sergeant major came quickly, and Livingston repeated Kane's question. Ogan shook his head.

"I'm not sure; we kept communications to a minimum. If they don't think we're coming, my guess is they'll decide to go after the cargo themselves."

"That's just great."

Kane said, "Well, all isn't quite that hopeless, Lieutenant." He nodded toward a map. "See here. Mr. Poole tells me there's a sizable village on our route. Urisomething."

The navigator plucked a pencil from behind his ear. "Uryupinsk," he said, circling it on the map.

"Right. We'll reach it in just a few minutes. Now then, you can probably find a vehicle of some sort there and make your way south. What's more, the charts say there's nothing but hills and fields for nearly a hundred kilometers in all directions. I can ditch this lady somewhere along the way and, hopefully, we can all link up."

"And if we stay with you, how close can you get us to Stalingrad?"

"Probably two hundred kilometers. At best, one-fifty, if God sees fit to give us a tail wind."

Livingston weighed the options, then turned. "Come on, Ken. We're moving out."

Gathering their gear, the men put on the German uniforms they'd been provided with, Lambert shivering violently as he changed. He felt better when he'd donned his animal skin fur coat, field gray fur cap, and parachute. Weyers checked each man's harness before they headed to the bomb bay. They waited there while Poole guided Captain Kane toward their destination.

Lambert looked at his thick arms. "I feel like the Monster of Frankenstein in this. I can hardly move."

"It's better than freezing," Weyers said. He looked at Livingston. "If I were you, sir, I'd take the landing on my good leg and roll to that side. You've got enough padding. Otherwise, if you hit with both legs, you may pop your bandages."

Livingston thanked him.

"Also," the South African said, "it's going to be cold out there, so I suggest we cover our faces." He looked at Lambert. "That includes keeping your mouth shut so your tongue doesn't freeze."

"That can happen?" the Frenchman asked.

"Tongue, eyes, nose—anything damp or exposed is going to take a hell of a lashing."

The copilot gave the men rags, Lambert stuffing extra padding into the front of his pants.

The plane had dropped steadily from its service ceiling of 10,800 meters until it was just 1,100 meters high. At four-forty, Copilot Abel came through the cockpit door.

"We're nearly over the village. Best be getting to the hatchway."

The men squeezed through the cabin into the nose section, where the copilot had pushed aside the remains of the bomb sight, navigator's table, and cheek-gun ammunition box. The men gathered around the wide, jagged gash in the hull, all that was left of the forward hatch. The wind was bone chilling and fierce.

Lambert swore. "Someone shoot me *now*!"

The copilot stood back. "I'll give you the signal! You've got about"—he looked at the captain, who nodded—"forty-five seconds."

Lambert tried to wrap his arms around his chest, but the coat was too stiff. Colon crouched, Weyers moved slowly from foot to foot, and Ogan rubbed his gloved hands. Livingston watched the copilot.

"Thirty seconds."

Livingston looked through the hole. Below, the dark terrain was broken by the occasional light of a home, a car, or a fire.

Soldiers keeping warm, he guessed. He wondered what they thought his plane might be.

"Twenty seconds!"

Livingston looked at the men. "I'll go first, then Weyers, Lambert, Ogan, and Colon."

"Ten!"

Weyers yelled through the cloth covering, "Don't hesitate! Go out, turn facedown, count to ten, then pull the cord. And remember to *give* when you hit. Don't try to *stay* on your feet!"

"Five!"

Livingston sat on the lip of torn metal as Weyers gave them a few more suggestions. He only half heard them.

"Three!"

He had to push out, just enough so his chute would clear the rim.

"Two!"

Weyers squatted beside him, ready to take his place the instant Livingston jumped.

"One—"

Livingston's heart punched hard and fast against his throat.

"Go!"

The lieutenant arched his body and slid from the rim, pushing back as he went through. He cleared the hatch and found himself on his back.

It was a sensation like nothing he'd ever felt, but it was also not at all what he'd been expecting. Instead of the stomach-turning drop he'd been anticipating, he felt as if he was floating on a loud, choppy sea. The air actually seemed solid, and it tore past him with fury that made him feel as though he were lying still. He couldn't see the B-17, nor, in the dark, did he see the other men; the droning of the plane was quickly swallowed up by the deafening roar of the wind.

So caught up in the jump was he that Livingston had to force himself to concentrate on what he was supposed to be doing. Remembering what Weyers had said, he drew in his arms and legs and did a slow, awkward somersault until he was facedown. He realized, then, that he'd forgotten to count. Because it had to have been at least ten seconds since he'd jumped—he couldn't be sure; time didn't seem to exist in this dark, dreamlike world—Livingston reached to his side and tugged on the ripcord.

Reality returned with a jolt.

He didn't see the parachute, but he heard and felt it. The fabric sounded like a flock of birds scared into flight, and even through his thick coat, the jerk of the harness was sufficient to kick the air from his chest. As he descended feetfirst, twisting slightly in the wind, the air was no longer so loud, nor so thick. *Now* he felt like he was falling.

He looked to his right, caught a glimpse of another chute some twenty meters off. Then he looked down. He recalled Weyers having said that if they saw trees, they should pull hard on the side of the chute toward them, so they'd drift in the opposite direction. But, as far as Livingston could see, there was nothing but open field below. He thought he saw a home or a farmhouse off in the distance, but it was too dark to be certain. He glanced down again, his eyes barely open to protect them from the wind.

Then he was on the ground, before he knew it. One moment it was barely visible, a bleak stretch of dirt mounds and withered grass; the next moment it was rushing up at him, like a bull he'd once crossed in Spain. He pulled in his injured leg slightly, took the landing on his right leg—

He was only on the leg for an instant. As soon as he touched down, the parachute dragged him down, onto his face. He had the wind knocked from him again, and it was several seconds before he could gather up the shroud lines, curl onto his back, bring his heels around, and dig in to stop. The chute drew him to his feet again, and he limped forward as he struggled to pinch the quick-release hook. When the chute finally came off, he scooped up the lines and hauled in the deflated canopy.

He turned, saw Weyers land with precision just ten meters away, followed by Colon. Both men undid their chutes without difficulty.

Weyers jogged over. "I've never seen it done quite like you did it, sir."

"Save it for your memoirs," he said, more disgusted with his own ineptitude than with Weyers's insubordination. He finished bunching up the canopy and handed it to Weyers. "Bury 'em. I'm going to see about the others."

"I saw Ogan come down about fifty meters past Colon. But I didn't see Lambert at all."

"It figures."

Livingston hurried off. As he'd suspected, they'd landed in a farm. The fields appeared to have been stripped clean, probably by the Germans before winter. He stopped to make sure that Colon and Ogan were all

right, and determining that neither of them had seen
Lambert, Livingston pulled off his glove, pulled the Luger in his pocket, and headed toward the house.

He circled wide, moving with extreme caution, then
froze when he noticed a light on the second floor go on.
He stood stone-still, and as the horizon began to shade
from black to dark blue, he realized that this was probably when these people got up. He continued searching,
his pace quickened.

As soon as he was on the other side of the house, he
saw a small barn—and Lambert. His chute was draped
from the dome of the silo, the Frenchman dangling face-
front beneath it. He was trying to reach back and climb
the shroud lines, but his bulky coat made it impossible
for him to turn or lift his arms.

The silo was roughly five meters high, and were he to
fall from that height, Lambert would certainly break his
leg. Livingston thought of going back and gathering the
other parachutes, to try to form a cushion. But the sun
was rising quickly, and there wasn't time. Propelled by
an oath, Livingston hurried toward him.

When Lambert saw him, he stopped struggling and
shrugged. Livingston motioned for him to be quiet, then
went around to the other side. A ladder was attached to
the lower bin, and it rose to the dome; the uppermost
rung was about two meters from the side of the chute.
Somehow, he would have to find a way to reach it.

He looked around, heard a horse whinny in its stall.

There were animals. That meant there must also be
hay.

Rushing inside, he felt along the dark walls until he
found what he needed: a pitchfork. Grabbing it from the
hook, he raced back outside.

The horizon was already a band of blue-green as he
started up the ladder. He climbed quickly, and, reaching
the top, latched the hook of Lambert's harness to the top
rung of the pitchfork, a thin metal bar. Leaning to the

side, his foot braced on the joint where the dome met the lower bin, he snagged the lines almost at once. Then he whispered loudly to Lambert.

"When I start to pull, you walk yourself around, on your heels. Just take it slow, understand? If the lines come loose, we're screwed."

"*Oui!*"

Holding the pitchfork so the tines were nearly upright, he slowly began to draw them around. Lambert's boots clumped and echoed through the empty silo, and Livingston prayed that no one in the house heard them. All the while, he had an odd sense of déjà vu, feeling the way he did when, as a child, he'd use a stick to try and work a kite free from the trees in Central Park. He tried not to think of just how *many* kites he'd lost that way. . . .

Livingston's arm began to cramp, and he relieved the strain by bracing the handle of the pitchfork on his knee. Finally, the shroud lines were within reach and, tossing the pitchfork to the ground, Livingston grabbed them. He looped them around the ladder and around his arm as Lambert inched over. He stole another look at the horizon, which was now a dull yellow.

It took just a few seconds more for Lambert to reach the ladder. The instant he grabbed it, Livingston undid the harness lest a gust of wind pull him off.

"You won't believe it," Lambert said through his muffler. "This only happened because I tried to *avoid* landing on the barn!"

Lambert was chattering from the cold and, having taken off his gloves, his hands were nearly frostbitten. After they were down, Livingston handed him his own gloves, then bundled up the parachute and stuffed it behind a skimpy bale of hay in the barn. They started toward the field; as they passed the house, a shotgun blast disrupted the still morning.

"Ahdyeen meenootah pahzhahloostah!"

Livingston looked toward the house, at the silhouette of a man standing in the doorway. He had no idea what the Russian had said; all he knew was that before he could reach his Luger, either Lambert or he would be dead.

Chapter Four

As the three men stood there, each waiting to see what the other would do, a second shot echoed across the field. This one came from the west; the short, stocky farmer turned, startled, and a second shot exploded, dislodging a small rock less than a meter from his foot.

He looked out and saw three men standing midway across the field, weapons drawn. Licking his lips, the farmer dropped his shotgun and raised his hands.

"Smart move," Livingston said, and came forward. A look of surprise crossed the Russian's round face.

Ogan, Weyers, and Colon arrived moments later.

"Whose shot was that?" Livingston asked.

"Mine," Ogan said. "We came to check—couldn't imagine what was taking so long."

The lieutenant nodded. "Glad you did."

"*I'm* just glad the Russian bugger didn't fire again," Weyers said. "If it were me instead of the sergeant calling the shots, I'd have nailed him."

"And not only would you have killed a potential ally," Ogan said, "but you'd have shot a man who apparently meant us no harm."

"How do you know that?"

"Because what he yelled was, 'A moment, please.'
Quite deferential."

"Deference—with a shotgun," Weyers said. "I'm not
comforted."

The Russian, a man Livingston guessed to be in his
early fifties, still seemed confused. He looked from the
men's military-issue coats to their faces. *"Nyehmyetski?"* he asked. *"Nyehmyetski?"*

Ogan said, "I believe, Lieutenant, he's asking if we're
German."

Livingston rubbed his chin. "Answer him."

"Nyet," Ogan said. *"Yah Angliski."*

The man's gloomy features seemed to catch a piece of
the rising sun. *"Da?"* The Russian was suddenly unable
to contain himself. Pulling Ogan by the hand, he led him
toward the house, motioning for the others to follow.
They turned to Livingston.

"I smell a fire inside," Lambert said, "and I'll bet
there's something warm cooking on it."

"We can't afford to stop now," Livingston said. "Ken,
find out if he's got a car or a truck somewhere."

Ogan stopped the man, and managed to make himself
understood. With obvious regret, the farmer said he had
no vehicles, only two horses.

"Ask him how far it is to Uryupinsk."

"Uryupinsk?" The Russian regarded Livingston. He
pointed past the house, held up two fingers. *"Dvah* kilometers."

Livingston looked at his watch. It was nearly six
o'clock. They were already late, and needed to find out
where they could get a car. Reluctantly, he motioned for
the men to follow the Russian inside.

The farmer's name was Alexandre Mekhlis, and his
wife was Caterina. They served the men bread and eggs.
From what Ogan could gather, their home and barn had
been used to billet German soldiers during their summer

advance. Before leaving, the enemy took most of the crops and destroyed what they couldn't carry, so the Russian troops wouldn't have it. The couple survived on what little their cows and chickens were able to produce. Livingston felt guilty about accepting their hospitality.

"The only reason they left the animals," Ogan said, after checking several words in his dictionary, "is because they want to use them to feed their armies later."

"When they retreat," Colon vowed.

Weyers grumbled, "Nix. The Jerries'll be eating lead before that."

Though he was bitter when he spoke about the German invaders, their host literally thumped his chest with pride when he talked about his *"chyeetiryeh sihn"* who had gone off to fight them. As far as Ogan could determine, the farmers hadn't heard from their four boys in over a year.

As Caterina offered the men helpings of porridge, Livingston glanced at his watch. Only a half hour had passed, though it seemed much longer; the stone hearth was warm, and the thaw, as well as the meal, had had an almost narcotic effect. But the convoy was due in just over thirty-six hours, and guilt began to gnaw at him.

He rose. *"Spasibo,"* he said, having picked up the word from the conversation. "Thank you."

Their host stood, bowed. *"Nyeh zha shto."*

"I guess that means we're leavin'," Weyers said, and he literally had to pull Lambert from the fire.

Alexandre offered to ride into town with one of them to see about a car. He said there were rarely any Germans around anymore, and that, if he asked the right people, it might be possible to buy, borrow, or even steal some kind of transportation. He added that he had a good idea where they could start their search.

As he was the only one who had ever ridden bareback, Lambert volunteered to accompany him. That suited him

more than walking with the others, and as the Frenchman reined one of the farmer's old mares onto the road,
and felt the warmth of the rising sun, he shuddered with
gratitude. However, his joy was short-lived, as the galloping of the horse sent frigid air riding up his pant legs
and coat. That had never happened to him in the Legion,
and he realized, bitterly, that he'd never ridden anywhere
that wasn't in or near a desert. Nor had the sands of
Timimoun or Idehan been as lumpy as the road to Uryupinsk. His buttocks slammed repeatedly onto the animal's bony back, and by the time they reached the village
at six, after nearly an hour, Lambert envied those who
were merely suffering from hypothermia.

Uryupinsk was as small and impoverished as Lambert
had imagined. Several shops were shuttered: the tailor,
the blacksmith, and the baker. After they'd dismounted,
Alexandre used vivid sign language to explain that the
first two shopowners had been taken by the German infantry to accompany them to the front; the baker had
been executed when he struck a soldier for stealing his
goods.

They stopped on the stoop of a small shop that ser-
viced the local farmers. Alexandre drove the side of his
fist against the wooden door; within moments, the shut-
ters creaked open on the second floor. Lambert saw fear
in the face above; when the man saw the Frenchman's
German uniform, the color evaporated from his ruddy
cheeks. Then he noticed Alexandre, and the trepidation
turned to confusion. The farmer called for him to come
down, and a minute later, a bolt was thrown and the
front door opened.

"Alexandre." The bearded proprietor clasped the
farmer's hand and shook it tentatively. "Come in, come
in." Alexandre entered and Lambert followed him. The
bearded man's eyes followed the Frenchman closely.

"It's good to see you, Mikhail!" Alexandre said.

"Is it?"

"Yes. You'll never believe what happened last night."

"Tell me it rained gold on your property. Tell me that you have come to your friend Mikhail to *spend* some of it."

The farmer beamed. "It rained, yes—not gold, but something nearly as good."

Mikhail's eyes finally shifted to Alexandre. "Does it have to do with this . . . Nazi?"

"Nazi? He is no more a Nazi than I am."

Alexandre launched into an explanation and, having no idea what the men were saying, Lambert walked around. There were several plows and stacks of pitchforks, hoes, and other implements. But there was no feed, and where the large barrels must have stood, there were now only dark, discolored circles on the floor. He assumed the Nazis had taken it for their horses.

After a short, excited explanation, followed by a brief discussion, the men came over to Lambert. Alexandre said something slowly—as though that alone would magically help the Frenchman to understand Russian—of which the only word that made any sense was *"mashinyu."*

"Le machine?" he asked in French. *"La voiture?"*

The Russians looked at each other and shrugged. Grabbing Lambert's hand, Mikhail led him out back.

There, in an alley, was a battered pickup truck. The windows were all shattered, and the seats were ripped up, but the tires were intact. Wondering why the Germans hadn't taken this as well, Lambert went over to examine the engine. As he passed the driver's side, he noticed a black medical kit on the front seat. Presumably, Mikhail was also a part-time veterinarian; which meant, as it did in many small villages in North Africa as well, that the man was also the local physician. Obviously, the Germans didn't know that or they might have taken him with the blacksmith and the tailor.

As soon as he raised the hood, Lambert saw why the truck was still there. A thick layer of frost coated the

battery, and the fan belt was stiff as iron. It would need
some work, more than the invaders had been willing to
spend. However, nothing he saw seemed beyond repair.

"*Le feu,*" he said to their blank expressions. "Fire!"

"*Pazhar?*" Mikhail asked, striking an imaginary
match.

"*Oui, pazhar,*" Lambert said as he pulled off his
gloves and began disconnecting the battery.

It was nearly 7 A.M. when, 150 kilometers to the
northwest, Captain Kane's aircraft ran out of fuel. The
pilot managed to guide the plane over a forest toward a
stretch of ice, and, dropping from a height of twenty
meters, the B-17 went skidding across the frozen lake.
Just two of its huge propellers had still been turning, and
upon impact, they shut down in a spray of ice and shattered metal. The force of the impact threw the aircraft
into a swift, dizzying circle. Disoriented, the men were
unaware that the awful grinding all around them was
more just the belly of the plane dragging across the ice.
The half-extended landing struts dug deep troughs in the
gleaming expanse, causing it to crack; the instant the
aircraft stopped moving horizontally, it sloped vertically,
the nose rising as water flooded through rents in the rear
of the fuselage. Within moments the plane was nearly
perpendicular to the ice, only the wings sprawling across
unbroken sections of ice preventing it from going under.

The radio operator and the navigator—who had been
sitting in the extra seat beside him—were caught in the
icy flood as the transmitter room went under. Though
dazed from the crash landing, and blinded by the thick
clouds of steam pouring in from the cooling engines,
Kane could hear their screams. But only for a moment.
Soon, there was only the roar of the rushing water and
the creaking of tortured metal.

"Abel! Abel, are you all right?"

There was no answer, and Kane took a moment to get

his bearings. He lay flat on his back in his seat, pinned by the armor plate that had become dislodged. Undoing his seat harness, he pushed against the metal slab.

He could see nothing to his right, and squirmed lower into the seat to try to get around the plate.

"*Abel*—are you in one piece?"

The captain heard a moan and, wriggling from the seat, felt about for the copilot's chair. He found it lying on its side, against the fuse panel beside the bomb-bay door. The force of the impact had ripped it from the two struts that held it to the floor.

The plane shuddered and dropped slightly, as the ice began to give beneath the starboard wing. Kane undid his companion's seat belt and checked his wounds. Abel's right arm was twisted behind him with a compound fracture; debris had raised deep gashes in his scalp, forehead, and shoulder. Kane suspected that he had suffered a concussion.

"Afraid I didn't do too well on this one," the pilot apologized. "I just didn't expect to lose those port screws before we touched down."

As he glanced down through the misty bomb bay, Kane saw the water rising quickly. The only way out was forward, through the hatch. Lifting Abel over his shoulder, the pilot used the bent seat struts as grips and climbed into the nose. He reached the torn hatchway and, Abel draped across his shoulder, jumped down. Laying the wounded man down and grabbing his collar, Kane dragged him behind as he started across the ice.

As he trudged away, the plane continued to shift and settle. Below him, the surface of the ice rippled ominously, and shifting the copilot onto his shoulder, Kane summoned his last reserves of strength and ran to the frozen shore.

Reaching it, he fell to his knees and lay the copilot on his back.

"Captain—" Abel moaned.

"I'm here."

"Where . . . are we?"

"On dry land. Just need to do a few repairs on the old flesh and bones, and then we can set out." Kane gave him a reassuring pat on the thigh. "Don't you worry, chum. Everything's just ducky."

After taking a moment to catch his breath, the captain rose. He glanced around. The first order of business was to make a splint for Abel, after which he'd have to find a warm place to leave him while he went to the main road to wait for Livingston.

In search of a suitably strong branch, Kane walked into the sparse wood beside the lake. He found, instead, a German patrol.

By the time Livingston and his men reached Uryupinsk at nine, Lambert had suspended the battery between a pair of hoe handles and was warming it over a fire. He had already used a hot, damp cloth to massage the ice from the fan belt, and was busy cleaning the battery connections.

"You missed all the fun!" the Frenchman said from under the hood. "The horse was terrible, and then the three of us were acting like deaf mutes, trying to understand one another, until *mon ami* Mikhail thought to try German."

"Who knew you'd also speak the part?" the merchant said.

"Now we're making good progress, and if the battery dries out, everything else should be fine."

Weyers surveyed the scene. "If you Frenchies are so damn resourceful, how the hell did Hitler ever knock you off?"

Lambert said matter-of-factly, "I wasn't there, *naturellement*."

Weyers took what little oil and gas Mikhail had and used it to fill the tanks, while Colon helped Lambert with the engine. Finally, after an additional half hour's work, and several heart-stopping tries, the engine did turn over.

Livingston and Ogan came outside, the sergeant major folding a black-and-white map Mikhail had provided. While the men piled into the truck, the lieutenant pressed a small wad of rubles into Mikhail's hand.

"We were given these in the event of an emergency. I want you to have them."

The Russian smiled and handed the money back. "Thank you, but no. I have nothing to spend it on, and besides, you may need it yet." He said emphatically, "*Help* our people, and that will be payment enough."

Thanking him, Livingston climbed into the passenger's seat. Colon was already behind the wheel, and the other men sat in the open back.

"You know where you're going?" the lieutenant asked.

Colon looked back through the shattered rear windshield. "Yes, sir. Out the alley, then left until sunset."

Livingston folded away the map. "Believe it or not, that's about the size of it. Let's move it out."

With that, Colon shifted into reverse and backed through the alley beside the shop, onto the hard, dirt road.

The *oberleutnant* in charge of the small mounted reconnaissance detachment looked from the pilot to the moaning copilot. Kane was sitting on the ground, trembling from the cold, his hands tied behind him; Abel lay sprawled beside him on the hard ground. In the distance, two soldiers were bravely crossing the chunks of cracked ice, headed toward the plane.

"We can help your friend," the ascetic young German said. "Tell us why you are here and we will take him to the medic. It is eight o'clock . . . we can have him there in less than an hour."

"My name is Robert F. Kane, Captain, Royal Air Force, serial number—"

The *oberleutnant* slapped him with the back of his

hand. "Idiot! Don't you realize that you will tell us, eventually, everything we wish to know?"

Kane's eyes grew hard. "My name is Robert F. Kane, Captain, Royal—"

The officer slapped him again, then drew the ten-inch dagger that hung from the belt beneath his greatcoat. The pilot rose defiantly, but the *oberleutnant* pushed him back down. The German grabbed a handful of the copilot's blood-matted hair and, raising his head, put the side of the blade to his throat.

"I'll ask you one more time, *Herr Kapitan*. Why are you here?"

Kane looked from the officer to his friend. He suffered a moment of doubt; he'd been with Abel for years. Yet he knew how scarce supplies were on the Russian front, and suspected they'd be executed in any case. There was no sense jeopardizing the mission. Swallowing hard, he said, "My name is Robert F. Kane, Captain—"

Teeth clenched, the officer dragged the dagger across Abel's flesh. Blood spilled out in a sheet, flooding onto the snow. The *oberleutnant* stepped over the corpse and towered over Kane.

"One last time, *Englander*. Why are you here?"

Kane looked at his dead friend. "Afraid we didn't do too well on this one," he said softly. Drawing a deep breath, he repeated his name and rank once again. Snarling, the officer kicked him onto his back and drove the dagger through the base of his neck.

A few minutes later, the two men from the plane returned with an armful of charts. On one, a small village had been circled.

"Uryupinsk?" the *oberleutnant* said under his breath. Puzzled, he summoned the *funkmeister* in charge of the field radio and contacted headquarters in Frolovo.

The ride was bumpy, but the truck held up as Livingston and his men traveled along the wide, dirt road that

ran southeast from the city. It was the major road leading
to Stalingrad, and though it was possible they might encounter German forces along the way, that was a chance
they'd have to take. Not only was this the quickest route,
but also, according to the map, the road would take them
through several small towns where they might be able to
purchase gasoline—assuming the Germans had left any
behind. Livingston wasn't optimistic. The first two towns
through which they passed had no gas, and the last had
no people at all, just fire-gutted buildings and fresh
graves. That was the price, Alexandre had said, of refusing to provide supplies to the enemy.

By late morning, Livingston was beginning to experience a vague sense of dispiritedness—largely, he felt,
because they hadn't yet found the B-17. As the fuel gauge
edged toward empty, Livingston would have welcomed
Captain Kane's optimism.

The men rotated every hour, with someone else taking
the passenger seat; having demonstrated in Algiers that
he was the best driver on the team, Colon remained behind the wheel.

It was Livingston, Lambert, and Weyers who were in
the back when, shortly after eleven o'clock, a German
cavalry unit came toward them from over a rise. The
soldiers in the front were pointing broadly in their direction.

Livingston counted the men as they neared. There were
fourteen in all, and they were approaching at a gallop—
obviously with a destination in mind. Quite possibly, it
had nothing to do with them. Then again . . .

He quickly thought it through. Maybe someone had
seen them in Uryupinsk or one of the other villages.
Maybe someone in Riga had guessed where they were
headed. Maybe the B-17 had come down smack in the
middle of General Paulus's camp.

Weyers stuck his gloved hands under his armpits to try

to warm them. "They look like they mean to have a
chat, Lieutenant. What do we tell them?"

Livingston looked around. There was an open field to
one side, and a wide stream to the other.

Nowhere to run.

Livingston said, "We haven't got papers, permits, or
a story that'll make us sound even remotely legit." He
leaned in through the shattered back window. "Private
Colon—if they stop, tear through them."

A smile touched the soldier's lips.

Weyers drove a fist into his palm. "That's *my* kind of
social intercourse."

"Lieutenant," Ogan said, "you realize that if we hit
any of the animals flush-on, it could crush us."

"I'm aware of that. But if we don't panic them, and
one of those men gets to his submachine gun, it'll do a
lot more damage."

Livingston and the others unpocketed their pistols,
then watched tensely as the troops neared. The nearest
inhabited village was roughly twenty kilometers behind
them. The lieutenant realized that there was no way these
soldiers were galloping toward it; the horses would never
last. The Germans were coming for them, a conviction
underscored when, still two hundred meters away, the
approaching *unterwachtmeister* held up his hand.

"It's us, all right," Lambert said.

Livingston lay on his belly between the men, facing
back. "You two take the flanks, I'll cover the rear. Colon! If we manage to break through, keep us in range.
We can't afford to leave any of them alive to report
ahead."

The private threw him a two-fingered salute, then
shifted into first. He pressed down on the gas and the
truck surged ahead.

There was a long moment when the cavalrymen
seemed frozen. Then, just before impact, the sergeant
reined his horse to the side. The others followed and the

truck sped through, half of the soldiers on either side falling in the first volley. But one soldier held his ground, tightly reining the horse with one hand, while firing at Colon with the other. The private ducked and the truck flew against the animal, which had reared in panic. The horse pirouetted, throwing the cavalryman through the broken windshield. The car hit the animal and swerved, skidding down the incline, spinning, and ending up sitting backward in the icy stream.

Livingston was sprawled in the back of the truck, though he'd lost his gun. He saw Weyers in the river, on his knees and shaking his head, but he couldn't see Lambert. Nor was there any time to search. There were shouts from the road as the *unterwachtmeister* tried to regroup his men; he heard someone moving in the cab but didn't know if it was one of his men or the soldier. The answer came in the form of a muffled gunshot, after which Colon sat up.

"Goddamn Kraut ball-buster!"

"How's Ogan?" Livingston asked.

The passenger's door opened and the Englishman slid out. "I'm all right." Suddenly, he bolted upright. "Christ! *Lambert!*"

Livingston looked over as Ogan rushed up the gentle incline. He saw the Frenchman lying unconscious beside the road, a clear target for the Germans who were dismounting and taking up positions on the opposite side.

"Weyers—Colon—cover him!"

Colon aimed through the windshield, while Weyers scrambled along the riverbank, swearing and trying to find his weapon. Spotting his own gun lying halfway up the slope, Livingston ran over and scooped it up. Then he lay flat behind a small boulder.

Several of the Germans opened fire, and Ogan dropped to his belly. They shot wide of Lambert; they obviously wanted him alive, to draw the others out.

The guns fell silent. Despite the crisp coursing of the

stream and the low idling of the truck, there was an eerie
silence.

"Give yourselves up!" one of the Germans shouted.
"There is nowhere you can go!"

Livingston looked back. Weyers had given up searching for his gun, was standing still, his chin resting in his
hand; Colon continued to lean through the windshield,
stiff as a statue. Suddenly, the South African began pitch-
ing pebbles at the cabin. Colon turned angrily.

Weyers put up a finger to his lips, then pointed from
the gas tank of the truck to the road. He threw his hands
apart, indicating an explosion.

Colon smiled and looked at Livingston, who nodded.
Colon reached into his pocket and flipped a box of
matches to Weyers, who had already opened the gas tank
and stuffed a handkerchief in. Watching them, Livingston hoped—prayed—that they didn't hurt all the horses.
The lieutenant motioned for Ogan to wait where he was,
then dug his toes into the soft bank: He'd have to be
ready to bolt the instant the truck was out of the gully.

Weyers signaled to Colon, who had moved behind the
wheel. When the private gave him the okay, Weyers ignited the fabric and put his shoulder to the truck. When
Colon hit the gas, Weyers gave the vehicle a hefty push.

Mud pelted him, but the South African kept shoving
hard and suddenly the truck was free, shooting up the
incline and onto the road. Inside, realizing that the enemy would have a shot at him if he left by one of the
doors, Colon turned, squeezed through the rear windshield, and shot across the back of the truck; he jumped
just as flame and shrapnel sprayed across the road.

The moment the truck blew up, Livingston ran ahead,
followed by Ogan. The roar of the explosion drowned
out the cries of the horses and men; it also did most of
the dirty work. None of the Germans was moving, and
many of the horses also had been killed.

Livingston looked across the field, breathed easier

when he saw that there were at least seven animals left. Most had fled; by a stroke of luck, one was held back by his dead rider. The man's boot was stuck in the stirrup and the horse was running in a tight circle, trying unsuccessfully to dislodge him. Ogan hurried over and snatched the reins. Pulling the dead man free, he mounted up and rode after the other horses. Livingston checked on the Germans while Weyers tended to Lambert.

Colon joined the lieutenant. "What's the story, sir?"

"All but two of them are dead."

"Want me to put 'em on ice?"

Livingston shook his head. "I need you to give Ken a hand."

Colon's eyes narrowed. "Are we going to *leave* them alive—sir?"

"The horses are your only concern, Private."

"Sir, with all due respect, may I remind you that it's quite possible these men will be found?"

"That's very likely. But what will they tell anyone? That we got away? German command will realize that anyway, when these men fail to report back. Now go help Ogan with the horses, Colon. We're wasting time."

Saluting perfunctorily, Colon ran to the field while Livingston took the IDs from the dead *unterwachtmeister* and four other men. He blindfolded the two who survived, and lashed them to a dead horse. He then found men whose uniforms would fit. Stripping the bodies, he changed and brought clothes to Weyers and Lambert. The Frenchman was sitting on the ground, rubbing the back of his head and scanning the carnage with pain-racked eyes.

"How is he, Wings?"

"Baffled, as usual."

Lambert looked back. "I won't even kick your balls for that remark. Whatever happened here, I like what I see, I'm alive to see it, and that's all that matters."

Weyers grinned. "Is it? Well, try these knickers on for size. We're going to have to make the rest of the journey on horseback."

Lambert's anguished eyes turned to Livingston. *"Vraiment?"*

The lieutenant nodded.

"With saddles?"

Livingston nodded again.

Lambert sighed. "Then it's not so bad. I'll be sore, but at least only the mount will be gelded."

After complimenting Weyers on his resourceful use of the truck, Livingston headed toward the stream, where one of the horses had doubled back and was drinking.

Livingston shook his head. If, in Uryupinsk, someone had told him that they'd be members of the German *kavallerie* before noon, he'd have told them they were crazy. But Force Five luck had held true, and for the second time in one day, nothing had gone as planned. He hoped that would change when they got to Stalingrad. If they did anything to the toxic gas but sink it straight to the bottom of the Volga, it would be the end of the city . . . and of Force Five.

Chapter Five

The horses were less efficient and far less comfortable than the truck.

In the truck, the men knew they'd get inside the relatively warm cabin every so often. Now there was nothing but a long day's travel into the bitter wind. When it came pounding off the plain, it was oppressive, causing the men to stop and turn sideways to avoid its full, frigid fury.

The horses also had to be rested and fed. No one in any of the villages protested when the soldiers commandeered meals for themselves and feed for the horses. However, all were downright amazed when, after they were brought to them, the German cavalrymen paid for them.

As they rode, Livingston was struck by the utter desolation of the countryside. Each village was more or less a self-contained society, only vaguely aware of towns up or down the road. Most of the people still got about on carts and horses, which explained the lack of good roads and the underdevelopment of the vast stretches of hills and plains between the towns. He mused that if the efforts being applied to the war had been turned to nurturing the Russian land and people, they'd be a most formidable nation.

By nightfall, as the weatherbeaten markers announcing Stalingrad dropped from triple to double digits, the villages became larger—and the German presence in most became pronounced. After a brush with a group of drunken soldiers outside of Anateka—Lambert sent them on their way with a pack of cigarettes—it became imperative to avoid the main road. However, the terrain proved so uneven that they had no choice but to abandon the horses and go the rest of the way on foot. They stripped off the saddles, weighted them with stones, cracked the ice of a small pond, and sunk them; they left the animals there as well. If the unbranded horses were discovered, it was unlikely they'd be traced to the missing unit.

It was well after eight o'clock when the men finally sat down beneath a rock ledge to get their bearings.

"That last village was Elistalovsky," Livingston said, consulting Mikhail's map. "That means we have to make our way around Stalingrad, get to the Volga, cross it, and hope that one of our contacts is still there."

"Ford the Volga without a boat." Lambert snickered. "We'd stand a better chance contacting General Paulus and offering to play poker for the city."

Weyers brayed, "With your luck, we'd lose the city *and* our shirts."

"Lieutenant," Colon said, "I'm concerned about what we do if the Russkies *ain't* waitin' for us."

"Then we just follow the river. Eventually, the German convoy will turn up."

"And what'll we use to sink it?"

"We'll have to find a way to get on board, punch a hole with explosives, or start a fire."

"What about Stalingrad?" Weyers asked. "We'll have to pass through German checkpoints."

Ogan answered, "The Russians usually try to sneak supplies into the city at night. We can probably pass as a patrol trying to keep them out."

"Bien!" Lambert said. "We get past the Jerries and get shot by the Reds."

"The Russians won't shoot," Ogan said. "The Germans are low on supplies as well. The Russians won't risk losing a fight and having their goods captured."

Weyers went off to urinate, muttering that no one ever lost his life by being prepared for a Russian, Czech, or Pole to do the *wrong* thing.

Deciding not to advance until after midnight, the men took advantage of their relative security to sleep. At 1 A.M., cold but rested, they moved through the fringes of the city.

The suburbs had fallen months before. The inhabitants had abandoned their burned-out homes, farms, and shops, and the Germans had pressed on to the city. Only when the men reached a bluff that overlooked Stalingrad itself did they pause.

This wasn't a city under siege. From all appearances, it was a dead city. The skeletons of modern buildings and factories stood beside the ruins of log huts, all of them shrouded in black smoke. Even at night, dark plumes could be seen churning up from the rubble, blotting out the cold clouds and full moon.

Weyers said, "You tellin' me there's people alive inside that?"

"Like ants," Ogan said. "The resistance . . . the life is all underground."

They started walking down. On the outskirts of the city, they passed the burned-out shell of a ten-story grain elevator. According to reports, that had been the scene of the area's fiercest fighting, the forty defenders having held out for ten days before being overwhelmed by sheer force of numbers. As they passed in silence, the edifice

seemed to call out to them, the wind moaning, weeping,
as it whipped through shattered windows and the huge
holes in the walls.

The Germans held nine-tenths of the city. Those who
saw the five men in cavalry jackets paid them no attention; no one wanted to go over and question them, lose
his place around a campfire. Though it may have been a
trick of the firelight, it seemed to Livingston that the
soldiers he saw were unnaturally thin and haggard.

By 4 A.M., a day after landing on the farm, and a full
day behind schedule, the men reached the high bluffs
overlooking the Volga. The winds here were vicious and,
from what they could see by searchlights on the German
bank, the waters were less inviting still.

The river was approximately one hundred meters wide,
with broken reeds, mud, and bomb craters lining either
shore. The splintered pier where they were supposed to
have met their Russian contacts was roughly two hundred
meters upstream and apparently deserted.

"It's only an hour until sunrise," Livingston said.
"We'd better move quickly if we want to cross while it's
still dark."

From behind a shattered antiaircraft gun that had been
destroyed in the Luftwaffe raids of August, Lambert and
Ogan took turns scanning the pier for signs of one of the
partisans. Weyers was sent back a few hundred meters,
toward the city, to keep watch, while Livingston and Colon went north to try to find a boat, since the few bridges
that spanned the river had been destroyed, and they'd
freeze if they tried to swim across.

Just beyond a sharp bend in the river, with the sun
rising on the opposite shore, the two men noticed several
small wooden rowboats tied beneath a crumbling dock.
Judging from the surroundings—a gazebo, benches, a
maypole—the boats must have been used for summer
holiday rowing on the river. Fortunately, they were only
visible in the early morning when the sun slanted directly

along the river; otherwise, they were hidden in the shadow of the dock.

Livingston and Colon hurried back to gather their companions.

"*Ah, bonjour,*" Lambert said, lowering his gun as they approached.

"See anything, Rotter?"

"*Non.* The reeds haven't moved, the water hasn't rippled, and the moonlight hasn't caught a puff of frozen breath."

"We'll go over anyway," Livingston said. "They may have decided to give us twenty-four hours before—"

The crunch of pebbles underfoot came from behind, and the men dropped and spun. Gazing back, they saw Weyers hurrying toward them. He was waving them on.

"Get the hell out, a bloody army's on the way!"

Livingston jumped up. "Are they after us?"

"Yes—but it's too long to explain. Just *move out*!"

The men ran along the bluff, then down the slope toward the riverbank. Breathless, they rushed to the dock and untied two of the wide rowboats; Weyers hopped into Lambert's boat, Ogan and Livingston rowing the second, with Colon watching their rear. The instant they started across, the boats were drawn downriver by the rapid current.

"Shit and damn!" the Frenchman bellowed, as the boats immediately turned their bows toward the south. "We'll go two meters down for every meter we go across!"

"Then row *harder*!" Weyers roared.

As he leaned into his oar, the boat began to pinwheel, scooting past the second boat, toward the bend—and the Germans beyond.

"*Slow down*, Weyers! My arms are too short to keep up!"

The South African slowed as the Germans came into

view. The boat stopped spinning but was still being
drawn quickly downriver.

In the other boat, Livingston studied the Germans in
the glow of the rising sun. They were watching over
their Karabiners, waiting until he and his men were
within range of the powerful rifles. The men might look
gaunt, but the lieutenant had no doubt that their eye-
sight was fine. He'd never felt more like a sitting duck
in his life.

When they were just over halfway across the river,
Livingston heard the German *oberfeldwebel* give the order to fire. He was about to order the men to jump over-
board and use the boats for cover, when he heard
shots—not from Colon or from the Germans, but from
the dock on the eastern side of the river.

The spray from the Degtyarev DP1928 light machine
gun drove the enemy back. There was a commotion on
the German side as soldiers shouldered their stolen
Soviet-made PPsh submachine guns and fired at the ramshackle pier. Livingston yelled for his men to put their
backs into the rowing before they got caught in the cross
fire. Suddenly, the shooting on the Russian side stopped
and someone bolted from a clump of reeds. With both
hands, the newcomer grabbed the bow eye of Livingston's boat and waded backward, toward the shore. After
the men had scurried up the rocky embankment, the
young man motioned for them to continue running, then
returned to the river and pulled the other boat to shore.
A grateful Lambert jumped to safety and followed his
comrades, barely pausing when he stumbled over the frozen body of a dead dog, one of five lying on the rocks.

When they were all atop the embankment, the young
man reclaimed his Degtyarev and yelled, *"Edetyeh syu-
dah!"* Leaping over the dogs, he led the men into a deep
trench that had been dug in the field.

As they lay there, catching their breath in cold, painful
gulps, Livingston studied their benefactor. He was very

young, still a teenager, of medium height. Even though he wore several layers of clothing, the lieutenant could tell he was powerfully built. He moved with confidence and agility, and though he was soaked up to the waist, he seemed heedless of the cold. He wasn't shivering, nor did his expression show any discomfort. It was a stoic face, the cheekbones and nose Asiatic, with a stubble of beard. His eyes were brown but seemed even darker, set deep beneath heavy brows. He looked as hungry and tired as the Germans they'd seen, but there also seemed to be a touch of nobility about the man . . . in the way he carried his head, in the alertness of the eyes, in the clear disregard he had for his own safety or comfort.

When they had all recovered somewhat, the man pulled a sack from a niche hacked in the hard dirt wall. He withdrew a wheel of cheese and a canteen, offering them to the newcomers.

Livingston shook his head. "Thank you, *nyet*. Are you Vlasov?"

The Russian took a swig from the canteen. "*Da*. Andrei Vlasov. *Kutahnybody sidyesi gavoreet puh Ruskyeh?*"

Livingston looked at Ogan.

"He wants to know if any of us speaks Russian."

Livingston shook his head. "Just English, German, or French."

Andrei didn't seem pleased. He capped the canteen, then pointed across the river. "Leonid?"

Livingston shrugged, but Weyers said, "Bad news, chum, but the Nazis have your brother."

Livingston shot the corporal a look. "How do you know?"

"That's what I was yelling about before. While I was watching, the Jerries caught a Russian."

"Jerries?" Andrei said with alarm. "*Nyemetsky?*"

"*Da,*" Ogan said. "*Nyemetsky*—the Germans."

"He was coming from a tunnel when they grabbed

him," Weyers went on. "From what I gathered, they'd been looking for this tunnel which the Russians've been using to ferry supplies all the way from the goddamn cliffs into Stalingrad itself. When they saw this Leonid fellow, they followed him and found the tunnel. I gather there were still Russians inside, though, because he tried to stall the Jerries. He told them there were partisans on the river, waiting for him."

"But he couldn't have known that!" Livingston said.

"That's just it. He lied, not knowing we were there. The Germans took him away, then came to check, which is when I took off."

"Where's Leonid now?" Ogan asked.

"I have no idea."

Livingston regarded Andrei. "Where is Masha?"

Pulling a foot-long dagger from a sheath he wore at his waist, the now distraught young man scratched a diagram in the earth. "Stalingrad," he said, pointing to a mark. "Volga." He traced the course of the river. Then he drew four ovals. *"Yat,"* he said.

Ogan consulted his phrase book. "The poison . . . the boats with the poison."

"Da—boats," Andrei said, then crossed out two of the ovals. As the men watched, puzzled, he drew a second line, which roughly paralleled the course of the river and ended in Stalingrad. *"Poeezd,"* he said. "Masha."

Ogan sat back. *"Poeezd?"*

Andrei nodded heavily.

"What is it?" Livingston demanded.

"Christ Jesus," he said. "What he said is that the shipment has been split up—that two of the gas tanks are no longer with the convoy."

"Where the hell are they?"

"On a train," Ogan said gravely, "bound for the heart of the city."

"A two-pronged attack."

"So it would seem."   .

Pointing at the tracks he'd drawn, Andrei said, "Masha."

"She's gone ahead to reconnoiter," Livingston said.

Breathing deeply, in a clear effort to control his emotions, Andrei pointed toward the city and said, *"Kak mazhna skayeya. Zavod!"*

"He's saying something about a meeting," Ogan said, "a factory." He flipped through the pages, then said haltingly, *"Yah . . . upzhdal na payezd . . . samalyawt?"*

"Da! Da!"

"That's what it is," Ogan said. "We're supposed to rendezvous with Masha at a factory."

There was a lengthy silence, after which Lambert said, "A train. How the hell are we going to dump a trainload of gas?"

"Assuming we can even get close to it," Weyers said. "It's probably an armored train, and protected up the bum."

Andrei poked Weyers. "Leonid," he said, then sketched out a circle. "Stalingrad." He handed the knife to the South African, urged him to make a mark in the circle.

Weyers shook his head. "I don't know where they took him. *Nyet!*"

Andrei looked imploringly at Ogan. The Englishman managed to explain, after which the partisan snatched the knife and, in a fit of fury, drove it over and over into the side of the trench. The other men watched in silence until, his anger spent, the Russian slumped down.

"Remind me never to piss him off," Lambert said with a stiff smile.

After a moment, Livingston motioned for the men to

gather in a tight circle. Andrei remained where he was, his knees drawn up, face between them.

"Obviously, we're going to have to split up," the lieutenant said. "Each group will have less firepower, but at least it will be easier to come and go without being seen."

"The thing is," Ogan said, "if either group fails, the entire mission fails. The Germans will still have enough gas to cover the Russian strongholds."

"Unfortunately, there isn't enough time to hop from one site to the other."

"No argument. I'm just saying there's no room at all for error."

Weyers was looking at the Russian. "Y'know, I'll bet this bloke's been here since yesterday, still as a broken watch, waiting for us while his brother made supply runs into the city." The South African faced Livingston. "We owe him. We can't just leave Leonid to die."

Ogan said, "I sympathize, Corporal, but where do you expect to get the manpower?"

"All I need is one man. Me."

"No," Livingston said, "no one goes anywhere alone. But I like the idea for another reason. We'll divide into three groups. Ken—you and Andrei will try to get to Masha and the train. Weyers and Lambert, you two will meet the convoy. Colon and I will go in and try to find Leonid, then wait here. If one or the other of the shipments gets through, we can be a stopgap."

"I like it," Weyers said, and when no one had any objections, Ogan went over and explained the plan to Andrei. At first, the Russian protested, insisting that he wanted to rescue his own "*brat*." But Ogan convinced him that Livingston and Colon were well suited for the task, and besides, he needed the Russian to help him get to the train.

Andrei didn't seem to hear the last part. He was

busy staring at Colon. *"Italianski-Americanski?"* he asked.

Colon stared back. "Something wrong?"

The others watched tensely as Andrei reached into his pocket; he withdrew a watch and opened the lid, showed Colon a photograph. *"Atyets."*

"His father," Ogan explained, looking at the picture. He asked Andrei, "And who is the other gentleman?"

"Italianski-Americanski. Houdini."

Lambert said, "The guy wasn't Italian—his name was Weiss."

"When in Russia," Ogan said, "people become what the government favors. Houdini obviously toured here, and Andrei's father must have met him."

"Terrific," Colon said. "We're facing death, and I gotta listen to some guy's life story."

"I *believe,* Private, he's trying to pay you a compliment. Obviously, Houdini meant something to Andrei's father, and to Andrei."

"Oh. Like a hero, you mean."

"Possibly."

Colon's expression softened. "Well, in that case— great. Thank him. Tell him we're gonna do an escape trick that'll put Harry to shame."

Ogan translated as best he could, and the Russian eased visibly.

The town of Novocherkassk, where Andrei said the transfer had taken place, was just two hundred kilometers away. Both the train and the convoy would reach Stalingrad as early as that evening.

That left just over half a day to intercept them. And to capture the train, which was the only way they'd get the gas far enough from the city. They couldn't even worry about keeping it out of Russian hands. Keeping it out of Russian lungs, off Russian flesh, was a more pressing matter.

After consulting maps that were stored in an iron box in the trench, the three teams set out. As they stood on the field, well beyond the range of the German guns, Andrei embraced each of the men. And each man, including Colon, returned the gesture, warmly.

Chapter Six

Through Ogan, Andrei told Livingston and Colon to wait until six-thirty before going across. That was when the night guard was relieved on the western bank; there was always a gap of two or three minutes while the new-comers were briefed and settled in for the eight-hour shift.

The two would be crossing much higher on the river than they had earlier. Andrei gave them a rubber raft that was kept in the trench for their regular passages; it bore the name *Nevsky*, one of the Russian gunboats that had patroled the river before the German bombers destroyed them all.

Andrei had also given them a password: *"Sorahk."*

Forty.

The number of men and women who died defending the grain elevator. Since they were dressed in German uniforms, if they had to deal with any Russians in the city, it was the only word that would help them.

Ogan, Andrei, Lambert, and Weyers all set out to the east, turning south once they were behind the guns and out of the view of the Germans. At 6:15, Livingston and Colon headed for the river. With field glasses provided by Andrei, Livingston studied the cliffs. When the watch was changed, they rushed into the river.

This crossing was utterly uneventful. A year before, the Germans would never have been so sloppy as to leave such a gap in their guard. But the prospect of spending another winter in Russia had obviously taken its toll on morale. Escott had told him that 200,000 Germans had already died here, and that Stalingrad had been referred to, in one German communiqué, as the "mass grave of the Wehrmacht." Livingston suspected that the only reason they pursued the Russians so doggedly, still, was because they knew that victory was their only ticket home.

The men paddled across quickly, hid the raft beneath the pier in the holiday area, then hiked up the bluff.

They'd decided that the best tack would be to go to the tunnel. There would still be soldiers about, and with any luck, Livingston could use his adopted rank of *unterwachtmeister* to find out where Leonid had been taken.

Reaching the top of the cliff, they walked to where Weyers had been stationed. As they neared the foot of the dirt road, they saw at least thirty soldiers gathered around a hole. There was a tree stump lying behind it, a false top to the entrance of the tunnel.

As they descended, the lieutenant noticed a severe-looking *hauptfeldwebel* standing beside an aide. The regimental sergeant major was thumping the side of his boot with a dry tree branch, watching the proceedings from behind thick glasses. As a senior NCO, he outranked Livingston, who was posing as a junior NCO. So much for walking over and demanding the information.

Thinking quickly, Livingston stepped up to the NCO and stood at attention.

"Reporting as ordered!"

The sergeant major peered through the fat lenses. "As ordered?"

"Yes, *Hauptfeldwebel*. By *Rittmeister* Krebs."

The *hauptfeldwebel* tapped his cleft chin. "I have never heard of him."

"We are just up from the Caucuses, *Hauptfeldwebel*. We heard that volunteers were needed to enter the tunnel and flush out the enemy."

"And has the cavalry nothing better to do than back up my infantry?"

"*Nein, Hauptfeldwebel.* The *rittmeister* simply thought that if the infantry were needed in the city, we might be able to relieve them here." He moved closer, said knowingly, "Our unit doesn't go into action until the ships from the Fatherland arrive. He thought it might be useful to get this business over with quickly."

"I see." The slender man studied Livingston a moment longer, then pointed the branch toward the tunnel. "We already have volunteers inside. And we have men on the other end, inside an abandoned factory." He smiled mirthlessly. "I give those Russian *hunds* credit for having dug and operated this tunnel without our knowledge for nearly a year. However, the end is near."

"Are you certain the enemy won't take their own lives?"

The noncom eyed Livingston suspiciously. "You have not seen much action, have you, *Unterwachtmeister*?"

"Yes, *Hauptfeldwebel*—a good deal, in fact."

"Then how is it you do not know the Russian mind?"

Livingston frowned; mercifully, the NCO did not wait for an answer.

"As long as the Russians believe they can kill one of our men, they will not take their own lives. Only when we smoke them out with tear gas do they shoot themselves. At the moment, we are trying a new approach. We are rounding up several of the men and women we've captured. When they're here, we'll begin shooting them until the men inside surrender."

Livingston didn't have to look to know that Colon had tensed behind him. He didn't blame him, but the last time the private had torn loose, in Algiers—when they were trying to steal a motorcycle—they'd been lucky to get away with their lives. Livingston looked back at the tunnel. As he turned, he fired a cautioning glance at Colon, whose eyes were angry slits.

"Let me go in there, *Hauptfeldwebel*," Livingston said. "I think I can bring them out."

"How will you do that?"

"Earlier, we overheard some partisans use a password by the river. I can use that to lure them out."

"What was the password?"

"*Pavadze,*" he said, "a nickname they have for Stalin. I can fire several shots, give the Russians the password, and convince them that our soldiers are dead and they should come out. That way, you will have them *and* the prisoners you've already—"

Livingston's words were cut off as a big, noisy Opel Blitz truck arrived with the prisoners. There were eight men and six women, all tied one to the other by their hands, so they couldn't run. Livingston had no idea whether Leonid was among them.

"*Hauptfeldwebel,*" he said urgently, "will you let me try?"

"I commend your courage, but I think not. We can't spare the rations to keep prisoners anyway."

"And what of the Russians in the tunnel?"

"They'll die too, of course."

"What I mean is, the tunnel probably hasn't a single support. How long before one of the enemy realizes that all he needs to do is start shooting to bring the ceiling down? How many of *our* men will survive such a cave-in?"

The noncom eyed Livingston. "It's possible." He cupped a hand to his mouth. "Hans! Tell the men in the tunnel to withdraw! I'll be sending one of them back in with a message to relay to the *wurm-stichig* Russians."

Livingston was caught off guard. "*Hauptfeldwebel*, please, allow *me* to serve the Fatherland—"

"No. You're quite right about the tunnel, *Unterwachtmeister*, and I thank you for your help. But these men have earned the right to finish the job they started."

Livingston looked at Colon. There was no choice, now, but to fight for the lives of the Russian prisoners. Livingston unbuttoned his holster as he backed toward where the private was standing. His plan was to kill the men nearest him, then get to the truck and arm the Russians. But as Livingston approached, he heard footsteps behind him; he turned and saw Colon walking swiftly toward the tunnel.

It was too late to stop him and, swearing under his breath, Livingston had no choice but to wait and see what the private was going to do.

Lambert's thighs still ached from the horse, and now his feet hurt from traipsing across the hard ground. Worse, because he was walking briskly to keep up with Weyers, his chest and sides stung with every frigid breath. And to cap off the morning, as the pair passed through a village, the slate gray skies opened and began dumping snow. The temperature plunged.

"Do you think we should steal a horse and cart?" Lambert asked through his chattering teeth.

The South African shook his head. "We need to be mobile. Besides, in this weather, a cart and a horse . . ."

He didn't bother to finish the sentence. He just sneered up at the sky and shook his big head.

Lambert knew what Weyers meant. They'd get bogged down within minutes, or else the horse would freeze to death. There was no choice but to walk, and the only thing that kept him going was rage: anger that the Germans in the convoy were probably warm and comfortable in their death-boats.

The morning dragged as the snow fell without respite.

Visibility was less than a few meters; when the winds kicked in, the cold drew tears from their eyes, and their vision was blurred even further. Both men were forced to walk with their faces averted, to protect them from the battering winds.

They proceeded blindly. It wasn't until Lambert slipped on a patch of ice that they realized they were on a lake. As Weyers helped him up, the Frenchman happened to look to the side, then screamed for his companion to turn around.

Nearly flat on its back now, the snow-covered B-17 looked like a white dragon, its tail fin the head, its fuselage the long neck, its wings two immense legs. The men slogged toward the plane, Lambert slipping several times as the winds howled across the open expanse and literally knocked him down.

Reaching the aircraft, the men crawled up the fuselage and entered the hatch. They stepped down gingerly because lake water had frozen along the length of the plane's interior, making it extremely slippery.

Though it was still well below zero, being out of the wind caused Lambert to shudder with relief. He pulled the stiff scarf from his face, then began stamping the ice from his boots and trousers. He peered down the darkened fuselage.

"*Alors*, you're the aviation expert. Could they have walked away from this?"

"Quite possibly. There was no fire, and very little damage to the fuselage. Captain Kane did a hell of a job bringing her in. There's a man I want to buy a dinner."

"The question is, why didn't we see them? They were supposed to make for the pier."

"Maybe they took shelter in the village. Not everyone is stupid enough to travel during a blizzard."

The airplane creaked and bent slightly; a hairline crack appeared in the ice beneath them. Lambert looked out a window.

"True," the Frenchman said, "but I wonder." He walked ahead, into the upside-down cockpit, and lit a match. "*Regardez!* The maps are missing."

Weyers glanced toward where the navigator had been sitting. "Maybe he took them. Or they coulda sunk."

"*C'est possible.* Yet—if they were stolen, it would explain how we were found out in Uryupinsk. It may also be the reason the Germans split the shipment of gas. Perhaps they figured out what we were up to."

Weyers's massive shoulders dropped. "If that's the case, then they'll be expecting us on the river."

"At the very least."

"What do you mean?"

"I mean, if they've found the cavalry unit we took on—which by now they surely have—they'll also know how we're dressed."

"We won't even get *near* the boats."

Lambert stamped his feet to stay warm. "*Alors*, we're not going to give up. We'll just have to figure out a way around it."

Weyers sat heavily on the ice. "Sure. Maybe the Japanese have the right idea after all. You go in not planning to come out. Makes things a lot easier."

"Not Le Rodeur," Lambert said. "He plans to come out, and does. Never failed yet."

Warming, Lambert reached up and felt around in the nook behind the cylindrical panel light.

"What're you looking for?"

"Abel's cigarettes, but they're gone. The Huns were here all right."

"How do you know? Maybe Abel took them."

"*Non.* He told me that he only smoked when he flew." Raising his fists, Lambert cried, "I promise, *mes comarades*, the enemy will regret ever having set *eyes* on this aircraft . . . or on me."

"You have a plan?"

"A plan? I don't *need* a plan, Wings, I am Le Rodeur. I *always* find a way."

Weyers had unholstered his gun to check it over; he scowled. "I hope so, Rotter, because it's beginning to look like your wits and my fists are all we've got left. Take a look."

Weyers handed Lambert the pistol, and he examined it: The chamber had cracked, a combination of the cold and shoddy manufacture. He quickly checked his own weapon, which was intact, and exhaled loudly.

Weyers grinned. "Confidence isn't as good as a working Luger, is it?"

Lambert said nothing as he holstered the gun. He didn't have to. The sigh had said it all.

An hour after setting out, Ogan and Andrei reached a point nearly six kilometers north of the city, where the Volga narrowed sufficiently so that a person could wade across. It wasn't what Ogan wanted to do, but there was no alternative. As Andrei reminded him, they had to cross sooner or later. And it was better now, under cover of the sudden snow squall, than later. At least this way, they wouldn't be seen by anyone on the other side.

Andrei removed his coat, shoes, and socks, and instructed Ogan to do likewise. With a few words and gestures, the Russian indicated that, unlike before, when he had gone in only up to his waist, the river here would be well over that. Their coats would absorb the water and freeze when they came ashore, weighing them down, and making it impossible to move.

Reluctantly, the Englishman followed Andrei's lead, then waded in quickly.

How the Russians did it, regularly, was beyond the Englishman's comprehension. How they avoided frostbite and gangrene—how *anyone* did—was also a mystery. He had heard of Tibetans whose feet were so tough they

could walk barefoot across sharp rocks and ice; perhaps
the Russians had a similar resistance to cold.

Ogan, like the Germans, did not.

The water bit like thousands of tiny needles. He felt
the burning chill on his legs, feet, and waist; nearly as
bad were the wind and snow that lashed his upper torso
and face. The wet snow also collected quickly on his
coat, which he held over his head, causing it to double
in weight. Ogan was glad, at least, for the current that
pushed and threatened to knock them down; it gave them
something other than pain to concentrate on as they
crossed.

When they came ashore, his chest was numb, his legs
were on fire, and his head throbbed viciously from the
cold. He pulled on his coat and rubbed his arms hard as
they walked, well understanding just why the Germans
were bringing poison gas to Stalingrad rather than digging in for another winter.

They followed the river north, until the snow became
blinding. Afraid of falling into the deep-drifting snow,
they took shelter in an abandoned German tank; they left
the hatch open, lest it freeze shut, and kept out the
weather by stuffing the Russian's coat in the cupola.

Ogan was glad to be out of the storm, and assuaged
his guilt by telling himself that the train would also be
forced to stop. Andrei muttered that he hoped his sister
and brother were all right, then went ferreting about the
tank for stores. He found neither food nor drink, but
there was a working radio, and Ogan flicked it on. Despite the storm, they were able to pick up a broadcast
from Germany, a speech Hitler had made the night before, at a dinner party.

The Führer was saying, "There stands a certain town
that bears the name of Stalin himself. I wanted to take
the place, and, you know, we've done it. We've got it,
really, except for a few enemy positions still holding out.
Now people say, 'Why don't they finish the job more

quickly?' Well, I prefer to do the job with quite small assault groups. Time is of no consequence at all.''

Andrei recognized the voice, and asked Ogan what Hitler was saying. Using his book, Ogan translated the gist of the speech. When he was finished, the Russian spat, then shut his eyes and went to sleep.

Chapter Seven

There were four soldiers at the entrance to the tunnel, and Livingston watched as Colon walked over to them. The private didn't speak much German, but that didn't matter: Colon was not a man who relied on words to make a point.

The four soldiers paid him little attention as he approached. As Colon neared the group, Livingston looked about, trying to decide where to make his own stand.

He decided on the truck. There were just three Germans, and if Colon did what he anticipated, they would give him little trouble. Turning, he walked over, all the while watching Colon from the corner of his eye.

When the private reached the tunnel, he said something to a soldier who was smoking; Livingston assumed that he asked the man for a cigarette, for the man reached into his coat pocket. He also bought himself an extra heartbeat of life: Colon knew where *his* hands were, so he shot the other two before gunning down the smoker. He was in the tunnel and gone before anyone else realized who had fired or where.

At the first report, Livingston drew and shot the sergeant major through the forehead. Then he stepped up to the cab and killed the driver and another soldier. He spun. There were just three other men, standing with shovels and picks midway between the truck and the dirt road. The lieutenant shot two of them before his gun jammed; tossing it aside, he ran at the third man.

The soldier had a pick and, to Livingston's surprise, he threw it like an Olympic hammer. The head hit Livingston's chest and knocked him down; the next thing he knew, the soldier had dropped onto his chest with one knee, and was flailing at his face.

Though the German was at least ten years younger and twenty pounds heavier, his blows were stiff, their impact muted by the gloves and layers of clothing he was wearing. Livingston bucked and tried to roll over, but the German straddled him and pressed his forearm across the American's neck, cutting off his air.

Livingston wasn't able to pull off his own gloves, and the blows he threw were dull and ineffective. He cast desperately around for something to use as a weapon, and spotting a rock, he was unable to wrench it from the frozen soil. Then he saw the dagger hanging from the belt of the soldier's quilted over-trousers. Overcome with rage, wanting to lash out with his fists, the German had neglected it. It was an oversight that would cost him his life. Grabbing the hilt, Livingston pushed the blade up, through the man's chin.

Blood poured onto Livingston's hands and coat as the German sat up. Stunned, the soldier rose unsteadily and felt the knife handle with disbelief. Then his eyes rolled back into his head and he twisted, falling across Livingston. The American pushed him aside, then looked down.

The bastard wasn't dead. He was staring up, wheezing, pawing at his chin, trying to dislodge the knife. The blood in the wound bubbled with every breath.

Livingston reached down and pulled out the blade. There was no time to do anything for the man. Throwing the dagger to the Russian prisoner so they could free themselves, Livingston took a P.38 from a dead soldier, shot the wounded man, and ran to the tunnel.

Colon liked tight places.

As a child in Pittsburgh, he'd loved storm drains. Crawl spaces. Closets. Hiding under beds. There was something dangerous and exciting about a hole or a close space—no room for error. Here, neither he nor the enemy could turn and run. They had to fight it out.

He moved through the pitch-black tunnel by wriggling along on his forearms. Progress was slow, not only because of the way he was traveling, but also due to the tunnel itself. While building it, the Russians had encountered roots and rocks that they hadn't bothered to dislodge. They slowed his progress. They had also encountered two building foundations, which they simply went around. There was no way to see these changes coming; one first had to run into them. Fortunately, the floor itself was relatively smooth, worn flat by countless people having wormed their way through with crates and sacks. He felt a welling of pride for the Russians when he considered that supplies could only be pushed through the tunnel. Each passage had to take at least an hour in the dark—something that would have given even non-claustrophobics pause.

When he heard German voices coming from up ahead, Colon stopped and listened, trying to figure out how far away they were. But it was impossible to gauge because sounds reverberated through the tunnel. However, as he crept along, he continued listening, for it occurred to him that other tunnels might connect with this one, and there was no time for a wrong turn. Though it caused his neck to cramp, he kept his head erect, face forward, to make certain he didn't miss the glow of any lights the Germans might be using.

Because he hadn't heard any German voices behind him after the shooting, he assumed Livingston had managed to take the others by surprise. He admired the Lieutenant enormously but wished Livingston would save his attempts at persuasion and reasoning for when he had kids. Germans were for shooting on sight.

A glint of yellow light caught Colon's eye, and he stopped and listened. The Germans up ahead were whispering—from the few words he could make out, they were wondering why they hadn't heard anything else from the men outside.

Colon grinned wickedly. He enjoyed surprises. Unsheathing his dagger, he crawled ahead slowly.

As he entered the last long stretch of tunnel, one of the soldiers heard him. It was the soldier farthest from him; the German craned around slightly and shined the light around his comrades.

"Loben wir Gott!" the German said with relief.

Praise God your ass, Colon thought as he shielded his eyes with his free hand. *"Das licht!"* he complained, not even certain he'd said the right word. He must have; the other soldier apologized and turned the flashlight away, then began asking questions.

Colon didn't understand what the soldier was saying, nor did he care. As soon as he was beside the nearest of the men, he brought his right arm up along his side and plunged the knife through the man's open coat, into his heart. Squeezing past him before the others could react, he cut the next man's throat with a backward slash. Dousing the light, the last man crawled ahead.

Certain the German would be desperate enough to use his gun, Colon backed up and lay low, behind the two dead men. He pushed his fingers into his ears moments before a shot reverberated through the tunnel; it was followed by a scream as the sound shattered the soldier's eardrums. Colon waited several seconds. The ground was frozen sufficiently so that only a thin layer of dirt was dislodged by the shot. When the echoes died, Colon felt around for the flashlight. Switching it on, he pressed on through the dirt that hung suspended in the beam.

Less than three meters ahead, the German soldier was lying on his back, his arms across his face, his head rolling slowly from side to side. Colon put him from his misery by sliding the knife between his ribs, then snaked around the dead man. When he heard movement up ahead, he stopped and yelled along the tunnel.

"*Sorahk!*"

There was a heavy silence. After a few moments, he said, "Goddammit, yer pal *Andrei* sent me!"

There was more movement ahead, coming in his direction. Placing the flashlight on the ground, facing him, he lay on his belly with his palms turned toward the beams. The sound stopped and, suddenly, the flashlight seemed to float into the air. The beam played over and around him, settling briefly on the dead man.

"*Shtah vi khatityeh?*"

"I don't understand yer lingo. I only speak English . . . American."

"*Amerikanski?*"

"Yeah. Amerikansi. I killski Nazis." Colon pointed behind him. "*Nyet* Nazis. Coast clear."

The light was turned then, and illuminated the Russian. The wan, grizzled face nodded once, then motioned with its chin for Colon to follow.

"*Nyet,*" Colon said, "they're waitin' for ya at that end. *Nazis.*"

He pointed behind them. The Russian understood, and indicated for Colon to go back the way he'd come.

That was easier suggested than done. Colon quickly discovered that as difficult as it had been to move forward, it was much more difficult going backward. It was impossible to turn, and in order to move, he was forced to push with his hands and flop back, like a fish out of water. His arms quickly cramped, but there was no other way to negotiate the tunnel.

A half hour later he emerged with the two Russians in a raging snowstorm. Much to his surprise, Livingston was nowhere to be seen. After checking the dead Germans to make sure that none of the snow-covered forms was the lieutenant, he looked from the river to the city. Knowing the lieutenant and why they'd come, he turned and ran toward the city.

When the B-17 shuddered and sloped backward at an angle, Lambert and Weyers decided it was time to go.

The South African hurriedly finished etching the names of the B-17 crew members in the ice, then joined Lambert at the hatch on the top of the aircraft.

It was nearly ten. They'd been there an hour, and the storm had abated somewhat. They surveyed the layer of snow that covered the lake. The drooping plane had caused a weblike pattern of cracks that reached nearly to the shore; they had no idea how badly the ice itself may have split.

"What do you think?" Lambert asked.

"Does it matter? We've got to go."

Lambert went first, sliding down the fuselage and then holding out his arms for balance. When the ice held, Weyers joined him, and they began their slow, cautious trek toward the shore. Only a few slabs of ice had broken off from the rest and, although several spots were unsteady, they crossed the lake with no problem.

As they were about to enter the woods, Lambert suddenly stopped.

"What's wrong?"

The Frenchman eyed a high pile of snow for several seconds more, then went over and started brushing it off.

"It's a pile of rocks," Weyers grunted.

"*Non,*" Lambert said. "It's a grave."

"Impossible. The Germans ship their dead home, and the Russians bring them to their families. Anyway, it's too large for a grave."

Lambert was unconvinced, and began removing the topmost stones. A sick feeling welled in his gut, and he began pulling the rocks away more quickly. As he did so, he began to pant—not from exertion, but from anger.

"Say, mate, what the bloody hell is *wrong* with you?"

Lambert didn't answer. He pushed over a large slab, then stood back. His entire body trembled with fury as he stared down. Stared at the corpses of the pilot and copilot.

There was crystallized blood on their white flesh, and their feet and hands were bare. Someone had taken their shoes and gloves.

Weyers gazed openmouthed at the bodies. "The Jerry scum. They . . . *executed* them!"

Lambert regarded the men for a long moment. Then, slowly, he began to cover the grave. Weyers helped him.

They were nearly finished before Lambert spoke. "Whoever killed them may still be in the vicinity."

"Probably a patrol—a small outpost guarding this section of the river. The Jerries haven't that many men to spare this far from the city."

"However many there are, they'll be made to answer for what they've done."

Weyers regarded Lambert through the fast-fading storm. "Are you sure that's the right thing, Rotter? Risking our lives when we should be concentrating on that shipment?"

Lambert stood back and stared at the grave. "I'm sure."

The South African turned. Through the trees, he could just see the snowy slopes that led to the bluffs overlooking the Volga. "Well, the convoy'll be coming this way eventually. I suppose it doesn't matter where we meet it."

Uncharacteristically silent, Lambert made a cross from fallen branches and jammed it into the stones. Then he led the way southwest, to the cliffs. When they reached the top, they stopped to study the riverbank. There, Lambert saw what he'd hoped to find.

Smoke, rising from roughly a half kilometer downriver.

A bunker.

His eyes narrow, mouth uncharacteristically mean, Lambert moved quickly across the snow-covered expanse toward the German position.

After Ogan and Andrei had warmed slightly, he asked Andrei why it was necessary to go north to intercept a train that was coming from the south. Switching on a small, battery-powered instrument light, the Russian found a pencil and pad and began sketching a map of the trains.

Although the tracks paralleled the river in the south, they went wide around the city and came in from the north. Andrei explained that a quarter century before, when the system was built, it was the only way the line could be constructed without disturbing the city. Moreover, fishermen who plied the waters near the city had complained that, if the tracks ran by the river, the noise of the trains would frighten away the fish. The circuitous route also allowed farms in the north to use the trains to ship crops into the city—though few did because of the expense.

The German train would have to travel southward for approximately four kilometers before entering the terminal—a straight run through largely open fields. Somewhere along that stretch was where they'd have to attack. Asked what made him certain the Germans would not unload the gas before that, Andrei replied that only the terminal yard had the cranes and other equipment they'd need.

When the storm let up, the men pushed the stiffened coat from the opening. They had to struggle to dislodge it, working their hands around the sides, smacking off the snow, and finally pulling it in. Andrei bent and cracked the garment, then forced his arms through the frozen sleeves.

Suddenly, his head cocked like that of a wary deer. He pressed a finger to his lips and sat stone-still. Ogan listened.

Now the Englishman heard them too. Voices. German voices. Most likely a patrol that had also been waiting out the storm.

Andrei snapped off the light and buried his face in his coat, motioning for Ogan to do likewise. The Englishman understood. Rising from the turret, their frosty breath might well be spotted by the Germans.

The voices grew louder.

"—was Gerhardt's tank. The cannon was sabotaged, so they just left it."

The soldiers fell silent; Ogan could hear their heavy breathing, the crunch of boots on the fresh snow.

Then the crunching stopped.

"Look, there, at the canopy," someone said.

"Marks," said another. "They look like scratches."

"Animals that took shelter perhaps? Squirrels?"

"If so, we have dinner."

The coat! Ogan thought. *It had disturbed the snow!*

The crunching and the voices came closer. "Wouldn't it be nice if it were a pheasant seeking shelter?"

"With our luck, it will be a *peasant* who took shelter."

"*Wahrscheinlich!* I wonder how they taste!"

Andrei nudged Ogan, handed the Englishman his pistol. He motioned for him to put the gun to his chest. Ogan shook his head violently. There wasn't any way he'd kill the Russian.

Andrei also shook his head. Then he raised his hands, and Ogan understood: Andrei would pretend to be his prisoner.

Reluctantly, Ogan agreed and, turning his face toward the opening, yelled, *"Achtung! Mein kamerad!"*

He heard the distinctive sound of rifle bolts sliding into place. "Who's in there?"

"Trompeterreiter Wilhelm Keitel. I have a Russian prisoner with me. We came in to wait out the storm!"

Ogan heard several sets of feet headed toward the tank. Two ruddy faces peered in and seemed satisfied with what they saw; they pulled Andrei out, then helped Ogan from the tank.

Ogan stood on stiff legs as the squad *oberwachtmeister* came over. The gaunt NCO wore a sparse beard and an unfriendly expression.

"Well," he said, "a hero and his captive. Explain yourself, *Trompeterreiter."*

Thinking quickly, Ogan said that his own company had been ambushed several kilometers to the north, and that he was the only survivor. He said he had managed to capture one of the Russians, and was bringing him in for questioning. The *oberwachtmeister* examined Ogan's papers, then looked the Englishman over.

"A hero," he said, "and a well-fed one at that. What did you have to eat, *Trompeterreiter*?"

"Sir, we killed and ate our horses. There was nothing to feed them, and they would have died anyway. We simply ceased being a cavalry unit and became infantry."

For a long moment, the NCO's face revealed nothing of what he was thinking. Then, suddenly, he broke into a broad smile.

"Very resourceful, Keitel. You will come with us, then, and will remain infantry. Ritzenthaler, Eichermann—take the prisoner."

Ogan watched as Andrei was pulled from the tank and pushed ahead. He resisted the urge to gun the men down. There were ten of them, plus the squad leader. Even if Andrei had a gun, it would be difficult to come out on top.

The squad marched through the snow, Ogan convivially sharing stories with the men as Andrei was repeatedly shoved into the snow and kicked by the soldiers who held him at riflepoint. For once, Ogan found himself wishing that Private Colon was there, and offered up a silent prayer.

As they passed the holiday area by the river, and turned to go up the dirt road that led to the city, Ogan's eyes suddenly went wide.

If there was a God, he thought, He had a curious flair for the dramatic. . . .

Chapter Eight

Upon reaching the mouth of the tunnel, Livingston heard a gunshot from deep inside. If it had dislodged any of the tunnel roof, Colon's retreat might be blocked, leaving them no choice but to continue ahead—right into the arms of the soldiers waiting at the opposite end. Rounding up a man and three of the fittest women from among the Russian prisoners, he communicated to them that he was going to the other side of the tunnel, and could use their help. They agreed without hesitation and, taking guns from the dead soldiers, the four Russians led the way.

The trip to the factory was uneventful, though Livingston noticed two packs of emaciated dogs running through the snow toward the river. He remembered the dead animals he'd seen on the other side, and presumed the dogs deserted the city whenever they ran out of food. If the animals found Stalingrad uninhabitable, he couldn't imagine how the Russians survived.

The group entered a wide, deserted square dominated by a larger-than-life-size statue of six children dancing in a circle. It was an incongruous sight amid all the carnage—charred wood jutting through the snow, bricks, and crumbled walls of buildings scattered around the square, twisted pipes and broken wire lying about. And yet, Livingston told himself, the statue was probably a sight that gave the defenders hope. Russian children had played here once before; they would play here again.

After crossing the square, Livingston followed the Russians down a broad avenue toward a towering gray tractor factory. As they neared, they slowed and walked quietly toward an open door. Livingston drew his pistol and entered.

He was inside a small room, a machine shop. Two young soldiers were squatting beside a lathe which, apparently, had been used to conceal the opening. Livingston approached and they looked up. When he was just a few steps away, he ordered them to raise their hands.

"What have we done, *Rittmeister?*"

"Just do as you're told," Livingston said, then summoned the Russians. The soldiers stared in stunned silence until the lieutenant had them bound to the lathe with electrical cord. One of them started shouting obscenities, calling Livingston a traitor, and was gagged; the other soldier looked frightened and said nothing.

Livingston bent over him.

"Early this morning, a man was captured at the other end of the tunnel, a young Russian named Leonid. Where is he?"

The youth swallowed hard. "They said they were going to question him and then take him to the gallery."

"Which gallery?"

"O–our *gallery.* Where things are . . . *shown* for the public."

Livingston felt a jolt. It couldn't be. It just couldn't be. He jammed his pistol in the holster; if he hadn't, he'd have used it.

"Where is this place?"

"It's—it's on the north side of the square."

Rushing outside, Livingston ran back toward the square. It probably hadn't been wise to leave the soldiers in the hands of the Russians, but at the moment that wasn't nearly as important as getting to Leonid before it was too late.

Passing the statue of the children, he turned down a small street on the northern side. He stopped short and stared at a sight he would never forget.

Seventeen men and six women hung naked from streetlights up and down both sides of the road. Around each of their necks was a cardboard sign that read, in both Russian and German, "We are partisans. We tried to kill German soldiers."

For several minutes, Livingston couldn't move. He gazed through the snow at the sadistic spectacle. The heels of several of the victims had been gnawed, probably by dogs leaping and nipping at them. But very little snow collected on them, meaning they were still warm enough to melt it.

The Germans must do this every day. Rise, eat, and execute prisoners.

His chest tight, Livingston walked along the street, looking up at each of the corpses. He felt neither the snow nor the wind, just the bile burning in his throat.

Yes, he thought, supplies were low. It was impractical to keep prisoners, other than the women who were kept for the soldiers, or the people who were used as bait, like the poor souls whom the *unterwachtmeister* had intended to execute. Livingston himself didn't know what he'd do with the two German soldiers at the factory. But this . . .

There was cruelty evident in the nakedness of the corpses. It was a final insult, to be stripped before they were hanged. He stopped below a young man who looked like Andrei. This had to be Leonid. The Germans obviously didn't spend much time questioning him. He'd been executed quickly because, in a day or two, it wouldn't matter what the Russians were planning or where they were hiding. In a day or two, they'd all be dead.

It occurred to Livingston, then, that that was why the
Germans wanted the men in the tunnel taken alive. They
were to be added to this gallery. Probably photographed,
their portraits sent back to the Führer.

As Livingston walked, he noticed a ladder propped
behind the box office of a movie theater. Opening it,
Livingston moved down the street, untying each of the
bodies. His fingers were numb, his eyes grew bleary from
the storm, but it didn't matter. Nothing mattered, save
for giving these tragic souls a final measure of dignity.

When he finally returned to the factory, he found Colon waiting for him.

"The Reds at the river told me where you went," he
said, then cocked a thumb at the two soldiers. "How
come these *organi* are still alive?"

Livingston walked over to the Germans. "That's a
damn good question." In German, he asked, "How in
God's name could you people *do* something like that?"

The soldier said nervously, "General P–Paulus said it
would be an—object lesson. The general s–said it would
cause the Russians to leave the city."

Livingston pulled out his gun. "Do you really believe
that *crap*? Has it deterred a single damn Russian?"

"I—I don't *know*."

"Did you put any of those people there yourself?"

"No—"

Livingston put the gun under the Germans' nose.

"*Yes!* Two or three—*please*! They said it would send
the enemy . . . a *message*!"

"And maybe it'll send a message to *your* countrymen
if I leave the two of you hanging outside with big holes
in your goddamn heads!"

"*Nein!* We had no choice!"

"You *had* a choice. What you don't have is *guts*."

The soldier said nothing more and tried not to shake.
He failed. Livingston saw tears in his eyes. The other
German was staring ahead, resigned to his fate.

Putting away the Luger, Livingston faced one of the Russians. He pointed toward the theater, to the captives, then made a shoveling motion.

"Take these bastards out to bury your people. Wait until tonight, if you have to, until it's clear." He pointed to the Germans, made a running motion with his fingers. "When they're finished, let them go."

"*Svabodni?*" a woman declared, turning an imaginary key.

"Yes. Free them."

The Russians were clearly unhappy. Livingston said, "You *must* do it. Let them go back and tell the others that *you* are not animals. Make the general think about what *they've* become."

Colon said, "He'll care?"

Livingston turned slowly. "*I* care. After what I just saw, it matters what *we* do."

Though the Russians didn't understand his words, they seemed to grasp his meaning. After talking among themselves, they nodded.

The lieutenant faced the Germans. "Tell your general what the people here are made of. Tell him they don't need to resort to barbarism to keep their home."

There was a smugness, a glow in the bright blue eyes of the gagged soldier. A small, crescent scar on his left cheek rose slowly as he smiled beneath the gag. He obviously knew about the gas.

Livingston grabbed the man by his jacket. "Smile, you cocky bastard, but you and your comrades are in here for the long haul. I'm going to see to that *personally.*"

Releasing the man, Livingston stormed outside. Colon joined him, raising his collar against the storm.

"You should've plugged him, sir. He ain't worth getting your bowels in an uproar."

"That's all right, anger keeps me warm. Besides, I had to have my say."

"Frankly, sir, I liked your first idea best. We should've taken 'em out and hung 'em up headless. T'hell with moralizin'. *That* would've scared the crap outta the other Krauts."

After returning to the factory to bid the Russians farewell, the Americans set out.

"Ten o'clock," he snarled. "Even time moves like it's made of ice here."

To lessen the chance of being fired at by Russian snipers, Livingston followed the same route Ogan and Andrei had taken. However, he hadn't expected to run into them outside the city.

There was no chance to avoid the men: Livingston and Colon turned around a bluff just as the German squad came from the opposite direction.

When he saw Andrei with his hands raised at the head of the squad, and Ogan in the middle, beside the *oberwachtmeister*, Livingston felt like he had when they'd paddled across the river. They were trying to go one way, but the current kept taking them another.

None of the men acknowledged each other as they passed. However, as Livingston and Colon passed the squad leader, the German stopped.

"Those men's shoulder straps," the NCO said to Ogan. "I thought you were the only one who survived the battle."

Livingston glanced back, saw Ogan hesitate. *Deny us!* he screamed inside. *Tell him we must have stolen the damn uniforms!*

But Ogan said nothing, and the NCO drew his gun. "I had a feeling about you." He yelled to his men, "Take them *all!*"

Because their clothing was so bulky, Livingston and Colon had been carrying their rifles rather than wearing them slung over their shoulders. Thus, before Livingston or Colon could move, three Karabiners and two pistols were leveled at them. Slowly, they put their hands on their heads.

The *oberwachtmeister* looked at each of the men. "You're not even German!" He scowled at Colon.

"Thank God," Colon said in German, and spat. The butt of a rifle came down on the back of his neck and dropped him to his knees.

"Since you seem so anxious to be heard," said the squad leader, "we'll start with you. Who are you and why are you here?"

Colon raised his face and spit again. This time the *oberwachtmeister* kicked him, and growling, Colon scrambled to his feet. The rifle brought him down again, and one of the soldiers put his boot on Colon's neck.

"You goose-stepping blue-eyed *porco*—"

The NCO took the rifle from the soldier and clubbed Colon twice in the side of the face. Livingston ran at him and a soldier kicked him in the gut. The lieutenant doubled over.

"Pick him up," the *oberwachtmeister* ordered. Livingston was pulled to his feet. "We will go someplace it's warm, and maybe you'll think more clearly. If not— I assure you, it will be a most unpleasant day for you all."

He ordered Livingston to help Colon, and as the men were marched back into the city, toward the German-occupied sectors, Livingston saw something that made his heart sink even further.

A German company had moved in and surrounded the factory. Their footprints in the snow told the story. They had come to the tunnel, found the dead soldiers, and followed the tracks made by the Russians, Colon, and him.

The Russians had a few pistols. The Germans would have submachine guns. The Germans in the factory would be killed—if not by the Russians, then by their own peo-

ple—and so would the Russians. If only he hadn't told
them to stay . . .

In six years of fighting, Livingston had never experienced anything approaching the desolation he felt now.
His only hope was that Lambert and Weyers would stop
the boats, Masha would somehow stop the train, and
winter would finish what the invaders had started. . . .

Leaving the South African behind, Lambert went to
the bunker. Weyers watched as the wiry Frenchman
strode ahead, bent low so that his chest was nearly touching the snow. However, something to the right caught
Lambert's eye and, suddenly, he turned from his path
and headed toward the Volga. Creeping from the woods,
Weyers looked toward the river and saw two soldiers
standing at a pier, guarding several barrels of oil and a
pair of four-man motorized assault boats.

Weyers hurried ahead and joined his friend. When he
arrived, the Frenchman pointed to one man. Sneaking
up behind them, Lambert pushed that man into the river
and held his head underwater, while Weyers broke the
other man's neck.

That part was clean and simple. So was hiding their
bodies under the pier, using their belts to lash them to
the pilings. However, Weyers was surprised when Lambert kept both of their machine guns, one tucked under
each arm.

"What are you doing?"

"Carry over one of these barrels for me," Lambert
said. "Open it near the chimney, pour some in, and then
run *comme l'enfer.*"

"Run like hell?"

"Into the woods. And stay there."

Now Weyers began to worry. "Rotter, what are *you*
going to be doing?"

"Standing right here, making sure none of them gets
away."

"Gets away? Half the *shore's* going to vanish when this blows. *No one* will get out of there alive!"

"And if *one* man does? How do we know it wasn't *he* who killed our friends? Hurry, Wings, before one of them comes out to piss."

Muttering under his breath, Weyers tilted the great, black barrel onto an edge and began rolling it through the snow.

The chimney of the bunker had been hacked in the ledge, a pan-size hole from which gray smoke rose along with the distinctive smell of burning oak. Bringing the barrel up the hill and down onto the roof, Weyers used his pocketknife to punch two holes in the top of the barrel. Then, digging a small channel in the wet snow, he lay the container on its side. When the first of the oily liquid began oozing down the trough, Weyers ran from the bunker. Right to Lambert's side.

"*Un fou!* What are you doing?"

"Helping you make sure none of them gets away."

Both men dropped to their bellies. The seconds became minutes, and they began to wonder if something hadn't gone wrong.

"It occurs to me," Weyers said, "that if they're using the fire to cook, we're dead."

"*Oui.* And if it's soup, or *rotkohl*, they won't even *taste* the petrol."

There were voices behind the bunker. The snow had stopped, and the two men watched as a pair of soldiers came out for a smoke and fresh air.

Weyers said, "If they come around front, they'll see that the guards are missing."

"I know." Lambert reached into his pocket. "Cover me."

"Why?"

Without answering, Lambert ran toward the bunker. Weyers licked his lips as he stared down at the gunsight. The soldiers were standing just beyond the left wall of the bunker, staring up the hill, away from the river. He was glad, at least, that they were wearing their fur pile caps with the headdresses that covered their ears. It was unlikely they'd hear Lambert.

Just then, one of the men pointed down. They'd noticed Weyers's footprints. The South African wriggled his body back and forth, tried to get as low in the snow as possible. He continued to watch as the Frenchman, instead of attacking the men, grabbed the roof ledge in front of the bunker and pulled himself up. Weyers prayed the fuel didn't blow up *now*.

A match flared in Lambert's hand. He cupped his hand behind the flame, set a handkerchief on fire, and dropped it down the chimney. Then he spun and dove from the ledge.

There was a very small explosion as the oil dripping down the chimney ignited. The roof lifted up slightly with a muffled roar, then collapsed back down, snow and rock cascading inward, toward the heart of the blast. The barrel was among the last of the debris to fall, but fall was all it did. Snow from the ledge had extinguished the fire, and it failed to explode.

Weyers jumped to his feet and ran forward. He shot the two men who had been standing out back, then stopped to cover Lambert, who had stopped running. Men were coughing and helping others from the wreckage, and Lambert was gunning the men down as they emerged. Holding his own machine gun waist high, Weyers kept a sharp watch for anyone who wasn't killed by Lambert's fire; the South African didn't have to shoot again.

When there was no longer any movement or sound, the two men cautiously approached the bunker from opposite sides.

The carnage had been complete. A few bodies had been torn apart by the blast, but the bulk of the men—at least twenty of them—had been gunned down.

"Tres bien," Lambert said as he surveyed the damage. He poked among the dead men, seemed to be searching for something. Suddenly, a look of triumph crossed his features.

"Voilà!" He held up a pack of cigarettes. "They are Abel's! These pigs did the killing, all right. I feel very good about this—very good indeed."

Lambert lit one of the cigarettes, blew out smoke—and lost it as Weyers grabbed him and pulled him behind the tree. A heartbeat later, the ruins erupted in a massive fireball. The tree was sheared just above their heads, and other trees, nearer the blast, were uprooted entirely. It rained particles of the bunker and ground for nearly a minute.

When the dirt, rocks, snow, flesh, and pieces of uniform had settled, Lambert shook off the debris and stood.

"*Mon Dieu*, how did you know?"

"I saw black smoke, and figured the petrol drum was finally smoldering."

Lambert looked back toward the wreckage. "It's good that you did, *mon ami*. These bodies seem much thinner than before." Lambert began pacing then, suddenly lost in thought. "But you know, this has given me an idea about how to deal with the boats."

"Really?"

"Yes," Lambert headed toward the river. "Come with me, we have much to do before our friends arrive."

Chapter Nine

The four men were marched to a largely undamaged office building, which served as a field headquarters for the advance units of the Sixth Army. There, they were turned over to *Generalleutnant* Edmund von Horstenau, and taken to a boiler room in the basement. Beneath the glow of a single bare bulb, the men were stripped to the waist, their hands bound behind their backs, their legs tied together; their legs were also tied to iron hooks that had been set in the floor. A rope was loosely tied to each man's throat and hung down his back. Behind them stood a burly soldier who, apart from the *generalleutnant*, was the only other man in the room.

Horstenau paced the small concrete chamber, ignoring the occasional roar of the large, iron burner behind them. There was an ivory cigarette holder in one hand and a short length of hose in the other. He put the holder between his teeth.

"You three are English. Or American perhaps?" His dark eyes were like little cameras, growing wide and narrowing as he studied Livingston, Ogan, and Colon in turn. When he reached Andrei, the lieutenant general sneered. "We know what *you* are, Russian dirt. Do you understand me? Do you speak a civilized tongue, animal?'' Andrei said nothing and the officer looked at the other men. "I expect stubbornness from this mindless thing, who shall hang in any event. But I have no desire to hang you alongside him. Cooperate with me, and you will be sent to a prisoner-of-war-camp outside Leningrad. You will be cared for until the Reich is victorious.'' He approached Ogan, stared at him down his long, slender nose. "*You* are English. You have that . . . look. That air of righteousness." He tapped one of Ogan's fingers with the hose. "And I see you are married. Do you want to make your bride a widow?" He dragged the hose repeatedly along his chin, then along his groin. "Or we can arrange it so that she will have to turn to other men for satisfaction. Which will it be, English? Pain? Or will you tell me how many others were sent in with you, and where they are now?"

Ogan said nothing, and Horstenau smiled around his holder.

"As you wish. Hang for a lost cause." He walked over to Livingston. "And you? Will you talk or die?"

"My name is Livingston. Lieutenant. Serial number—"

The German brought the hose across Livingston's neck. He fell to his side, his teeth clenching as he landed on his shoulder.

The officer smiled. "You see? It's a simple but effective means of persuasion. The blow hurts, but not nearly as much as being unable to break your fall."

The officer nodded to the man in back, who came forward immediately, grabbed the rope attached to Livingston's neck, and pulled him to his feet.

The officer went to Colon. "You spit at the *oberwachtmeister*. Do you have the courage, now, to stand alone again—to be wiser than your comrades?"

"*Kussen* my butt," Colon replied.

The German frowned. "Butt?" he repeated the English. Then he smiled, clapped once. "*Butte!* I see."

The smile remained as he undid Colon's trousers. "Yes, I will be happy to oblige you."

The pants dropped to the floor, followed by Colon's shorts, and the officer stepped behind him. The hose slashed across him; Colon gasped and his legs trembled, but he didn't fall.

"Admirable. But before we are finished . . . *kissing*, you will scream. *And* you will talk."

Andrei and Ogan continued to stare ahead, but Livingston watched as the officer beat Colon. The private dropped to his knees after the third blow, and was pulled up by the noose; he fell again on the fourth blow, his face striking the ground and leaving a smear of blood when the big soldier yanked him to his feet. Livingston watched to keep his hate strong. If a miracle occurred and he had an opportunity to strike back, he didn't want to do what he'd done at the factory; he didn't want any feeling that was remotely human to get in his way.

The beating lasted for twelve blows. When it was finished, Colon somehow managed to climb to his knees, and then to his feet. His entire lower back and the upper part of his thighs were bloody and raw; there were deep gashes on his forehead and chin.

But he stood, and when the lieutenant general came around from behind, Colon stared flush into his eyes, spit blood at him, and wheezed, "Kiss it again, f–faggot."

Horstenau's eyes narrowed and widened furiously. Slapping Colon's jaw hard with the hose, he lifted his chin with a finger. "I will, young man, I promise. Right before we hang you in the gallery."

He stepped back from the men. "I will return in a half hour, *meine Herren*. Use that time to consider carefully what you will say then. If one of you tells me what I wish to know, all but the Russian will be spared. Otherwise, thirty-three minutes from now, you will all be hanging from lampposts, food for the dogs."

The Germans left, and as soon as the iron door shut, Colon fell to the ground, unconscious. Livingston lowered himself to his knees and backed toward him. The private's head was close enough so that he was able to reach his temple.

"His pulse is strong," the lieutenant said. "The guy's made of iron."

Ogan sat heavily, his legs folded under him. "That won't help when they take us outside. What do you suppose the 'gallery' is?"

Livingston told him, and when he was finished, the Englishman's features were dark. "From the people who brought you the Blitz, another innovation in the art of war."

"More innovative than you think," Livingston said. "When I cut the bodies down, I saw a generator at the other end of the street. Scarce as fuel is, the sons of bitches actually use the street lamps to light the bodies at night."

While he was speaking, Livingston stood and tried to wriggle his wrists free of the ropes.

"I tried that while our friend was whacking Colon," Ogan said. "They won't give."

Livingston stopped and looked around. "There's got to be *something* we can do!"

"We can always spoil his fun by hanging ourselves," Ogan said only half in jest, eyeing the noose around Livingston's neck.

Livingston looked from the Englishman to Colon. "You know, there may be something to that."

"What, suicide?"

"No. The ropes."

Livingston dropped down and backed over to Colon. He was able to reach the knot around his neck, and began to work on it."

"What are you going to do if you get it?"

"Loop it through the metal hook."

"And?"

"Pass one end to you, and one end to Andrei so the two of you can pull. Look, the damn things aren't cemented there, they're just hammered in. If I can get the hook free, I can come over and try to undo your hands."

Pulling frantically at the knot, Livingston was able to work a finger into one of the loops, and managed to undo the knot. He sat down, passed the rope through the iron hook, then maneuvered to each end in turn. With a small flick of his bound wrists, he passed one end to Ogan; Andrei, however, was too far.

"Never mind. I may be able to do it myself." Livingston reeled in the rope and grabbed it tightly behind him. "Ready?"

Ogan nodded, and leaning forward, both men pulled upward so the rope formed a V, with the hook in the center.

"No good," Livingston said, "there's too much slack."

"Let me see what I can do," Ogan said, sliding the rope through his own hook in order to gain some added tension. The men began pulling again; ironically, it was Ogan's hook that eventually gave.

"The weakest link," Ogan muttered as he hopped over to Livingston. Backing up so they were hand to hand, he began working on the lieutenant's wrists.

Moments later, Andrei was beside them, his hands free. Ogan and Livingston stared at him.

"What the hell did you do?" Ogan asked.

Andrei allowed himself a rare smile. He held up his forearms, made two fists. His wrists expanded to nearly twice their normal size.

"Slipped out," Livingston said. "Incredible."

"*Nyet* incredible," Andrei said as he stopped and began pulling the ropes from the lieutenant's feet. "Houdini."

Ogan and Andrei picked up Colon and lay beside the

burner, where it was relatively warm. Then Livingston
went to the door and examined the lock.

"I don't suppose you can handle this too, Andrei."

The Russian shook his head.

Ogan rubbed his bare arms. "It wouldn't matter, really, sir. We'll need clothes and arms if you plan to leave
the building. The only way we're going to get guns is
when the lieutenant general comes back."

Livingston nodded, and the three men went over to
the burner to stay warm. The lieutenant found a rag lying
over a pipe, and used it to clean Colon's wounds; then,
restless, he went and stood by the door. However, as he
waited for the Germans to return, what he heard was not
at all what he'd expected to hear.

Early in June 1941, as part of the ill-fated French Sixth
Army, Lambert had fought the Germans on the Seine.
The battle for France had been all but lost by then. Troops
had been surrendering all along the front, and the Ital-
ians had declared war against the French, joining the
German invasion.

Along with refugees from the Fourth and Seventh Armies, Lambert had formed a guerilla group that proved
effective for several weeks, harassing the southward-
moving Germans along their flanks. With the fall of
France, Lambert had joined de Gaulle's Free French
Forces in London, where he'd remained until he was re-
cruited by Force Five.

The defense of the Seine had been unmemorable,
largely because so many troops were ordered to retreat
rather than attempt a defense. The few companies like
his own that did make a stand had been quickly decimated and forced to scatter. However, Lambert had been
particularly troubled because, when there was still time
to mount an offense, his commander hadn't allowed him
to try a plan he'd worked out with several other Foreign
Legion veterans.

"We can *stop* them!" he'd told Captain de Chagney in his tent. "They won't bother to search the riverbed!"

The elderly officer had huffed, "You've only fought in the desert, Lambert. I won't trust the fate of twenty-two divisions to your plan!"

"What about the fate of *Paris*? If the enemy crosses here, the city will be theirs!"

But the captain had been too busy to listen, too busy loading his staff car with maps and reports. The city had fallen, and de Chagney, along with most of the ex-Foreign Legionnaires, had died when the surviving French troops were surrounded, divided, and gunned down outside of Chartres.

Lambert's plan had been simple, and he'd been aching to try it ever since: to place petrol tanks underwater and, when the German army was well into the river, shoot holes in the containers and set the fuel afire.

Not that the situation on the Volga was exactly the same. Though they could start a fire that would stop the ships, it might not sink them. In that case, each man would get on board one of the vessels by posing as survivors of the bunker blast. They'd found sticks of dynamite buried in a concrete-reinforced pit in the bunker; going below, they'd sink the ships using the explosives. Lambert calculated that one stick fore and one aft would be sufficient to drown each boat without rupturing the tanks.

"And if they don't believe there are still partisans in the woods?" Weyers asked. "If they think *we* started the fire?"

"Two men doing so much damage? *C'est absurde!* Trust me, Wings, nothing will go wrong."

"Trust you! The last time you said that was before we left for Algiers, when you were sure that bloke wouldn't find you with his wife. How close did he come to blowing your head off?"

"That was a fluke. On occasion—on very *rare* occasion—a beautiful woman will blind me. But never a Nazi. They are not only as unpleasant as rain, they are as predictable.''

Weyers still wasn't convinced, but as he had no other plan, he agreed to Lambert's proposal.

The first order of business was to collect pieces of wood from the bunker, then dry them using swatches of the dead men's uniforms. Fortunately, the outpost had been a typical field facility, and the men found sufficient remnants of wooden tables and chairs for the job. They lit a fire outside, staying close to it as the noon sun failed to make its presence felt. There was also, Lambert was glad to see, a powerful transmitter. When they were finished drying the wood, he found the twisted remains of its antenna, yanked off the wire, and began winding it around his arm.

"*Zut!* Only twenty meters' worth.''

Weyers held up a length of wire. "Here's more we can use.''

"That's another ten meters or so. We need at least forty for two separate lines.''

"There are hammocks. Can we knot them together—''

Lambert shook his head. "The colors are too light. Lookouts on the boats may see them.'' The men began lifting slabs of stone and wood. "Not even a length of clothesline, or nylons for the women. What kind of army do these people run anyway?''

"The kind with supply lines stretched thin as a Scot's shilling,'' Weyers said.

Lambert kicked a shattered chair, then stared out at the river as the winds caused eddies of snow to dance across the banks. "Well, we'll only be able to cover the middle of the river. We'll weight the ends of the wires with stones to hold them in place, then hide on opposite shores with a drum or two apiece. If the convoy tries to sneak around, we can dump oil in the gap before we go aboard.''

Weyers agreed, and bringing the materials to shore, they began knotting what Lambert dubbed "Le Maginot en Miniature"—though as Weyers was quick to point out, if it didn't stop the Germans any better than its big brother had in France, they and Stalingrad both would be finished.

Chapter Ten

There was shooting from somewhere outside the boiler room.

Livingston had placed his ear to the door, wincing as the cold burned his flesh. The gunfire was several blocks away, but Livingston liked the sound of it: not just Lugers and German 98ks, but Russian Sudarevs as well. When the Germans attacked the factory, the Russians must have counterattacked near here; he felt a welling of satisfaction at the courage and simplicity of the strategy.

Fired by the Russian assault, Livingston set Ogan and Andrei to the task of trying to dismantle the boiler. A worn, black brute of a tank, it had a pair of rusted iron pipes and a cross-pipe jutting H-like from the top. Ogan pulled the bent hook from the floor and began scraping at the joints where the center pipe was attached to the others; Andrei lashed one of the ropes around it and pulled each time Ogan scratched away. The quarter-meter-long pipe wouldn't be much of a weapon, but it might be something they could use to work off the hinges of the door.

It was a long shot, but that wasn't the point. Livingston didn't want his men sitting around. If the battle came this far, he wanted them to be on their feet, ready for action.

Andrei hadn't asked about his brother, and Livingston hadn't offered any information. Perhaps the Russian assumed Livingston hadn't learned anything. Perhaps he hoped to find him here. Perhaps he simply didn't want to have his worst fears confirmed.

Andrei continued tugging at the pipe. There was a groan. *"Predityeh!"* the Russian barked.

Ogan hurried over and continued scraping at the joint. "It's going to give! *Pull!*"

Livingston came over and grabbed the rope. He wrapped a length around his wrists and braced his heels against the boiler. He and Andrei pulled in unison, and the corroded iron snapped. Thin wisps of steam entered the room through the break, showing the feeble way the boiler had been warming the building. Ogan immediately climbed on top of the tank and put his shoulder to the bar. It bent up, he pulled it down, and he pushed it up again. The rusted iron gave easily, and Ogan handed the length of pipe to Livingston. Stomping down on one end, he flattened it, then used it like a crowbar to try to loosen the hinges.

As he pried at the bolts, he could hear the gunfire getting closer. There were muffled shouts: German voices from just outside the building. Then he heard Russian voices. They seemed a bit farther—

Footsteps and gunfire sounded on the stairwell, along with more German voices. The Germans were retreating! There was nothing downstairs but the boiler room. They were going to have to come in here for cover.

"Ogan! Andrei! Over here, quickly!"

The men abandoned the boiler as Livingston directed them to positions around the room. He gave Andrei the pipe and positioned him right beside the door. Colon, just regaining consciousness, was moved to safety behind the boiler, while Ogan crouched on the other side

of the door with a length of rope. After smashing the
light, Livingston squatted beside Andrei with the other
end of the rope.

The gunfire had reached the door. Keys clattered in
the lock. The door swung in.

Rifles and pistols firing, three Germans backed in.
They were unaware of the darkness and saw neither Andrei nor the rope Ogan and Livingston suddenly pulled
taut behind them, knee level. Andrei swung the pipe and
one soldier flew from the room, his skull shattered, while
the other two tumbled over the rope. One of them was
Horstenau.

Livingston jumped on the *generalleutnant* and Ogan
fell on his companion.

"Welcome back, you miserable sonofabitch," Livingston said through his teeth. He rose and snatched the
pipe from Andrei. "Here's a kiss *you'll* never forget!"

Livingston swung the pipe like a golf club; the German's head snapped viciously to the side. Ogan dispatched the other man with two blows square in his nose.
Then the prisoners rose and peered through the smoke
of the gunfire.

Four Russians stormed into the cellar, a tall, slender
woman in the lead. They took up positions behind a fil-
ing cabinet and the banister; when there was no return
fire from the boiler room, they rose slowly.

"Force Five?"

Before Livingston could answer, Andrei bolted through
the doorway. "Masha?"

The woman handed her submachine to one of the men
behind her. Running over, she embraced her brother
tightly.

"Andrei," she said softly.

After a moment, she stepped back and touched his
cheek. Unsmiling, she began speaking to him quietly.
Livingston heard Leonid's name mentioned; from An-

drei's darkening expression, he knew that she'd seen the bodies in the gallery.

When she was finished, Andrei turned and went to the corner beside the boiler.

Masha faced the others. Looking at her now, Livingston could see that she was considerably older than her brother, at least in her early thirties. She had dark eyes and long, black hair streaked with white dust. Her parka was old and ragged and also covered with powder.

"I am Masha Vlasov," she said in thickly accented English. "Are you Livingston?"

"I am. Thank you for coming."

"You are fortunate. We used the tunnel to get to the factory, where we hoped Andrei would be waiting with you. Those who were there had seen you led away, told us what happened." Her voice grew hard. "When the Nazis arrived, they volunteered to stay behind, draw the enemy to them, so we could come and get you."

Livingston looked down. "I wish I could thank them."

"You can, Livingston. Help me stop the train, and they will not have died needlessly." Her eyes softened slightly. "Tell me. Was it one of you who cut Leonid and the others down?"

Livingston said that he had done it, and Masha thanked him sincerely. "All is not black," she said. "There are, yet, those who have honor."

The other Russians introduced themselves. Sergei was a brute of a man who was nearly as wide as he was tall; Piotr was as gangly a man as Livingston had ever seen. But their eyes burned with purpose, and he felt good knowing what they were on his side. The Russians offered the men their coats, but, thanking them, Livingston said that their own German uniforms might serve them better.

While the three men recovered their clothes from a corner of the room, one of the Russians stripped the *generalleutnant* and gave his uniform to Andrei. At first, the young Russian refused to put it on; only after a few strong words from his sister did he relent.

As Livingston pulled on his coat, he asked Masha what the situation was with the train.

"It is not good. The Germans have stopped, for now, to repair a small section of track we destroyed well outside the city. But the cars are heavily armored, and there are soldiers on board the train—at least sixty. We did not have people or arms sufficient to take it."

"That means the boats are probably carrying a few companies as well."

"How many men did you send there?"

When Livingston told her, the woman's expression soured. "Two! What can two men do against a convoy?"

"Probably more than two dozen. All along, it was our plan to get on board *somehow*. An all-out attack against a convoy, speeding upriver, would have been useless."

Ogan came over. "Don't worry. They're extremely able men."

"Let's worry about the train," Livingston said. "How long until it gets moving again?"

"Tonight, perhaps. Very early."

"And how long until it reaches the terminal?"

"Tomorrow, I would guess. Early in the morning. The Germans will be moving slowly, to watch out for sabotage along the track."

"What's the terrain like in between?"

"Mostly flat. A few hills—and one bridge, just outside the city."

"How high?"

"Ten meters, maybe. But you can't blow it up. If any of the tanks fall from the bridge, they will certainly break."

"And if we attack the train outright," Ogan said, "they'll cut us down. Doesn't sound promising."

"No, it doesn't," Livingston agreed. He took the Karabiner from the unconscious *generalleutnant*. "But we'll worry about that after we've had a look at the train.'' He walked over to Colon, who was sitting with his back to the wall.

"You look like hell, Private."

"Feel like it too."

"Can you walk?"

With Livingston's help, he struggled to his feet. Wiping blood from his cheek, he went to get his clothes. "Show me a German, sir, and I'll *run* to plug a knife in him."

"Good man," Livingston said.

Dressed and armed, the makeshift unit left the cellar and cautiously made its way to the street. Gunfire could still be heard at the factory, and it took all of Livingston's self-control not to go and help the beleaguered Russians. The temptation clearly tore at Masha and her countrymen as well. However, they all understood that the survival of the city came first and, bent low and staying to deserted side streets, the group cautiously picked its way around the fighting, heading toward the northern end of the city, the terminal, and the tracks beyond.

"It figures," Weyers moaned. Only one of the two assault boats started, and they'd planned on having two to deploy the wire.

"Lousy German industry!" Lambert said. "Just make sure *this* one doesn't fail, or we'll have real problems."

While Weyers ran the engine, Lambert doffed his boots and three layers of socks and waded into the river. It was the only place where the rocks weren't frozen to the ground. After fetching an armful, he raced back to shore. Dropping the stones beside the boat, he held his bare feet over the smoking, rattling engine.

"I swear, monsieur, I would rather be in *hell* than in a place which has winter."

"Hey—if your plan doesn't work like you say, you may get your wish."

"It will work, Wings. Next time, I think I'll take myself a partner who doesn't *doubt* so much."

Weyers snorted. "Yeah, I can just see you and Colon. You'd kill each other inside of two minutes."

Satisfied with the engine, Weyers checked the fuel tank, swivel bracket, screws, and drive shaft of the motor, making sure they were free of ice. With one boat running smoothly, Weyers went to the other. The engine still wouldn't turn over, and he performed the same cleanup of ice and mud. When it still didn't start, he stood back.

"Is it beyond repair?" Lambert asked.

"I could search the rubble for tools, if you think that's how I should spend my time."

Lambert checked his watch. "The convoy will be here by two o'clock at the earliest. That only gives us three hours. It will be better, I think, if we concentrate on our preparations."

Weyers stepped into the boat and, after they had soaked the wood with oil, he chugged out into the river. The Frenchman lay one rock-weighted end of the line in the water, some fifteen meters from shore. As the South African motored across, Lambert fed the wire and wood into the river. The current bent it into a gentle arc, but the line held. They came to within twenty meters of the opposite shore before it played out.

Lambert put his face to the river and said gleefully, "We've *got* them, *mon ami. Regardez!* The waters on either side are too shallow for a corvette or frigate."

"That's fine, but what if they try to run the blockade?"

"They won't risk burning and sinking. And for all they know, there are partisans waiting to shoot them as they go through."

"But if they *do* run it?"

Lambert made a face. "Then we signal them to stop and take us aboard. While they're busy navigating through the fire, we'll give them a little water to think about.''

Weyers picked at a callus. ''I still say it's got as much chance of working as a fisherman in the Sahara.''

''Be *optimiste*! If nothing else, we'll be warm before we die.''

Weyers frowned as they turned back to collect the oil drums. There were nine in all: They put four along the eastern side of the river, where Lambert would be stationed, and five on the far side, where Weyers would be. They hid them all behind mounds of snow, and punctured the tops, just to be ready.

The men were finished just after one o'clock. Lambert left Weyers on the western shore, with instructions to light the line as soon as the convoy was in sight. The ships would stop—and Lambert, waiting downriver in the boat, would deploy the second line behind them and set it ablaze. The men would then dump the remaining oil and set it on fire, after which Lambert would collect Weyers. If the convoy didn't go down, they'd go on board.

It was nearly three o'clock when Weyers saw lights far down the river. For over two hours, he'd sat on the ground, feeling like Lambert as he thought of nothing but the cold, each minute passing with awful, numbing slowness. He wished he could light the dynamite, watch it explode, just to have something to do. The lights were a godsend, and the instant he saw them, he jumped to his feet.

Grabbing the box of matches in his coat pocket, he headed to the bank, crouched behind a rock, and watched the convoy's progress. A horn sounded from the lead boat: two blasts, then silence. The lights continued to near; then there were two more blasts.

Suddenly, the lights slowed. It was a straight run of river; there was no reason for caution.

''C'mon, ya Jerry blighters, what the hell's wrong?''

The lights stopped. There were two more blasts from

the ship's horn, and with a jolt, Weyers realized what
they were doing: signaling the bunker and waiting for a
return blast, an all-clear.

How could we have been so goddamn stupid?

Thinking back, Weyers recalled that somewhere in the
wreckage he'd seen a hand-cranked siren, like the one
the boats were using. The bunker was on Lambert's side
of the river. Did he know it was there? Would he even
think of going to get it?

Weyers dismissed the idea of lighting the fires now;
they might burn out before the enemy arrived. The only
thing to do was to get to Lambert and regroup. It was
some thirty meters across, and he felt that he could survive the cold, could fight the current. What choice did
he have? Rising, Weyers hurried across the shingle and
slogged into the river.

At once, the fabric of his coat and trousers began to
soak up water. Each step became more difficult, and
Weyers was soon forced to strip both garments off. The
frigid water stung his legs, shot through his cotton cavalry shirt, and burned his chest. Up to his neck in the
rushing river, he writhed in torment as he walked. Then,
when he was barely halfway across, his legs went numb
and seemed to vanish from beneath him. Going under,
he twisted with the flow, screaming from the shock of
the cold closing in around him. Water flooded his mouth
as he went down, and his last thought was that this had
been the stupidest plan in which he had ever taken
part. . . .

Chapter Eleven

Livingston didn't know quite what to make of Masha.

Unlike Andrei, who alternately brooded and sobbed about his brother, Masha said nothing. Her expression was unchanging—the eyes remained hard, the mouth straight and stern. When she spoke, her voice was even, without emotion. He didn't understand how anyone could keep so much pain inside.

Before the afternoon had passed, he learned just how she dealt with her sorrow.

It was nearly one, when many of the patrols rested for lunch, and Masha was leading them through a section of town that had once been a pleasant residential area of three- and four-story apartment buildings. Most of the building fronts were still standing, many because they were propped up by the rubble of their fire-gutted interiors. The group was sticking close to the facades, listening for voices or gunfire, when enemy soldiers entered the street from the other side. Livingston's men sunk into doorways, alleys, or behind steps. The young woman and Piotr ducked inside a building.

Watching from an alley, Livingston saw them scale a pile of debris and make for the enemy position. The lieutenant vaulted a shattered brick wall and hurried after them while the rest of his men opened fire on the unwary Germans. Two soldiers went down at once, and the others took up positions in buildings and behind telephone poles, street lamps, and trees.

Behind the buildings, Masha and her companion moved quickly and quietly, the woman exhibiting catlike grace and balance as she climbed over and around debris. She remained in the lead as they approached the last mound of rubble; as a result, she was the first to see the potato masher when it was hurled from the other side.

"Get down!"

Masha screamed as she flung herself behind half a bathtub lying nearby. Livingston dropped to his belly behind her and covered his head. Shrapnel clattered against the tub. Livingston and Masha were spared; out in the open, Piotr was not.

Masha opened fire from around the tub, shooting at the mound, and Livingston scrambled ahead on his belly, trying to get closer. A pair of Karabiners appeared, firing blindly over the mound while Livingston approached.

Instead of coming in over the rubble, Livingston backed down the side of the mound and crept around the one that was hiding the Germans. He came in behind them and, kneeling, shot them both in the head. After throwing one of the rifles out to Masha, he took the other and crawled through the adjoining building.

The Germans were clearly visible through the shattered glass of the front windows. Stopping behind a charred sofa, the only piece of furniture in the room, Livingston aimed at the nearest man, and noted where another was standing nearby. Both fell in quick succession, followed by a third and a fourth. Livingston hadn't shot them; Masha had, from behind him.

Livingston made for the shattered front door of the building and, caught in a crossfire between Livingston and his men, the remaining two Germans went down.

And as he stepped into the street, Livingston saw how Masha handled her sorrow.

Her lips tightly shut, expression still neutral, she began beating one of the dead men. Andrei and Sergei said nothing. They went back and checked on their comrade, and after making certain Piotr was dead, laid him on the ground behind the building and covered him over with pieces of brick and concrete. The dead Germans were left where they lay, as a warning to others.

When the men were finished, they waited silently until Masha was done. Her blows were brutal; she kicked, she punched, she used the butt of her gun on the corpse. And when she was finished, she turned and rejoined her comrades—calmly, as though nothing had happened.

"I know how she feels," Colon said as he passed Livingston. Though his speech was slurred, the lieutenant was glad to see that his eyes burned with their old intensity.

The loss of Piotr was sobering, more so because there were only six of them left. As they rested in the back of a bakery, sharing some cheese and chasing rats from the crumbs, Masha said that gathering more people was out of the question. By day, patrols such as the one they'd just encountered fanned out through the city. Avoiding them would be a feat in itself, let alone trying to get to every cellar and cranny where partisans might be hidden.

While they rested, Masha told Livingston a bit more about the train. The flatbed car to which the gas tanks had been chained was sandwiched between the engine and an armored car. The armored car had a turreted 76.2mm gun on top, for long-range firing, and small ports whose metal doors could be opened and used by the soldiers inside. There were seven such windows on each side of the car. There was also an armored caboose and a spare engine in back.

"Sounds like we've got our work cut out for us," Ogan

said. "We're going to have to find a way to get into the engine."

"That's what I've been thinking," Livingston said. "We take the controls and run it backwards, away from the city."

"Right. The engine would certainly be a defensible position."

"But what do we do then?" Masha asked. "We can't hold out forever."

"If we can get to the engine, we don't have to," Ogan said. "In London, Escott calculated that this new, heavy gas will have an effective range of approximately three kilometers. If we capture the train and derail it where the track runs through the farmland, we can open the containers without the gas reaching the city."

"And hold our breaths for a very long time," Colon remarked.

They continued their journey from door to door, stopping at one point when they ran into a sandbag and barbed-wire barricade stretched across a broad avenue. The impasse hadn't been there the day before; Masha guessed that the Germans were trying to seal off roads that led to the railroad station. They tried another street, but soldiers were also in the process of sealing that route.

Masha led them to a small pond nearby, where a stone bridge afforded cover. They ducked behind one of the supports.

"We have two choices," she said. "We can attempt to go through one of these barricades, or we can try to approach the bridge along another, less direct route."

"And crossing that bridge is the *only* way to get us to the tracks?" Livingston asked.

Masha nodded.

"What's the less direct route?"

"An approach from the west side, through the rail yards."

"Is it safer?"

"If the yards are crowded with trains. Otherwise, there will be a lot of open space to cover, and it will depend upon where the guards are standing and which way they are facing. There's a diagram in one of our bunkers. If we're going to try that approach, it would be best to stop and plan it."

"Is the bunker far?"

"A few blocks."

Livingston rubbed his two-day growth of whiskers, then reluctantly approved the stopover. Time was short, but precision in this phase of the operation was also important.

As they moved out—one at a time, around the pond, with Livingston bringing up the rear—the lieutenant was distracted by something that Colon had mentioned before: that several people would have to be close to the gas tanks in order to open them.

Never could he remember ever having worked so hard, and all for the privilege of dying.

When Lambert was certain the convoy was slowing, he used a piece of wood to backpaddle the boat into a clump of reeds. He didn't dare use the engine; the noise or the fumes would have been noticed. Peering through the moss and vines that hung over the water from a gnarled beech tree, he watched as the boats signaled again, then stopped.

Obviously, they weren't going to move until the signal was returned. Even if he had a siren, Lambert had no idea what to send back, whether the convoy expected the same signal, or something different.

He stayed calm, decided it didn't matter. The important thing was to get the fires going, to delay the convoy, to lure a search party over and get on board.

He looked upriver. There was no movement on the shore where Weyers was hidden; it was clear he didn't intend to deviate from the plan. The river was now an enemy. Lambert couldn't yell the change of plans to Weyers and be heard; he couldn't fire his pistol, or the Germans might hear; he couldn't rush over, or the Germans might see.

Suddenly, his concerns became academic as Weyers shot from his cover and splashed into the water.

"What in God's name is he doing? *L'imbecile!*"

The Frenchman watched with horror as Weyers labored through the torrent, tearing off his coat, getting caught in the flow, and going under.

Lambert pulled on the starter cord, but the engine wouldn't turn over. He tried it again, but it still wouldn't start.

Swearing, he jumped from the boat and ran along the bank. As he peered into the dark river, Lambert wasn't even certain he'd be able to see Weyers, let alone save him. Though it was only half-past three, the sun was already low behind the hills, casting long shadows. Any movement on the water's surface could have been the figure of a man.

He raced through the snow, his legs heavy, eyes searching desperately for a sign of his friend.

Then he saw it. A hand sticking up from the water. But it wasn't being carried downriver, and Lambert soon saw why: Weyers had managed to snag the line, and was holding on to it.

Climbing into the second assault boat, which was still moored to the pier, Lambert pulled it back several meters, upstream of where his friend was. When Lambert climbed in, the current carried him toward the line, the Frenchman using the tiller to guide it to the center of the river. He came close enough to Weyers to grab his wrist and, reaching into the river, found his belt and managed to pull him in.

The South African's fingers were bent stiffly around the wire, and it came in with him. As the boat twisted madly downriver, Lambert pinched Weyers's nose shut, put his mouth to the South African's pale blue lips, and blew hard. Weyers responded, and a few seconds later he breathed in again, and then a third time.

After the fourth breath, Weyers stiffened and gulped down air. Lambert pulled off his coat and wrapped it around his friend.

"You'll be all right, Wings. Le Rodeur has things under control."

Patting his friend on the chest, Lambert looked frantically about for something to stop them from being carried toward the convoy. There was nothing in the boat but the seats, the motor—and the line Weyers had dragged in. The rocks were still attached to the ends, and though they weren't heavy enough to serve as an anchor, they might have another use.

Checking to make sure the wire was tied firmly around the flat stones, Lambert got to his knees. They were approaching the beech tree where he'd been hiding and, swinging the rope over his head, bolo-style, he let one end go. It caught a branch, but when he attempted to reel the boat in, the line snapped. Cursing, the Frenchman tried again to turn the engine over. The starter rope barely drew a sputter.

Swimming for shore was out of the question. Weyers was nearly blue, and was too large for Lambert to tug behind him in any case. However, it occurred to Lambert that they did have *one* chance.

First he had to lighten the boat. Loosening the clamp screws that held the motor in place, he let it fall back, then lowered himself over the stern. The water rose to his chest and the cold shocked him as it had before. But he was able to skid along the bottom and slow the boat; at the same time, he began working it sideways, toward the shore.

It was difficult to breathe, the frigid waters causing his chest to contract. He stumbled several times, but the boat steadied him; eventually, the water was only up to his

knees, then his shins. He staggered ashore but didn't
stop. Fear kept him going. Afraid someone in the convoy
might have seen them, Lambert pulled Weyers from the
boat and dragged him up the embankment. He headed
for the bunker. Though they were nearly one hundred
meters downriver, it was the only hiding place around.

As he struggled ahead, Lambert thought he heard the
sound of motors. The frigates had probably lowered
launches, sent them to see what the problem was. The
men riding them would probably be armed to the teeth.

The sounds grew louder, and were definitely engines.
There was no way he'd make it to the bunker before they
arrived, and he realized that his tracks, in the snow,
would lead the Germans right to him. Panting, his flesh
frostbitten, he stopped to try and focus his thoughts, to
concentrate.

The boats. The river. The bunker. The dynamite.
There was nothing he could use to stop the Germans.
With just the one gun, he might be able to hide and snipe
at a few of them, but ultimately, they'd prevail. Trying
to convince them that they'd survived the bunker attack
was out of the question: Weyers was in no condition to
surrender on his own, and if they couldn't get into different boats, the plan was useless.

The boats. The river. The bunker—

The dynamite!

Shaking his head violently to try to clear the throb-
bing pain, Lambert ran ahead. It didn't matter, now, if
they knew what he was doing. The important thing was
to do it before they could stop him.

Scrabbling the last few meters on all fours, he reached
the bunker and, after wrapping himself in the coat of one
of the dead men, Lambert went to the reinforced pit. It
was out back, away from the bunker in case of fire or
attack. Collecting armfuls of dynamite, he started toward
the bluff overlooking the river. Realizing he'd left his
matches in his coat, he swore, stopped, and began

searching the pockets of the dead men. After losing precious minutes, he found a box, then looked back.

Two launches were about two hundred meters from the shore. Lambert cursed again. There was no way he could get up to the cliff, do the job, and get back for Weyers before the Germans arrived. If he went back, he risked not stopping the convoy. If he went ahead, Weyers was a dead man.

He went back.

As he ran, out of breath, he saw the Germans pointing at him. Lighting the fuses, he began heaving the dynamite at the boats. The shallows and the shingle erupted furiously, raising pillars of rock and water. One of the boats was overturned, and those soldiers who weren't killed by the blasts were dragged by the current. The other boat turned and tried to fish the men from the water.

When Lambert reached Weyers, the South African was beginning to come around.

"Very noisy," he whispered.

"Don't . . . add . . . to it," Lambert gasped as he dropped beside him. His legs were weak and trembling. "Can you walk?"

"If not, I can crawl."

"*C'est bien*, because I can't carry you."

Lambert took Weyers's arm and helped him to his feet. The big man took a step, then grabbed Lambert's shoulder for support.

"Sorry, Rotter. Just give me a second." Weyers took several deep breaths, then took a few more steps.

"Let me know when you can stand on your own."

"Why?"

"Because I used up all my explosives. I need to get more."

Weyers told him to go ahead and, his own step uncertain, Lambert left his companion behind.

He had just finished pulling the rest of the dynamite from the pit when Weyers arrived.

"Take these," Lambert said, pushing a bundle of sticks into Weyers's arms.

"And do what? We can't just chuck them at the ships."

"I don't intend to. Just trust me."

Realizing what he'd said, Lambert looked up at Weyers.

"This one *will* work. Whether the ships move or stand still, we've got them."

Their arms full of explosives, the men trudged along the shore. Every muscle in Lambert's body ached, and his head was pounding. But on the bright side, he told himself, at least the convoy hadn't moved, and no other launches had been sent out. Either they had radioed for assistance from a battalion upstream, or were planning to launch a more organized raid. In any case, it gave him ample time for what he had in mind.

The bluffs along this stretch of the Volga weren't as high as they were upriver, the tallest of the crags reaching only some twenty meters. But, like the other cliffs, they were fraught with fissures, caused by eons of water seeping into the rock, freezing, and expanding.

They'd do in the place of a bona fide drill holes.

Once on top, Lambert got on his knees and began burrowing in the snow. Finding a large crack, he traced its course along the length of the cliff. Satisfied, he lined it with TNT, pushing in a stick every meter.

"Going to make like little beavers, are we? If we can't burn the river, we'll dam it."

"Why not, monsieur?"

"No reason. Only, why didn't we think of this in the first place?"

Lambert went back and began packing snow around the base of each stick. "Because it isn't *parfait*. It will stop the ships, but it won't sink the cargo. Hopefully," he said, "we can get to that later."

Convinced that the sticks wouldn't tip over, Lambert stood and fished the matches from his pocket. "Now go. These are short fuses, and a minute after I light them, most of the cliff is going to bid us *adieu.*"

Water had frozen on the South African's lashes. He rubbed it away. "Forget it. I'm staying with you."

"*Non!* There's nothing you can do—"

"Like hell! Suppose you slip and break your goddamn leg? How are you going to get away?" Weyers made an angry face, the dark lines heightened by exposure and exhaustion. "You saved my life, Rotter. In South Africa, that'd make us brothers, and brothers stick together."

Lambert seemed uncomfortable. "*Tres bien,*" he said quietly, "and—thank you."

Striking one of the matches and shielding it from the wind, Lambert touched it to each stick in turn. The fuses hissed wickedly, and when he'd ignited the last of them, the two men turned and ran down the sloping backside of the bluff. When they were nearly to the bottom, the ground heaved violently, a massive pop punched hard at their eardrums, and they threw themselves forward, into the snow. The explosion echoed up and down the river valley, punctuated by the dull thumping of boulders hitting the snow and the noisy rain of dirt and pebbles.

It was nearly a minute before either of them lifted their faces from the snow.

"Rotter, are you all right?"

Lambert had landed hard on his chest and wheezed. "Hitler should feel like I do." He pulled his arms beneath him and sat up. A layer of small stones fell from his back. "This being pelted with rocks—it's getting to be a habit with us."

"Better rocks than bullets."

"*C'est vrai.*" Lambert looked around. Snow was still falling from the blast, a cool, glistening rain that felt good on Lambert's face. After several minutes, the men stood and, making their way through up the bluff, which was now peppered with rocks of all sizes, headed back toward the cliff.

Looking down, Lambert felt as though he'd just won the war. A causeway stretched most of the way across the river. It was uneven, and some of it barely broke the surface, but nothing larger than a rowboat would be able to pass over or around it.

A smile split the Frenchman's cheeks.

"You did it," Weyers said, slapping him on the back. "Damned if you weren't right about *this* one."

"Did you doubt me?"

"Frankly," Weyers said, "I did. Severely." He sat heavily on a jagged slab of rock that had been torn up by the blast. "The question is, what do we do next?"

Lambert sat down beside him. "My guess is they'll try to dig up the dam. When they do, virtually every man will be assigned to the detail. And when that happens, we simply go on board and finish the job we started." Lambert looked back, toward the woods. "As for the immediate future, I suggest we go somewhere, light a fire, dry off, and find something to eat. I've a feeling it's going to be a long night."

Chapter Twelve

Masha, Livingston, and the others left the streets and took to the cellars.

The woman led them through a series of dark basements connected by short, narrow passageways that were little more than rat holes. They stopped to drink in one, where a still-functioning boiler beneath a German outpost had melted the snow and formed one of the few pools that wasn't utterly rank.

The Germans may have claimed to control these areas of the city but, Masha whispered, the Russians had been most effective using these tunnels to make their way behind enemy lines and pick off soldiers.

The cellar network ended under the stage of a music hall. Masha said that she and Andrei knew the building well: Their father used to manage it, and they were aware of crawl spaces and closets the Germans would never find. It was there, in fact, in a scenery pit beneath the stage, that the network of tunnels had been begun. The building hadn't been destroyed because General Paulus admired its beauty, the marble columns outside and bas-relief friezes inside. He vowed that when he took the city, he could make this his headquarters; in a communiqué, Hitler had vowed that he would make Stalin dance on the stage before executing him.

Masha said that she had vowed to raise a new Stalingrad with the nineteenth-century edifice as the centerpiece.

The group emerged beneath the stage and, after making their way through the stacks of furniture and costumes, they were in a basement, facing a life-size portrait of Lenin. The painting swung around in the middle, admitting them to a stairwell that led to a long, narrow room. The walls were brick and the floors were covered with mismatched scraps of carpet.

"It was built by a man who ran this place before my father," Masha said. "He was a czarist, and after the Revolution, my father let him and his family hide until they could escape Russia."

"You come from a long line of heroes," Livingston said.

"Not heroes," she said emphatically, "but lovers—of our people, and of our city."

She lit candles in the room while Andrei went upstairs to stand watch. For the first time since they landed, Livingston felt safe, able to let down his guard. But he couldn't relax. It was two o'clock—less than a day before the gas would be unleashed upon the city.

Masha went to a wooden desk which, along with two small beds and a large washing basin, were the only objects in the room. She took a map of the city from the center drawer and unrolled it beneath a candle. Livingston and Ogan looked down.

"Here are the six roads which lead to the terminal," she said, pointing to them in turn. "Presumably, all are blockaded. Here is the bridge." She used a pencil to sketch the span in profile. "It is an iron trestle, with five supports—one at each end, one in middle, and two halfway between each end and middle."

"How long is it?" Livingston asked.

"Fifty meters."

He looked at the map. "So trains come over the bridge, into the terminal, then down and around under the bridge to the yard where cargo is unloaded."

"Yes."

"And you said the bridge is ten meters high—just enough for trains to pass under into the unloading area." The lieutenant scratched his head. Slats of melting ice fell from the sides. "Do you know anything about running trains?"

"No."

Livingston smiled. "I should have had Weyers stay with us. Sonofagun can run anything." He began pacing. "We have to assume that there will be soldiers all over the place. Which means that even if we get close to the bridge, odds are good that they'll spot us."

"Even if we came through the terminal, they would have seen us," she said. "We'll just have to take our chances."

"Agreed. The question is, can we even get close enough to the damn thing to blow it up? How much do you have in the way of explosives."

"Very little. There is some dynamite in one cache, a bit of petrol, and a few bazooka rockets—but no launcher."

"If what you say about the bridge is true, just a stick of dynamite or two is all we'll need." He stopped his pacing, studied the map intently. "Do you happen to know if the locomotives are coal-driven or electric?"

"They are old steam locomotives."

"Damn."

Ogan looked at the lieutenant. "Why? What did you have in mind?"

"I was thinking that if we could pack one of the locomotives with explosives and move it under the bridge, we could blow the thing to kingdom come. But if the locomotives are all coal-driven, it would have to be stoked—no way we could do that without being seen."

Ogan pointed to the map. "Can we come at the bridge from the other side?"

The woman shook her head. "We'd have to cross the open track. The Germans would see us for certain."

Livingston continued to stare at the map. "I wonder—what if a few of us were to launch a diversionary attack from somewhere in the rail yard?"

"While the rest of us do what?" Ogan asked.

"You said you hid out in a tank before. What was wrong with it?"

Ogan shrugged. "It was covered with snow. For all I know, it simply ran out of petrol."

"The German tank on the river?" Masha asked. "We clogged the cannon with mud and it split. It's no good to anyone."

"Maybe it is for us," Livingston said. "Ken—how far upriver was it?"

"About a quarter kilometer."

The lieutenant looked at the map. "Masha, what's the best way to get there?"

She thought for a moment. "Since the Nazis have discovered our one tunnel to the river, the only way is to take the tunnels in the destroyed residential district here, just one block from the back of theater." She traced a path with her finger. "Then go through the park to the river. But there is only open space after the park—very dangerous."

"We'll have to risk it. Ken and I will go. We'll get the explosives, take the tank, and while you draw fire from the rail yards, we'll ride right up and blow the damn bridge to scrap iron."

Masha regarded Livingston with a mixture of admiration and disbelief.

"Don't worry," the lieutenant said. "It's a German tank. They'll think we're coming to help."

"You'll need new clothes," she said. "If you approach the tunnel in those uniforms, there's a good chance you'll be shot before you come within shouting distance."

Ogan said, "There's probably something you can use on the costume rack?"

Colon snickered. "I saw a coupla tutus."

"I meant street clothes."

Livingston said, "We'll check. What about the explosives?" he asked Masha. "Where are they?"

"In a butcher shop, beneath a pile of rotting dogs. Germans will eat raw horseflesh, but not dogs." She allowed herself a rare smile. "We gave up the food to ensure that the weapons would be safe."

Livingston returned the smile, though it was tempered by the knowledge that she was telling the truth.

The group retired to the property room beneath the stage, where the men found civilian clothes. Though they were too large, intended for comedy skits, it was all the men had to choose from.

"It's funny," Masha said when they were finished, "but with clothes too large and torn, and with these caps, you *look* like Russian peasants."

Livingston slid his gun into a shabby overcoat. Despite the condition of the clothes, and the fact that he would be much colder wearing them, he was glad to be out of the German uniform. Now he felt like he was dressed for a fight, not anonymity.

While they dressed, they discussed their timetable. Masha and her people would enter the yards on the western side and begin widespread fire in exactly three hours. At that time, Livingston and Ogan would come from the east with the tank. If for some reason the tank didn't make it, the two men would have to approach the bridge without it. Livingston reminded Masha that even if the gas was released just on the other side of the bridge,

fewer Russians would die than if the gas was released in
the heart of the city.

"The password is the same?" he asked as they walked
toward the backdoor of the theater.

"Yes. I do not know who will be in the tunnels, but
a woman named Nona is in command. She will help
you."

Livingston and Ogan embraced the Russians.

"You want to hug me too, sir?" Colon asked Livingston.

"Only if you're wearing a tutu."

The private smiled, then wished his companions luck.

Masha checked to make sure there were no patrols
outside. When she returned, Ogan and Livingston hurried into the street.

The snow was blinding after the darkness of the theater, and in the courtyard, the two men crouched behind
a large, bronze mask of tragedy while their eyes adjusted.

Masha watched them through a peephole her father
had installed years before. A strong wind gusted by;
when the swirl of snow was gone, so were the men.

It was just before five when, with the last of the daylight to his back, Lambert went to the woods in search
of dinner. At once, he spotted two striped squirrels. They
were side by side, clutching a tree, facing down and nib-
bling on snow-covered ivy growing from the trunk. As
Lambert raised his gun, the squirrel nearest him looked
over, spun, and fled up into the bare branches; the animal behind it looked over, froze, and caught the bullet
that was meant for its companion. Blood sprayed across
the tree and the animal fell.

"It's like war," he muttered as he trudged ahead.
"You took the bullet fate had intended for your buddy."

Not that it mattered to Lambert which squirrel they
ate. At this point, it didn't matter whether the squirrel

was even cooked. Licking his lips, Lambert ran to fetch
the small animal. Unfortunately, Lambert was not alone.

Glancing into the trees, Lambert noticed a wolf standing in the dark shadows. The Frenchman slowed to a
walk.

"You go and chase the other squirrel," he yelled.
"This one's *pour moi*."

The wolf glowered back at him, its green eyes and
gray head moving with Lambert's every step. When the
Frenchman reached the squirrel, the wolf voiced a guttural growl.

The Frenchman's palm began to sweat around his pistol. He stared at the wolf and knelt slowly, his eyes never
leaving those intelligent, green eyes staring back at him.
When Lambert finally gazed down, he frowned.

The blast had decimated the small animal. There was
nothing left but the tail and hindquarters, barely enough
to serve as an appetizer for—

"Le Loup. Porquoi pas?"

Laying the decimated squirrel on the ground, Lambert
smiled as he backed away slowly. . . .

Weyers sat back from the fire he'd made. "I've got to
hand it to you, Rotter. I've never eaten wolf." He spit
out a chunk of fat. "It's greasy, and there's a lot of gris-
tle, but . . . it's not bad."

"It's better than camel," the Frenchman said. "They
taste as bad as they smell."

The South African looked over at the gutted carcass.
"Too bad we don't have the time to skin it. The pelt
would make very nice gloves or boot lining."

Lambert wiped his hands on his jacket. "Unfortunately, we have to go and see what our friends are up to.
How do you feel?"

"The fire's worked wonders, but I can't remember
when I've hurt so much *everywhere*."

Lambert noticed the raw, red blisters on Weyers's

hands and, after examining them, lifted Weyers's shirt.
There were huge patches of caked, red skin on his side
and neck.

"Frostbite."

"So?"

"It does not look good."

"What're you talking about? You're a French-Arab
from the desert. You wouldn't know frostbite from a map
of Cape Town!"

"*Peut-etre*. But I do know gangrene, and I'd watch
those spots around your waist and under your arm. They
could become infected."

Weyers pulled down his shirt. "I'll see a bloody doctor on my next day off." He winced as the fabric scraped
his skin. "I'll also take some bandages from the ship's
sick bay if we go on board."

Lambert rose and kicked snow on the campfire. "*Al-
lons*. We've got our half of a city to save."

With a last, longing look at the smoldering embers,
Weyers plucked his coat from an overhanging tree limb
where he'd left it to dry, then followed Lambert to the
bluff.

The Frenchman was surprised to find that not a single
soldier had come to examine the rock slide. The Germans must have concluded that whoever made the strike
had done their job and fled. Lambert looked downriver,
and was also surprised to see that a large force had landed
at the bunker and that the convoy had moved much closer
to it. There were dozens of soldiers standing on the decks
of the two ships, sleek, gray frigates each of which had
a diamond-shaped antenna atop its single mast.

"That's strange," he said.

"What is?"

"Why bother coming just a little farther when they
can't get through?"

The answer came when he heard a deep grinding sound
coming from somewhere behind the rubble of the bun-

ker. The two men listened for nearly a half hour as the sound came closer. Then, two phalanxes of soldiers appeared, dressed in winter camouflage uniforms. They were carrying kerosene lanterns, studying the ground for mines. Between them was a pair of huge, treaded trucks.

"Sweet Jesus Christ," Weyers moaned.

Lambert was silent. The Germans weren't going to give up. They were going to finish the trip on land.

"We should've sunk the ships when we had the chance, Rotter."

"*Ca va.* I didn't think they had the stinking *resources* for this." He stole a look at the skies. "Please, God, let it snow again."

"Save your prayers for when we need 'em. Those are Opel Maultiers. Remember the half track we had in Algiers, the one that rode up and over everything? Well, these are even tougher. Nothing short of a 100mm howitzer will stop those treads."

Lambert's mouth went dry. He was oblivious to the cold, to his battered muscles. All he saw were the trucks being turned around when they reached the riverbank while, under the glow of the ship's spotlights, a large crane at the stern of each frigate began to pivot.

"The bastards are supposed to be out of fuel, Wings. They don't have enough to run monsters like those."

"Maybe they had just enough. They don't expect to be here much longer."

Lambert kicked at the snow, then drove a palm against his forehead. "*Quelle l'ane!* Dammit, *think!* Why is nothing coming?"

"Because we're both dead on our feet—"

"*Non!* We must think of something, or a *city* will soon be dead, *period.*"

"Can we use more dynamite? Blow up the trucks?"

"We'd never get near them."

"Does that matter, as long as we get close enough to disable them?"

"It's an option," Lambert said laconically.

"Seems like the only one," Weyers continued. "They have to go through the woods. We could wait there—"

"Wait!" Lambert said. "The woods—*oui*. Something *is* coming to me!" He grabbed Weyers's arms. "Wings, what happened to me before?"

"When?"

"At the lake."

The South African's beefy face twisted in thought. "You mean, when we first got there?"

"Oui!"

"You fell."

"And *why* did I fall?"

"Because you didn't—" The South African paused and stared at the Frenchman. Suddenly, the big mouth turned up. "Good God, Rotter—yes. I think you've got something there."

Lambert fired a look back at the bunker. "How long do you think it will take them to load the trucks? An hour?"

"At least."

"And another hour to get through the wood?"

"About that. Those trucks are tough, but they aren't very fast."

"Magnifique!"

The Frenchman left the bluff and started back through the woods. Weyers lumbered after him. Lambert was at once delighted—and angry for having doubted himself.

The question now was no longer what they would do to try to stop the shipment. The question was whether they had a chance in hell of succeeding.

Chapter Thirteen

Livingston and Ogan reached the tunnel just after three. Because so many German soldiers had apparently been reassigned to the train and terminal, there were few men about. It was also considerably colder, which Livingston was certain influenced the Germans' will to leave their outposts to patrol.

The tunnel was located in an outhouse. Upon stepping inside, Livingston yelled the password down the hole and waited; in less than a minute, a boy clambered up.

He was no older than fourteen, and there was a German helmet strapped to his head, an old German P.08 tucked in the waistband of his trousers. He spoke no English, but when they asked for Nona, he was able to tell them, through gestures, that she had been killed the night before in a gun battle in the park. In fact, using hand motions, the boy informed them that, after that fight, he was the only one left alive.

Livingston put an arm around his shoulder and commended him. But the boy seemed uncomfortable, making it clear by his posture, by the way he held the gun, that he considered himself a man. The lieutenant understood, and quietly pulled back.

Using his dictionary, Ogan told the youth where they

needed to go and, leading them down the rank hole and
through the tunnel, the boy took them to the butcher
shop. Moving aside the dead dogs—German shepherds,
Livingston was gratified to note—the men found a trapdoor. Opening it, they descended a rickety ladder to a
small basement, where there were five sticks of dynamite, rockets, and a can of petrol.

"Like the woman said," Livingston sighed, "it's not
much."

"If we take the rockets," Ogan suggested, "and abandon the tank when we set the explosives, it'll still cause
a hell of a blast."

Livingston agreed. When they climbed from the small
storage room, the boy made motions that he wanted to
go with them.

"Zdyehs?" Ogan asked.

The boy gestured behind him. *"Zdyehs . . . pa-
tyerya."*

"What'd he say?" Livingston asked.

"I told him that his place was here, but he says that
the battle here is lost."

"Can't really blame him for feeling that way. He had
a hell of a night. Find out his name, Ken."

Ogan asked. "Vladimir," the youth said. "Vladimir
Ilyich Tsigornin."

Livingston offered his hand. "Welcome to Force Five,
Vladimir."

After emerging from the tunnel in a devastated police
station, Vladimir led Livingston and Ogan across the
street to the park.

Like everything else in Stalingrad, the park hadn't been
spared the bombs of the Luftwaffe or the guns of the
Wehrmacht. The iron fence had been shattered, swings
were a mass of broken sticks and tangled chains, and the
benches were overturned or split.

Running around the twisted fence, the men ducked

behind a sandbox, which had been overturned and broken down the middle, forming a pyramid. Trees and debris blocked the opposite side of the park from view; for all they knew, enemy soldiers might be encamped there.

Indicating that the men should stay where they were, Vladimir flopped onto his belly and wriggled toward a kiosk in the center of the park.

Livingston watched as a boy pitted himself against the threat of battle-seasoned German troops. Vladimir's courage brought a lump to his throat. Suddenly, the youth stopped; Livingston heard them too: German voices coming from somewhere on the other side of the debris. An engine joined the voices, followed by the clatter of wood.

Vladimir hurried ahead to the kiosk, then looked back at the men. He moved his fists as though he were pulling on a rope.

"They must be setting up a barricade," Ogan said. "They probably came here after securing the area."

"That figures," Livingston said. "They're probably looking to contain the Russians in as small an area as possible before bringing in the gas."

"Do we wait or do we take them?"

"We can't afford to wait, but the question is, how do we *get* to them?"

Apart from a few benches, the park to the left and right was completely open; there was nowhere to set up a cross fire. The matter was resolved, suddenly, horribly, when Vladimir rose. His gun tucked in the back of his waistband, his hands held high over his head, he began walking toward the voices.

"Yah galuhdyen!" he yelled to the Germans.

There was a flurry of movement behind the fence, followed by a long, terrible silence. Then a gun was poked through the fence.

"Kommen!" one of the soldiers yelled.

The boy had evidently hoped one or more of the sol-

diers would look over the pile of broken fences and concrete and make himself a target for Livingston or Ogan.
It was a brave but naive move, the lieutenant felt. Shooting at a gun might drive it back but not remove the threat.
He racked his brain for a way to attack the well-hidden
enemy.

"We can't let them take him!" Ogan said urgently.

"No," Livingston agreed, "and we can't let the enemy stay there either. Here's what I want to do. You see
where the fence is curled up and lying on its side?" Ogan
looked to where Livingston pointed. He nodded. "Whatever they drove to get here is over there. I'm going to try
to get to it."

"And do what?"

"Gun it," Livingston replied, "run them down. I'll
need you to cover me. When I start out, fire at the gun
and drive him back. As soon as you hear the vehicle start
to move, get as close to the fence as possible." He
cocked a thumb toward the flour sack at Ogan's side. "If
you have to, use a stick of dynamite to take them out."

Ogan nodded and, after taking a deep breath, Livingston sprang from behind the sandbox.

The instant he did so, Ogan opened fire and drove the
gun back. Simultaneously, Vladimir dove behind a tree,
drew his pistol, and began shooting at the fence. The
exchange lasted only a few seconds, but it was enough
time for Livingston to reach the park side of the scrap
heap. Flopping down, he took a moment to catch his
breath.

Suddenly, just a meter away, the top of the rubble was
pushed over by a German boot. Looking up, Livingston
saw a Kubel on the other side, a small Jeep-like car.
However, instead of the spare tire that these vehicles usually carried on their sloping hoods, this car boasted a
tripod-mounted MG 34 machine gun. It swung toward
Livingston, and would have cut him in half if Ogan hadn't
managed a remarkable shot, cutting down both the gun-

ner and his companion in quick succession. The gunner
fell across his weapon, pumping his only burst into the
hood of the car. The engine fell silent.

Cursing, Livingston crawled back, taking shelter behind the nearest tree. He still had no idea how many
soldiers were there, nor did it matter. Attracted by the
exchange, other soldiers came running toward the park.

Vladimir ran from one tree to another, drawing fire.
A bullet tore into his arm, but he was able to fall behind
a fat tree trunk. Having seen where two of the soldiers
were, Livingston fired several rounds, but the rubble
protected them.

Ogan looked over at Livingston, and the American
pointed to the Kubel. The machine gun seemed to be
still usable, and it was their only hope. Ogan and Vladimir both nodded, then shot at the Germans' position
to keep them back as the lieutenant bolted up and over
the woodpile.

Livingston landed on the front of the hood, at the foot
of the gun. Because the car was facing away from the
Germans, he slid down to the cobbled street. Looking
back, he saw a soldier running toward him; there was a
hollow, clumping sound as the German vaulted up the
flat back of the car and ran across the seats to take the
place of his fallen comrades. Livingston climbed to his
knees, and there was a moment when the German was
staring down the long barrel of the machine gun and
Livingston was looking up the barrel of his own pistol;
the pistol coughed first, and the soldier fell backward.

Livingston stole a look around the car. There was
only one man left of the original complement, and he
had begun making his way to the other side of the street,
away from the Kubel. The reinforcements, twenty of
them, were running toward him, double time; the surviving soldier was gesturing behind him, toward the
Jeep.

There was no time to waste. Jumping onto the hood, Livingston spun the gun around, threw the ammunition belt over his shoulder, and opened fire.

The Germans were too far from the protective doorways, too cold to think clearly, and too tired from battle. As a result, Livingston cut down most of the men on the first sweep of the gun. The survivors fell to their bellies and died reaching for their Karabiners.

Standing on top of the debris like an eagle scouting prey, Vladimir coolly shot the soldier who had tried to run. Then he ran down to check on the other soldiers.

While Ogan made certain Livingston was all right, the Russian kicked each of the soldiers. Two had survived; before Ogan or Livingston could stop him, Vladimir shot them both in the forehead.

Ogan ran over. "What the *hell* did you do that for?"

Vladimir seemed to understand. Nodding, he moved his wounded arm up and down the street. *"Da,"* he said gravely. *"Hell."*

The sergeant major said nothing more.

Noticing Vladimir's wound, Livingston insisted on taking a look at it. The bullet had only grazed the skin, and pulling his arm away, Vladimir rubbed snow on it. He insisted that he was fine.

Ogan said, "He doesn't want to miss out on the chance to do some more killing."

"You're probably right. And how do you *expect* a fourteen-year-old to react to all of this? With understanding?"

Ogan didn't answer. He looked down, sighed heavily, and walked away.

As they picked their way from doorway to doorway, Livingston realized that what made Stalingrad unique wasn't just the unusual heroism or barbarism. The entire struggle was surreal: dark gray streets, ruins, and skies splattered with blood. It was an environment in which people were reduced to something less than human, to dull, gray, killing machines.

"Hell," he said quietly.

When Masha had first mentioned the rail yards, Colon's spirits had soared.

As a child growing up in Pittsburgh, he'd often played in the rail yards. It was either that or the steelyards, and security was tighter at the mills. So he and his friends would tightrope-walk along the tracks, smoke or drink in abandoned boxcars, rumble with rich kids who had no business being there, play chicken with incoming trains, and at night, climb the power lines, set caterpillars or worms on the live wires, and bet on whose would burn the longest.

He'd felt privileged to be there then. In storybooks and in the movies, kids had to go to playgrounds, where they always did the same things, saw the same sights, played with parents looking on. But the rail yards were constantly changing, with new cars to explore and new freight to examine. And best of all, if you were careful, you never had to deal with any adults.

Now that they were at the edge of the rail yard, Colon felt his heart begin to race. He was home, and there wasn't a German soldier on the planet who could match him here. For that matter, as long as his body smarted with every step, as long as the beating he'd received was fresh in his memory, he was convinced that there wasn't a German on earth who could match him anywhere.

It was possible, though, that there was a woman who could match him. As he watched Masha go ahead with Andrei to reconnoiter, he felt certain she was the equal of any street tough, football player, or soldier he had ever met. There was an art to moving in a dangerous situation, and she knew it. She was probably as smart as any Communist could be.

She stopped behind a signal box and motioned to Colon. He and Sergei ran forward, Sergei joining Andrei behind a stack of cross-ties, Colon sliding to Masha's side.

She said, "Ahead is the bridge. This is where it becomes—how do you say it? Tricky?"

Colon looked out, saw the bridge roughly a quarter kilometer away. As they'd expected, soldiers were marching along the length of the span. Colon could also make out soldiers at either end of the trestle.

"Tricky's a good word, but from where I sit it's more like puttin' yer head in a lion's mouth. They've got a clear shot at every car in the yard. If we just run in and try to snipe at them, we're cat food."

Masha's voice hardened. "You say nothing all day, yet now you complain that it's too dangerous—"

"I *ain't* complainin'! I'm just sayin' that if we run in to draw their fire from the lieutenant, we won't be comin' out."

"You have a better idea?"

"Matter of fact, I do." Colon absently tapped his ear with his pistol. "It seems to me the thing t'do is warm the Hun slugs."

"Pardon?"

"Light a fire. Get their attention somewhere else, so that when we start shootin', they'll really have their hands full." Colon pulled matches from his pocket. "Take it from me, Masha. In the right place, a little heat can work wonders on a pack o' worms."

Masha considered this, then waved the other two Russians over and interpreted as Colon explained his strategy.

The last thing Lambert wanted was to do heavy labor. But, as he said to Weyers when they reached the lake and were struck by the enormity of the task, "The Germans will not turn around, no matter how nicely we ask. We'd better get to work." And so, under the light of the rising full moon, they began what Lambert described as "one of the most important landscaping jobs in military history.''

Lambert had Weyers take care of the lake. That was the least creative job. The South African was a good man, but he didn't have the soul of an artist. Creating a new shoreline was a different matter. Lambert felt that he would be better equipped to create the illusion that a portion of the lake was, in fact, solid earth. He thanked God it was dark. The enemy might not give the terrain a second thought.

Weyers went into the B-17 and came out with the pilot's seat. Turning it upside down, he used the backrest as a shovel, scooping snow from the other side of the plane—where the disturbance wouldn't be noticed—and dumping it near the shore. There Lambert smoothed it out, making it seem as though the shore came five meters farther into the lake than it did. When the snow was smooth and level, he gathered rocks and leaves and scattered them about.

That part of the job went quickly.

''That was easy,'' said Lambert. ''Now comes the hard part—creating the detour.''

Still panting from his exertions, Weyers muttered a string of oaths damning ''the easy part'' as he followed his partner into the woods.

One large tree had snapped nearly in two during the storm, and it was relatively simple to twist it from its trunk and drag it to the lake. But there were no other trees, and there was still a stretch of some seven meters to cover—seven meters of real shoreline before the false one.

Lambert checked the time. He began to grow anxious as Weyers tried to push down smaller trees and was unable break them. The Frenchman wasn't even sure that little trees would do the job. The plan wouldn't work if the trucks didn't leave the real shore and go onto the lake. If they used small trees, the trucks would roll right over them.

Then it hit him.

With deep sorrow, followed by a touch of nausea, Lambert went to where the two men from the B-17 were buried.

"You're not," the South African said.

"I am," Lambert replied, and began removing the rocks from the graves.

"This is sick, mate. *Very* sick."

"I know. But can you think of an alternative?"

After hesitating, Weyers said softly, "No. And I've got to believe they'd have understood. In a strange way, I guess they might even have been honored."

Bending, he scooped up an armful of stones and followed Lambert to the unblockaded stretch of shore.

Chapter Fourteen

The cap of the gas tank was frozen shut. By the time Livingston and Ogan managed to work it off, their hands were torn and bleeding; they poured in the contents of the container, and only hoped it was enough to get to the bridge.

Despite the cold, the tank started without much difficulty. It was a large, green Panzer III, and all three were able to fit inside comfortably. Because the cannon had been destroyed, and the ammunition had been taken from the hull machine guns, there was sufficient room for everyone; there was also nothing for Ogan and Vladimir to do but sit while Livingston drove. His face pressed close to the observation window, Livingston backed the tank down to level ground and guided it along the riverbank.

As they rode toward the city, Ogan found a letter tucked folded into the pistol port in the side of the turret. He held it up to the fading light by the porthole, and began to read.

"It looks like the Germans are in worse shape than we imagined." Yelling to be heard above the grinding of the gears, he said, "Listen to this. 'Dearest Father and Mother: Nothing has changed since my last letter to you. Night after night, we sit in our tents, listening to the aircraft engines and trying to guess what supplies they will bring us. Last night we got black pepper and prophylactics, but no food. We are short of all supplies. Each man is given a hundred grams of bread, and watery soup, which we try to improve by stirring it with bones from horses that we dig up. Some of the soldiers actually get to kill and eat horses, but my division, being motorized, is not included in this plan. We are also low on firewood, and because petrol is so difficult to come by, we can make only limited trips into the city to fetch kindling. Ironically, the Russian pigs are able to stay warm at night by burning the ruins of their own buildings. In the morning, when they are fresh, we are frozen.' ''

Livingston said, "I don't hurt for them."

"Wait, there's more. 'Though we continue to fight, there is word that Russian reinforcements are on the way: Rokossovsky from the north, and Vatutin from the west. If this is so, then the sad truth is that we have not yet seen the worst of this war.' ''

Livingston's ears perked. "So that's it, then. The reason for this mustard-gas operation. They don't want to have to fight the armies as well as snipers in the city."

"So it would seem. But why do you suppose Escott and Sweet didn't tell us that reinforcements are coming?"

"Probably because they're top secret. That's why only the Germans know."

The tank rocked and lurched up the dirt road, past the tunnel where Leonid had been captured, then pressed on into the city.

The streets were virtually deserted now, all German personnel having been diverted—probably to guard the shipments. Livingston began to dread what they'd find at the terminal, though he took some consolation from the fact that at least he'd sent Colon ahead. By the time they arrived, there might not be a railroad, let alone any Germans.

Things would have been easier if it hadn't snowed. The wooden cars were damp and the cross-ties were covered with lumpy sheets of ice. Still, Colon felt that the plan would work.

Though the fuel had probably been drained from the cranes and other machines in the service area, kerosene lamps were still hanging from several of the cars. The Russians covered Colon as he moved around and under the trains, draining the lanterns into a rusty bucket he'd found.

When Colon returned, he told the others that he wanted to try to get to the service area in the middle of the yard.

"You're mad!" Masha said. "What's wrong with the cars here?"

"They're too wet. Look." He pointed ahead. "There are three cars coupled at the service platform, under a ledge. They'll be drier, an' if I can get them to burn, the wooden building'll go up too."

"But how will you *get* there?"

Colon studied the terrain. "Whatta we got? Three . . . four freight cars side by side, an open stretch of track, then a turntable, more open track, and then the service area."

"After the freight cars, you'd be out in the open."

"Not me. You guys."

"What?"

"Yeah, an' the open space won't matter, because the Heinies'll be lookin' somewhere else."

Masha shook her head. "I'm sorry, but I don't understand."

Before answering, Colon studied the terminal. It was on the other side of the yard from the service area. Outside the main building were two water tanks and a tower that contained sand for use on icy tracks.

"Look," he said, "we do *two* diversions. Those supports on the sand tower look like they're as old as my grandmother. The thing'll burn like dry leaves."

"So? Once the fire reaches the water towers, it will be extinguished."

"By then, it won't matter. When the legs start to burn, you three run in the other direction, toward the service area, and torch the trains there. We'll have a fire in the north, a fire in the south, and the jerks won't know which way to turn. Meanwhile, we all meet back here and start a fire from the west. They'll think they've got the whole Russian army comin' down their throats."

Masha considered the plan. "There are problems. How will you take the kerosene over?"

"You can thank your countrymen for that." Colon disappeared into the boxcar and returned with an empty vodka bottle. "I noticed it before. I'll use it to make myself a little cocktail."

"And there's something else. By setting this fire before Livingston arrives, you will alert the enemy that there are saboteurs among them. Is that wise?"

Colon gestured toward the bridge. "Hell, they're expectin' us already. Besides"—he glanced at his watch—"it's less than fifteen minutes before the lieutenant arrives. It's about time we started making things hot for these Kraut bastards."

Masha consulted the others, and they agreed to the plan. After mapping a route that would take him under as many cars as possible, and then waiting until the sun had slid behind the terminal, Colon filled the bottle and set out.

The sound arrived long before the trucks themselves. Tucked behind a thick clump of saplings, Weyers and Lambert had been watching the dark lake. When Lam-

bert wasn't studying the shore, wondering if there were
any last-minute touch-ups he should make, he stared at
the B-17. The wind obscured the plane with clouds of
snow; the hazy image reminded Lambert of a mirage.

But the graves were real. The stiff, obscenely slashed
bodies of the pilot and copilot were real. His hate, too,
was real.

He was glad to finally hear the rumbling. It meant that
there was no more time to second-guess their handiwork,
to worry whether or not it would fool the Germans. Now,
it was all in the laps of the gods.

The grinding of the treads was accented, now and then,
by the snap of branches, the thud of trees. The distant
glow of the lanterns through the trees was like fireflies.

"God help us if they're just running everything
down," Weyers said.

Lambert hadn't needed to hear that. "God help us is
right. If the barrier doesn't work, we have only one re-
course left."

"And what's that?"

Lambert muttered, "Snowballs."

Soon the men could hear the crunch of the soldiers'
boots. They huddled lower behind the trees.

The first truck surged into the clearing like a lion
bounding from its lair. It shot over a ridge of snow and
slammed down on the ground, the treads kicking up twin
plumes of snow. The second truck leapt into the clearing
some twenty meters beyond, the two lines of soldiers
marching alongside them both. Under the bright moonlight, the men could also see the trucks' vile cargo quite
clearly: two huge, cylindrical yellow tanks boldly marked
GIFTGAS. Poison gas.

After the trucks emerged in the clearing, Lambert began to worry that the second truck was too far behind
the first. If one sunk right away, there would be enough
time for the other to stop.

Too late to worry, he told himself. There was nothing to do now but sit and watch.

The driver of the lead truck turned to avoid the tree they'd put down, and Lambert's spirits rose. The truck swung toward the lake, then slowed as he approached the graves. The driver peered out the side window, shouted to a major, a chemical warfare officer, walking beside the truck.

"Herr Regierungschemiker—do you think these are ours?"

"Nein."

Lambert's heart was thudding against his throat as the driver shifted gears. *"Mon Dieu,* please, *please—"*

"Wait!" the officer shouted, cupping a hand to his mouth. "Don't run them down. The rocks may be *frozen.* They'll rip the bottom of the truck! Go *around* the graves!"

Acknowledging with a wave, the driver shifted gears and turned the truck toward the lake.

Lambert watched, cursing as the windswept clouds and the snow billowing from beneath the treads obscured his view. The first truck was no longer visible, and he felt a surge of hope as the second truck disappeared into its wake. But that hope died as, like a monster from the depths, the first truck reappeared, rolling up from the lake and back toward the shore.

"The bloody ice is holding!" Weyers snarled. "How is that possible?"

"I don't know—"

Weyers jumped to his feet. "Hell, they're not getting away. I'm gonna go and jump on the goddamn lake my—"

The rest of his exclamation was drowned out by a deep, resounding pop from deep within the white cloud of snow over the lake. It was followed by the sounds of splashing water.

Now Lambert rose. "The second truck must have gone under!"

Both men watched through the trees as the driver of the first truck stopped, jumped out, and ran toward the lake. Now that the treads were still, the Frenchman could see what had happened. The front end of the Maultier was jutting straight from the water. All around it, soldiers were helping their fellows from the lake.

Lambert shook his head angrily, like a dog with a bone. "I won't let one truck get through."

"What are you going to do?"

"Just stay here," the Frenchman said, and ran from the woods.

The South African raised his gun, watching as Lambert forged through the snow. The Germans were too busy pulling each other from the water to notice another man in a German uniform. If they had, Weyers was ready to buy him every possible second.

Lambert covered the fifty meters to the truck, then ducked inside. Throwing the truck into reverse, he waited until it began edging backward, then flung himself out the door.

There were shouts as men saw the truck coming toward them, and oaths as it picked up speed. The huge Opel hit the lake with a thump, then stalled. It sat there for a moment, and then, as though a trapdoor had opened beneath it, the truck plunged through the ice. The surface of the lake rippled and cracked, men shouting and vanishing as the frigid waters swallowed them. The turbulence sent the other truck over onto its back, trapping the tank of mustard gas beneath it. Steam rose from the engines of the two trucks, large bubbles bursting where they sank.

A few men who had stayed on the shore shot at Lambert, but Weyers's return fire sent them retreating to the far side of the lake, where they took cover behind a string of boulders. Picking himself up, the Frenchman ran for the clump of trees.

"That was good," Weyers said as he continued to shoot at the Germans, "but why didn't you *take* the damn truck? We could have dumped the gas somewhere, and then we wouldn't have had to walk back to Stalingrad."

Lambert drew his own pistol and fired several rounds. "I wanted the gas *gone, mon ami*. I did get this, though." He pulled a crumpled map from his coat. "It was lying on the seat. At least we'll be able to find the most direct route back to the city."

Weyers and Lambert picked off several soldiers who managed to pull themselves from the water. Then, still firing, they began their retreat.

Exhausted as they were, the Frenchman couldn't help but smile. "You know what's most amazing, Wings? That we actually managed to follow our original orders."

"How's that?"

"What was our mission?"

"To sink the gas."

"And what did we do?"

Weyers frowned as they stopped firing and began to run through the woods. "Look at it a different way, Rotter."

"Ah, the voice of the pragmatist."

"Call me names if ya want, but tell me who *really* sunk the Jerries—us or the B-17 crew?"

Lambert's smile evaporated. "*C'est vrai.* It *is* they who deserve the medals."

Only the howling of the wind, the lengthening shadows of late afternoon, and their thoughts of the brave fliers accompanied the men as they made their way in silence through the woods.

The tank lumbered past a row of ramshackle log huts on the outskirts of the train yard. It was nearly five, and the sun was down. There was less than two hours before the train reached the terminal.

The railroad workers once lived at this end, men whose lives were directed by the howl of incoming trains. The trains would call and, regardless of the hour, the men would go out and pamper them.

Ironically, Livingston thought, these men and their kind understood discomfort and sacrifice. Unwittingly, in modernizing the railroads, Stalin had prepared his people for the deprivation that was to follow.

After passing the nine shacks, and the huge iron and rubber bumpers that marked the end of the rail line, Livingston maneuvered the tank onto the tracks.

Ahead, roughly an eighth of a kilometer away, was the bridge. Soldiers stood shoulder to shoulder along its entire length, and also as far as he could see on either side.

The tracks slipped by. Now and then, a soldier would look back at them, then turn away. Because he was driving a German tank, no one gave him a second thought.

Vladimir hugged the dynamite to him. Ogan had managed to explain the plan, telling the boy that they'd park the tank beneath the bridge, light the fuses, then evacuate. But Vladimir shook his head, said that he didn't want to run the risk of the tank's containing the blast. He wanted to make sure the bridge came down. And the only way to do that was for him to get out and slap the explosives beneath the trestle.

The plan was extremely dangerous, from Vladimir's point of view. But neither of them could deny that it would be more effective. Nor could they have talked the Russian out of it if they'd wanted to. Indeed, as they neared the bridge, Vladimir seemed almost buoyant, eager for the chance to strike back at the enemy.

When they were just two hundred meters away, Ogan pushed at the hatch. There was a moment of concern when it refused to budge, but it gave when Ogan and the youth both put their shoulders to it.

Ogan went to the pistol port, did his best to draw a bead on the bridge. The clank of the hatch drew some attention, and soldiers who turned now continued to look down at the tank.

"We've got them asking questions," Ogan warned.

Livingston handed Vladimir the matches. "Good. Because it's time to give them some answers."

Livingston and the Russian shared a long, respectful look, after which Vladimir lit the dynamite. The fuses cast a bright, blinding light through the tank, and Livingston had to shield his eyes to see the terrain ahead. An *oberst* had been summoned, and was leaning imperiously on the railing, shouting down. Several soldiers, rifles held across their chests, stood at his side.

Livingston said, "He wants us to identify ourselves, Ken."

"If you can swing me to the side just a bit, I'll be happy to oblige."

Livingston turned the wheel slightly, and the tank moved ahead diagonally. The maneuver gave Ogan a clear view of the bridge, and though the tank was rocking vigorously, he managed to spray the target area with gunfire. Livingston was pleased that though Ogan was a professional bleeding heart, he also knew when to stanch the flow.

The railing stopped most of the bullets, but a soldier and the *oberst* went down.

"Good job," Livingston said.

Livingston straightened their course, but when the tank was just a few meters from the bridge, he swung diagonally again.

"Give them another round, Ken. I don't want them shooting down the hatch."

Ogan slapped in his last clip and fired slowly at the bridge. Two more soldiers fell, and a few Karabiners poked through the rails, one shot blazing through the observation window, right past Livingston's cheek. But then they were under the bridge and Vladimir hopped up through the canopy.

"Good luck!" Livingston shouted as the boy climbed onto the turret, the dynamite blazing in a bundle under one arm.

Livingston stopped the tank and watched through the observation port as the boy looked for a place to lay the sticks. He tried to wedge it in a V-shaped joint between two of the girders, but the metal was too thin and the bundle wouldn't balance there.

Livingston licked his lips as the fuses shrank. There were shouts from above, and the clatter of boots. Soldiers were running from the bridge toward the wall that bordered the lower tracks.

They were coming down.

Aware of the soldiers, Vladimir rattled a fist in frustration. He squinted into the darkness above, studied a platform where the shoe connected the middle support to the span. He looked back at Livingston and, with a smile, used his foot to slam the hatch shut.

"Vladimir! What the hell are you doing?"

"He's climbing, sir! He's going up the support!"

"They'll cut him in half!" With a snarl, Livingston threw the tank into reverse. "Ken, can you cover him?"

Ogan was already looking out the port, and began shooting at the soldiers as they tried to come down the wall onto the lower tracks. Suddenly, the healthy shout of the pistol was replaced by a soft click.

"Empty," Ogan said with disgust.

Livingston continued to back up, watching as Vladimir scaled the girders. He lay the dynamite on the small square of metal. Swearing, Livingston threw the tank ahead.

"Ken, get ready to open the—"

The roar followed the blaze by a heartbeat. It hadn't come from the bridge but from the terminal, from a rickety wooden tower.

"Must be Colon!" Ogan shouted.

Livingston nodded as he pressed the controls, trying to get every available ounce of speed from the tank. He looked out as Vladimir just clung there in the shadows, his grim expression illuminated by the flickering fuse.

"Hold on, kid, just hold on!"

Suddenly the world went white, as the bridge, the soldiers, and part of the terminal flew in pieces into the air.

Chapter Fifteen

Blinded by the blast, Livingston plowed into the wall.
Several soldiers fell as the stone edifice crumbled; Ogan
and Livingston themselves were thrown back as the tank
came to rest at a sharp angle. Grabbing the controls, the
lieutenant pulled himself up, spitting out dust and particles of stone that had been blown through the observation
window. There were shouts and gunfire all around them,
followed by a hard rapping on the hatch of the tank.

"Lieutenant! Are you okay? *Lieutenant!*"

Reaching up, Livingston threw back the hatch. A Karabiner was thrust into his hand.

"Here's one for the sergeant major too," Colon said,
handing down another rifle.

"The bridge?" Livingston said.

"Ain't nothing there 'cept air." He smiled. Spinning,
he sprayed gunfire behind him, then looked back into the
hatch. "Come on, sir. We can't let Masha and her pals
fight this thing on their own."

Livingston accepted Colon's hand and climbed through
the hatch.

The rail yard was an inferno, flames rising from the
cars, repair platform, and terminal, an inferno peppered
with white flashes as fuel or ammunition exploded.

"It was somethin'!" Colon enthused. "The sand tower fell right away, set off fuel or explosives or whatever the hell they had in the terminal. Took a pisspot fulla Krauts with it."

Livingston commended him and, as he helped the dazed Ogan from the tank, he scanned the wreckage of the bridge. There were bodies and parts of bodies lying amid the rubble. He didn't see a trace of Vladimir but knew there was no way he could have survived.

Through the smoke of the smoldering bridge, Livingston could see Masha and her people advancing across the tracks. "Come on," he said, "we've still got a train to catch."

While Ogan and Colon set up covering fire, Livingston climbed from the tank, ran across the tracks, and stepping over a pile of bodies, scaled the wall on the opposite side of the track. Colon went next, grabbing a second Karabiner as he ran, and, holding both waist high, fired from the hip at anything that had a uniform and wasn't dead. When Livingston and Colon had taken up positions on the far side, Ogan scurried across the tracks.

By this time, reinforcements were pouring from the terminal. Livingston guessed there were at least one hundred soldiers converging on the rail yard, most of them stepping over the wounded and the dead, taking up positions behind smoking rubble or still-flaming trains.

Livingston said, "We'll have to hurry. As soon as they realize there's only a handful of us, they'll charge us."

"Then we can't let 'em realize that," Colon replied, firing across the tracks.

Masha and Sergei came running past the destroyed bridge. They dropped flat beside Livingston.

"Fine job," he said, then frowned. "Where's Andrei?"

"He had an idea." She pointed to a smoking locomotive and freight train that had begun inching toward them from well down the track.

"With all the smoke and fire around, no one saw him stoke it. He felt it would give us extra cover."

"Good idea," Livingston said as the old, black locomotive chugged toward them. "I suggest we take advantage of it."

Everyone but Colon turned and started toward the north.

"Private! Let's move it out!"

"You go, sir! Someone's got to cover for Andrei!"

Colon lay there and watched as the burning train headed toward the wreck of the bridge. Soldiers retreated as the fiery train picked up speed, most of them diving to their bellies as the locomotive hit the twisted girders with a grating smack. It threw them in all directions, the impact also derailing the train. The locomotive skidded off the terminal side of the track bed, dust and stone flying as it plowed into the shattered wall below. The other cars slammed into the engine and folded one into the other, throwing slats of wood and burning embers in all directions.

Glancing down the track, Colon saw Andrei approaching from behind the wreckage. He was covered with blood and dragging a leg.

Leaving one of his guns behind, Colon ran toward the tracks. Before he'd taken more than a few steps, however, a burst of gunfire brought Andrei down.

"No!" Colon stopped, aimed, and shot at a German soldier who was lying behind an overturned truck. A German helmet ducked back and Colon continued toward Andrei.

Watching from the other side of the tracks, Livingston and Masha set up a protective fire as Colon knelt beside the Russian. He put his ear to Andrei's chest, felt his wrist. Screaming, he ran across the tracks, toward the German side.

"Colon!" Livingston hollered.

The private either ignored him or didn't hear him.

Oblivious to his own pain, the deep wounds from the beating, Colon ran around the flaming train and up the shattered wall to the overturned truck. The German's rifle came around the fender, but Colon swung his own Karabiner, using it like a club, to smack the other gun away. Then he flipped the rifle around, aimed, and fired twice. He looked down for a moment; satisfied, he turned and ran back across the track, scooping up an armful of rifles as he crossed.

"That was a damn foolish thing to do," Livingston said when Colon rejoined them.

"I know, sir, but Andrei bought us time. His killer *needed* to die."

There was no disputing Colon's logic and, after making sure that Masha and Sergei were all right, Livingston distributed the extra guns, then led the team into the field beyond the tracks. Despite what had just happened, the Russian woman's face was as impassive as ever. He couldn't help but wonder if it would remain so when, at last, they came face-to-face with the cargo that had cost her so dearly.

The team proceeded in leapfrog fashion. Two of them stayed behind at all times to cover their backs. When the other four had gone approximately one hundred meters, two of them would peel off and the other two would catch up.

They'd gone just over a kilometer when they saw the train.

It was coming out of the large, low moon, and looked like something a child might have designed using toy soldiers—overcrowded and overarmed. There were soldiers riding on the locomotive, standing on the injector pipe, holding on to the handrail, and hanging on to the window. There were also men on the flatbed car, surrounding the two gas tanks, and there were rifles pointing from the ports of the armored car and caboose. There were even soldiers standing on the couplers and on the front of the locomotive.

"Looks like they're expectin' company," Colon said.

Livingston agreed. The Germans were indeed prepared for a massive assault, and the lieutenant bitterly regretted that he wouldn't be able to give it to them.

Livingston looked around. The track passed through a plain that sloped gently toward them, to the west. There was a barren, snow-covered field to the north of the tracks; to the south, several broken carts and a rusted plow. Beyond the implements was a ramshackle shed and more acres of white terrain. The burned skeleton of a barn was well in the distance.

In just a moment, the men in the train would spot them. Livingston ordered the team behind the sled. After surveying the field one last time, he joined them.

"The way I see it, we've got to concentrate on the locomotive. If we can take it and run the train backwards, fine. Failing that, let's at least try to uncouple it. If we have to, we'll start shooting holes in the gas tanks, release the stuff here. With any luck, it won't drift far."

The ground began to tremble as the train neared.

"You're gonna want someone shootin' from the other side," Colon said. "I'll go."

"No. We attack from this side. At least we've got cover. We'll go after the men on this side of the locomotive, and whoever's in the cab. We'll worry about the other side when we get on board."

As they crouched beside the shack, Ogan sidled up to Livingston. "For what it's worth, sir, I think you've done a hell of a job getting us this far."

"It was all of us," Livingston said, glancing over at the Russians. "Everyone did their job."

Masha was watching the tracks from around the corner of the shed. "They're slowing!"

"Someone must have radioed ahead," Ogan said, "or maybe they saw the smoke from the terminal."

"They're stopping," Masha said. After a moment, she added, "That's strange."

"What is?"

"Before, they were pulling an engine in back. Now they are not."

"Freight trains usually travel wit' a spare," said Colon. "They must've dumped it to conserve—"

"Soldiers are coming from the armored car and flatbed," Masha interrupted. "They're walking along tracks."

"They *must* have gotten word about us," Ogan said.

"I vote we attack," Colon added. "If they pin us here, this isn't gonna be a happy fight."

Livingston looked around. Colon had a point, but he didn't relish attacking more than three dozen soldiers. The rotted carts offered no defense, and going inside the shack would be suicidal. He pursed his lips and wormed over to Masha's side.

"I'd give my right arm for a hand grenade," he said as the Germans fanned out, obviously intending to surround the place. "I don't like the odds, Masha, but it looks as though Colon's right. We're going to have to take the offensive, and hope that one of us gets close enough to the tanks to put a few holes in them."

"Agreed," she said.

"We'll let them get a little farther from the train, so they can't use it for cover."

Colon said, "Wouldn't it be a kick in the head if we go ahead and get killed—and Rotter and Wings failed?"

"A riot," Ogan said. He gripped his rifle tightly and forced a smile. "But Rotter didn't fail, God bless him. He and Wings probably sunk the ships and then went looking for a sunlamp."

"Or a dame."

"Or a train!" Livingston said. "I'll be goddamned, will you look at this?"

The others rolled out slightly so they could see. The

Germans also stopped and turned, watched as a lone locomotive rocketed along the tracks. Lambert was leaning from the window, illuminated by the steady fire from his MP38, which he was directing at the soldiers on the tracks. An *oberst* standing in the cab screamed for the soldiers to board.

Masha said, "That was the spare locomotive."

"He's got one hell of a head of steam," Ogan said. "He's going to ram them."

"Let's give them something to think about on this side," Livingston said.

Diving sideways, clear of all obstacles, Colon began shooting. Before the Germans had turned back to face the attack, his bullets killed five of them. The two Russians went around the shack, firing as they ran toward the train, while Ogan and Livingston covered them from behind the shack. Half the Germans who had left the train were dead before the others could organize to meet both fronts.

On the locomotive, the *oberst* pushed at his engineer, and the train began to move again.

"We can't let him through," Livingston said. "Go after the damn locomotive!"

He came from behind the shed and, following Colon, ran down the other side of the tracks. Ogan ran after Masha and, from the corner of his eye, Livingston saw the Russian woman spin and go down. Sergei looked back; Ogan waved him on as he slid to her side.

"Go ahead," she said, clutching her thigh. "I'm all right."

"Are you sure?"

"Yes! *Get the train.*"

The ground was quickly staining red beneath her. "We'll be back for you," the Englishman said, and hurried forward.

Livingston was still firing, still waiting for the train to pass, when plumes of red began spraying from the backs and legs of the Germans the *oberst* had left behind. Lambert had come within range, and was stitching the few men who survived with bursts from his pistol. Clearly, all that mattered to the *oberst* now was outrunning Weyers's locomotive.

Ahead of Livingston, a bullet from the German train knocked Colon onto his back. A stream of gunfire also forced Livingston, Ogan, and Sergei to seek cover on their respective sides of the track. As the train roared by, the few guns still active in the caboose kept them pinned where they were.

When the train had passed, Livingston rose.

"Damn! *Damn!*"

He glanced ahead at Colon, who waved weakly. Then he looked at Weyers's engine, which was racing toward him. Throwing his rifle over his back and jamming his pistol in the pocket of his Russian coat, he ran toward the track.

"No!" the South African yelled. "Don't try it!"

"Like hell I won't," Livingston said under his breath. As the locomotive passed, the lieutenant reached out and grabbed the ladder behind the coal tender. The maneuver nearly dislocated both arms, but he held on. Locking his feet around the rung, he got a better grip and then pulled himself up into the coal bin. Hurrying across the scraps of coal that remained, he climbed into the cab.

"That was *tres* impressive, sir," Lambert said, "but I'm afraid you will never play the piano again."

Livingston rubbed his right shoulder. The warmth from the open coal furnace felt good. "What the hell are you two doing here?"

"Seeing the countryside, sir."

Livingston frowned. "The gas—"

"We took care of it, lieutenant. As for being here, we located the tracks thanks to a map we took from the Germans. We thought it would be the best way to meet up with the rest of you. We rode a hand cart until we discovered this locomotive a few kilometers back." He cocked a thumb toward a transmitter in the control panel. "We were not far away when we heard someone from the terminal radio ahead about a fire. It didn't take a genius to figure out the rest."

"You saved our skins," Livingston said as he looked ahead at the German train. "What are you planning to do now?"

Weyers said without turning, "We're going to stop them, sir."

"That's fine, but you can't derail them. This close to the terminal, they can still get the gas into Stalingrad."

Weyers moved the throttle and they gained slightly on the train. "I have no intention of derailing them, sir. This is a Gelsky train, sir. We've got a coupler in front. Rotter," he yelled over his shoulder, "I'm gonna need more fire! I'm really pushing her now."

Sighing, Lambert grabbed a shovel and began feeding coal into the open furnace. Livingston helped by picking up chunks and throwing them in.

Soldiers in the caboose began firing at them as the locomotive gained on them. The engine clanged as bullets struck inside and out; Livingston and Colon bent, but Weyers continued to stare ahead. He didn't flinch even when the window exploded and showered him with glass.

"All right," he said when just a few meters separated the two trains, "I'm going to make my move!"

Livingston stood and watched as they closed, slowly, on the caboose. And he realized, then, that Weyers had no intention of hitting the train at all.

The lunatic was going to try to grab it.

Chapter Sixteen

Weyers was literally nursing the throttle as he approached, edging the stick forward, then back. He was no longer gaining in meters but in centimeters, the caboose within arm's length, the couplers brushing.

The South African gave the locomotive a jolt and the couplers connected. The instant he heard the distinctive clack of the latch, Weyers yelled for the men to brace themselves, then pulled on the air brakes.

Though prepared, the three men were hurled against the control panel. The locomotive squealed violently and, climbing back to his feet, Livingston could see sparks flying across the snow; the smell of ozone filled his nostrils.

The locked trains ground to a halt. Looking ahead, Livingston could see the ruined bridge and flaming terminal.

"Tug-o'-war time," Weyers said, and threw the locomotive into reverse. The wheels screamed and pistons howled as the engine began creeping backward. "Give me more fire, Rotter!"

Lambert and Livingston began tossing more coal into the furnace. Over the din, the lieutenant could barely make out the *oberst* screaming at his men.

"What's he barking about?" Lambert asked.

Livingston stopped shoveling and listened.

"What is it, sir? Can you make it out?"

Swearing, Livingston grabbed his rifle and scampered up the control panel to the shattered windshield. He paused and said, "Cover me, Rotter. The sonofabitch is going to uncouple the trains."

Squeezing through, the lieutenant leapt over the steam dome and sidestepped the whistle. Lying down behind the smokestack, he hooked his feet through the handrails that ran along the top of the locomotive.

The locomotive was higher than the caboose and the armored car, and he had a relatively clear shot at both. The few soldiers left in the caboose were trying to make their way forward; after Livingston picked the first two off, the others retreated. Return fire from the armored car flew wide of Livingston's position, the portholes having been designed to cover only the sides of the train. The smokestack rendered the 76.2mm gun on top useless. Leaning from the cabin, Lambert drove back the few soldiers who came out to try to get a clear shot.

Weyers's engine began to pick up speed, and the entire train started rolling backward.

"Just as I figured!" Weyers cheered. "The bugger's all but run out of coal!"

Suddenly, the train lurched to a stop again as the engineer on the German train applied his own brakes. As soon as it did so, a handful of men came from the locomotive, pale, surreal figures in the stark moonlight. Two of them set up a cross fire on the smokestack, while a third and fourth made their way onto the flatbed. Before ducking to safety, Livingston saw that they had chain cutters.

There were two massive chains holding the gas tanks side by side on the flatbed. One was draped across the front, one across the back. The *oberst* intended to unload the gas here, and probably try to haul it into the city.

"Lieutenant!" Weyers yelled. "He got us that time. It'll be a few minutes before I've got the *oomph* to override him!"

"We don't *have* a few minutes!" Livingston yelled. "They're dumping the gas tanks!"

"Like hell they are!" Lambert yelled, bolting from the cab door like a human cannonball. "Not after all we've been through!"

The Frenchman followed a spray of gunfire as he ran along the side of the train. Gunfire from inside the armored car, however, sent the Frenchman jumping back against the side of the locomotive.

"Maybe some other time, *oui*?"

"Stay put," Livingston said. "Just keep an eye on the back of the flatbed—don't let them uncouple it!"

Save for the coughing of the locomotive, there was silence as the Germans worked on the chains at the back of the flatbed. The armored car obstructed his view completely, and rushing them would be suicidal; he could do nothing until the soldiers went to release the chains in front.

As he lay there, the cars once again began to ease backward under the pull of Weyers's engine. The German locomotive complained, but it wasn't able to hold its ground. Black clouds rose around him, and the heat of the engine roof began to burn his coat. He knew he wouldn't be able to stay there for long.

Lambert walked backward, alongside the train. He stayed wide enough to keep an eye on the coupler between the flatbed and the armored car; the gas tanks prevented the Germans from having a clear shot at him.

As they began to pick up speed, Livingston saw movement below, on the western side. Inching over, he saw three soldiers using the shadow of the train to try to reach the caboose and uncouple it. Livingston shot down at them, and the men ducked between the cars. Shifting quickly to the other side, the lieutenant got Lambert's attention. He held up three fingers and pointed to the coupler; nodding, the Frenchman stopped walking. As the coupler section passed, he shot the men dead.

The locomotive screeched and slowed again. Smoke poured from the German locomotive as the engineer obviously stoked his engine with everything he had left. It was then, over the din of the engines, that Livingston heard the order he'd been dreading: With a steady wind blowing in from the north, the *oberst* told the men on the flatbed to release the gas.

The valves were in the back, where the men already were. There was no way Livingston could stop them from atop the locomotive: He'd have to go forward.

"Lambert! Up here!"

Even before the Frenchman had climbed the ladder, Livingston had gone to the front of the locomotive, swung down to the headlight in the center of the boiler front, and jumped onto the back of the iron-plated caboose. Reaching up with his pistol, he fired into one of the ports, then ran up the ladder in back to the top of the car. Gunfire cracked from behind him as Lambert kept the soldiers in the armored car from opening the rear door. Just then, Livingston heard a yell from behind as a sudden down draft swept the dark cloud from the smoke-stack into Lambert's face. Livingston turned just in time to see the Frenchman's rifle slip from his hands as he reflexively pressed them to his eyes.

Livingston had no choice but to continue, and scurrying along on his belly, he reached the end of the caboose, crouched, and jumped to the armored boxcar.

Weyers's engine was beginning to win the battle again, and under the strident cries of the *oberst*, Livingston could hear the soldiers working frantically to open the tanks. As the train had passed earlier, Livingston had seen that the valve screws were driven by wheels twice the size of a manhole cover. It would take a few minutes to crank it open.

Livingston raced ahead. Just as he rounded the turret containing the 76.2mm guns, a soldier's head appeared at the far end of the car, along with a Luger; it cracked twice and a bullet caught Livingston in the side. He fell onto his belly and, despite the pain, managed to crawl back behind the turret.

The train was picking up speed, heading away from the city. Livingston leaned on the turret, waited for the soldier to show himself again. There was more yelling, this time from the flatbed. He wormed forward on his good side, slowly, painfully, half expecting to see smudges of gas rise above the roof of the boxcar. It hurt worse than the wound to think that they'd come this far, only to be a few bullets away from succeeding.

But instead of the gas, he heard shots from the flatbed, and then from the western side of the train. Looking over, he saw Ogan and Sergei crouched behind a snowbank, firing at the soldiers. Livingston dragged himself forward, peered over the edge of the car. The four soldiers were hiding behind the tanks, shooting back. The *oberst* came out and was firing as well.

They'd forgotten about Livingston. He'd make them wish they hadn't. Leaning on the top rung of a ladder, he rose to his knees.

"Gute nacht, meine herren!" he said and, raising his pistol, shot from the hip. They fell in turn, the *oberst* dropping to the side, between the flatbed and the locomotive.

Painfully lowering himself to the flatbed, Livingston went to check on the forward chain when the engineer came from the locomotive and began firing—not at Livingston, but at the gas tanks. Two of his bullets struck one of the tanks, and a greasy, yellow smoke began to drift from the side.

Livingston shot the engineer, then, dizzy from the loss of blood, fell beside the tank. Grabbing the chain that was still attached to the tanks, Ogan pulled himself up.

He climbed between the flatbed and the locomotive and, grabbing the lever that linked the couplers, pulled up. There was a loud snap, a surge of speed, and the German locomotive began to recede and slow.

Ogan came over. Livingston was coughing, unable to hold his breath. Putting his arm across his back, Ogan rose and was nearly knocked over by the tanks, which, held by just one chain, swayed precariously as the train picked up speed. Dropping to his knees, the Englishman crawled to the side of the flatbed and heaved Livingston over. The lieutenant landed in the snow, and Ogan followed him off.

The sergeant major landed on his shoulder and rolled through the snow. When he got his bearings, he saw Livingston lying several meters away and hurried over.

When he arrived, Livingston managed to prop himself on an elbow. Together, they watched as the train, racing now, headed back toward the fields trailing a thick column of black smoke and, below it, a thinner column of yellow poison. He lay back.

"Weyers—Lambert. Did they get off?"

"Naturellement," said the Frenchman.

The two were plodding over from the south. They'd obviously bailed out before Ogan and Livingston.

"That's what I like," Livingston said. "Men who stick with something to the end."

"There was nothing else we could do," Weyers said as he squinted through the fading light at the train.

"Besides, Lieutenant," said Lambert, "we did our job. We assumed that you were capable of doing yours."

Livingston managed a weak smile and lay back. He looked up at Weyers, who was towering above him. There were dark circles around his eyes and grime on his cheeks and forehead, his face was drawn, and he was panting heavily. But Livingston couldn't remember when he'd seen a more satisfied smile on anyone's lips.

Sergei joined the group.

"The others," Livingston said. "How are they?"

Ogan told him about Masha, then asked Sergei about Colon. The Russian pointed to his left shoulder. "Colon—*mnyeh zdyes balna.*"

"Shot in the shoulder," Ogan said.

Lambert said, "Between that and the prison, there is one man who will be sore come morning."

Just then, there was a grating sound from well up the tracks. The men watched as, in the distance, the runaway train hopped the track, dragging its deadly cargo with it. The furnace exploded and, amid the billowing black smoke, the yellow fumes twined slowly, wraithlike, from the wreckage. It hung low over the wreckage; only the fringes of the cloud were disturbed by the wind.

"It'll dissipate slowly," Ogan said, "but I doubt that it will get anywhere near the city."

Lambert shook his head. "All this, an' a train wreck too. *Mes amis*—it's almost like *Noel*!"

Weyers and Ogan helped Livingston back to the shed, where they were joined by Colon and Lambert. The men lay Livingston down beside Masha and, after bandaging his wound with fur torn from the pockets of their coats, they went outside and began forming the boards of the cart into a sledge.

Though they didn't think the Germans would come after them in the dark and subzero temperatures, they had to leave. The gas cloud was creeping toward them. Under the full moon, the low-lying poison almost seemed to glow as it rolled along, a meter above the ground.

"I've seen mustard gas before," said Weyers as he lay Livingston on the stripped-down cart, "but whatever the Nazis did to make it cling like that is vile."

"I wish we could take back a sample," Ogan said. "Maybe there's a way to counteract the stuff."

"We've *got* the way," replied the South African. "It's

called *leaving*." He looked across the field again, shuddered like a child. "And the sooner, the better."

Their destination was a car factory less than a quarter of a mile from the Volga. The Russians had converted it to a tank factory, and the Germans had burned it; however, because it was so far northeast of the city, neither the Russians nor the Germans had bothered basing people there. Nevertheless, as a place for exhausted refugees to spend the night, it was ideal.

The snow had melted slightly during the day, and it had frozen again when the sun went down, giving the team a hard, slick surface for the sledge. Though the trek was demanding, and the temperatures bitter, there was no wind, and they completed the trip by dawn. Livingston couldn't believe it had been just two days, exactly, since they'd arrived in Russia. But again, as in Algiers, despite everything that had happened—or *because* of it?— they had been two of the most rewarding days of his life.

After settling in amid the charred machines of the cavernous factory, they fed on hares Weyers and Sergei had shot. At the express request of the South African, Lambert was barred from participating in the hunt.

After resting for a full day, the group headed for the Volga. The sight that greeted them caused them to stop in their tracks.

A wave of Russian infantry was moving in from the north: on gunboats, down the shores, through the fields, and along the bluffs. In the distance, the commandos could vaguely make out T-70 light tanks, and the heavier T-34s; trucks carrying rocket-launchers and stacks of 132mm rockets; and rows of sleek 45mm field guns. On the other side of the river, the armies that had been holding the line there were now advancing southwest, toward the German batteries that guarded the river.

"Holy Moses," Weyers muttered, his exclamation speaking for his teammates, who stood in awed silence. Masha and Sergei broke down and cried.

The group was spotted by a young lieutenant at the front of the lines, who ran ahead with five men. When they saw that several of the party were wearing German uniforms, they drew their guns and approached more cautiously.

Sergei went forward to talk to the men and, as the armies continued to march by, he explained what had happened. When he was finished, the officer pushed back his cap and whistled once. He saluted Livingston, who returned the greeting, then sent one of his men to fetch a medic. Another was dispatched to brief General K. K. Rokossovsky.

In less than a minute, the general's tank had pulled to the front of the lines. The ruggedly handsome Rokossovsky climbed from the open hatch and, after embracing the two Russians, offered each of the Force Five team members his hand. Lambert also accepted an offered cigarette.

Through Masha, he said to Livingston, "We'd heard of the gas and feared that we would find a dead city. Your courageous actions will long be remembered."

The medic arrived and, after tending to Masha and Colon, treated Livingston's wounds. The lieutenant lay back on the sledge. As far as he was concerned, the bulk of the healing had already been done. These fresh, well-supplied Russian troops would make life miserable for the invaders. He knew the Germans wouldn't roll over and die, but he knew too that they would never take Stalingrad. He looked down the river, squinted into the rising sun, and smiled.

"What's so amusing?" Ogan asked.

"The sun. It's warm. And there's no wind."

Ogan looked around. "An aberration."

"No," Livingston said, drinking in the sight of the soldiers marching past, then shutting his eyes. "A new day."

Chapter Seventeen

The Admiral's Pub was empty this early before lunch. There were ships to attend to, campaigns to plan, fish to catch, and businesses to run. Only soldiers on leave could visit during the late morning, and there were very few of those.

Lambert, Weyers, and Colon were sitting at the bar, nursing beers and wounds.

"Can you believe that mad bastard won't let them surrender?" Weyers asked.

Lambert took a swallow of beer. "Nothing the Führer does surprises me. He was *un idiot* for going into Russia in the first place."

"We weren't?"

"Ours was a noble cause," Lambert replied with a flourish. "Theirs was loathsome."

"But ya gotta admire their guts," Colon said. He was seated at the far end, munching pretzels. "Man fer man, those Krauts ain't pushovers."

"And so many of them are going to die," Lambert said. "How many are left at Stalingrad? Over two hundred thousand?"

"More, I think." Weyers threw his head back, did some rapid calculations. "I make it they'll need about

six or seven hundred tons of supplies each day just to
survive. Even if Hitler could round up the goods, the
Luftwaffe can't spare the planes to carry them in.''

Lambert raised his beer. "To advance planning," he
said. "May the Germans continue to leave it all in the
Führer's capable hands.''

Someone sat heavily in the stool beside Lambert. The
Frenchman looked over congenially. His expression
clouded.

"I heard you blokes were here. I was afraid we'd miss
ye.''

In the dark pub, the red beard of the newcomer looked
like a mass of sandstone. The eyes were even harder.
The fists resting on the faded mahogany were harder still.

Lambert sighed. "Captain Thorpe. How decent of you
to welcome us back. I *know* you are a *tres* busy man.''

"Very.'' Two other men moved over from a table in
the corner. One carried a blackjack, the other was rubbing a pair of brass knuckles.

Thorpe took a sip from Lambert's beer.

"By all means, help yourself," the Frenchman said.
He looked at Colon, who was staring stiffly ahead at the
life preservers hanging behind the bar. Weyers was half
turned to Lambert, watching from the corner of his eye.

The old bartender came over. "What can I git ye
gents?''

"Towels," said the captain. "A lot of them.''

"I beg yer pardon?''

"I said *towels*. Y'know—the kind ye use to mop up a
mess.''

The bartender looked from the captain to Lambert.
The Frenchman shook his head. "Don't bother. We're
going outside.''

"No, we ain't, Rotter.''

The five men looked at Colon. Thorpe snickered.
" 'S'matter, mate? Afraid of a fair fight?''

Colon finished his beer. "Bartender, set me up another."

The captain's bushy red brow drooped angrily. "I asked a question, ye Yankee runt. Are ye afraid to fight *fair*?"

"Bartender," Colon said, "you happen to know any American football scores here?"

The burly Scot spun off the stool and walked to the end of the bar, his two men in tow. He leaned on the bar, next to Colon. "Ye were the one who set up that dirty fight, scumbag. I want *you* in particular. Now, are ye gettin' up like a man, or do I have t'*drag* ye from yer seat?"

Colon picked up the fresh stein and took a mouthful of beer. He faced Thorpe—and as he spit the brew into his eyes, brought the stein down hard on Thorpe's hand, which was flat on the bar. The captain howled, and Colon swung his left fist in the man's belly. Thorpe bent at the waist and the glass came down on his head.

As soon as Colon hit the captain's hand, the seaman with the blackjack raised it—only to have Weyers catch his wrist with one hand and break his nose with the other. The sailor stumbled over an anchor and slid to the floor. Lambert beat the third sailor to his feet and, ducking an awkward swing from the man's brass knuckles, locked an arm around his neck and yanked him around, where he met Weyers's massive fist. The seaman seemed to hang on the South African's knuckles for a moment, then fell straight to the floor.

Weyers went over to Colon, who had popped his bandages and was holding his shoulder, wincing.

"You all right?"

"*No!* I really wanted to *kill* the big bastard!"

"I think he means your shoulder," Lambert said as he put several pound notes on the bar.

"Yeah, that's awright. I'll get it fixed."

The bartender walked over. He had been watching

from the door, one foot on the wharf. "Thanks for not bustin' the place up."

"We're not like that," Weyers said. "We're not rowdies."

"Mais non!" Lambert said. "Do we look like the kind of men who would beat up fellow soldiers?"

The bartender studied each of their faces. "Frankly—no." He looked down at the three moaning sailors, then picked up the pound notes Lambert had placed on the counter. He folded them into the Frenchman's hand. "But I've been listening to the things you've been saying—and the next time you *do* fight the Jerries, give them a shot for ol' Dale Rupert. God bless you all."

Lambert was genuinely touched. Weyers leaned over the bar and shook the old man's hand. "Count on me to deliver," the South African said.

"Algeria . . . Russia," the bartender continued. "Any idea where you'll end up next?"

"I wish I did." Lambert smiled. "But they like to surprise us."

Weyers and Lambert headed to the door; Colon paused and, looking down at Captain Thorpe, bent and grabbed a handful of the man's beard. He pulled the round face toward him and lifted the lid of one eye. *"Excremento!* Before we go, there's one thing I want t'say. If we *ever* have the bad luck t'meet again . . . it's *Mr.* Yankee runt to you. Got it, sea biscuit?"

Thanking the bartender again, Lambert went over and pulled Colon onto the dock.

"You know," he said as they walked from the Thames, "compared to Russia, winter in London feels almost—balmy!"

"Speaking of Russia," Weyers said with a frown, "we really shouldn't talk so openly about what we do."

"In the crowded underground, we shouldn't. But in a deserted tavern?"

"Hey, for all we know, that bloke in there might've een a spy."

"Monsieur Rupert? *Impossible!* He was genuinely roud of us. I'll bet he taught some very severe lessons) the Hun in the last war."

"Maybe. But tell me, Rotter. What Englishman in his ight mind *ever* parted with a quid?"

"You're being paranoid . . ." Lambert bit off the rest f the sentence and stopped suddenly. *"Merd."*

"What?" Weyers asked.

"How long have we been back?"

"The plane landed one and a half days ago. Why?"

Lambert pointed, and the others stared at Escott's fa-iliar black sedan rushing along Dill Street. The car topped heavily beside them, and the portly inspector got ut.

"I'm glad I caught you," he declared. "You're needed ack at the hotel at once. We've got rather a serious roblem."

"Where?" Lambert asked.

Escott looked around at the deserted pier. "Norway."

"Norway!" Lambert cried. *"Merci a Dieu.* We'll reeze!"

Weyers and Colon looked at each other and shook their eads. "The man doesn't mind dying, as long as he's varm," the South African said.

Scowling, Escott impatiently motioned the men into he car. And behind them, leaving the shadow of the oorway of The Admiral's Pub, Dale Rupert hurried to he telephone at the back of the bar.

Watch for

Destination: Norway

next in the Force Five *series
coming soon from Lynx Books!*